Praise for *Panic*

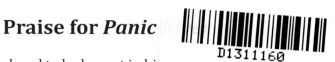

"Elliott Foster has dared to be honest in hi. Set in familiar Upper Mississippi River locales, his novel takes us to the secret interiors of familiar faces and their outdoor lives. His exploration of marriage, family, sexuality and gender identity is courageous, insightful, and compassionate, and his story has cliff-hanger qualities that make it a page turner."

> — Emilio Degrazia, Minnesota Book Award winning author of *Billy Brazil* and *Seventeen Grams of Soul*

"Foster's hero is a man in pain, and the way forward hurts even more. But walls come down, hearts open, and there is such pleasure in sharing the journey."

> — Sandra Scofield, National Book Award finalist and American Book Award winning author of *Beyond Deserving* and *Swim: Stories of the Sixties*

"*Panic River* is a marvel: equal parts salient, searing portrait of Middle America and taut, orchestrated page-turner full of family secrets that don't stay buried for long. Foster offers up an exquisitely-crafted panoply that grapples with American angst, toxic masculinity, identity, and the expectations we face every day of our lives, all handled with tenderness and deft skill. Yes, this is a luminous novel; I'll happily follow Foster wherever he goes next."

> — Robert James Russell, author of *Mesilla* and *Sea of Trees*

"Elliott Foster became the voice of Minnesota cabin land with Whispering Pines. Now he crosses the river into rural Wisconsin with his darkly droll novel, *Panic River*. Foster writes characters that are so real and lovably imperfect that you want to shove anyone who bullies them down a staircase. The spark has been dwindling between Corey and his husband Nick, who has not been telling the truth. But in turning the pages I discovered that Corey and his family have more secrets of their own than there are deer in Barron County. And so begins the panic-filled hunt for the real meaning of Corey's inheritance."

> — Catherine Dehdashti, author of *Roseheart*

"... Novel readers who choose *Panic River* for its theme of a middle-aged gay man facing his demons and much-changed circumstances will uncover the roots of these connections and will learn how they evolve. They will find *Panic River* a powerfully evocative, thought-provoking consideration of how life moves on, how freedoms evaporate and re-form, and how one man makes difficult choices that bring him full circle in an unexpected way."

– Midwest Book Review

"... Overall, this book was a fascinating read about love, tough love, and all of the complicated relationships that happen when a person decides to be him or herself. Well-written with all types of little life lessons thrown in, this book was engaging and entertaining. A book well worth reading, geared towards young adults to adults."

– Kristi Elizabeth, San Francisco Book Review

"Elliott Foster has written a tremendous novel, at once a testimony to courage and friendship and family bonds, *Panic River* is also wickedly intense and psychologically riveting. It is, in other words, the sort of novel that touches on every reading pleasure."

– Peter Geye, author of *Wintering*

For my father,
who, in the midst of his life's deepest pain,
guided me through mine.

Art washes away from the soul
The dust of everyday life.

Pablo Picasso

Also by Elliott Foster

Retrieving Isaac & Jason (Calumet Editions, 2019)
Whispering Pines (Wise Ink Publishing, 2015)

PANIC RIVER

ELLIOTT FOSTER

CALUMET EDITIONS

Minneapolis, Minnesota

"Faceless" by Corey Fischer
1988 Stockholm Art Fair
High School Division
Third Prize

The sandy-haired boy at the center of the artwork stood scarcely camouflaged near the top of a rugged oak, his fingernails dug deep into the crevasses of its bark. His tiptoes touched a sturdy branch while one arm seized the trunk. It was a long way to the ground. He appeared to be looking out across the wide river valley, but only the back of his head was visible. His facial expression was hidden from view.

The abstract oil painting filled the canvas with muted colors—grays and beige—with a sliver of crimson on the open palm of the boy's free hand and several drops of the same color suspended toward the earth, below. There was enough detail to grasp that the boy had mounted a middling hardwood burrowing its tentacled roots into the thinly cloaked ground of an island. Brown river water flooded its base and birds of prey circled in the sky. Leafless branches radiated from the trunk—shielding the boy from above, supporting him from below, and beckoning him farther out from the trunk.

In the distance a church steeple, slender and white, towered above a village resting along the riverbank. Still, the boy's face remained hidden, his gaze fixed toward the far horizon. From this distance, the town was blurred in tones of sable and soot, except for that lone, ivory spire. From his post in the treetops, the steeple must have seemed small to the boy. From here, it wasn't clear—was the boy searching for something on the horizon, or taking delight in having climbed to the top of the world?

The Wounding

July 2012

1

After dropping Nick at the airport Friday morning, Corey Fischer glanced down at his cell phone and tapped the Pandora app. A mélange of jazz began streaming through the car's speakers. He checked himself in the rear-view mirror. Not bad for thirty-eight. He still had a full head of sandy brown hair although his face clearly needed moisturizing. Corey wondered why his skin had weathered so much faster than Nick's. After all, they were the same age and had been together almost twenty years. They both looked better than most of their straight friends, though, especially the ones with kids.

Corey pulled the gear into drive and followed the slow line of cars toward the exit from MSP. He sped up once he entered the freeways, heading back toward the condo he and Nick shared in Minneapolis overlooking St. Anthony Falls. Corey loved to stand on the condo's balcony and stare at that cascading water, often losing his sense of time.

Above the falls he could see the placid tributary that looked virtually the same as it did when first chronicled in western literature by Father Louis Hennepin, the Recollect friar who named the falls after his patron saint, Anthony of Padua. Below the turbulent waters, however, the Mississippi changed dramatically—opening up into a steep gorge of muddy brown water pooled artificially deep ever since the creation of lock and dam number one a few miles downstream. Corey knew the river's history and often strained to imagine the Mississippi's naturally flowing rapids over massive boulders, now hidden far below the river's murky surface.

Corey wondered what he would do for the next few days with Nick out of town. He hadn't found time to think about it, since he had been worrying constantly about their money quarrel two nights ago. The row had left Corey feeling small—Nick looking down on Corey due to his superior height, carrying on with his familiar grievance about the disparity in their incomes, insisting that Corey look for a higher paying job. They made up later that same night after two rounds of Belvedere and tonic, poured heavy with a splash of elderflower. They had sex on the sofa, initiated when Nick grabbed Corey's hips and flipped him onto all fours up against the cushions. Corey submitted to Nick's drunken aggression, allowing his clothes to be removed only far enough to expose what Nick wanted to see, and use. Corey never could resist Nick's impressive manhood, that coarse black hair brushing against Corey's smooth skin. Afterward, they shared a bottle of Vigonier over Vietnamese food delivered to their doorstep and eaten directly from a pair of white pint-sized boxes.

He was looking forward to some time apart from Nick, but he also didn't want to spend the weekend alone. He had the day off from work, with no concrete plans until his next shift at the museum Monday morning. Maybe he'd enjoy some quality hours at the studio. His latest painting was certain to be his best, and he was itching to complete it.

On the other hand, he also found himself thinking lately of his mother. Her birthday was coming up next week, and it had been a year since his last visit. For once, maybe he should put some time in with her, even if it meant dealing with his dad face-to-face. He picked up the phone, searched for his mother's name, and sent the call. The music inside the car faded when she answered.

"Hello?"

"Good morning. May I speak to the lady of the house?"

He could picture an emerging smile.

"Corey? Is that you?"

"Yes, Mrs. Fischer, it is I—your favorite son."

"Oh, I almost didn't recognize your voice. It sounds like you're in a tunnel."

"That's because I'm talking to you through the car speakers. It makes me sound important."

She laughed. "Well, I'm just glad to finally hear from you."

He winced, trying to remember the last time he had called. It was at least two weeks since hearing her quiet voice.

"I was wondering what you guys were up to this weekend. If you're not busy, maybe I could come down?"

"Yes, please. We're not busy at all."

"Good. I need to finish some work at the studio first and then pack a bag. But I can certainly be there in time for supper."

"Oh, Corey, that'll be wonderful. I'll call Frank at the office and let him know."

"Okay, I'll see you around five."

"Drive safely."

"I will. Talk to you soon."

He arrived at the studio in Northeast, an old Polish neighborhood full of vacant warehouses where artists could afford the cheap rent. As he clumped up the worn stairway to the third floor, he realized that his desperation to paint made his promise to visit Pepin feel compulsive and he regretted it, and in regretting it he felt disloyal. This would've been the perfect opportunity to stay home and paint. Lately, there had been too little time for doing what he loved. With budget cuts at the museum, Corey often shouldered the toil of two staffers for the salary of one. His days were filled with tours and preparing upcoming exhibits. He longed for the freedom to spend hours in this studio. He put the key into the lock, startled to feel it already open.

He timidly pushed the metal door, tense in his shoulders despite the familiar scent of the hundred-year-old space with its concrete floors, exposed brick walls, and large, single-paned windows through which the Minnesota winter winds seemed to flow uninhibited. Corey was relieved to spy Carol at her potter's wheel, her unmistakable long blond hair cascading down toward the middle of her back.

"Morning. I didn't expect to see you here today."

"I'm going in late to work. I wanted to finish up this piece and get it into the kiln. This is gonna be the one that puts me on the map, Corey. What do you think?"

"I think it's terrific—definitely your best work."

"Thanks, love."

"This is the one where you're experimenting with the new glazing technique?"

"Yeah. I'm about to apply the white glaze, then finish with this color—it's a mix of Gerstley borate and K-44 Royal Purple Stain."

"I love it." Corey was on the verge of telling Carol about his trip to Pepin but switched into work mode instead. "Oh, I hate to be a downer, but you may have a shitload of paperwork once you get to the museum."

"Really?"

"Yeah, I got verbal commitments late yesterday from the Whitney and MOMA. You get the fun task of filling out formal requisitions."

"No worries. I'm excited that we're prepping this exhibit. Arshile Gorky has never been displayed in Minnesota before. It'll definitely be a hit."

Corey loved discussing art with Carol. She was the only person who appreciated his life's calling. Nick didn't have the patience, at least not anymore. On occasion, Nick would feign interest, listening to stories about a visiting exhibit or the contrast between Expressionism and Fauvism, between Munch and Matisse. He became far more animated, of course, when the conversation turned to pop culture, fashion, or his own job at the bank.

"I'm sure it will be, Carol. And it might just shine an overdue light on Gorky, not to mention surrealism in general."

"And the Armenian Genocide."

"That too."

"Say, I took a peek at your easel over there. You're working on something pretty impressive yourself, mister."

"You think?"

"For sure. It reminds me of *Grounds of the Chateau Noir* in the British Museum. Julian and I saw it on our anniversary trip. There are definite similarities—the cottage entangled in branches obscuring the sky, and the touch of orange that Cezanne used to lend vibrancy to the green of the trees."

Corey was familiar with that painting and of course was imitating Cezanne's style, as a means of teaching himself to go deeper into impressionism. But the cabin and woods he cast onto the canvas were images of his own—seared into his memory from childhood, of a place he hadn't visited in more than twenty years.

"Huh," Corey said. "I read that Gorky went through a Cezanne period... did you know that?"

"No. Looks like you two have something in common then."

Corey didn't mind the flattering comparison to an artist who was known for painting vivid images from childhood. He was particularly taken with Gorky's distinct technique but disturbed that such a magnificent talent would take his own life after suffering a succession of tragedies at the age of forty-four, only a few years older than Corey was now. In the span of a few years, Gorky's studio had burned to the ground, he was diagnosed with cancer, and he broke his painting arm in a paralyzing car accident. As if that were not enough, his wife then left him for fellow painter Roberto Matta and took the children with her. Corey couldn't fathom a person sustaining so much loss, all at once. He hoped his own depression would never take him that far.

Once Carol left, Corey stood in front of his easel and began to paint. Lately, he had been attempting to master a far more abstract style. On the canvas he experimented with both color and light, applying hatched brushstrokes to convey images of people, structures, and landscapes with figures dissolving toward an invisible point of disintegration at the edges of the frame. His current project was a dark-hued image of a cabin set in the midst of a gloomy woods. The presence of a hunter in the distance was only guessed at from the faded orange hat atop what appeared to be a man. He spent an hour adding slight touches to the painting—the faint brown hint of a deer amidst the trees, blanched horns atop its skull, a noticeable spurt of crimson from its side.

Yet, he struggled. Like Cezanne, Corey had attempted to paint this same scene multiple times—from different angles, in varying mediums, and with diverse amounts of natural light. Still, perfection eluded him. Or perhaps, the expectations he set for himself as an artist were as unrealistically high as those in most areas of his life. Corey stared at the canvas and decided he'd done enough for today. Then, he washed out his brushes in the sink. He looked up and noticed a flyer for the West Texas Art Fair in Marfa hanging on the wall. Why hadn't he thought to travel there while Nick was away? He envisioned visiting his "painting friends," as Nick called them, and checking out two up-and-coming artists whose compositions were being considered for a minor exhibition at the museum. But he could already hear the director denying his request. "There's no room in the budget for that," she would say. And he knew better than to travel there as a personal expense, given his recent fights about money with Nick. For a moment, Corey contemplated a furtive escape—telling no one and paying for the imagined trip with cash from his studio safe, funds he had accumulated from selling paintings over the years. He didn't necessarily feel good about concealing that money from Nick. Corey had always considered himself a good person, at least as honest and moral as the next guy. Yet lying about this one thing—his secret stash—felt like equal justice, a fair arrangement given how many times Nick had lied to him.

Then again, he had already committed to visiting his parents. It was too late to back out now. Besides, the weatherman had forecast a beautiful weekend, and the drive would be relaxing. He returned to the condo to pack a light bag. His contemporary home with Nick was a distinct contrast in style with the studio. The converted nineteenth century flourmill housed units with surprisingly modern design and décor. Corey figured out soon after moving in that the condo was a perfect metaphor for Nick's life—a beautiful façade covering a fragile, aging foundation. After gathering his things in a Louis Vuitton overnight bag, Corey sent a short text to Nick alerting him of the plan to visit Pepin.

Within thirty minutes, the confines of the Twin Cities were behind him and Corey headed south along the Great River Road. The farther he traveled, the more the tensions from his work-week ebbed, only to be replaced with anxieties about seeing his parents. And, about Nick. Arguments between them had become more frequent, often triggered by Corey's lack of trust. With each successive spat, he felt tremors of uncertainty about their bond traveling along invisible fault lines buried deep within their relationship. Nick's last-minute news of the Miami business conference over the weekend in particular seemed suspect. But, as usual, he had an explanation—his boss unexpectedly canceled and asked Nick to take his place.

After passing by the confluence of the Mississippi with the St. Croix, Corey turned the AC off and rolled down the windows. On this bright July day, boats were aplenty with people fishing, waterskiing, and tacking their sails. The river's pungent scent wafted into the car carrying a flood of memories, especially ones involving Billy. The two of them had spent a considerable part of their childhood along this muddy river—fishing, canoeing, and exploring her shores. Corey kept his right hand on the steering wheel while lifting his left from the open window frame of the driver's side door. He playfully lifted his arm up and down to feel the power of the wind upon his skin. After resting it on the door frame, Corey's eye caught a glimpse of the tattoo on the underside of his forearm. He smiled at the memory of how it got there.

He had acquired the tattoo in the summer of '96 after the fifteen hundred mile drive to LA with Billy who was following his girlfriend and future wife to California after college. Drained after the three-day ride and sweaty from the summer heat, they parked at Dockweiler State Beach, then raced to be the first to touch the Pacific, both of them diving into the sea. That night, after a few too many shots of tequila and several Coronas, Corey asked the Latino tattoo artist to inscribe "friends for life" on his arm. In a drunken, ingratiating effort, Corey mistakenly slipped into the language he had mastered in college—Spanish. It was Billy who caught the irreversible mistake, halfway through the inking of *amigos de por vida.* He looked at Corey, then at the artist, and urged them to go ahead, to finish what had already been started. "And when you're done," Billy added, "I'll take the exact same thing."

Population 837. Corey shook his head upon seeing the familiar sign. He couldn't imagine living in a town this small again, after spending the past twenty years in Minneapolis. At first glance, nothing had changed. The same houses in the same places. Who knows, maybe the same cars sat out front of each of them too. He passed by the Third Base Bar—"The Last Stop Before Home"— and the Kwik Stop. As a kid, he had spent most of his hard-earned money in this convenience store. Billy had too.

He turned onto Pine Street and saw the tall white steeple of St. Bridget's staring down at him. In the distance sat the house where he grew up, where his parents had lived for the past thirty-five years. It was a rambler made of brown brick with a large picture window hung across the front, providing an unobstructed view of the river. Corey smirked upon seeing the gray satellite dish on the roof. Apparently, Frank was still too cheap for cable.

Corey pulled into the long driveway and parked to the far left, in front of the detached double car garage adjacent the back of the house. As far as he knew, his parents still only had one car. And Frank would of course be pulling his car in on the right, if he wasn't home already. Corey turned off the engine and looked into the backyard. It too was the same as he remembered. A freshly pruned hedge lined a perfectly cut lawn, a freestanding screen porch and a work shed the only obstructions. There was never even a swing set here during his childhood. When it was time for play, his parents sent him down the street to Billy's or to the playground across town.

He stepped out of the car, grabbed his bag from the back seat and walked over to the house. He entered the back door and saw his mother in the kitchen.

"Hey, Mom."

"Corey, I didn't hear you pull up. Come in, come in."

He crossed the threshold, dropped his overnight bag at the door, and wrapped his mother up tight in a hug.

"Geez, put me down. You'll hurt your back."

He set her feet gently onto the kitchen floor.

"You feel lighter. Have you lost a little weight?"

"I wish."

"Well, you look fantastic."

She smiled with pursed lips and patted her brown hair that concealed a faint wisp of white. He thought she looked as pretty as ever—those gentle brown eyes, her trim figure, and the smooth skin across most of her face.

"Frank not home yet?"

"No, he'll be a while. Friday night with the boys at the Legion, you know."

"Good, we'll have some time just to ourselves. What's new around here?"

She showed him a recent embroidery and jars of maple syrup created from her own taps, both intended for this year's county fair. Through the living room window, his mother also pointed out a fresh bed of annuals she and Frank had planted underneath a birch tree in the front yard.

"Dinner might be a while. You know your father."

Corey nodded his head.

"You're probably thirsty from the drive. Hungry too."

"What's for dinner, anyway? Wait, let me guess. Pork chops in herb sauce?"

Ginny laughed at the inside joke. "It's the best thing I make."

"Dad says it's the only thing you make."

"Oh stop. I make plenty of good meals for that man, and a variety of them too."

Corey laughed along with her. The predictability of his mother's cooking was an accepted truth within their small family—both the limited menu range and its provincial, simple appeal. Dinners at the Fischer house would never be confused with the cuisine at the world-renowned Harbor View Café down the street.

"Come help me in the kitchen. We'll take some drinks and snacks outside."

Corey obliged. He made lemonade from a powdered mix while Ginny whipped up her famous gherkins wrapped in cream cheese and shaved corned beef. He hadn't tasted those in years. He had disparagingly described them to Carol once as "Wisconsin Sushi," but now he couldn't wait to pop one into his mouth.

Ginny walked over to where Corey was stirring lemonade in a large plastic pitcher.

"You need to add more sugar, dear."

She always said that, no matter how much had already been poured in.

"Mom, it's already sweeter than a sugar boat on a river of honey."

He winced the moment the adage left his lips. She gave him a look.

"I know where that came from. See, I always said you were more like your father than you'd admit."

He emptied the remainder of the sugar jar into the pitcher, then put it and a pair of plastic cups onto a tray along with the gherkin rolls and walked outside. They each took a seat in the screened-in porch. Corey poured two tall glasses of the lemonade and handed one to Ginny.

"To good health."

"To good health."

Corey drew a sip from his lemonade, then shoved an entire gherkin wrap into his mouth.

"So, how's Nick?" Ginny asked, as Corey swallowed, then almost choked on his food. His parents had only met Nick briefly, when they were in Minneapolis for an insurance convention years ago. At the time, Nick was introduced to them as Corey's roommate.

"Um, okay. He's actually in Miami on business."

"Oh. He travels often, right?"

"Sort of. It depends."

He couldn't remember his mother asking about Nick before. "You guys" was the closest she ever came to including him in her questions.

"You should bring him down here sometime... to Pepin. He should see where you grew up."

Corey double-checked his lemonade, wondering if it had been spiked. Then he looked her in the eye.

"Mom?"

She set down her drink, then folded her hands and rested them in her lap.

"I can't speak for your father, of course, but I'd be fine with it. How many years have you two lived together now, a dozen?"

"Eighteen, to be precise."

"Well, the world is changing, and I'd just like to see you more often."

Frank's car pulled into the driveway, interrupting their conversation. As he got out of the car and walked toward them, Corey noticed few changes in his father's appearance these past twelve months. He seemed as lean as always, except for a slightly protruding beer belly. Frank was in decent shape for sixty-one. But his skin now looked ashen, with deep wrinkles that made him appear ten years older than he was.

"Corey, the big city art dealer. How are you, son?"

"Fine, Dad. You?"

"Been a long week. Ginny, is dinner ready?"

"Almost. I can have it on the table in twenty minutes. But I didn't expect you home this soon. Everything all right?"

"Of course, everything's fine. Can't I come home early and see my only son? I can shoot the breeze with the Legion boys any time. Come on, Corey, let's go inside." Frank pointed toward the house. "How about a drink?"

Corey sensed that his father didn't need another, but he obliged. Frank made them each a martini, dry with an olive.

"So, what's new up there in the big city?"

Corey talked about the museum's current exhibit, some recent flooding in Duluth that sent animals fleeing from the local zoo, and the legislature's decision to build a billion-dollar stadium for the Vikings.

"Christ. A billion dollars? For that horseshit team? Well, I hope everyone's happy with how your tax dollars are swirling down the drain."

Corey laughed at the reaction he expected. "I know. A lot of us are upset."

Frank nodded and swallowed the rest of his drink. "Another?"

"Sure." Corey could see his mother in the kitchen, but she avoided making eye contact. Frank turned away and poured a second round of drinks with shaky hands. Corey sat deeper into the sofa, the strength of that first martini helping him to forget the tensions he'd obsessed about during the long drive.

"I hear you've also got a political battle brewing," Frank said.

Corey sensed a familiar mocking tone in his father's voice, like when he drunkenly mocked Corey as a teenager about going out for cross-country instead of football.

"Yeah. I assume you're referring to the referendum on same-sex marriage?"

Frank laughed and continued mixing their drinks, but he didn't turn around. "The boys at the Legion have more colorful words to describe it."

"The pundits say it's likely to pass."

"Is that right?"

"It's a little bit confusing, though. If you're against gay marriage, you vote yes and if you're for it, you vote no. I'll be voting no, of course."

Frank turned and walked across the living room wearing a look of mild defeat. He handed Corey his drink, inadvertently spilling some on the floor.

"Good for you, but I don't think we should talk about this anymore tonight. You know how we feel about that subject."

"Okay, but you brought it up." Corey considered dropping the subject, but then continued on. "Ya know, did you ever consider that maybe you and Mom have different feelings on that topic— gay marriage?"

Ginny continued slicing fresh-baked bread at the kitchen counter.

Frank still stood above him and looked Corey directly in the eye. "The church's teachings are clear, Corey. Ask any priest. Sex outside of marriage, and particularly with another man, is an abomination."

"The church forbids a lot of things, Dad."

Corey's eyes remained locked with his father's. Neither looked away. Frank finally uttered a small laugh.

"You're right about that. Now, let's drop this and have a nice meal."

As if on cue, Ginny called them to supper. Corey walked quietly into the kitchen and sat down in his traditional seat adjacent his father.

"Oh, honey," Frank said, "this smells delicious. Pork chops with your mother's herb sauce?" He playfully nudged Corey's arm and smiled.

"Now stop it, both of you. I found the meat on sale at Pedersen's. And the vegetables are all from Sally's garden next door."

"It looks terrific, Mom. Thank you."

They ate and exchanged pleasantries amidst an invisible layer of tension. Finally, there was a moment of silence when no one seemingly had anything to say. Corey set down his fork, then rested his arms on either side of his plate.

"Look, on that topic we discussed earlier, I know how you feel and what the church has to say about it. But soon marriage equality is going to be legal in Minnesota, maybe everywhere. And when it is, my marriage to Nick will finally be official here in America."

Ginny looked at Corey, then at Frank, and then straight down toward her plate. Frank chewed slowly on a mouthful of pork, then swallowed and turned to face Corey.

"Your marriage?"

"Yes, we had a small ceremony in Canada three years ago when it finally became legal there."

Frank wiped his lips with a cloth napkin, then set it back on his lap and stared.

"You got married three years ago, and you're telling us about it now?"

The question caught Corey off-guard. He had no reply.

"And I suppose Nick's folks were there to cheer you on for this so-called marriage?"

"No, but his mother did send us a gift."

"I see." Frank laughed and shook his head. "Must not be Catholic."

"Lutheran, when they attend. Does it matter?"

"Figures. They're probably not familiar with key scripture, like a man shall not lie with another man, and each man should have his own wife."

"Seriously? It's 2012. Do you watch the news?"

"Oh I see it, but that doesn't make it right."

Corey didn't respond. Ginny stayed quiet.

"Let me just say this, Corey. You're our son, and we did our best to raise you right. But we wouldn't have come to your pretend wedding even if we had been invited. And we certainly won't be sending you a gift." Frank looked down at his plate, then picked up his fork and aggressively stabbed a piece of pork. Before lifting it to his mouth, he pointed the forkful at Corey. "I won't condone it."

Corey looked at Ginny but knew better than to ask now for her to express her own thoughts. He looked back toward his father.

"Condone? You don't condone my marriage?"

"That's right."

"Who says that kind of thing to their own son?"

"It's how we feel."

"Well maybe I don't condone the shitty husband and father you've been for the past forty years."

Frank forcefully set down his fork. He looked straight at Corey, swallowed his meat, and cleared his throat. "Get outta my house, and don't come back." Then he rose from the table, walked down the hallway, and slammed the bedroom door.

Ginny began to shake, her head buried in her hands. Corey fell back in his chair. He noticed his overnight bag still sitting unpacked next to the kitchen door. His departure would be easy. With only two drinks and some food in his stomach, he felt alert enough to drive.

"Well, you heard the man. I'm no longer welcome in this house." His eyes began to tear.

"Corey, please…"

"No, Mom. His words were crystal clear. I'm sorry, but I've gotta go."

Ginny remained in her chair, crying, as Corey walked out the door and drove away.

"Nick, call me as soon as you can."

Corey tried reaching Carol at work and Billy in California—both to no avail. He left messages instead. He needed to talk to someone about the gravity of what his father had said—"don't come back." It felt like one of those watershed moments that can't be undone. He would never return to the house where he grew up, and he was unlikely to see his mother again either. She was not one to drive all the way from Pepin, alone. That loss might be too great to bear.

Why did he push the issue at dinner, especially with his father already a half-dozen drinks into his night? Sure, Frank taunted him about it first, probably thinking the referendum would fail in Minnesota like it had everywhere else. Why did Corey have to provoke him by telling Frank about the marriage to Nick? And why do that in front of his mother? Surely, at least she deserved better than that.

Fifteen minutes outside of Pepin, Corey saw the sign for Maiden Rock and pulled off the road into the rest area. He fumbled with his bag and found the prescription Xanax. He popped a little white pill into his mouth, swallowing with his own saliva. Outside his window, he spotted the towering bluff from which an Indian maiden allegedly had leapt to her death. Whenever passing by here as a kid, Corey would beg his mother to pull over and read aloud the story of Maiden Rock emblazoned on the historical marker at the roadside pullout. Even now, he could hear her mellow voice retell the legend of an Indian girl, the daughter of Dakota Chief Red Wing. The maiden had fallen in love with a young warrior who belonged to the rival Chippewa tribe. The Chief declared he would never condone a union between his daughter and her lover. Then he had the warrior killed. So the maiden climbed to the peak of a tall bluff, right above where the marker now stood, and jumped. Something about that story fascinated Corey as a boy. He alighted from the car—today, as a full-grown man—to read it once more.

After he finished reading, Corey walked to the edge of the overlook, facing the river. He strained to remember what his therapist had taught him—how to ward off the worst of his depression. But those tips didn't seem to work tonight. In the past, despair had snuck up on him like a fungus. Tonight, it punched him right in the face.

Another car pulled into the rest area, and a young couple stepped out to read about Maiden Rock. The guy put his arm around the young woman. She slid hers around his waist. They stared at the sign with vibrating lips, pulling each other in tight as they read along. Corey wondered how many people who'd read this sign could relate to the Indian maiden, how many people had ever considered taking their own lives. Corey had, the first time he learned that Nick had slept with another man. He never acted on that desperation, but the notion had crossed his mind. He remembered wanting to call his mother that night he found out about Nick. But he couldn't. At that point, he hadn't yet even told her he was gay. Instead, he pictured himself straddling the railing on the Tenth Avenue Bridge, vacillating between life and death. But unlike the girl in the Dakota legend, Corey had stepped back and found a way to move on.

After arriving home to Minneapolis, he tried once again to reach Billy, Carol, and Nick. None answered the phone, so he left more messages. He dropped his bag on the floor and fell backward onto the bed, rubbing his temples and breathing through his nose. He considered taking another Xanax, but the doctor's orders were clear—never more than one per day. Instead, he walked straight to the liquor cabinet, poured himself a generous Belvedere tonic from a new bottle, then returned to the bedroom and unpacked his bag. A few minutes later, he sat down again on the bed with his half-finished drink. He looked around the room. Being home was a comfort, though less so without Nick who was a thousand miles away and inexplicably inattentive to his phone.

He looked up and noticed the set of framed photos atop the dresser. The first one took him by surprise, though he had walked past it nearly every day. It was taken in 1986 during his First Holy Communion inside St. Bridget's. He stood proudly between his beaming parents, their only child now entitled to receive the body and blood of Christ. Or, as Billy called them, "crouton o'christ and the holy shiz."

The second photo was taken in Thunder Bay, Ontario in the spring of 2009—Corey and Nick smiling and wearing dark-blue suits. He focused on Nick's smile, which appeared to be genuine. Nick's thick brown hair was cut short for the ceremony, a three-day shadow lay like straw down both cheeks and surrounding his mouth. Corey thought Nick looked even more handsome in that photo than on the day they had met in college all those years ago.

They were flanked in the photo by Carol and Julian. Julian had obtained an on-line ordination from the Universal Life Church and officiated the nuptials.

Julian.

Why hadn't Corey thought of him before? Nick and Julian worked together at the bank and had been best friends since college. If the conference were as important as Nick suggested, Julian must be there too. Corey grabbed his cell phone and scrolled down to find the number. He rose from the bed, with drink still in hand, and paced back and forth.

"Hello?"

"Julian, it's Corey."

"Hey, buddy. What's up?"

"Have you seen Nick? I need to talk to him."

"No. I'm at dinner with Carol. It's our anniversary. Maybe he's out with the guys after work?"

"But aren't you at the conference?"

"What conference?"

"The one in Miami."

"That doesn't start till Tuesday. I'm flying out Monday night. I think Nick's on the same flight."

"But I dropped him off at the airport this morning. He said there were sessions taking place over the weekend."

Silence from the other end of the line.

"Julian? Are you there?"

"Oh, I forgot. There were some events ahead of the main conference, but I'm not part of them. It makes sense that Nick flew down today."

Corey felt his device buzz and held it away from his ear to see who was phoning. Nick's cell number flashed across the screen. Corey dropped Julian's call without saying goodbye.

"Nick, where are you?"

"Um, Miami. You took me to the airport this morning, remember?"

"But Julian's not there, so why are you?"

"How do you know Julian's not here?"

"I just talked to him. He's out to dinner with Carol."

"Oh, I see. Is that why you sound so upset? Because Julian is on a date with your girlfriend?"

"This isn't the time for your stupid jokes, okay?"

"Fine, sheesh." Nick paused. "Corey, have you been drinking? You're slurring your words."

"No!"

Corey set his near-empty glass atop the dresser.

"And why do I have so many missed calls from you? Everything okay there in Pepin?"

"Everything is not okay. And I'm not in Pepin."

"What?"

"I'm back at the condo. You'd know if you'd listened to any of my messages."

"Wait a minute. Slow down. You sound like you're about to lose it."

Corey explained as Nick listened without interruption. A minute later, Corey heard a voice call Nick's name on the other end of the line.

"Who's that?"

"Oh, I've got the news on here in my room."

"I don't think CNN knows your name. Who's there with you?"

"No one's here with me. I just told you—it's the television. Now I know you've been drinking because you're hallucinating."

Corey questioned himself for a moment. After all, he'd already downed three drinks tonight but was accustomed to having five or six. Nick constantly complained about how moody and depressed Corey would get after three or four and would nag him relentlessly for each drop of alcohol he consumed after that.

Then Corey had a flash of recognition—Evan, from the bank. The guy he met at the company holiday party before Nick awkwardly steered Corey away. The guy he once saw sneaking out the stairwell of their condo building. The guy who left an anonymous voice message for Nick on their home phone. It was Evan's distinctive voice there in the Miami hotel room. Corey knew it as surely as he knew himself.

He abruptly ended the call and threw his phone toward their wedding photo. It missed, landing with a whack and skidding across the tiled hallway floor. He remembered taking a leap of faith when Nick promised that he had changed his ways. That's the only reason Corey finally had agreed to marry. Now, it was all a lie. He fell onto the bed and wept for several minutes, then rose abruptly to his feet, intent on fixing himself another drink. As he walked away from the bed, Corey glowered at the framed pictures atop the tallboy, then took the two at which he had been staring and chucked them toward his damaged phone. Glass splintered everywhere. He walked across them resolutely toward the bathroom, seized an orange bottle of Ambien from the hall closet and returned to the liquor cabinet where he grabbed the nearly full bottle of vodka.

His cell phone vibrated atop the glass shards in the hall. He walked toward it and barely saw Carol's name through the shattered screen. He picked it up and answered without saying hello.

"Corey? Are you there?"

Even though Carol's was a longed-for voice, he could barely say "yes" through his rage.

"Julian said you called sounding upset and that you might have been drinking?"

He wasn't able to speak. Either the alcohol or the weight of tonight's disasters prevented him from summoning the right words.

"Corey! Tell me where you are, and I'll come over."

Carol wouldn't understand. And he didn't know what to tell her. He simply whispered that he had to go, that he would call her back tomorrow. Then he ended the call and dropped the phone onto the floor.

Corey headed toward the living room and sat down on the sofa with the vodka bottle still gripped in his hand. As he dwelled on his father's words, he took several deep swallows. As he pictured Nick fucking Evan in a Miami hotel room, he took a few more. Then Corey thought about his mother sobbing at the dinner table hours earlier, and he swallowed the very last drop.

There was a knock at the front door followed by a familiar, grating voice.

"Nick? Corey? Is everything all right?"

Mrs. Randall was a charming old widow, but she could also be annoying as hell and way too nosy about other people's business. In calmer times, Corey enjoyed her animated stories about growing up black in the South during Jim Crow. But there was no way he could deal with her tonight. He walked quietly across the living room, ignoring her repeated pleas through the condo door. He ran into an end table with a thud, but at this point he didn't care if Mrs. Randall heard it. He wasn't about to answer the door.

Once inside the bedroom, he sat down atop the bed and tried to open the plastic container still clutched in his hand, spending almost a minute fumbling to remove the childproof lid. He dumped the remaining pills onto the comforter, then picked them up with one hand, dropping them into the open palm of the other.

He paused upon seeing the ink on his forearm, just below the wrist. Corey moved the pills to his opposite hand, away from the tattoo, then tossed them into his mouth and swallowed. A few got stuck in his throat, making him feel as if he might gag, so he stumbled back to the liquor cabinet and took a burning swig of rye. He walked back toward the hall and noticed his phone. Through the cracked screen, he could see two missed calls from Nick and an unexpected one from the landline at his parents' home.

Now they want to talk to me? "Fuck you all," he said aloud. He then hazily remembered the empowering feelings of revenge that had filled him during those moments when he imagined jumping off the Tenth Avenue Bridge.

Corey collapsed onto the bed, placed headphones on his ears, hit shuffle on his device, and took one long, last look at the Kahlo replica hanging on the wall. *The Wounded Deer* may have been her most painful and revealing work. He then lay back and closed his eyes for what he had hoped would be the final time.

Corey awoke the following afternoon, lying on a bed in the psych ward, initially oblivious to his whereabouts. He felt the touch of a person's hand atop his foot, a rough caress. Someone was whispering his name.

"Corey," he thought he could hear, the sound as if his name were being shouted under water.

"Corey," he heard again, a bit more clearly.

A third utterance triggered him to open his eyes, still not certain of who he would see. The most important people in his life were hundreds or even a thousand miles away. But he had the sense that one of them was calling to him. He looked at the person standing at the foot of his hospital bed.

"Billy, what are you doing here?" His voice was raspy, and a burning sensation filled his throat.

"Funny, I was about to ask you the same thing."

Corey looked left and right and down toward his feet, then noticed the woman in blue scrubs sitting on a chair near the door to the room.

"Who's she?"

The woman didn't look up from her magazine.

"That's the gal who felt me up before I came in. Said she was checking for sharp objects, but I think she mighta just been sweet on me."

Corey laid his head back against the pillow and rolled it back and forth.

"I'll take that to mean you liked my joke?"

"Billy, I'm sorry. I, uh…"

"It's okay, man. No need to say anything right now—unless you want to."

"But how did you get here? How did I get here?"

"You, my friend, got a ride in the ambulance, courtesy of my 911 call. I, on the other hand, shelled out a few hundred bucks for the red-eye from LA."

Corey grimaced.

"I didn't mean it like that. Sorry, just trying to lighten the mood. I did have to lie my way in here, though. I convinced them I was your brother."

Corey gave him a look.

Billy smiled as he moved from the end of the bed and up toward Corey's side. Suddenly, he looked more serious. "You almost died last night, Corey. Do you know that? Is that what you wanted?"

Corey closed his eyes and forced out a tear. He slowly shook his head back and forth.

"Good, 'cause I don't want that either. Nobody does."

Corey opened his eyes and began to utter a retort, but then stayed silent.

"Look, I don't know everything that happened, but I did listen to all of your messages. What a shitty, shitty night. I can't even imagine."

Corey looked away, toward the window. The realization that Billy flew through the night to be at his bedside was about to make him cry.

"Listen." Billy tugged at Corey's arm, summoning his face.

He obliged.

"We're gonna work through this together, okay?"

Corey looked at Billy and nodded his head, yes.

"Good. Even though I can be a pain in the ass, you know I've got your back. You're stuck with me—whether you like it or not."

"Why are you being so nice to me?"

"Seriously? Because I care about you, ya dumbass. And if you ever pull a stunt like that again, I'll kill ya."

Corey laughed. "What a relief to see that the real Billy showed up. I was getting a little nervous about this ultra-sensitive, proper guy hovering over me like a mom."

Billy continued holding onto Corey's arm.

"The real Billy? I'll show you the real Billy."

He pulled Corey's arm from underneath the blanket and gently turned it over, then laid his matching tattoo next to Corey's. Billy inhaled and brought himself in close, looking Corey in the eye as emotions spilled over their banks.

"This is the real Billy, the one who got a fucking tattoo on his arm in a language he can't even read just so it would match yours, my friend for life."

Inheritance

November 2013

1

Friday

Corey loved to run and had the body to prove it. His favorite route began along East River Road, crossed the Mississippi atop the Lake Street Bridge, then cruised down to Bohemian Flats before hitting the heart-rate challenge up to the West Bank. He prided himself on his fitness. After all, how many forty-year-olds could take this hill at a full sprint?

He preferred to slow down at the end of each run, though, to catch his breath before walking across the Stone Arch Bridge and back to feel the cool mist of St. Anthony Falls spray across his face. Unlike most runners, Corey thought deeply on his jogs, rather than zoning out and becoming one with the pavement. He liked to feel driven forward by distant memories. Nick warned him that it was unhealthy—dwelling so much on the past—claiming that Corey's obsession with the back-story of his life interfered with handling the present.

Given the past few days rife with upset customers and missed deadlines in his new job at the art gallery, Corey was happy to get in a run after work. He lamented losing his position at the museum in the wake of last year's lengthy hospitalization. At least next week would be mercifully short, only three days of work before the long Thanksgiving holiday weekend. Nick had suggested going north to visit his parents again this year. But Corey wanted to stay in town and spend the extra days working in his studio. He was finishing a new painting that he intended to submit to the State Arts Board. He had told Nick that he wanted a more low-key holiday this year, rather than another noisy Thanksgiving meal with Nick's family. He should have foreseen Nick's reply—"At least I have a family that wants me to come home."

His heart racing and his legs drained from the steep grade as he approached the shadow of the Guthrie overhang, Corey thought about what a damn bully Nick could be sometimes. That's when his toe caught on some protruding pavement, and he found himself flying, hands spread out ahead of himself. His left wrist and kneecap hit the asphalt first. The right side of his body and his head landed on the grassy edge, missing the hardened footpath by inches. Dazed, he looked up to see if anyone had witnessed the tumble. The pain surprised him, first in the wrist and then the knee. Sand embedded in his palm sent throbbing ripples up through his arm.

When he stood, a stream of blood ran from his kneecap down his shin, pooling at the top of his sock. He then grabbed the side of his torso, wondering if he also might have cracked a rib. He began to feel light-headed. He saw a park bench a few feet off the trail, walked over to it, and sat down.

"God." Gently rubbing his leg near the edge of the wound, he winced as the ripped skin with entrenched pebbles chafed against his touch. He wiped off what he could on the grass below and the rest on his sweaty shirt.

Corey considered his wounds.

The grains in his hand would require careful extraction, the deep gash on his right knee, possibly stitches. He summoned a few calming mantras.

Universe, I belong to you.
Deep in my soul, I am love divine."
Words in my ear, nothing can conquer my heart.

Then he rose from the bench, looked both ways down the path, and began the walk home. With every step, blood seeped from the wound on his knee. He could feel the heartbeat in his hand, pulsing all the way up to the pinched muscles on his face. It was in times like this that Corey felt bitter about being forced to give up booze.

He reached the front door of the condo building and punched a code into the keypad to gain entry. Though he would normally climb all three flights of stairs, today he opted for the elevator. As the door opened, he almost ran straight into his neighbor, Mrs. Randall.

"Oh! Corey, you scared me."

"I'm sorry. I wasn't paying attention. Here." He stepped back and allowed her to exit. Before he could enter the elevator, she grabbed him by the arm, thankfully the uninjured one.

"Good heavens, what happened?"

He gave her a quick recap as the elevator doors tried to shut, but Mrs. Randall kept them open with her forearm.

"Oh, what a shame. Here, I'll take you up to your unit."

"No, that's very kind of you, ma'am, but I can manage."

"I insist. It looks like you've lost some blood, and I don't want you to faint here all alone." She pulled him inside as the alarm bells rang on the elevator from its doors being forced open. Corey had nothing personal against Mrs. Randall. He even felt sorry for her, being a widow and all. But she could be such a damn gossip. Some days it was entertaining. Right now, he wasn't in the mood.

The doors shut, and Corey pressed number four.

"I'll make sure you get inside where Nick can bandage you up. He's home, you know."

"Yes, ma'am. He works from home on Fridays."

"How nice. Harold always had to go to the office, you know."

"Yes, the workplace is changing, Mrs. Randall."

"I'll say. Harold never missed a single day of work in his entire life… did you know that?"

"No, but I'm not surprised." Corey had heard that fact several times before.

"It sure must be a perk not having to leave home and still get paid. Heck, I see Nick even has people bringing work to him here at the condo during the day."

He was about to ask Mrs. Randall what she meant by that comment when the elevator doors opened, and she ushered him into the hall.

"Here we go." She practically dragged him toward his own condo. "Nick!" She yelled the name twice from several doors away. The woman sure had speed for being north of eighty. She pounded on the door. "Nick, come quick. Corey needs your help."

Corey handed her his key just as Nick opened the door.

"Jesus, what happened to you?"

Mrs. Randall threw Nick a stern look.

Corey glanced down and cringed at the sight of the blood-stained T-shirt. "Had a little accident."

"A *little* accident? I'd hate to see how the other guy looks." The old lady uttered a generous laugh as all three of them stepped inside.

"Let me see that."

Corey winced at Nick's hard touch.

"I've got Mercurochrome in the medicine chest back in my apartment. That's what I used to put on Harold's scrapes. I'll go get it."

"Not necessary," Nick said. "I can handle things from here, Mrs. Randall. Thank you for bringing him in."

"Okay, but we don't want things to get worse and end up having to call an ambulance again."

"I promise he'll get it under some water and cleaned up fast. We're meeting our friends Julian and Carol for dinner in forty minutes."

Corey pulled his hand from Nick's grip. "We might have to cancel. I think I need stitches."

"What?"

He lifted his knee, then bared his other wrist. "I'm gonna have to flush out these pebbles."

"Good Lord, did you fall?" Corey marveled at Nick's knack for asking the obvious. Yet, everyone thought Nick was the smarter one?

"Yes, he was running near the falls," Mrs. Randall explained before Corey could.

"Geez. At least it wasn't worse, right?" Corey cocked his head, uncertain whether Nick was making the best of the situation or just being an ass. He looked at Mrs. Randall, then decided to hold his tongue. This was exactly the type of situation they had repeatedly addressed in therapy—Corey taking Nick's comments too personally, then overreacting with an angry reply.

"You're right, I guess it could've been worse. At least I didn't go ass over teakettle straight into the falls."

"Exactly." Nick put his hands on Corey's shoulders and looked down on him. While Nick's four-inch height advantage was an attractive trait when they had first met, now it only made Corey feel inferior. "You go on, little man. Take a shower, and put a bandage on your leg. You'll feel better after cleaning up. I'll call Julian to see if we can push our reservation back by half an hour."

"I'm not sure a bandage will be enough."

"He'll probably need stitches," Mrs. Randall added.

"Corey, it isn't that bad. Don't be such a baby. Remember that time you thought you were having cardiac arrest, and we spent half the night in the ER only to find out it was a panic attack?"

"So you're saying these wounds are in my imagination? Look at my leg. I'm bleeding."

"And it will stop once you sit down, wash out the dirt and apply a bandage. Now, go. And thank you again, Mrs. Randall. I think everything here is under control." He steered the neighbor lady toward the front door.

"Okay, but call if you need anything." After Nick agreed, she turned and walked reluctantly out of the condo.

Corey hobbled toward the bathroom and turned on the shower, spinning the dial all the way hot. The 1930's-era building had plenty of charm, but it took a while for hot water to reach the fourth floor and mix with the steady stream of cold to produce a warm shower. He undressed slowly, careful not to rub fabric across his wounds. He went to toss his soiled running gear into the hamper but stopped when he noticed two towels at the bottom. He lifted them up and immediately remembered Mrs. Randall's comment about someone visiting Nick during the work day. He thought about walking back into the living room and confronting Nick, but he knew from past experience that first he would need more proof. Nick was smart and could explain away almost anything.

Corey also remembered that the housekeeper had cleaned the condo that morning as she had every Friday for the past three years. That meant Nick's window of opportunity was small—between the time she left and Corey returned home. That must've been the sequence. It was inconceivable for the housekeeper to have missed a pair of used towels in the bin. She was thorough—that's why Nick had hired her. She scrubbed every surface, scoured every tile, and always placed the hamper's contents into the wash. She never missed a task.

While Corey didn't mind a mess, Nick gravitated toward clean and orderly. Clothes either hung in the closet or were piled neatly in the laundry. The kitchen sink never held a dirty dish for more than five minutes. Last man out of bed had to make it and replace the decorative pillows atop the comforter. The only item regularly out of place? The Hoover Wind Tunnel T-Series Plus. Sitting in the front closet while either of them was home, the high-end appliance rested on the tile adjacent to the front door when the house was empty. Nick demanded that they vacuum the carpeted living room each morning before work, pulling the brutish device behind them toward the entryway, literally sweeping themselves out the front door.

Corey lifted the towels to his nose, expecting an unfamiliar scent, but dropped them back into the hamper when they revealed no clue. He threw his own dirty clothes on top of the towels and began thinking of questions he might ask Nick later, aimed at catching him in a lie.

He wrapped a fresh towel tightly around his waist, then looked into the mirror and cleared a small circle in the steam. What a mess. He grabbed a tweezers and plucked several granules of dirt and grass from just above his ear. Thankful that he had avoided scraping his forehead in the fall, he turned on the sink faucet, diverting hot water from the shower, and splashed the flow with his fingertips until it too felt sufficiently warm.

"Oh my God," he said aloud as soon as the stream of water hit his wrist. With his right hand, Corey awkwardly pried pebbles from his left. He pulled various-sized grit from his scraped skin and threw them into the trash. He was grateful that the abrasion stopped short of piercing the tattoo on his forearm.

The bathroom door burst open abruptly, causing him to inhale. "Jesus, you scared me."

"Sorry. You're the one who shut the door, and you know how it needs a good shove to reopen."

"Well now that you're here…"

Nick interrupted. "I forgot to tell you. Some guy named Larry Preston called this afternoon. Wouldn't leave a message. He said to call him back at your earliest convenience. Here." Nick set the sticky note atop the vanity, then turned to walk out. "I see it's a 715 area code. Must be one of your indiscreet lovers from the distant past." Nick laughed.

"Wait. I need your help." As Corey turned to hand the tweezers to Nick, the knotted towel slipped to the floor. He stood fully naked.

"Corey, there's no time for *that* now, Jesus. Get in the shower, and don't make us late as usual."

Nick disappeared into the living room before Corey had a chance to explain that he wanted help with his wounds, or to ask about the number of showers Nick had taken that day. Corey wondered—would Nick really have brazenly brought another guy into the condo? He tried to picture Nick, eagerly going at some faceless guy right on their bed. Of course, like usual, Nick would be on top.

Corey shook his head and set the tweezers atop the scribbled piece of paper, then picked up his towel and hung it behind the bathroom door. He stepped slowly into the tub and closed the sliding glass shower door behind him. After tempering the hot water with a modest amount of cold, he pushed his face directly into the spray. A stream washed away the dirt and coagulated blood. He reached for the bar of soap and gently worked up a lather. As the stinging subsided, his thoughts turned to the message from Larry Preston. That was a name he hadn't heard in a while.

He wondered how Larry even had this number—perhaps from Billy?

Corey emerged from the shower and finished cleaning his wounds. He grabbed the first aid kit from the vanity. Mrs. Randall was right. Stitches were undoubtedly the better option for his knee and one less likely to leave a scar. But how would he convince Nick who thought the wound wasn't that bad? Their plans had been made long ago, and reservations at Chez Toulouse were booking six weeks out. Canceling dinner and running off to urgent care would only create a shit-storm with Nick.

"Julian says the reservation can't be moved," Nick yelled from the hallway. "We need to leave in fifteen minutes. Don't make us late."

Corey didn't bother to reply. He patted his wounds dry with a tissue, then located a flesh-colored patch from the kit, placing it gingerly across the abrasion on his wrist. Next he pulled the paper backing from a butterfly bandage. He pushed the edges of the skin on his knee together to close the gash, wiped away the fresh flow of blood, and rolled the twin tentacles of the compress to bind his wound. It wasn't until after dressing his injuries that he noticed the antibiotic lotion in the bottom of the first aid case. He pondered removing the two bandages, applying the protective cream and starting all over again, but he felt an urgency to return Larry's call before Nick's fifteen-minute deadline expired.

He walked to the bedroom closet and pulled on a collared paisley dress shirt, wearing it untucked over a favorite pair of Ben Sherman jeans purchased on their 2011 trip to London. He pulled them delicately over his bandaged knee, then sat on the bed and dialed the phone, pulling on a pair of socks using his shoulder to hold the device against his ear.

"Good evening, law offices."

"May I speak to Larry Preston, please?"

"Speaking. How may I help you?"

"Hi. This is Corey. Corey Fischer? I had a message that you called."

"Corey, how the heck are ya? What has it been, five or six years?"

"I'm guessing five, sir. I had dinner at your house when Billy and I were back for our fifteen-year class reunion."

"That's right. You should stop by and see us next time you're back home."

"I live in Minneapolis now, Mr. Preston. *This* is my home." Corey winced, thinking his reply might have been a bit cold.

"Of course it is. I just meant... Well, I'm calling for a rather serious reason."

Corey heard Nick turn off the television in the other room. He cut to the chase. "Is it Billy? Did something happen to him?"

"Billy?" Larry paused.

"Yeah, I thought maybe you were calling about him."

"No, no. Billy's fine. He's fine. I talked to him last night."

"That's a relief."

"Yeah, Billy's doing great. You should go out and see him. Boy, does he ever have a nice place not far from the beach."

"I will, sir. I just haven't had the chance."

"I know. We all get so busy. Anyway, that's not the reason I called." Larry hesitated and took a deep breath.

Corey waited.

"I'm very sorry to say this, Corey, but I'm calling about your father. He passed away this morning. He had a heart attack at your family's cabin while getting ready for tomorrow morning's deer opener."

For a moment, Corey didn't breathe.

"Your mom received a call from the Barron County Sheriff saying they fielded a 911 alert about a man lying face down in the yard. By the time the EMTs arrived, he was gone. I'm very sorry."

Corey remained silent.

"Are you still there, son?"

"Yes, Mr. Preston. Thank you."

"Please, call me Larry."

"Have you talked to my mother?"

"Yes. We paid her a visit this afternoon right after she called. Of course, she was on her way out the door to meet with the priest. As she got into the car, she rolled down her window and asked me to call you with the news."

Corey wasn't surprised. It had been two months since he spoke with his mother, a year and a half since he had seen her face. How was it even possible for that much time to have passed?

"Corey, you still there?" After a pause, he asked again. "Corey?"

Hearing his name the second time, Corey emerged from reflection. "Yes, I'm sorry, Mr. Preston. Larry. I was distracted by someone here in my condo."

"You might want to call your mother. She mentioned that her sister was coming down from Eau Claire to stay the night."

"That's a relief," Corey said—perhaps too coldly. "Yes, I'll call her."

"She's also waiting for your father's body to arrive at the funeral home from Barron. You may want to get here as soon as you can." Larry continued after hearing no reply. "There's one more thing. The funeral will be on Monday morning, or at least that's what I'm speculating based on my sixty years of observing you Catholics and your traditions." He paused. "Geez, I hope that didn't sound disrespectful."

"No worries. It's my parents' religion, not mine—at least not anymore."

"Okay, then, assuming the funeral is on Monday, we'll have a reading of the will on Tuesday morning here in my office, the very next day."

"That's fine, sir. I'll make sure to let my mother know so she'll be there."

"That's kind of you Corey, but she already knows. I mentioned it to her at the house this afternoon. I'm telling you because you'll need to be present for the reading as well."

"Why? Can't you find one of my father's insurance buddies to serve as the witness or whatever it is you'll need?"

"I apologize. I guess I'm not being very clear today. You'll have to pardon me... it's been a rather long week." Larry cleared his throat. "I need you to be present for the reading so you can hear what your father is leaving you in his will."

"I can help you with that one right now, Larry." The fogginess in Corey's brain that emerged upon hearing the news of his father's death evaporated. "I won't have to be present for the reading because I'm certain my father didn't leave me a goddamn thing."

Just as Corey's tone on the phone call changed, so too did Larry's. "Now, I know that you and your father weren't on the best of terms."

"Not on the best of terms? That's putting it mildly."

"I'm sorry about that. I really am. But you still need to be at the reading of Frank's will. He left you something of significance, and you need to be present to hear it. I wrote that will, after all, and I know what it says. You and your mother are the only listed heirs."

"What is it? What did he leave me?"

"Now that would contravene my vow of ethics if I were to tell you over the phone. I'm sorry, but you're gonna have to be here in person on Tuesday morning to hear me read it out loud."

They exchanged goodbyes and ended the call. Corey sat on the edge of his bed. The weight of all he had heard sank in. His father was dead. The heart attack itself didn't surprise him, but the suddenness of it did. He gave no thought to regrets because there were none.

"Corey?" Nick poked his head into the bedroom. "Ready to go?"

"Yeah." He rose and walked toward the door.

"Were you talking to someone? I thought I heard you rambling on in here."

"I returned Larry Preston's call."

"Who?"

"Larry Preston. The message you handed me, remember?"

"And?"

"And what?"

"So who is he? Is he related to that friend of yours out in California?"

"Yeah, Larry is Billy's father."

"So, what did he want?" Nick uttered each word slowly, distinctly, harshly.

"Oh, he was just calling to let me know that Frank died."

"Frank? You mean, your father?"

"Yeah, that's the one."

"Oh my God. What happened?"

"Heart attack. Boom. Done."

"Jesus. I, uh, I'm sorry."

"Why are you sorry? You didn't even like him. Hell, you barely knew him."

"Well, it seems like I kinda did know him, from all the stories I've heard in our therapy sessions. Anyway, I'm sorry."

"Thanks. Do you want to get the Jeep and pull around front? I need to use the bathroom before we go. I'll meet you outside."

"You still want to go for dinner?"

Corey walked past Nick into the bathroom without answering and firmly shut the door. Inside, he rested both hands on the edge of the sink before lifting the left one aloft. He had forgotten for a moment about his injury, but pushing his wrist against the porcelain brought a sharp reminder. He stood upright, reaching for the medicine cabinet. Like he had done every single day for the past year, he twisted the cap off the semi-clear orange bottle and shook a single white pill into his hand, then tossed it into his mouth and swallowed. Fluoxetine, twenty milligrams. He wasn't even all that sure it did any good. He certainly felt less despondent than in the past, back when it seemed impossible to lift himself out of sadness. He remembered feeling heavy and almost unable to move during the worst moments—after discovering Nick's infidelity, incurring his father's bullying, and failing as an artist. Nick always claimed that Corey was just being dramatic, that he should "pull himself up" and "think positive thoughts for once." Nick didn't understand the weight of the sadness pinning Corey down. At times he couldn't even will himself to do the things he loved most—to paint, to read, or to run. It took a crisis for the doctors to diagnose his misery and prescribe an anti-depressant. He couldn't honestly say that he felt any happier than before starting the meds, but at least he no longer experienced the despondence from the lowest period in his life.

He looked in the mirror and ran four fingers through his thick brown hair, the hair he had inherited from his mother. He also had her eyes, her slender build. No one ever doubted their genetic ties. His thoughts traveled to her. What must she be thinking and feeling right now? Despair? Relief? Was she waiting for his call? Perhaps, but just as likely she expected awkwardness in their first conversation following Frank's sudden death. She did have Larry deliver the news, after all, instead of placing the call herself.

Corey wasn't ready to talk with his mother yet. He wasn't even certain of his own emotions. He wondered if hollow is how other people felt, at such an inevitable but unexpected moment, when you first learn that one of your parents has died. He had contemplated it intellectually, of course, but never in his heart. Now, he felt surprisingly indifferent, maybe even a bit liberated. He tried to envision his father's final moments, apparently walking from the cabin to his car, then lying prostrate on the ground clutching his chest. Corey abandoned those thoughts when he couldn't fully visualize his father being that vulnerable. Though Corey hadn't seen Frank in more than a year, surely he appeared roughly the same, perhaps his hair a bit thinner and his nose a deeper shade of red. Corey had looked his father in the eyes a million times—Frank always demanded it. But now he couldn't picture Frank at all.

The ring of the cell phone jolted him. He lifted the device from his pocket and saw Nick's name flash across the screen. *Impatient as usual*, he thought, before accepting the call.

"I'm on my way down, relax."

"Come on, we're late. What's the hold up? Can you please be…" Nick's voice disappeared mid-sentence. Corey ended the call and shoved the phone back into his pocket. Like most every day for the past twelve months, Nick's constant nagging suffocated him. Tolerating his over-the-top monitoring required enormous amounts of energy. At his worst, Nick's condescending presence exceeded the limits of Corey's medication.

He grabbed a pair of dress shoes from the closet and sat down on the bed to put them on. After tying the laces, he stayed seated for a minute and took a few deep breaths. He looked at the painting on the bedroom wall, the unavoidably large replica of Kahlo's *The Wounded Deer*. It was Corey's favorite piece of art. It had been a birthday gift from Nick ten years ago. What happened to that guy—the Nick who went above and beyond to show his love? He recalled Nick's tenderness in those early years, how he paid attention to Corey, and to his interests. Just before Corey's thirtieth birthday, Nick surprised him at work where they dined in the museum's café, and then Nick spent two hours following along with a school-group tour that Corey had led through the permanent exhibits. Sitting in the office afterward, Nick perused the oversized art books and asked Corey which piece he liked best. He remembered reaching for the specific book, turning to a page near the back and showing *The Wounded Deer* to Nick. He explained that Frida Kahlo was his idol. You could stare at any of her works for the longest time and still never see everything she painted. He remembered Nick asking why this piece in particular spoke to him. Corey was elated to talk about his favorite piece of art, explaining that he could feel the inner pain Kahlo was trying to convey.

At the time, Nick seemed interested in Corey's art, as he persisted with questions about the deer and the arrows protruding from its body. Corey remembered telling him that Kahlo actually had a pet deer of her own and that she was quite fond of it. She painted other works using that deer as a model too, but this one was unique. Corey remembered moving to the other side of the table and bringing the book closer to Nick, pointing to the painting's background—its trees with barren branches and a raging sea in the distance. Also, the word "karma" was scribbled in the left corner, possibly a reflection of how Kahlo saw herself—doomed by fate to a difficult and shortened life. She was only forty-seven when she died, Corey explained. He blurted out that he saw a little bit of his own past in her wounded deer. He also noted how he admired Kahlo's artistic effort, the way she put so much emotion onto the canvas. It's what he strived to do in his own work as well. One week after that exchange with Nick, Corey arrived home from work on a Friday night. He recalled how the unexpected darkness inside the condo unnerved him.

"Surprise! Happy Birthday!"

He remembered lights coming on all at once and how it scared the shit out of him. Nick was standing in the kitchen with Julian and Carol. All three donned party hats and walked toward him with a cake and thirty candles. Later there were presents, including a large, rectangular-shaped object wrapped in brown paper and a bow that Nick set down at Corey's feet.

After barely stripping away a thin swath of wrapping, Corey recognized what was inside. He laughed now, remembering Julian's incredulous reaction—"What in the hell *is* that?" It was a replica of *The Wounded Deer*, the same one Corey was now staring at in their bedroom.

He faintly heard Nick honking the horn of the Jeep Cherokee outside the building. He got up and left the condo. As he walked toward the elevator, he was reminded of the pain in his knee. Why hadn't he at least thought of taking an Advil? Too late. He exited the building and circled around to the passenger side. It hurt to bend his knee when climbing into the seat.

"Ready?"

Corey suppressed a sarcastic reply. "Yep."

"How's the knee?"

"If you really want to know, it needs stitches. That's where we should be going instead of your plans with Carol and Julian."

"My plans? You and your girlfriend Carol wanted to try Chez Toulouse since well before it opened. Don't pin this on me."

"Well, you could show a bit more compassion, Nick. In addition to these injuries, my father just died, remember?"

"You haven't spoken to the man in over a year, and I didn't see you shed a single tear. I'm sorry about your dad, I really am. But I asked you back at the condo if you still wanted to go to dinner. You didn't answer. You just walked away and got dressed."

"Fine," Corey conceded. "We'll see how the evening goes. But you'll be driving me to urgent care after dinner if things get any worse."

Nick looked over at Corey, then focused again on the road ahead. "Doctor Parker on duty, as usual."

"What do you mean by that?"

"Calm down, it was a joke. Sort of. I mean, I have taken care of you on more than a few occasions when you needed my help." Corey stared straight ahead as Nick drove. Sometimes Nick did, sometimes he didn't. "Remember Munich, 1998?"

Corey recalled their college graduation trip to Europe, relieved not to be talking any longer about his injuries or Frank's death. They had spent three weeks in the heart of the continent, hiking and eating and drinking their way across five countries. How could he ever forget the two nights in Munich?

"Yes, unfortunately. What I remember was trying to keep pace with *you* sampling every variety of beer in the Hofbrauhaus, with nothing more than half a pretzel in my stomach."

"Man, were you ever sick. I remember you turned green."

"Very funny. To this day I don't remember how I got back to the hotel, but I can vaguely picture you bringing me water, a piece of bread, and some pills."

"They made you feel better, didn't they?"

"Yes, but for all you know they could've been placebos. Or worse, poison."

Nick rolled his eyes and laughed. "I had a helluva time communicating with the German pharmacist down the street. She didn't speak a word of English."

"Then how could you be certain what you were buying?"

"She and I understood each other well enough with non-verbals. I showed her a photo of you from my wallet, held my head, and wailed like a dying freak pointing toward our hotel." Nick re-enacted the scene, then regrabbed the steering wheel.

"I'm surprised she didn't scream and call the police." Corey laughed at the memory, and at Nick's poor acting.

"Yeah, that display might have scared most people. But given my age, nationality, and our proximity to the beer gardens, I'm sure she'd seen it before."

"It sounds like you portrayed me accurately," Corey said. "I really felt like I was gonna die."

2

Friday

Nick tossed his keys to the valet and entered the restaurant with Corey trailing several steps behind.

"Sorry we're a bit late," Nick said as he reached the table at which Julian and Carol were seated, his thumb pointing backward. "You know how the princess can be when she's getting ready for the ball." Julian laughed. Carol poked him in the arm with her elbow. They rose from their chairs, embracing Nick and Corey in turn.

"Hi guys, my apologies," Corey said. "It's been a long week."

"No problem," Julian said. "We went ahead and ordered drinks. I hope your tastes haven't changed. We asked for the usuals."

As if on cue, a waiter appeared with Pinot Grigio for Carol, an IPA for Julian, a vodka tonic for Nick, and an iced tea with lemon and mint leaf for Corey.

"Belvedere, I hope?" Nick wore a look of deep expectation.

"Yes, sir," the waiter replied, holding the empty drink tray in one hand, the other arm perched in the middle of his lower back. Dressed in a starched white shirt and dark slacks, with freshly shined black shoes, the waiter looked nearly identical to his fellow servers working the room.

"I was relieved when they had it," Julian said. "I know your high-class taste when it comes to liquor."

He and Nick had been friends since business school. They golfed in the same foursome, hunted together with Nick's brothers every autumn, and often joined other junior executives in downtown bars at four thirty on weekdays. Corey suspected that Nick and Julian also covered for each other when one of them needed a believable excuse for arriving home later than expected.

Nick took a long sip and exhaled. "Ahhh."

"Is yours okay?" Carol asked Corey.

"Perfect, thank you. I'll just have to pace myself so I don't overindulge," he said while lifting his glass toward his lips. "It looks like I'll be the designated driver." Then, after a light sip, "Again."

Nick smirked. "Yes, I get to be the wild one tonight. Julian, you remember back when Corey used to drink? When he used to be more fun?" Corey bit his lower lip, even though he knew his reaction empowered Nick, like a puppeteer pulling strings with only the words from his mouth.

As Corey set his glass on the table, Carol noticed his bandaged wrist. "What happened there?"

He followed the direction of her gaze. "Oh, I had a nasty fall while running this afternoon. Scraped myself pretty good." He lifted his palm higher so Julian could see it too.

"Geez, man. That must hurt."

"He's fine," Nick interrupted. "Don't baby him."

"Yes, Julian. It was pretty painful. Still is. But it's nothing compared to the gash on my knee. We'll probably head to urgent care after dinner." He pushed back from the table.

"Jesus, Corey, keep your pants on. No one wants to see your other injury."

"I'm just stretching my leg, Nick, if that's all right with you. It's getting a bit stiff."

Nick tipped his glass, swallowing more than a sip of his drink.

"Yikes, your knee as well?" Carol asked.

"A pretty deep cut, actually. It's covered with a butterfly bandage for now, but I'm sure the doctor will recommend sewing it up."

"Good Lord, you've had quite a day," Julian said.

Corey glanced at Nick who was looking away from the table. He thought about mentioning the other part of his bad day—Frank's death—but stayed quiet.

Carol changed the subject. "So, we haven't seen you guys since Governor Dayton signed marriage equality into law. Isn't it exciting? Now everyone can legally wed the person they love."

"Here here." Julian lifted his glass. "To the spread of love in the great state of Minnesota."

"*Sante*," Nick said, lifting his tumbler as everyone at the table clinked glasses.

"Are we celebrating something special tonight, folks?" The waiter returned, standing tall at the side of their table. Deftly handing off an empty tray to the silent assistant to his right, both of the waiter's hands were folded behind his back. He flashed a toothy grin. Corey saw Nick smile back just as broadly. He had grown used to Nick's habit of ogling every attractive man that passed by.

"Just friendship and the expansion of love," Julian said.

"Very nice." The waiter recited the evening's specials, delivered with the confidence of a Broadway performer and the deliciously detailed descriptions of a seasoned storyteller. Chateaubriand with haricot verts, Coq a Vin in a reduction of Bordeaux, and his own professed favorite of the evening—Duck Confit prepared extra crispy.

"It should be called Duck Confat," Nick said as the waiter contributed a gratuitous chuckle. "I mean, have you seen how much grease they drain off those things? Ghastly. Delicious, yes, but still—disgusting." Julian and Carol looked into each other's eyes as they laughed at Nick's joke. Having recited the specials, the waiter moved on to another table.

Corey looked up from his menu and was reminded that, other than Billy, these were his closest, most enduring friends. Carol was still the effervescent girl he met in college. He always thought that she and Julian were an odd pair, though. Not that

Julian wasn't handsome—he was. But he seemed a bit bookish. Their stark difference in height also made them look incongruent, standing side by side. Yet, after sixteen years of marriage, they still seemed smitten.

It was no surprise that the foursome hung out together after all these years, despite Corey and Carol's sexual encounter in college. It was Carol and Julian who introduced Corey to Nick. Corey had been living in a singles dorm during senior year. Carol had texted to let him know that they would be going on a double date that coming Friday, and that he had no choice but to say yes. He called to protest, noting that the last three guys she set him up with had been complete disasters. She laughed and told him that this one would be different. The new guy was a friend of Julian's and super hot—a swimmer with a muscular physique. Corey dropped his objection and showed up at the restaurant on Friday night. He found Carol and her boyfriend of two years already snuggled into one side of the booth. Julian explained that his friend would be there within minutes. He promised that the guy was funny and smart. Carol added that she had tried to set Nick up with her sorority sister, but he had made clear his preference for men.

Corey could still picture Julian waving Nick over to their table as Corey stepped out from the booth to shake hands with the handsome stranger. The date was a success, the very first time Corey had gone home after meeting a guy and feeling like this could be *the one*. Nick was the most handsome man Corey had ever seen. He had a confident, masculine air about him that Corey found attractive.

Corey attended every swim meet during their senior year in college and professed his love within a month. He couldn't believe that this lanky Aquaman had said that he loved Corey in return. Their relationship felt different from any before, far beyond the first longings Corey had felt for the foreign exchange student during high school. He used to watch Nick fly down the lanes of that pool, awestruck by his raw power, by each deliberate cupping of the water in his strong hands. Yet that was not the strength he admired most. Nick seemed comfortable in his own skin, with who he was as a man. Nick had a perceptible depth, serenity, and sense of purpose unencumbered by fear of others' judgment. Corey remembered Carol and her girlfriends fawning over the qualities they collectively found so attractive about Nick.

"He's definitely a keeper, so witty and fun."

"Those muscles! That hair! Why wouldn't you date him?"

"Check out those long fingers. You know what that means."

Captain of the swim team, Nick exuded strength and sensuality in one fluid rhythm—graceful, like the way he cut through water in the pool. Corey still remembered how he fell in love in a split second just like Nick's flip-turns halfway through a hundred-yard sprint.

Carol posed a question to the table, interrupting Corey's faraway thoughts. "So are you two going to get married again, now that it's official here in the state?"

"Well, are we?" Nick looked at Corey.

"I don't know. Is that a proposal? It sounded more like a deflection."

Nick shrugged his shoulders, raised his eyebrows, and twisted his lips into a non-verbal smirk. The rest of the table fell silent before Carol jumped in to offer a toast. "*Santé!*"

"But isn't it passé now to be in favor of marriage equality?" Julian asked. "Only the zealots remain opposed." The other three nodded in agreement. "I mean it's all one giant conspiracy, if you ask me—one last insulting harassment on the poor gays."

"How do you mean?" Corey asked.

"Well, think about it. You've survived Stonewall, the AIDS epidemic, legalized discrimination. And now society wants you all to hang up the swinging single life and get married? To one person for the rest of your lives? Haven't you people suffered enough?"

Corey laughed along with everyone else.

Carol persisted. "I know it's a big deal legally and all, but for you two it must seem automatic, even uneventful since you were already married in Canada."

"Uneventful?" Corey asked.

"Well, how long have you guys been together? Almost two decades?"

"Three happy years," Nick deadpanned. Only Julian laughed.

They resumed perusing their menus. Corey had already settled on the salmon with *pomme de terre*. The waiter returned to the table and took dinner orders without writing a single note. The topic of marriage never resurfaced. Instead, the conversation focused on work and plans for upcoming winter vacations. Corey said little, barely listening to Nick and Julian's explanation of a recent reorganization at the bank. For some reason, Nick's "three happy years" comment brought him back to wondering about his mother. Did she have that many happy years with Frank? In their entire forty-year marriage, was she content more than 10 percent of the time? And what did she feel now, sadness or relief? He had no idea. The broken relationship with his parents these past sixteen months carried him further and further away from knowing how she felt about anything. He no longer precisely knew her thoughts about Frank. And he couldn't say for certain exactly what she felt toward her only son.

Nick was on his second vodka tonic, half-way to his normal total for the night. With every sip, he seemed more relaxed, less abrasive. To Corey, this was a predictable and welcomed change. For all of Nick's faults, at least alcohol had a calming, humanizing effect on him. He drank to the edge of inebriation, but rarely lost control.

After emerging from deep thought, Corey's eyes met briefly with Nick's. Then he looked away. He felt an itch on his knee and indiscreetly used his fingernails to scratch the edge of the bandage through his jeans. Worried that he had detached the edge of the bandage where it had previously stuck to his skin, he considered slipping off to the restroom and inspecting the wound underneath. The tickle running down his shin bone might be a renewed stream of blood.

"So, Carol, what's going on at the museum?" Nick asked.

She glanced at Corey, then turned back toward Nick. "Oh, not much really."

"What do you mean?" Julian asked. "Tell them about how great the Gorky exhibit is going. You talk about it all the time at home."

Corey reached out and touched Carol's hand. "It's fine, really. I'd actually like to hear about it."

"Well, we've had record numbers pass through the museum. I've seen quite a few people come back multiple times. It might just be the most popular and meaningful collection we've ever exhibited."

"That's terrific," Nick said. "Tell us more about it."

Carol looked at Corey for a non-verbal cue, and he urged her with furrowed eyebrows to continue.

"People seem quite drawn to *The Artist and his Mother*. There's always a crowd surrounding that work."

"Is that the one where the boy is standing next to the seated woman, and she looks white as a ghost, but with missing hands?"

"Yes, Julian, but her hands aren't exactly missing. They were just washed over or whited out. Critics say it symbolized the inability to feed herself during the Armenian Genocide. After all, she did starve to death right in front of Gorky when he was only fourteen years old."

"Well that's depressing," Nick said.

"Perhaps, but it's a stunning piece of art, arguably one of the most powerful paintings of the twentieth century."

"It took Gorky almost sixteen years to paint it." Corey couldn't help but chime in. He had read practically everything ever written about Gorky back when he worked at the museum, back when he was the lead curator for the anticipated exhibit. Carol looked at Corey and smiled.

"Does that mean we'll have to wait another decade and a half for you to finish your own masterpiece, like Gorky?" Nick took a long sip of his drink while still maintaining eye contact with Corey.

Carol continued. "The other piece that garners quite a bit of attention is called *Agony*."

"I don't think I was as fond of that one," Julian said. "I found it thematically dark and confusing."

"Indeed, it is completely different from the painting of Gorky with his mother. It was completed only a year before the artist died and represents the height of his surrealist phase. Gorky used a vibrant red palette for this one, along with an incisive pulling together of line and form to depict pain, suffering, and death."

"Sounds delightful. I predict I'll prefer the painting of the mother, like Julian."

"But that's just it, Nick. You can't help but look at them both, possibly even at the same time. We deliberately hung them side by side which has never happened with these two paintings before."

Corey envied the excitement in Carol's voice.

"The two works reveal vast differences in Gorky's principal styles and between the use of vibrant color versus pale ones, between abstraction and surrealism. Yet, the paintings are a perfectly matched pair in one important respect."

Nick and Julian listened intently. Only Corey knew what Carol would likely say next.

"Each is an elegy to Gorky's parents. He painted the one in tribute to his mother, obsessing for thirty years after her passing to achieve perfection. *Agony*, on the other hand, was completed quickly, less than a year following the death of his estranged father, and only one year before Gorky took his own life by hanging himself in the backyard."

Nick cleared his throat.

"As long as the dinner conversation has grown so despondent, it might be a good time to share some bad news we received today."

His tone had grown quiet, more serious.

"Nick?" Carol asked. "What's going on?"

"Well, since we're already discussing the death of estranged fathers, we should tell you that Corey's dad passed away this morning too. We got the call before coming here."

"Oh my God, Corey. I'm so sorry." Carol choked up as she spoke.

"Geez, man, you have our deepest sympathies," Julian added. "You guys should have called us and canceled. This must be a shocking blow."

Corey finally looked up.

"Thank you. As you know, my father and I weren't close. I haven't spoken to him in over a year."

"This must be so difficult," Carol said, "after what he said to you last year. I still remember it."

"It definitely caused a rift—my father's cruel words and my mother's silence."

Carol got up from her chair and enveloped Corey in a tight embrace before going back to her seat.

"In fairness," Nick chimed in, "It was mostly his father. Frank was never the most open-minded man in the world. Corey's mom is lovely, though. Quiet, a bit complacent perhaps, but nothing like his father."

"How is your mother holding up?" Carol asked.

"I, uh, haven't spoken with her yet. I literally got the call from a family friend as we were heading out the door. Mom was at church, then going to the mortuary. My aunt is with her for the night."

"Again," Julian said, "we're so sorry. Is there anything we can do?"

"Thanks, but everything will take care of itself. My father was a planner. That's the one good thing I can say about him. He'll have tended to every detail in advance, right down to the type of food served at the reception."

"Yeah, I think this will be hard on Corey's mother. Frank was the centerpiece of her life. She made his meals, ironed his shirts, and basically waited on the man hand and foot for forty years. She put up with a lot and catered to his every whim." Nick's declaration of insight into the Fischer family dynamic brought a look of surprise to Corey's face. Perhaps Nick had listened to all of Corey's complaints and stories about his parents. "I didn't know her terribly well, of course, given our estrangement, but the few times I met her she was exceedingly nice. And pretty too. In fact, I'd say that Corey takes after Ginny in all the best ways."

An image of his mother's face appeared in Corey's brain. He always thought she was the most lovely woman he knew. Even as she aged, her beauty deepened along with all of her "worry wrinkles," as Ginny called them. Corey looked right past them.

"That's what everyone always said when I was growing up— that I take after my mom. Most meant it as a compliment, but when pointed out by my father, it was intended as a critique."

"And now he's gone, so we should bury that bitterness with him," Nick said. "No sense dwelling on the past."

Corey turned to look at Nick. For once, couldn't he just nod politely like everyone else instead of telling Corey what he should or shouldn't feel? He turned toward Carol and Julian instead of speaking his mind to Nick.

"I'm glad I look like my mother. She's a beautiful woman, especially her long brown hair. Well, at least it was long for a while."

"What do you mean?" Carol asked.

"When I was younger, she let it fall to the middle of her back. Occasionally she might pull it into a bun or a ponytail, but she was always perfectly coiffed and took pride in making herself look nice. It's funny—sometimes I would watch her through the doorway of my parents' bedroom as she sat in front of the makeup vanity, brushing her long auburn locks, seemingly miles away in thought. I always wondered what she was thinking about as she combed her flowing strands over and over, sometimes smiling, sometimes just staring into the mirror. I never asked."

Nick interrupted the story to detain the passing waiter and order another drink. "Anyone else?"

Carol and Julian declined. Corey too.

"Do you mind if I tell the rest of my story now?"

"The rest? I thought that was it."

"Go ahead, Corey," Carol said. "So, what happened?"

"I remember the day I came home from school, in eighth grade, to find her crying at that same table. Her head lay in her hands, her long hair now shockingly short. I tapped on her bedroom door and asked what was wrong. She straightened up in her chair upon hearing my voice. She wiped her eyes with a tissue and spoke to me by looking through the mirror. She wouldn't turn around. 'I'm fine, honey,' I remember her saying. 'A little emotional today, that's all.'"

Corey paused to take a swallow of iced tea. Nick sat silent in his chair, not even reaching for his drink. Corey had never shared this story with him before.

"Why was she crying?" Julian asked.

"I knew before she said a word, before she even looked up at me through the reflection in the mirror. It was her hair," he said, gesturing in the air behind his ear. "I couldn't stop staring at it, or at least the space where it used to fall. 'What happened to your hair?' I asked. She told me that she had gotten it cut short and asked what I thought. 'It's different,' I said. Looking back, that was a stupid thing to say, given how upset she had been. But at the time, it was the best I could do."

"Why did she cut it off?" Carol asked.

Corey raised his eyebrows, then took a deep breath and exhaled through his nose. "She assured me that my dad would like it. 'This was his idea,' she said. 'Your father thought I was getting too old for ponytails and long hair, that I needed a fresh look. I'm sure he's right.' And that tells you an important fact about my parents. They both always thought he was right."

Once dinner ended, they split two desserts between them—crème brulee and tart de pomme with iced cream. Nick and Julian each had a glass of port while Carol and Corey ordered herbal tea. Proclaiming themselves stuffed, they left the restaurant and retrieved their cars from the valet. Corey felt his phone vibrate and saw that Billy was trying to call. He sent it to voice mail. Carol and Julian's car arrived first, and they left. When Nick began chatting with the handsome twenty-something valet, Corey listened to the message from Billy who offered his condolences about Frank. He also offered to fly out for the funeral. Corey sent a quick text thanking him but assuring Billy it wasn't necessary. Instead, Corey promised that he'd come out to California for a visit, sometime after Christmas.

"Hey, the Jeep's here. Who are you texting?"

Corey looked up and hit "send" at the sound of Nick's voice.

"I'm not texting anyone." He knew better than to tell Nick the truth, especially after so many drinks. Nick repeatedly accused Corey of being infatuated with Billy, even suggesting that they probably gave each other hand-jobs back in high school. Neither was true. "I'm just seeing which is the closest urgent care or emergency room." That lie triggered the argument Corey expected. Nick put up a fuss, but ultimately Corey insisted. As the designated driver, he had full control and drove them straight to the ER.

Nick reluctantly followed Corey inside the hospital. They made their way toward registration following color-coded signs. Each of them was familiar with the layout of the ER and the process of walking in wounded, from Corey's prior panic attack.

The chaos this evening took Corey by surprise. The waiting room was filled with people. A toddler sat in his mother's lap crying, holding a bandaged hand close to his chest. An entire family of what Corey assumed to be Somalians hovered around an elderly man. They were talking excitedly in a foreign tongue. A few people were asleep in plastic seats, and an elderly couple sat quietly in the corner sharing a sandwich and Styrofoam cup of coffee, with the man occasionally stopping to check his pulse. There wasn't an empty chair in the room.

Corey approached the desk while Nick waited several steps behind. The intake nurse assessed his emergency as *low* on the scale. "It might be an hour or more before you can be seen," she said. Corey was glad Nick wasn't close enough to hear that. He took the registration form and led Nick to a stand-up table on the other side of the room. He grabbed one of the pens attached to the table by a metal chain. With the pain in his wrist still acute, Corey held up the pen and asked Nick for help in filling out the form. Nick obliged and began completing the items he could with shaky hands—name and address, social security number, date of birth. Corey explained again how the injury happened, in detail, and Nick transcribed a shorthand version.

Then he conducted a rapid-fire quiz, asking Corey to answer yes or no to a long list of maladies. "Diabetes? Cancer? Coronary Heart Disease?"

Corey told Nick to stop playing games and to lower his voice. He should know all of the answers to those questions already.

"Ever tested positive for an infectious disease, such as HIV/ AIDS?"

The answer was no, but thankfully there was no question about STDs. Corey had never told Nick about the gonorrhea diagnosed in his sophomore year of college. It had been treated long before they met, back in Corey's wilder days after first coming out as gay. Recognition of his sexual orientation had come slowly during freshman year, but once acted upon Corey became unleashed. As a sophomore, there were plenty of one-night stands. He met men by answering personal ads in the paper and at eighteen-plus nights in the clubs. There were a few actual dates and a one-month romance, but most encounters were purely for sex.

On occasion, Corey engaged in things more risky—anonymous hook-ups in a public restroom and once on a path along the riverbank just downstream from his dorm. He had a particular weakness for the bad boys—the ones who wore leather or displayed tattoos. Piercings and facial scruff were equally fierce turn-ons. Carol referred to it as Corey's "punk rocker" phase.

He slowed down a bit by the end of junior year, fearing that a sudden fever and appearance of bumps in his mouth meant that he had caught another STD. He was relieved when the nurse said it was nothing more than canker sores and that he should try eating a healthier diet. Once he met Nick, Corey put his feral desires and lifestyle behind him. He became a willingly loyal partner.

"Family health history?" Corey looked at Nick but gave no verbal reply. Was Nick so affected by vodka that he had already forgotten about Frank's death? "I'll fill that in for ya. But I don't know why they need your parents' health status to stitch up a wounded knee. Ridiculous."

Corey looked at the elderly couple once more. They had finished eating and were quietly waiting their turn. He noticed they were holding hands, and he wondered why they were there. Corey considered the woman's face. He had long ago abandoned painting portraits in favor of landscapes. But something about her countenance made him stare and think about casting her onto canvas. Maybe it was her strong cheek bones, or perhaps it was the devotion he imagined inside her as she sat in this desperate hospital waiting room, sitting by her man.

"Okay, let's see," Nick continued as he turned the paper over. "Insurance company name and group number, or name of the person responsible for payment? Oh, I guess that'd be me." Corey kept staring at the elderly couple in the corner. He wondered if bitterness in a relationship wanes over time. Do people soften with age? Would Nick ever stop holding his role as the family provider over Corey's head?

He thought about how he and Nick had reached this point. A year after graduation, they had rented an apartment together. Nick landed a coveted entry-level job at a bank while completing his master's degree. Corey had turned his museum internship into a paid position, and their high-rise flat was the envy of their growing network of friends. Corey remembered telling Carol that he thought he had struck gold with Nick—a handsome man with a good job who professed his love for Corey freely, and often. Nick also urged Corey to pursue his art, to eschew getting an advanced degree or a higher-paying job. He encouraged Corey to get his own studio. "The world needs to see your talent," he remembered Nick saying. Nick made more than enough money to support them both. "Someday, when you're a world-renowned painter, I'll retire early and we'll live off your fame and success."

Corey swallowed that promise just like one of those catfish he and Billy used to snag back in Pepin, the ones that bit into deceptively delicious bait. For the first few years, it was like living a dream. He sublet a small studio and spent untold hours crafting new works. A few pieces earned spots in local art shows. But there were no breakthroughs. For several years he entered pieces in the State Arts Board's Essential Art competition. Twice he made it to the finals, but he never won first prize. Yet, Corey was happy, and the support from Nick was pivotal to his budding career as an artist.

"Marital status? Hmmm. It doesn't list any choices, just a blank space. Do you think they mean single versus married, or happy versus miserable?"

Corey refused to laugh. "Married. You were there with me when we each said 'I do' and Julian pronounced us husband and husband, remember?"

Nick looked as though he were going to say something, but then turned back toward the form. Corey was troubled by the look on Nick's face. What was he thinking—that he regretted getting married? Despite last year's drama, Nick seemed committed to continuing their relationship. He did recall Nick's shocking suggestion three years in, however, to open up their relationship to allow for having sex with other men. "It's pretty common," Nick argued at the time, "so why not?"

Corey reminded him of their agreement to be monogamous. Nick pushed back, saying that he hadn't sown his wild oats in college like Corey did. "Maybe it's not entirely out of my system." Corey stood his ground—a commitment was a commitment. Nick relented, but that conversation lingered in Corey's mind for a long time to come, and it undermined Corey's confidence in Nick's vow of fidelity.

He also recalled the first indication of cheating, a few years later. He had gone to surprise Nick at the gym with plans for dinner at a brand new café. He scoured the weight room and running track. There was no sign of Nick, yet his vehicle was in the lot when Corey arrived. He headed for the steam room on the off chance that Nick was taking a sweat break between routines. He was. Corey discovered Nick sitting naked next to a fellow gym rat, their hands in each others' laps, barely shrouded in the mist. Each covered up with a towel after the door opened and Corey stepped inside.

Corey turned and abruptly left. Nick called after him as the door closed, saying "It's not like that." But yet, it was. Corey left the gym and waited in his car, vacillating between anger and self-pity. He saw Nick exit the building ten minutes later, freshly showered. Corey emerged from his vehicle and walked over to confront Nick.

He remembered demanding they talk about it right then and there. Nick persuaded him to at least get inside the car, given the bitter temperature outside and the presence of people coming and going from the gym who might overhear their argument. Corey recalled mocking Nick for suddenly being concerned about what people see and hear him doing in public. No sooner had Corey stepped inside the car when Nick began to sob. He apologized through his tears, saying this was not who he meant to be—a cheater. Nick's contrition did little to temper Corey's ire, especially when Nick offered that he "couldn't help it."

"Bullshit," Corey had said.

It took several minutes for Nick to pull himself together and unravel the truth. He claimed that he had something important to share, something he had only told one person to that point. From the time he was eight until roughly fourteen, his older brother's friend forced Nick to be his "girlfriend." The guy made Nick promise never to tell anyone. The first time it happened, the guy snuck into Nick's bedroom during a sleepover, feeling around beneath the sheets and massaging Nick in places he had never been touched before. After that, Nick was persuaded to perform orally and then to receive his brother's friend from behind, even though it hurt like hell. As Nick's story unfolded, Corey's fury dissipated like the frost on the clearing window ahead of him.

Corey asked Nick why he hadn't told someone. Nick said he had told his brother after the third encounter, but his brother called Nick "crazy" and said that the friend was a starting safety for the school football team. "He's not a fag!" Nick never contemplated telling anyone else, certainly not his parents.

Corey remembered reaching out to Nick in the front seat of the car, pulling him into an affirming embrace. His mind volleyed between shock and sympathy... and also uncertainty as to how that difficult past related to Nick's present promiscuity. In that moment, Corey remembered offering forgiveness. In the days that followed he insisted that they seek therapy, and Nick obliged. Over the ensuing months, as the layers of Nick's shame and guilt revealed itself in unquenchable thirst for self-esteem, Corey's love and compassion for Nick grew apace.

And yet, in the ensuing years, doubts persisted. Corey willed himself to trust that Nick was at work when he was supposed to be and abiding by a vow to skip the steam room at the gym. He considered demanding that Nick only work out in the small exercise room at the condo, but remembered Carol talking him out of it. "You're going to have to trust him," she had said. Corey wondered how that could be possible. What if Nick cheated again? And unless he was stupid enough to get caught, Corey would never even know for sure if Nick was being faithful.

Nick's voice brought Corey back to the registration form.

"Any current medications?"

"Fluoxetine." Nick should've known the name of the drug because he was the one responsible for Corey being on it. It was his affair with Evan in Miami that sent Corey into that tailspin last year—or at least Corey's suspicion of an affair. Nick never did admit to it. He convinced Corey that the entire thing was in his imagination and that the suicide attempt was further proof of mental illness. Corey was the one who needed help, Nick argued. Nick was not the one to blame.

Corey only conceded that Nick was right about one thing— that Corey had no proof of the affair. But he wasn't the only one who held suspicions over the years. Rumors trickled back to Corey about Nick sharing his body with other men. There was even talk of an on-going thing with a closeted married man from work, Nick's employee Evan. Corey thought he spied Evan in their condo building once, when Corey came home unexpectedly early from a museum event in Chicago a few years back. He had recognized Evan from one of Nick's holiday work parties, remembering the strong vibe Corey had detected—his gaydar was rarely wrong. Corey was instantly taken aback as they crossed in the lobby. Evan looked awkwardly at his watch and quickly left the building.

Corey remembered walking straight into the condo and finding Nick in the bedroom standing shirtless, zipping up the fly of his jeans. Corey demanded to know if that was Evan he saw in the lobby. Nick feigned ignorance and suggested that if it was Evan, then perhaps he was visiting someone else, possibly getting some action on the side with one of the neighbors. Corey scoffed at the obvious lie, saying that he doubted Evan wanted to be ridden by a cougar like Mrs. Randall when the one he was really after was Nick.

Looking back, Corey realized the strategy of pushing Nick into a corner always boomeranged. Nick returned fire with all-out war. He yelled at Corey for being "dramatic and wrong," swearing that Evan was straight. "He's married for God's sake," he remembered Nick angrily protesting. "Evan wants pussy." The fight lasted ten minutes. Corey ultimately had no proof and Nick gave no ground. In the end, it was Corey who had to apologize for insulting Nick, who agreed to forgive Corey—this time—but told Corey that he needed to remember who pays the mortgage and both car payments along with virtually everything else while Corey was "finger painting" all day. Corey relented and said no more. But he remembered from that point forward being on a continuous search for answers to a gnawing suspicion—that Nick was a cheating bastard. Corey would smell T-shirts from the hamper. He spied on Nick's phone when he was in the shower. And occasionally he would rifle through Nick's briefcase in the middle of the night.

Tonight, that same cheating bastard stood beside Corey in an emergency room, continuing to ask questions from a registration form.

"Okay. Last question—any allergies?"

Corey stared straight through him with a piercing gaze that made Nick ask whether Corey had just seen a ghost.

"No, but I'm done answering these stupid questions. Come on, we're leaving."

"What? We're almost done."

"I'm done now. Let's go."

"Wait a minute. You seemed fine a second ago. Is it something about allergies? I didn't think you had any. What's the big deal?"

"No, I don't have any, but yes that question is a big deal, all right?"

"I'm at a loss here, Corey. You wanted to come to the ER, so we came to the ER. Now, all of a sudden, you want to leave? I don't want to be here any more than you do, but I think you owe me an explanation. I've been filling out this stupid form for the past fifteen minutes."

"Fine. I'll tell you what I'm allergic to. I'm allergic to the memory of my dead father, that's what. I want to get him out of my mind, but he keeps showing up, and it's making me sick to my stomach."

"Whoa, whoa, whoa. What are you talking about?"

"When I was eight years old, I first learned what my father really thought of me, though I didn't understand it until years later."

"What do you mean?"

Corey released a deep sigh. "I was heading toward the Kwik Stop with Billy to buy junk food for our sleepover. I came flying into the house and asked my mom if I could have five bucks. She was sitting in her recliner reading a magazine. She told me to look in my father's wallet. Frank had the day off and was working in his basement shop. I could hear the muffled sound of a circular saw from down below. I ran to my parents' room and reached for his wallet sitting atop the dresser. I held and admired that smooth leathery pouch for a moment before spreading it open in search of a five-dollar bill. His medical emergency card floated out and fell to the floor."

"I reached down to get the card and was about to put it back when I decided to look at it more closely. I knew what it was. I'd seen my mom's card a few times while rummaging through her purse, but never Frank's. I can still picture what it said. His blood type was O. He carried 185 pounds on a five-foot-ten frame. Then I scanned past the details of age, address, and next of kin. The word "allergies" appeared, followed by a long blank line. On it, my father had written "queers" in permanent black ink. It caught me off-guard, but I didn't know why. I folded the wallet shut without taking any money, then put it back on the dresser in the exact position where I had found it. I left their bedroom and headed for the bath, feeling as if I were about to puke. Then I went into my bedroom and shook a bunch of coins from a ceramic pink piggy bank and ran out of the house back toward Billy's.

"At the time, I didn't know exactly what I had just seen. But I knew that the strange and horrible-sounding word was wrong, and that it made me uncomfortable. It wasn't until years later, in college, that I thought about that incident again and knew the truth—that my father was allergic to queers. My father was allergic to me."

Nick released the almost-completed registration form from the clipboard and let the pen fall back atop the table. He crumpled up the paper, threw it into the trash, and put his arm around Corey.

"Come on. Let's get out of here and go home."

3

Saturday

They left for Pepin the following morning at eight. Because of the late-night emergency room visit, Nick insisted that Corey drive so he could nap. He also demanded that they take Nick's Jeep because it was more comfortable than Corey's Prius on a long drive.

Nick was asleep within minutes. Corey turned the radio to a classical station, hoping that would drown out Nick's snoring. He sipped tea from his travel mug and focused on the road ahead. The sounds inside the Jeep became little more than white noise, and his mind drifted ahead to thoughts of arriving in Pepin. For the past sixteen months, he truly thought he'd never see that damn town again. His father's command had been clear—get out of this house and don't come back. How strange to be traveling there now, with no preparation for what lay ahead. His father wouldn't be there, of course, but how would the year-long chasm affect the reunion with his mom? Would they even discuss it, or did Frank's intervening death close the door on that episode?

He continued driving south on the four-lane highway before crossing the river into Wisconsin and following a state highway the rest of the way. The overcast November skies mirrored Corey's mood. Memories of that awful night last year kept returning to his mind. He tried thinking of something else, anything else. Yet he couldn't help but dwell on them. As he reflected on it now, maybe it was his mother who set the whole calamity in motion. After all, it was Ginny who first mentioned Nick, encouraging Corey to bring him to Pepin. If she hadn't been so cavalier in her offer, maybe Corey wouldn't have felt emboldened to confront Frank.

He remembered the conversation beginning on a friendly note. He had talked about the art studio and the museum. There was also discussion of a few local news items. Yes, that was the catalyst—Frank's mention of same sex marriage on the Minnesota ballot. In retrospect, Corey could have stopped there, should have stopped there. Why had he felt empowered to push further at that particular moment? Was it the alcohol? Was it because he was almost forty and it was time to take a stand? He couldn't say, and now it didn't matter. Frank's death meant that the words spoken that night could never be taken back or explained or atoned.

Corey slowed the Jeep for a four-way stop. The sudden braking awakened Nick. "Where are we?"

"Almost there. Another half-hour to go."

"Oh." Nick rubbed his eyes before looking at Corey. "Why are you crying?"

Corey wiped away the tear he hadn't felt escape down his cheek. "I'm not crying. Just deep in thought."

"About what, or will I regret that I asked?"

"This is my first trip back to Pepin since, well, you know when. It brings back painful memories."

"You mean about Frank's cruel statement?"

"Yeah. I'm trying to piece together how it all happened, and whether it could have been avoided."

"Corey, you did all of that in therapy. We even role-played how you might confront your father. But now he's dead, so why are you torturing yourself? Frank isn't going to be there."

"Maybe that makes things worse, okay? I did all of that talking and processing at the hospital and in therapy. But now that I'm actually going back home, the whole thing feels suddenly real."

"Fine, let's go over it again right now. I don't want you falling apart in front of your family."

Corey stayed silent.

"Come on, out with it."

He relented, reluctantly retelling the events from last year. He lingered over minor details—drinking the sugary lemonade with Ginny, his father mixing drinks with unsteady hands—and rushed through important ones, like his decision to reveal his Canadian marriage. Nick listened without interrupting. Corey's voice became more animated and high-pitched as the sequence of scenes led closer to Frank's cruel declaration. He tightly grabbed the steering wheel at the very moment he replayed the part about picking up his overnight bag and walking out of his parents' house. Then he noticed the speedometer on the Jeep—ten miles per hour over the limit. He tapped lightly on the brakes to slow down, then looked over at Nick for a reaction. Nick had been respectfully quiet throughout Corey's umpteenth retelling of this story, which was a refreshing change.

Nick was sound asleep.

Like that watershed evening over a year ago, Nick wasn't there when Corey needed him. He was tempted to swerve to the left so that Nick's head would hit the side window, giving him what he deserved. The road was curvy on this part of the drive, and they were going fifty-five miles an hour. But there was no sense instigating drama. The therapist repeatedly told him that self-created crises were Corey's greatest pitfall. He looked out the window toward the Mississippi and considered the river that had been flowing past him for his entire life. He imagined that one day he might even get swept away from Nick and drown, caught in a sharp drop-off like those in the shifting sandy bottoms of that same river where Corey swam frequently as a boy.

Here he was—driving along in silence on a two-lane Wisconsin road headed toward a reunion with his mother, a funeral for his father, and with Nick callously asleep. Nick's insensitivity reminded Corey that the story of the worst night of his life had not ended when he left his parents' house. That part—his father's declaration—was only the beginning. A cascade of emotions had welled up inside him on that difficult night in 2012, and Corey could still summon them today as he drove toward Pepin. He recalled how the therapist in the psych ward had convinced him that two massive issues, hitting him simultaneously, was too much for anyone to bear. Corey shouldn't feel bad any longer about trying to take his own life. Most of the time he accepted that advice, but today he once again succumbed to a feeling of defeat. Goddamn you Nick, he wanted to shout right now—just like back then. He again gripped the steering wheel hard, wanting to escape from this Jeep, from these memories.

Corey willed himself into thinking something more positive. He started by focusing on those who helped him on that life-threatening night. The last thing he could remember, even now, was smashing his phone and those photos onto the tile floor and draining Nick's last bottle of Belvedere. Between that and waking up to feel Billy caressing his foot through the blanket, he recalled nothing. Of course, Mrs. Randall happily told him all of the uncomfortable details months later. Initially she had come to his door upon hearing the breaking glass but returned to her own condo once no one answered and she heard no further suspicious sounds. But she had sprung up from her recliner upon hearing the first siren blaring from the street, alarmed as it drew near. She had pulled back the curtain on her living room window and seen the first responders rush out of the fire truck and enter their building, below. She opened her door and peeked into the hallway to smell if there was any hint of smoke. That's when the paramedics came rushing out of the stairwell, heading straight for her, demanding to know which condo belonged to Corey Fischer. "That one." She pointed dramatically in her retelling of the tale to Corey. "Hold on a second, I have a key!"

Billy had filled in the other missing pieces for him. Upon receiving Corey's desperate voice message that July night while getting home late from a job site, he had tried repeatedly, unsuccessfully to call Corey back. Sensing that his best friend might be in danger, Billy called the Minneapolis Police Department telling them it was an emergency. Billy had also tried calling Nick, but the calls went straight to voice mail. After receiving only vague, limited information from the police dispatcher in the ensuing hour, Billy drove to LAX and boarded the red-eye to Minneapolis.

The last person to provide missing details of that night was Nick. He defensively discussed it during therapy months later. He confessed that after Corey hung up on him and wouldn't accept his return calls, Nick went out for a drink and dinner with Evan. Nick had assured both Corey and the therapist that his interactions with Evan were platonic and strictly business. Corey didn't believe it. Nick acknowledged seeing Billy's number flash across the screen of his phone a few times, but he sent them to voice mail. He figured that Corey had complained bitterly to his best friend, and Nick wasn't interested in being chewed out by Billy. Then, he had turned his phone to silent, to enjoy the rest of his evening in peace. He did listen to Mrs. Randall's call Saturday night after returning to his room. He caught a flight home mid-morning on Sunday and took a cab straight to the hospital. When Corey refused him entrance to the room and the hospital staff refused to budge, Nick left the hospital and went home.

Corey and Nick reached the city limits of Pepin twenty minutes later. Silent, meditative chants had returned him to a state of zen by the time Nick awoke from his morning nap. Nick was insistent that he needed to address some important work e-mails about a brewing HR crisis, so Corey left him at the motel for an early check-in. Rather than rushing to his parents' house, Corey drove around town to see a few favorite haunts from his childhood. First up was the Kwik Stop, the place he'd been a million times before with Billy. He stopped to buy a cup of coffee, only to cringe at the slightly burnt taste the moment it hit his tongue. Sadly, the nearest Starbucks was forty miles away.

He pulled over to the curb across the street from Pepin's Community School. It was the one and only school he attended from kindergarten until graduating from twelfth grade. From this vantage point he could see the football field where he would go on Friday nights during high school with his father to watch the varsity team, led by strong safety Billy Preston on defense. At times, Corey asked if he could go to the games with a friend instead, but Frank insisted on this being a father-son ritual. Unfortunately, that ritual always included Frank haranguing Corey about not trying out for the team, for choosing to run cross-country instead. Later, after enduring Frank's embarrassing loud-mouthed jawing at the referees, Corey would happily part from his father at the end of the game and wait for Billy to emerge from the locker room. The two of them would then walk to the Kwik Stop for an ice cream sandwich to celebrate victory or commiserate in defeat.

He then drove past the Preston house and wished he would see Billy step out from the front porch and onto the lawn.

After driving past all of the landmarks he could remember, Corey then turned the Jeep toward his childhood home. Cars filled the Fischer driveway, one each for Corey's three sets of aunts and uncles. He knew that the next two days would be filled with the presence of family from the Geraghtys, his mother's side. There would of course be visits from his father's few friends too. Like Corey, Frank had been an only child, and the Fischer branch of the family tree was almost barren. He parked across the street, turned off the ignition, and sat for several minutes rehearsing what he might say once inside the house. He reached into his bag and downed a Xanax with the lukewarm dregs of his convenience store coffee.

Corey felt nauseous. He strained to remember when and what he last ate—oatmeal with brown sugar and raisins at seven o'clock before leaving home. He restarted the Jeep, looked out the window to make sure no one had noticed his arrival then took off. He decided he wasn't yet ready to go inside. He needed some time on his own to breathe so he headed north out of town, toward Stockholm seven miles away. It had been a refuge for him as a teenager, at least once he had his driver's license. Corey would drive there on Saturdays when he could, and always by himself.

He didn't even bring Billy along. Stockholm was a place he enjoyed on his own and with people for whom he felt a kinship—artists. Despite its small size, the town was filled with unique galleries and stores selling the wares of painters, potters, and other craftsmen whose studios dotted the landscape of the surrounding hills and valleys in Wisconsin's driftless area. On the drive down that morning, he and Nick had passed through Stockholm without stopping, and Corey remembered seeing a sign advertising Small Business Saturday. Though not as big an event as the art fairs he loved attending in Marfa, Texas, he was certain to find the village shops open. There might even be some deal on an interesting piece of art. At a minimum, it would give him time alone, more time to prepare for encountering his mother.

He found a lucky parking space on a side street off the main drag, then bought a savory egg sandwich and bottle of juice at the Bogus Creek Bakery. He recognized the woman behind the counter as the mother of a childhood friend. Thankfully, she didn't remember him. He would have enough reunions later in the day. He walked up and down the town's two main streets. Several of the shops were the same ones that had been there for years. He perused photography and textiles at Ivry Treasure, small hand-crafted pieces at Hugga Bugga, and amazing woodwork and hand-blown glass at the Purple Turtle. He quickly lost track of time, surprising himself when he looked at his watch, and realized that he'd been walking around town for almost an hour.

A surprise text from Nick—asking how things were going—made Corey think he should head back toward Pepin. He texted back that things were fine and that he would be at his mother's house for a while longer, but that he'd be at the motel later in time for dinner. Corey stopped in one more store, the Humble Moon Folkstead. The Humble Moon specialized in functional art and furniture, all made by local artisans. He watched as a woman was demonstrating her hand-crafted jewelry. It was a medium that had never really intrigued him before, but her craftsmanship was mesmerizing, and he only wished he could stay another hour.

He got back on the road and was in front of his mother's house ten minutes later. His stomach had calmed down. As he alighted from the Jeep, the sharp smell of raw walnuts assaulted his nose, making him smile. He remembered hiding behind the woodpile with Billy as kids and whipping the soft green husks at the Neidermeyer twins as they walked, then ran past the house. Aunt Mary and Uncle Jim met him at the back door. They enveloped him in a tight group hug, both of them telling Corey how sorry they were for his loss. Mary also commented about Corey seeming to have lost a little weight. Of course, she must have heard all about his madness from the year before. He suppressed the instinct to turn and run. Instead, he followed them into the house.

Inside the kitchen, he met another aunt and three cousins. Though he had not seen any of them in a few years, their welcoming embraces and kind comments erased some of the angst that had been building up inside him all morning. As he approached the living room, Corey noticed the familiar oak bookcase. It had stood in the same spot for as long as he could remember, and it held a series of framed pictures that hadn't been moved for years. He focused on a sepia-toned photo from Frank and Ginny's wedding, the couple flanked by their own parents wearing vacuous stares. He passed quickly over the one from his high school graduation, reminded again how glad he was to have saved up some money in college to fill that hideous gap between his two front teeth.

He paused at a replica of the very same framed photo he had smashed to pieces over a year ago—Frank and Ginny smiling broadly in front of St. Bridget's, with Corey in his Sunday best in-between, celebrating his First Communion. He couldn't pull his eyes from the image of his mother's face, mostly because of her smile. She still wore her hair long then, her brown eyes gleaming and looking downward toward her son.

"Corey?" The distinctive, raspy voice came from his left, so close that he swore he could feel her breath on his neck. It was warm inside this house overrun with relatives, yet Corey shuddered with a chill. He turned to face his mother, feeling a twinge of pain in the back of his jaw. In the time since he had last seen her, Ginny seemed to have aged a few years. Her auburn hair held waves of ash. He noticed that she wasn't even turning gray but maturing directly to white. Her smile was the same as the one in the photo on the shelf, though, wide and sealed tight, masking teeth tinged with a faint shade of yellow. She leaned down to crush her cigarette into an ashtray on the table, then took a step closer and swathed her son in a timorous embrace.

He received her and rested his hands loosely on her waist. He spied her smoldering cigarette, inhaled her familiar perfume. He then looked up toward the hallway that led to the master bedroom, half expecting his father to appear and tell them to break it up. He told her how sorry he was for her loss. Corey didn't cry, self-conscious at being the center of attention from so many gawking relatives. He and Ginny released each other as if on cue from a director off-stage. There were no tears in her eyes either, as she sat back down in her usual spot. She reached for a cup of coffee while he brought a folding chair over to her side.

"I'm also sorry I didn't come sooner. I didn't get Larry Preston's call until late last night."

"Oh, don't worry about that. I didn't expect you to." He winced, unsure how to interpret her comment. He had only called her infrequently after the blow-up the year before. About every three weeks he would dial the number he still knew by heart. He would always call on a weekday, usually between three and five, knowing he would catch his mother home preparing dinner. Like clockwork, Ginny answered every time, and Frank was never at home. Their conversations had been cordial, though not entirely warm, not intimate in the way they had talked when he was just a boy. They always discussed the weather, his job at the gallery, and anything new in Pepin which was hardly ever at all. After six months, she stopped asking Corey about reconciling with his father or coming home.

"You won't be surprised to hear that your father had everything planned out in advance—the visitation, the funeral, and two

burial plots in Calvary Cemetery. Larry tells me all the legal matters are taken care of too. That's Frank. He never overlooked a
single detail in his entire life."

Corey nodded and reached for her hand. He was surprised
by her calmness, her serenity. "Well, I'm here now, Mom, and am
happy to help out. Just tell me what you need."

"You came alone?" Her question surprised him.

"No. Nick's downtown at the Riverview. I wanted to come
here right away. I'll bring him to the visitation tomorrow. That is,
if you don't mind."

"I don't mind at all, Corey, but why don't you also bring him
by the house tomorrow morning after church." Corey expected
her to ask him to come with her to Mass as well, but she didn't. He
agreed to arrive at ten. They looked at one another without saying anything more, soon joined in conversation by other relatives.
Over the course of the next hour and a half, he twice caught Ginny
staring at him. He was glad that she was looking the other way
when he occasionally stared at her.

Those stares confirmed for Corey again how much he resembled his mother. In addition to having her same soft facial features
and faintly freckled skin, they shared a similar temperament—
shy and unassuming, never arrogant or bossy. Neither dominated
a conversation, back then or now. Even when it was just the two
of them alone, Corey and Ginny might go several minutes without
speaking, yet Corey understood that things between them were
fine. Sitting here in the living room, seeing his mom again for the
first time in over a year, he hoped that would still ring true.

Soon, Corey felt the effects of all that morning coffee on his
bladder. He carefully extricated himself from a conversation with
Aunt Mary, then walked down the hallway toward the bath. After
shutting the door, he quickly unzipped his pants and sat down on
the toilet, instinctively respecting his mother's admonition to sit
instead of stand when he peed. He felt instant, gratifying relief,
then opened his eyes again and looked around the small room.
How strange. He used to shower every day in that tub, comb his

hair and brush his teeth in front of that sink. Now, it had been years since he had done any of that.

On the way back from using the bathroom, Corey paused at the entrance to his old room. Then he turned the knob, walked inside, and closed the door behind him. It clearly wasn't his room anymore. For years it had been left largely unchanged, and Corey used it whenever he came to visit overnight. But at some point since his last trip to Pepin, Frank had converted the room into an office, even though he never actually worked from home. Where Corey used to have posters of his favorite rock bands and a Hardy Boys mystery book cover, now hung a pair of mounted antlers and a framed copy of Frank's diploma from UW-Eau Claire. It reminded Corey of the intense pressure his father exerted upon him, an expectation that Corey would attend the same college as Frank.

But Corey had other plans as a high school senior. He wanted to go somewhere else. With a 3.6 GPA, a 31 on his ACT, and a portfolio of drawings and watercolors that won awards from the county fair, he applied for and was granted early admission to the University of Minnesota. He remembered the day his acceptance letter arrived in the mail. He secreted it away to this bedroom, plopped down on his bed, and ripped the thick packet wide open. He clenched the edge of a pillow between his teeth to muffle the excitement after the first sentence which began with, "We are pleased to inform you." The only remaining hurdle would be convincing Frank to let him go. Corey remembered applying for every possible scholarship, investigating how he could pay for college on his own, in case Frank refused to fund anything other than Eau Claire.

It was during school conferences in December of his senior year that his plans were revealed, sooner than Corey had planned. He had sat with his parents at a table, hearing his counselor announce that he had been awarded a substantial art scholarship based upon his award-winning work. When Frank made a snarky comment about not knowing that Eau Claire even had an art program, the counselor wore a funny look, then clarified that the award came from the U of

M. Corey remembered feeling flush after noticing his parents' conflicting facial expressions. Ginny beamed. Frank furrowed his brow. Before Frank had a chance to protest, the counselor spoke about the prestige of the university and its renowned art curriculum—among the best in the nation. "From there, Corey can write his own ticket," the counselor had said. Ultimately, the weight of the scholarship prevailed. Despite his oft-professed hatred for Minnesota, Frank begrudgingly acceded to Corey attending college at the U of M, which would cost Frank half as much as Eau Claire. In September of that year, Corey happily packed his bags and moved upriver.

With a smile on his face from that memory, Corey turned to open his former bedroom door. He stepped slowly into the hall, instantly spying his mother still seated in her chair but looking his way. He stopped and stood frozen for several moments, again triggered toward a memory from his childhood, the only other time he had stepped gingerly outside of his bedroom and locked eyes with his mom.

At the time, he was eight years old. He had been in bed for half an hour, but not yet asleep, clandestinely reading a comic book by flashlight. The back door slammed, and Corey flipped off the light. He knew who it was and that there was little leeway for staying up past his designated bedtime. It was always dicey when Frank returned home after a night of drinking. If all went well, he would be merely obnoxious. Most of the time, however, he was downright mean. Like the time when his newspaper wasn't on the coffee table ready to read—Frank rolled up the rag and threw it across the room at Ginny. Or the time when there wasn't enough ice in his tumbler, complaining that the scotch was too warm to drink—"almost fucking neat."

But the night Corey now remembered was perhaps the worst of them all. He had heard Frank yell Ginny's name, the words loud and slightly slurred. At the sound of his father's voice, Corey leapt out of bed and peered outside his door, able to see down the hall and into the living room but no farther. Corey heard his mother tell Frank she was coming into the kitchen, and he saw her snuff out a freshly lit cigarette. She was reaching for the air freshener when Frank staggered into the living room and sniffed the hazy blue air. All these years later Corey could still hear their argument and remember what was said, the words and actions imprinted deep into his eight-year-old psyche.

"Goddamn it. You know I don't like walking into a house full of smoke. I put up with that filthy habit of yours, but only if you take it outside."

"I didn't think..."

"You didn't think what? That I'd be coming home?"

"No, Frank. Of course, I knew you'd be home after a long day of work and a few drinks with your friends." His Friday routine was predictable, except for that night when he unexpectedly arrived home an hour earlier than normal.

"Oh, I get it. The drinks. You didn't think I'd realize you'd been smoking because I'd be too damn drunk."

"Honey, come in the kitchen and let me heat up some meat-loaf. It's my mother's recipe—the one you like." She started to walk past him but didn't reach the kitchen.

"Ouch!" Frank grabbed a fistful of her shoulder-length auburn hair.

"Why do you have to get me so mad, after I slave all day at work and take a couple hours to catch up with the boys, huh?"

"Frank, please. You're hurting me."

The elevated voices magnetically drew Corey from where he stood, opening his bedroom door wider, ever so slowly, to avoid any noticeable creak of the aging hinges. The Fischer house wasn't all that old, vintage 1960s rambler, but it was made cheaply with hollow core doors and the lowest quality hardware.

"Frank, let go. Please!"

Corey stepped outside his door, his heart beating one hundred times per minute, not even sure now why he had alighted from his bed.

"You're going to wake Corey!"

"I'm going to wake him? You're the one screaming like a god-damn little girl."

Corey stood fully in the darkened hallway though flat against the wall, like the tightly nailed baseboard trim at his feet. He stared toward the threshold between the two rooms, where he could clearly see his father's back. His mother was kneeling in the living room, her bare feet hidden from view but presumably resting across the metal carpet strip and part-way on the kitchen linoleum. Frank stood over her, a shock of her hair still firmly in his grasp.

Their eyes made contact and locked for mere seconds, Ginny's already brimming with tears and Corey's filling with his own like a flash flood. Between them, they spoke not a word, but he understood every thought that his mother conveyed—*get back in your room, forget about this, and go to bed*. He retreated but continued to hear his parents' words flowing through the thinly-insulated walls as he stood crying inside his darkened bedroom.

"And what if he does wake up? So what? You want him to know you were smoking? For God's sake, Ginny, he coulda walked out of his room even before all this commotion and seen you sucking on that cigarette. Is that what you want?"

Ginny's sobs choked her ability to speak.

"What kind of mother are you? And what about me? Do you like making things uncomfortable for me in my own home, the home I pay for by slaving away at work?"

She succumbed to the emotions of the moment, arriving where he probably intended to drive her all along. Sniveling, Corey heard her say, "I'm sorry, Frank."

"Okay," he replied with an exasperated huff. "I hope you'll think more clearly before you try and light up in the house, our child asleep in the very next room and me about to walk in the door." Corey could hear Frank assume his traditional place at the table and envisioned him unfolding the cloth napkin next to his place, setting and tucking it into his sweat-stained white shirt.

"Now," Frank said in a lighter, almost happy tone. "I'm ready for that meatloaf."

Corey returned to the motel and found room number five. As promised in Nick's text, the door was unlocked. Nick lay on the bed with his back propped against the wall. He looked up from his laptop as Corey collapsed beside him and sighed.

"Went that well, huh?"

"Peachy." Corey provided highlights.

"Sounds heavy."

"It was. Better than I expected, but still surreal."

"Come on… let's get out of here," Nick said.

"Where are we going?"

"Aren't you hungry?"

"A little, I guess. I snacked a bit at my mother's but didn't fill a plate."

"Okay. Let's see what this town has to eat. And along the way you can show me around. Maybe I can finally see where you grew up?"

Corey's mood lightened as he followed Nick out the motel room door. While Nick drove, Corey narrated a summary of the various landmarks they passed in town—the Laura Ingalls Wilder Museum, Villa Bellezza Winery, and the world-famous Harbor View Café. "Their food is the best I've ever had—the halibut in black butter caper sauce might be the best meal on the planet."

"I remember you telling me about it. My boss agrees with you too—that the Harbor View has the best food in the world. Sounds like the place we should eat tonight."

"Well, our timing is right. This is closing weekend for the Harbor View. After tomorrow, they won't open up again till spring."

Next they drove out south of town. Nick asked Corey where in the hell they were going.

"I'm gonna show you Tiffany."

"Who's Tiffany?"

Corey laughed. "It's not a she, it's a place—a wildlife refuge to be more specific."

Two miles out of town, the landscape changed dramatically. A tall grove of pine trees separated the end of tilled farmland and the beginning of a nature preserve. Corey explained how the area was a haven for wildlife unmatched in the upper Midwest. At the confluence of the Chippewa and Mississippi Rivers stood a vast floodplain that provided thirteen thousand acres of state-protected bottomland and hardwood forest teeming with waterfowl, deer, and scores of other wild creatures. Corey recounted how he and Billy would camp and canoe here as kids, embarking from the boat landing south of town and pitching their tent on a broad sand bar a mile upriver. Those were some of his fondest childhood memories.

Nick noted the seemingly endless horizon of the Tiffany Refuge from his vantage point in the Jeep. Though now muted in tones of brown and gray, he said that it probably looked even more beautiful in summer with green in the trees and wildflowers sprinkled across the bottoms.

"It really is. And up that road there," Corey pointed toward the east, "you'll find an Amish settlement and three ghost towns."

"That's cool. It's not nearly this interesting where I grew up. You were lucky to have all this, Corey. My brothers and I could've had a lot of fun exploring these rivers and trails."

"Yeah, if you'd have grown up in Wisconsin, you could've been cool like me. You'd say bubbler instead of fountain, oh my garsh instead of uff da, and you'd understand that chocolate milk doesn't come from brown cows."

Corey finally elicited a laugh from Nick.

They turned around at the Chippewa River boat launch and headed back toward Pepin. Once again inside the city limits, Corey had Nick drive them past the school, the old creamery that used to serve frozen treats, and down the length of Main Street. He pointed out Larry Preston's law office and the tiny greengrocer who had somehow defied the trend toward big box stores and still served the Pepin community six days a week. He also nodded his head toward the First National Bank where Frank had worked for nearly forty years selling insurance as a licensed agent. Corey had often visited Frank's modest office, just to the right of the tellers, where customers could easily transact their financial business in one single stop—life, auto, home and annuities. Frank always claimed that he "sold it all and sold it well." He was apparently the bank's top grossing agent in all of Wisconsin. Endowed with natural salesman abilities, he also benefitted from the lack of competition. The only other full-service insurance agent within a thirty-mile radius worked across the river in Wabasha. Few if any folks in town would even think of crossing the river to give their hard-earned money to an unscrupulous insurance salesman from Minnesota, not when there was one available right here in town.

"I'm getting hungry."

"Turn here, yeah to the right." Corey guided them toward the river, down a steep street running toward the marina.

"Wow, those are some big boats. I had no idea people had anything that size around here." Though the slips out on the water were empty, a number of large vessels sat dry-docked and wrapped onshore.

"There are boats of every size here in summer—for sailing, fishing, even houseboats."

"At least this town has *one* redeeming quality."

"And that is?"

"From this marina, there's a spectacular view of Minnesota across the river."

"Funny. I wonder if my father ever thought about that. He hated everything about Minnesota. Always did."

"That's pretty harsh."

"Hmmm. And irrational too. He wouldn't even let us watch the Mary Tyler Moore show, because it was set in Minneapolis."

Nick shook his head. "That's a bit extreme."

"Yeah. He got it from my grandfather. That man ate, slept, and breathed everything Wisconsin—most importantly, cheering on the Green Bay Packers. I once heard him say that our state produced the finest beer, wild game, and women in America—in that order."

"Minnesota has those things too."

"Not in Frank's or my grandfather's eyes. As much as they loved Wisconsin, they loathed Minnesota, especially when it came to football. When I was a kid, the Vikings were the better team, and that really pissed Frank off."

"So, if your father hated Minnesota so much, why did he live in a house where you could look out the front window and see it across the river?"

"Who knows? Maybe he figured that the Mississippi was like the River Styx, the only thing standing between the hallowed hills of Wisconsin and the very gates of hell."

At the end of the street, Corey told Nick to hang a left. He pulled into a parking spot across the street from the Harbor View Café.

"Looks busy," Nick said.

"Well, it's definitely worth the wait." Corey felt a twinge of guilt at not asking Ginny to join them, but he knew she was hosting other relatives at the house. He could always bring her back here for an early dinner before the visitation tomorrow, if she wanted. The feelings of guilt melted away once he entered the café. For some reason, this two-room restaurant had always given him a feeling of comfort, of home. The staff was exceedingly friendly—the hostess still knew him by name. She offered her condolences about Frank, then showed Corey and Nick to a table near the window.

"The menu is on the blackboard. Seriously, anything you choose will be delish."

"Any recommendations? You mentioned the halibut earlier."

"Definitely the halibut, above everything else. I promise you won't taste anything like it anywhere else in the world."

"What else?"

"The pork shank, the beef tenderloin smothered in wild mushrooms, or the chipotle chicken breast. I'll be getting one of those four things myself."

"Who knew we'd find Chez Toulouse on the River, here in the middle of Farmville, USA?"

The waitress took their orders, and Corey gave Nick a recap of his time at the house with Ginny. Soon, their food arrived at the table, and their conversation waned. Corey looked out the window and anticipated the coming days with a visitation, the funeral, and reading of his father's will still ahead. He chewed his food slowly and gazed out past the marina, the sun now fully set behind the hills on the other side of the great river.

4

Sunday

On Sunday morning, Corey and Nick arrived at the house short-ly after Ginny returned from Mass. She wore a thrift store black dress when she met them at the door.

"Good morning. Come on in."

Corey entered first and connected with Ginny in a brief hug. Over his shoulder, Ginny said, "Nick. It's good to see you."

"Nice to see you too, Mrs. Fischer. I'm very sorry for your loss." He extended his hand to Ginny, which she beheld for a moment before shaking it.

"Thank you. I just put on a fresh pot. Have you two eaten?"

"We had something at the diner before coming over, Mom."

"Well then, Nick, why don't you go into the living room while Corey helps me bring out the coffee." She pulled her favorite Fire King mugs from the cupboard while Corey found the serving tray and silver set exactly where they had always been kept. He carried the cups, cream, and sugar atop the tray, following his mother into the living room as she held a plate of warm muffins. He almost ran right into her back when she stopped abruptly at the edge of the living room. From this angle, Corey could see Nick sitting expec-tantly in the brown recliner. Of the half-dozen places in the room to sit, he had chosen Frank's customary chair.

At Ginny's prompting, Corey regaled her with the latest proj-ects at his studio and the gallery. Then she asked the same questions of Nick who spoke at length about recent successes at the bank and an expected promotion once his boss retired at the end of the year.

"Thank you for taking time away from work to come down."

"Not at all, Mrs. Fischer. I'm happy to be here."

Throughout their exchange, Corey listened closely for hints of subtext, any clue to the direction in which the conversation might be heading, either good or bad. As far as he knew, Nick and his mother had only met twice, both times when Ginny accompanied Frank on business trips to Minneapolis. Yet he sensed in Nick an inexplicable familiarity with Pepin. Nick had driven straight to the Fischer home this morning without asking directions and got up to use the restroom down the hall as if he'd been here before.

During a brief pause in Nick's lengthy retelling of a recent employee scandal at the bank, Ginny looked at Corey. "Would you mind running downstairs and throwing a few pieces of wood into the stove?"

"Sure, Mom. Be right back."

Nick and Ginny continued talking as Corey descended the basement stairs. Once, he had tried to picture in his mind what an actual one-on-one conversation between the two of them would be like without him in the room. That is, if Ginny could even get a word in edgewise. He stepped onto the cold concrete floor and surveyed the spacious basement. The entire footprint of the home was exposed in this undivided room, with a washer and dryer in one corner and pantry shelves along the back wall. The rest was nothing more than a man cave. His father's workbench filled one entire wall, and the wood stove rested at the opposite end. In the middle sat a small grouping of furniture—a tattered brown sofa and mismatched recliner, each anchoring a braided rug with a small television sitting atop an end table. Corey figured this was the last TV with rabbit ears in America.

Reaching into the pile for two good-sized pieces, Corey remembered the many times he was asked to help haul or cut wood for this damn stove as a kid. As he lifted the piece of wood up to his nose, the scent of cut hickory brought back a vivid memory from one particular Saturday morning in his youth. In it, Frank had roused him from bed at seven, asking Corey to move the woodpile from one side of the basement to the other. Then Corey was to sweep up any loosened bark and scattered dust, so the basement wouldn't become a haven for mice.

He did as he was told, while Frank worked to repair the exhaust pipe on the stove. It had been producing residual smoke inside the house. After finding no problems with the basement pipes, Frank grabbed a beer from the spare fridge saying that he was going up on the roof to inspect the chimney. In just under an hour Corey had moved an entire cord of wood. Sweeping timber fragments and dirt took but five minutes more. He went upstairs, ran outside, and ascended the metal ladder resting against the eaves at the back of the house. His father stood atop the asphalt roof peering down into the smokestack.

He remembered announcing that he had finished the task and asking whether there was anything else before he biked over to Billy's. Frank answered Corey's questions with two more. Had he moved the whole pile? Swept up every scrap of wood? He assured his father that the basement floor was clean enough to eat off. "Good," he recalled Frank saying. "Now, move it all back. It's easier to load when the wood is within reach of the stove. Oh, and bring me another beer before you start. Working in this hot sun is making me thirsty."

Subdued by the memory, Corey placed the cut hickory into the stove and brushed a few shards of wood off his pant leg. Then he walked toward the other end of the basement to use the makeshift bathroom in the corner. Years ago, Frank had enclosed the toilet in a small cubicle of painted plywood. Four posts provided the frame, with the plywood starting a foot off the floor and stopping a foot below the ceiling tiles. Corey always refused to bring his friends down here, for fear they'd see that his family essentially had an outhouse in their basement.

A sink sat just outside the door. Corey stopped to look into the mirror, then stepped inside the hedged-in stall and unzipped his pants. Above his head was an air vent. Above that, the living room where he had left Ginny and Nick to themselves. He faintly heard his mother's voice through the vent, something to the effect of "Tell Corey about your marriage." Then he started to pee.

Nick's response, if there was one, got drowned out by the splash of Corey's urine hitting the water in the stool. What in the world could they be talking about? In that moment, Corey simply couldn't pee fast enough. He considered stopping the flow, but the relief in emptying his bladder felt too good. It certainly wasn't the first time he strained to eavesdrop on a conversation through an air vent in this house. As a kid, whenever he overheard his father through the metal grate in his bedroom, his ears perked up and his breath fell silent. Sometimes the voice was angry, other times serene. Corey's entire body would clench and hold still, waiting for clues as to which mood was present on any particular night.

He remembered the first time that he heard his mother's yielding moan through the vent in his room. Her voice sounded more of pleasure than anguish, like a mild tugging when plucking a rare flower. He knew what that meant right away, and sure enough the rhythmic sounds through the air vent ebbed and flowed like the tides on the river that night, the same waters Corey could see in the distance out his bedroom window, the spring moonlight reflecting off the rippled surface and enhancing the serenity of the night.

His bladder now empty and his fly zipped back up, Corey flushed the toilet and lowered the lid. Then he stepped on top of it, bringing himself closer to the ceiling vent so he could hear the voices above the swirling water in the toilet bowl. Nick was talking now. "Thanks again for letting me inside to talk, even though it didn't do any good in the end."

Corey couldn't hear Ginny's response. Her voice had grown soft. He stepped higher onto the porcelain back cover of the toilet. "It was complicated, Nick. You wouldn't understand."

After that, Corey heard no more voices. But Ginny and Nick probably heard him, because just as Corey pushed himself higher toward the metal grate, his foot knocked the cap off the stool, and it went crashing to the concrete floor. Corey saved himself from an injurious fall by grabbing ahold of the top edge of the sturdy wooden compartment, then lowering himself back to the ground.

The ceiling above him creaked with the sound of footsteps moving quickly toward the top of the staircase.

"Everything all right down there?" Ginny asked.

"Yeah. I'm fine. The toilet kept running after I flushed, and I dropped the lid on the floor when I went to check the thingy in the back of the stool."

"Okay. You could've used the bathroom up here, you know, instead of that rustic one."

"Thanks. It's all good. I'll be up in a minute."

Through the vent, Corey heard Ginny and Nick talking about the plans to have Thanksgiving dinner at Nick's sister's house later in the week. He picked up the toilet cap, surprised that it hadn't busted in half. He left the stall, washed his hands in the utility sink, then dried them off on a hanging towel. That's when he saw it— the very first painting he remembered completing with a sense that he might be really, really good at art. The framed piece hung in the laundry area, directly above the high-top table where his mother regularly folded towels and clothes. He stared at it for a moment, curious why he had forgotten about this important part of his development as an artist. Of course, it had been twenty-five years since he had created it. For a while it hung upstairs in the hall. Ginny—or Frank?—must've moved it down here sometime since. At least it wasn't rolled up and hidden in the attic.

Corey remembered the night of the unveiling in ninth grade. After his father had parked the car in the lot, Corey jumped out and ran toward the school. Inside, fluorescent lights shone brightly as parents poured in to peruse their students' creations in "Art Talent Show – Featuring Our Talent." Musical solos, sculptures, and paintings filled the school.

A new visual arts teacher had come to town at the beginning of the school year, and she pushed Corey to experiment with different media. While applauding his gifted drawings, she said that his artistic eye transcended form, that he likely had the ability to work equally well with oils, watercolors, or clay. He did, and he fell in love with painting, often staying after school with two other students specifically invited by the new teacher to learn techniques by watching her work.

Corey had found his passion.

He would watch his instructor briefly, then turn toward his own canvas and try to re-create her strokes, her choice of color, but with his own unique subject matter in mind. He gravitated toward portraits—faces, really. At first he used torn-out pages from magazines, transposing the countenance of famous people—Cher, Schwarzenegger, Marilyn Monroe—into his own imagined visage of how they really looked, how he pictured them feeling inside. Corey's teacher was initially speechless, but eventually saw what her pupil was intending to create—unspoken emotion on the canvas that revealed what the magazine pictures couldn't. She calmly and confidently told him "well done," then encouraged him to sit down and paint some more.

Corey remembered standing in the middle of the hall during the show and gently pushing Ginny forward to take a closer look. He glanced too at his father, urging Frank on with his eyebrows toward the painting hanging on the wall. His parents stared for several moments, cocking their heads one by one, to regard the unfamiliar style from slightly varying angles. In the background Corey had painted a landscape, with the right side bathed in muted sunlight and four blackbirds set randomly in the sky. Moving toward the left of the canvas the background colors darkened, with nightfall setting on that edge of the painting, the birds replaced with four spots of distant starlight. The two halves of the painting seemed at first glance to hold symmetrical, reverse images with the stark, bright likeness of a person dividing the scene.

A feminine face was the unmistakable focal point, though her aspect too was riven, sewn together with invisible precision right down the middle of her head. The left eye looked fearfully toward something outside of the frame, as if she had seen a horror film or was being chased by a wolf. The right side of her face appeared placid, the eye barely open and her smile turned slightly upward—the look of someone who had just sipped a fresh-brewed cup of jasmine tea.

He remembered Ginny telling him that it was beautiful and asking him to describe it, in his own words. Ginny's soft voice barely registered above the din of the crowded school hall. He told her that she should know who it was. Frank took a wild guess, saying that she looked kinda uptight on one side, "just like Diane, that gal from the TV show, Cheers." Corey remembered laughing, his father's conjecture not even close to the truth. It humored him, and also affirmed his purpose. Corey wanted people to have to study his art for a long time before seeing everything he had poured onto the canvas. He remembered turning once again toward Ginny, imploring her to offer a guess of her own. After shaking her head and looking toward the wall with furrowed brow, she said that the face looked a little bit like her own mother, at least in the shape of the head. "It most certainly is grandma's nose, and she has that same length and color of flowing brown hair. But," she noted, "the person you painted looks far more complex."

"It's you, Mom. I painted a picture of you." Ginny cast Corey a look of curiosity, then stared once again toward the wall.

Ginny said she was flattered. Frank wasn't as impressed, asking why half of her face seemed contorted. "It looks like you've got chicken pox and are about to cry."

Corey listened to his father's observation without feeling scorn, waiting to hear if either parent saw what was staring back at them from the wall. He finally explained that it was called *abstract art*. His teacher had given the work an A. He lifted the corner of the canvas to reveal the grade marking in bright red ink. Ginny offered him a broad smile, thanked him, and drew Corey into a tight embrace. Frank pulled on his chin and widened his eyes before turning away and suggesting that they go see what some of the other kids had done.

Corey rejoined his mother and Nick upstairs.

"Hey, I noticed my ninth-grade painting is now hanging above the laundry table downstairs."

"Oh, yes. I look at it every time I fold towels."

"Didn't it used to be pinned to the wall, up here?"

"It did, for many years. But I always complained to Frank about how it wasn't hung where I could see it, other than passing it on my way between rooms."

"So he relegated it to the basement?"

"He wanted to hang it somewhere that would give me time to look at it and reflect."

"Huh. And I see it finally got a frame."

"Your father made that frame all by himself, right down there in his workshop."

Corey didn't know what to make of that. He also refrained from a confrontation as to what they were discussing while he was in the basement. Later he'd ask Nick directly. Besides, it seemed like he couldn't get a word in anyway. Ginny was uncharacteristically chatty. He'd never seen her like this before—ever. She talked about the recent school bonding bill, how the town was divided fifty-fifty, and how she felt strongly that the measure deserved support, even though she and Frank were long past the stage of having a kid in the Pepin schools.

She grew a bit more animated on the topic of St. Bridget's Parish. A new priest—Father Frisch—would be officiating Franks' funeral, seeing as Father Murphy got reassigned by the archdiocese. In the end, it wasn't Father Murphy's chronic drinking that did him in. Rather, the church council drew the line at fornication. After discovering that the rectory's live-in housekeeper was doing more than keeping house, they called down to Milwaukee, and the playful priest was packed up and gone within a week.

"And for all those years, Father Murphy was always your father's favorite," Ginny said with a light laugh.

On and on she went, from topic to topic. Soon, Corey and Nick were caught up on every major story and scandal to rock the village of Pepin for the past twelve months. For a moment, Corey had the sensation that he'd never moved away. Everything felt familiar again. Eventually, Ginny must've tired herself from all that talking. She asked if they'd mind if she went to take a brief nap.

"Not at all. We can go to the motel, then come back when you're ready."

"Well, only if you need to lie down too. But if you don't, I was wondering if you might do me a huge favor."

"Of course. Anything."

"I hate to ask, but if it's not too much trouble, I could really use your help going through your father's work bench downstairs and boxing up anything of value."

"Why wait, right?" Nick's bluntness caused Corey to cringe.

"No, it's just that with the bonding measure getting defeated, I thought I'd donate Frank's tools to the wood shop at school. I'm never going to use any of those things, so why not give them to someone who will?"

"That makes sense, Mom." Corey looked toward Nick for assurance. "We're glad to help."

"Great, thank you. But, could I press my luck and ask for one more thing?"

"Why not?" Nick asked, before Corey could formulate a response. It may have been the very first time he recalled his mother putting her own needs first and asking others to help out.

"I thought maybe one of you could sort through the work bench while the other one spends time in Frank's office. If there's anything bank-related, I'd like it returned to them. There's also a closet full of suits and work shirts in there. I'd just as soon get those boxed up and donated to the parish thrift store."

"You get some rest, Mrs. Fischer. We'll have this done by the time you wake up."

"Oh, thank you boys."

"Yeah. Leave it to us."

"Okay. I only need a short nap, no more than an hour. And heavens, if I'm not up by noon please wake me. I already made us chicken salad sandwiches to eat before the visitation. We need to get there by two to start setting up."

"No worries. We've got plenty of time."

Corey's uncle Jim arrived later that afternoon. Corey and Nick rode to the visitation in the back seat of Jim's car. Ginny sat up front. A box full of photos and framed insurance awards sat in the trunk. Beyond sorting through Frank's home office, Corey hadn't offered any direct help to Ginny in preparing for the visitation or funeral. He didn't even know what suit his father was being buried in—he'd find out soon enough when they arrived at the funeral home and saw him lying in the casket.

The funeral director walked them through the agenda. After two hours of receiving guests, the director would ask everyone to find a seat and there would be a brief program—a prayer by Father Frisch, then time for folks to say a few words about Frank's life. The director then looked at Corey and told him that if there was an unusually long pause without anyone coming forward, that would be a good time for someone in the family to come up and offer their own recollections.

Corey's mind churned. He couldn't expect his mother to rise in front of the crowd. It would have to be him, his father's only child. At least he had a few hours to think of something—anything—positive to say about Frank.

"Now," said the director, "if you'll follow me, I'll show you into the gathering room. Perhaps it's best if the others," nodding toward Jim and Nick, "stayed behind for a few moments, so you two can pay your respects to Frank privately."

Ginny followed the funeral director, and Corey followed his mom. Jim took a seat in the entry while Nick stepped outside to get better reception on his phone. Corey saw the large gray coffin at the far end of the room as soon as he passed through the door. The color surprised him. For some reason he expected dark brown. Ginny and the funeral director blocked Corey's line of sight to the head of the casket. For the moment he couldn't see his father's face. As they approached the casket, the style also surprised him—plain. He thought that a life-long narcissist would choose something gaudy and extravagant to house his final place of rest. Perhaps it was Frank's cheapskate tendencies that won out in the end. Or maybe, Corey fantasized, his mother swapped out the coffins at the last minute, saving more money for herself.

And then he saw his dead father, or at least the top half of him. Frank's hands lay folded atop his belly. A rosary snaked with perfect placement in between his fat fingers. He wore a dark-blue suit with a white shirt buttoned to the neck, and a red and gray tie rested atop his chest. His silver hair was combed as Corey remembered, parted on the left side with a trimmed tuft of thinning hair combed back toward the right. His face wore no expression. Corey had pictured Frank forcing a smirk through his dead mouth, but instead the line formed by his lips was perfectly straight. He would go to his grave looking neither blissful nor cross, but instead looking like nothing at all.

Corey continued to stare at his father, half expecting Frank to open his eyes and yell "gotcha!" But the only movement inside the casket was Ginny's hand caressing Frank's cheek. The tenderness of that gesture startled him. He didn't recall seeing many displays of affection between his parents as a kid. Aside from hearing their lovemaking through the air ducts and watching Frank hold Ginny as she cried over her own father's death, he never gave a moment's thought to their lack of physical touch until right now. Was Ginny merely going through the motions in front of the funeral director, or did she truly have feelings of warmth or heartbroken ache for this man who was more often cruel than comforting to his family?

Ginny stepped away, leaving Corey to face his father alone. The funeral director followed her toward the door as well, leaving plenty of space for Corey to breathe, think, or even yell if he chose. He continued his stare but had difficulty staying with a single, consistent thought. There were so many unspoken words, unanswered questions in his mind. Anyone close to Corey and Frank's relationship could predict every single one. The torrent of feelings and questions ultimately narrowed into a single thought— *this is it*. This would be the final time he would ever look upon his father's face, the final time he could say something in his physical presence. And yet, Corey couldn't find the words. Forgiveness, anger, regret, understanding, and disgust. He wanted to tell his father all of it, and this was his only chance. But, nothing. In the end, he couldn't summon the courage to talk back to the man whose affirmation he desperately wanted and whose expectations Corey could never meet. Perhaps those failings were Corey's. Perhaps they belonged to Frank. Or perhaps, he would never know. He stared silently at his father's dead face for another few seconds. Then he turned to walk across the room toward his mom.

With help from Uncle Jim, Corey and Ginny began to assemble two poster boards filled with photos of Frank since childhood. At four o'clock, people began arriving. They signed the guest book and came in to see the family. Ginny and Corey greeted a semi-steady stream of mourners, mostly local residents and Ginny's extended family. All expressed their sympathies; some offered friendly anecdotes from the past. A few asked about the circumstances surrounding Frank's unexpected death. He was only sixty-two years old.

Corey recognized a few neighbors and people from the bank where Frank worked. He was embarrassed not to remember the high school shop teacher, Mr. Hannum, who knew Frank through the Knights of Columbus. Corey spent five minutes listening to Mr. Hannum recount a number of volunteer fix-up projects that he and Frank had worked on together over the years. He sure was going to miss Frank's sense of humor and good fun. Corey nodded and forced a smile. Then he said thank you to Mr. Hannum for being Dad's friend.

He was surprised to see his former art teacher approach him next. Though they hadn't spoken in twenty years, he recognized her right away. He felt awkward when she reached out for a hug. All these years later, he still thought of her as his teacher more than a comforting friend. Corey gave her a brief recap of his work at the gallery. She seemed very enthused to hear him describe what he had worked on in his own studio and encouraged him to ignore the absence of awards or recognition in art contests and to keep on painting and exploring his naturally gifted ability.

As soon as Corey broke away from the art teacher, Nick grabbed him by the arm and spun him around. An unexpected warmth filled him the moment he saw Julian and Carol. He had no idea they planned on showing up.

"We wouldn't have missed it, Corey."

He hugged Carol tightly for almost a minute. It was good to see a familiar, friendly face. In the absence of seeing his best friend, Billy, having Carol there in support was the next best thing. They only had a few minutes to talk before the funeral director interrupted, telling Corey it was time to get people seated for the program of remembrance. Once Ginny joined him up front and the crowd was seated and quieted down, the director introduced Father Frisch who led the crowd in a lengthy, solemn prayer. After that, a steady stream of people stood up and offered words of remembrance. Some were funny. Frank's fishing buddy recalled the time Frank thought he had a massive fish on his line and was pulling so hard on his pole that when the line snapped he fell "ass over tea kettle into the river. Sorry for the language, Father, but that's what really happened."

A few speakers expressed gratitude. The mayor recognized Frank's ten-year stint as a volunteer village fireman. The president of the parish council lauded Frank for his tireless service to St. Bridget's as a communion server, catechism teacher, and pre-marital counselor to engaged young couples. Corey wished he could have been a fly on the wall for one of those sessions— what sage advice had his father offered to those young men about fidelity and honoring a wife?

There were so many speakers that neither Corey nor Ginny needed to rise or say a word. While he was thankful, the situation surprised him. He had no idea that his father touched so many lives, that anyone would stand up and say a kind word. Near the end of the program, Corey began to wonder whether he even knew his father well at all.

One last person walked toward the lectern, accompanied by an older woman. He wore dress slacks and an off-white shirt with a plain blue tie around his neck. He walked arm in arm with the woman all the way to the front, and she stood by his side as he readied himself to speak.

Corey leaned over and whispered to Ginny, "Isn't that Todd Schultz?"

"Umm hmm."

"He was in my class, well sort of. Why is he here? We weren't even friends."

"No, but he and your father were. Shhh, now listen."

"Hello. My name is Todd," the man said slowly, choking up with emotion. "Frank was my best friend."

Corey glanced at his mother for a sign of non-verbal explanation, but she simply smiled while watching Todd speak. He remembered Todd from childhood. While they had started out as classmates in grade school, Todd's Down Syndrome led him on a different path with special services and a separate track for reaching high school graduation. Along the way, Corey was always polite when Todd approached him or tried to talk, but he never went out of his way to befriend or get to know him.

"We played checkers together on Saturdays. Well, not on hunting or fishing Saturdays, but all the other ones. Yeah, we played checkers." Todd paused for a moment, as that memory seemed to bring him happiness and made him more composed. "Yeah, I won most of the time, but Frank was still pretty good." Todd said the word *pretty* as if it had three long syllables. "I'm really sorry he died. He was my best friend." Then Todd began to weep.

Father Frisch joined Todd and his mother at the front, and they walked away together. The funeral director thanked everyone for coming, and people slowly began filing out of the room. Nick made his way up to join Corey near the front.

"Hey. I was thinking we could take Julian and Carol to that Pickle Factory place. They'll think it's a hoot."

"You guys go on ahead. I need to take Mom back home. There's a couple of things I need to go over with her before tomorrow."

"Okay. I'll catch a ride with Julian. I guess you'll have to find a way back to the motel later?" Nick's question almost sounded like a declaration.

"It's only six blocks. I think I can walk."

A trio of relatives stayed at the Fischer house longer than Corey had hoped. He felt tense when Ginny asked them to stay for dinner. He wanted to speak with his mother, alone. Thankfully they declined, eventually said their goodbyes, and left. Ginny insisted on making beef stroganoff for dinner, Corey's favorite meal growing up. He insisted on helping. He figured it would be easier to broach some difficult topics if they had a mutual distraction to keep from having to look each other in the eye. Ginny asked him to man the stovetop and brown the strips of chuck roast.

"Are you sure Nick and your friends don't want to join us? I have enough meat to feed them too."

"They'll be fine down at the Pickle Factory. Besides, I wanted to talk to you about a couple of things, alone."

"Oh?"

"Yeah. For starters, I overheard you and Nick talking earlier—when I was in the basement stoking the wood stove."

Ginny paused, then continued chopping onions on her cutting board.

"I wasn't trying to eavesdrop. Your voices came through the vent. But I didn't get the full context, so I was hoping you'd tell me more about that conversation."

"Corey, it was a difficult period. I've tried to apologize several times."

"What period?"

"Well, I thought you said you overheard us."

"I did, but only a small part. I heard you tell Nick that he should talk with me about my marriage."

Ginny stopped chopping, but still gripped the knife. She didn't reply.

"But if you were telling him to confess about being a cheater, like Frank was, save your breath. I already know about that."

Ginny set down the paring knife, wiped her hands on a dish towel, and turned to face her son. He couldn't tell if the tears in her eyes were spawned by emotion or the fragrant yellow onions.

"I didn't know about that, Corey. About Nick, I mean. That makes me sad if he's treating you that way. You deserve better."

He was tempted to say *you deserved better too* but refrained. For now, he focused on his own challenging marriage. "Then what was it you two were discussing about my relationship with Nick?"

"That's a topic you need to raise with him. It isn't my place to interfere."

"Well, it sounds like you already did." Corey regretted his accusatory reply.

"Honey, whether you believe it or not, I have your best interest at heart. But I think you should ask Nick about that subject. Now, what else was on your mind?"

She turned back to attend the onions.

"Fine." Corey paused. "Todd Schultz. How did he know Dad?"

Ginny smiled. "Todd is a special boy. Well, I guess he's actually a man, seeing as he's your age. Anyway, several years ago your father joined the church council. During one of the meetings, someone mentioned how Mr. Schultz had unexpectedly passed away. They weren't Catholic, of course, but something about the situation motivated Frank to go and visit Mrs. Schultz and offer his help. He apparently took to Todd, maybe because Todd laughed at Frank's silly jokes."

"Sounds like the guy has a horrible sense of humor."

Ginny laughed. "Maybe so. With his father's death, Todd really needed a friend here in Pepin. I guess Frank sorta took him under his wing."

"So Dad was trying his hand at doing charity work, something generous for mankind? What a guy."

"Well, at first I thought your father had found a new project. But it quickly became apparent that the two of them enjoyed their time together. I think they genuinely became friends."

"Todd sure thought so. His talk at the visitation was moving. I didn't see that coming."

"Sorry. I should've told you about Todd before now. It just never came up on our phone calls. And, to be fair, you didn't come home much the past ten years, so you didn't see what was happening."

"Well, good for Todd. And for that matter, good for Frank. He finally got the adoring son he always wanted."

"Corey, it wasn't like that."

"Wasn't it? According to Todd, it sounds like the two of them had a pretty special bond—the type of bond a lot of fathers have with their sons."

Ginny brought her chopped onions over to the stove and dumped them into the frying pan over which Corey was hovering. She turned off the burner, then set the pan aside. She rested her backside against the kitchen counter, folded her arms across her chest and waited until Corey turned to face her.

"Listen," she said, "I can't explain or apologize enough about your father. Yes, you two had a difficult relationship."

"That's an understatement."

"But now he's dead, and it's time to move on. If not for your sake, then do it for mine."

"What do you mean—for yours?"

"I put up with the two of you fighting and avoiding each other for far too long. If I'd have been stronger, then maybe I could've done something to fix it. But I couldn't, or didn't. It's time to put the feud with your father to rest."

"It's not that simple for me, you know?"

"Corey, you're forty years old. How much longer are you going to carry on this grudge match? Until I die too? Or you?"

He couldn't believe the blunt words coming from his mother's mouth. "I didn't start that battle, and I sure as heck never figured out how to end it. For Christ's sake, Mom, I was only a kid."

"Please don't take the Lord's name in vain in this house, Corey—in my house."

"I'm sorry. But what about you, Mom? You were locked in a struggle with Dad for the better part of forty years too. At least you had a choice. You were an adult. You chose to spend your life with that man."

For a split second, he swore that Ginny's hand flinched toward his face. For the first time in his life, he thought she might slap him. Instead, she dug her hands deeper into her sides. And then she began to shake.

"You have no idea what you're talking about. And tonight's not the night for me to explain it. I think we've said enough."

"Mom, I'm sorry. I didn't mean to upset you. I, uh…"

"I'm tired. We're both tired. It's been a very long day. And tomorrow will be even longer. We're going to be burying your father."

"I know. I know."

"I think I just need to rest. I'm not even hungry any longer."

"That's okay. I can finish making dinner."

"No, please. I think we should call it a night. There's still some chicken salad in the fridge if you'd like to make a sandwich. You're welcome to eat here or take it back to the motel. But right now, I need to take a bath and go to bed."

"All right. I understand, but at least let me clean up a little."

"There's no need. I'll just put the ingredients in the fridge. Maybe you and Nick can come by tomorrow and we'll finish making the stroganoff then."

Corey looked at his mother, stunned and not knowing what else to say. Ginny picked up the pan of beef and onions, covered it with a lid and placed it on the top shelf of the fridge. She pulled out the chicken salad.

"It's okay, Mom. I'll go join Nick and our friends at the Pickle."

Ginny placed the food back inside the fridge. She offered a tepid hug and wishes for a good night's sleep, but the embrace left Corey feeling detached. He walked out the door and headed toward the motel. When he looked back at the house from one block away, Ginny had already turned off the porch light.

He walked past the Pickle Factory but never intended on going inside. He kept on walking. While thinking about the exchange with his mother, he felt that a line had been crossed and that he was now floating in uncharted waters. For the first time in his memory, Ginny had chosen to stop preparing an evening meal, and the two of them were going to bed without dinner. And for the very first time in his life, he understood that her hidden pain just might be as considerable as his own.

5

Monday

Corey was a mere spectator at the funeral the next morning. He played no active role in planning or conducting the service. He gave no eulogy, recited no poem, read no verse from the New or Old Testaments.

There was a final visitation an hour before the service, but Corey chose not to approach the casket until the very end. When the time for commencing the funeral was near, Corey stood next to his mother with his arm around her shoulder. Conversation in the church fell silent as the funeral director tucked in the casket lining, then closed the lid for the very last time. Ginny cried—a little. She may have been the only one. And that would have been just fine for Frank. "It's more important to be respected than loved," he always said. Corey wondered if his father accomplished even that.

He took a seat next to Ginny in the front row. Nick sat beside him. The choir sang "Ave Maria" as the last mourners filed into St. Bridget's and took their seats. Corey looked back to see Carol and Julian seated in a middle row. Carol mouthed the words "love you," and Corey said "you too" softly in return. He also noticed Mr. and Mrs. Preston sitting a few rows closer to the front. Larry offered a small wave of his hand. Corey smiled and turned to face the front.

"When is this show gonna start?" Nick whispered. "We're already five minutes behind."

Although Corey remembered admiring Nick's penchant for punctuality when they first dated in college, over the years it had grown tiresome. In this setting, he thought it completely rude. He chose not to reply. He wouldn't even look in Nick's direction.

"Maybe someone should go check on the priest. I saw him enter that door behind the front of the church. But don't send the altar boy, or we might be delayed even further."

Corey turned to face Nick. "What is wrong with you? Show a little flippin' respect."

"Calm down, it's just a joke. Well, actually, it's not really a joke given what's going on in the Catholic Church."

"Keep your voice down. Or better yet, shut up."

"I'm just trying to lighten things up. You look tense, and I thought you could use a little humor."

"That may be, but your so-called humor is inappropriate."

"Geez. Sounds like I might've hit a nerve—maybe the joke was a little close to home?"

"You, of all people, shouldn't be making jokes about sexual abuse."

Though he had been an altar boy as a kid, Corey had never encountered anything remotely untoward. And it felt good to take a shot at Nick who sat back and didn't say another word.

Ginny touched Corey gently on the arm. "Everything all right?"

"Yeah. Nick's just quizzing me about the church and who's who behind us."

Once the song ended, Father Frisch emerged from the sacristy, then turned on the microphone at the pulpit and invited the congregation to stand. A group of Frank's friends from the Knights of Columbus served as honorary pallbearers. They walked alongside the casket, which rode atop a mostly-hidden metal cart, as the funeral director pushed it from behind. Father Frisch carried out the funeral liturgy to perfection, never missing a note. The homily was kind yet vague. The priest and congregation sang all of the traditional Catholic calls and responses. A young soprano from the choir offered a comforting rendition of "On Eagle's Wings." The Mass proceeded like all those Corey had attended years before. Not much was unique to Frank Fischer's final service, yet there was an odd comfort in that. Corey anticipated each reply to the priest's promptings as if he'd never left the church all those years before. "And also with you. It is right to give thanks and praise." Perhaps he had said those responses enough times in his youth that he'd be able to recite them all the days of his life. He was mildly surprised and even embarrassed then, to discover that the dictated responses had changed somewhere along the line. "And with your spirit. It is right and just."

Corey's mind drifted during Mass. He pondered the altar at the front of the church. Why hadn't he ever painted this scene before? He had certainly stared at this baptismal font and the random statuettes and relics for hundreds of hours growing up. Yet the scattered items never stood out to him as focal points in and of themselves. Rather, everything here in St. Bridget's appeared as backdrop, the scenery at the back of the set for this religious play.

When it came time to rise for communion, the priest strode down and offered it first to the family, before returning to the altar and awaiting the line of mourners to file past the casket, open their mouths wide, and receive the Holy Host. As Corey bent over to set the padded knee-rail onto the floor for prayer, he heard the heavy wooden doors of the church open and shut behind him, obviously the arrival of someone quite late for the service. Like the inability to avoid rubbernecking at an accident scene, he turned his head toward the back of the parish and recognized the latecomer. Then Corey smiled, more broadly than he had shown on his face in a very long time.

After the service ended, he rushed to the back of the church and found Billy in the very last pew. Their embrace lasted nearly a minute. Though they spoke often by phone, they hadn't seen each other since Corey's hospitalization over a year ago. The fact that

Billy flew in from California on short notice as a show of support for the second time in a year was surprising, and yet not so. Billy had always been there for him when needed. Why should the death of Corey's father be any different?

Billy released him from the bear hug just as Ginny joined Corey at the back of the church to begin greeting mourners paying their final respects on their way out of St. Bridget's. A graveside burial was next, where a small crowd gathered in close as the priest sprinkled holy water on Frank's flower-covered casket before lowering him into the grave. Then it was back to St. Bridget's for a basement lunch. Corey once again stayed close to his mother. He sat with her at a table alongside his grandma and two aunts and uncles. A church lady brought over a pot of coffee which she poured into ceramic white cups. Corey fondled his cup with a feeling of strange familiarity. He hadn't sipped a beverage from one of these iconic mugs in decades. Combined with the bare furnishings of the basement, which hadn't changed one bit in Corey's entire life and where he'd spent untold hours participating in youth group activities, he felt like he had now truly arrived home.

He made eye contact with Billy who sat at a table with his own parents across the hall. He also noticed Nick sitting with Carol and Julian at a table in the back. He felt amused when he saw his loud-mouthed cousin Janice sit down next to Nick. *Serves him right*, Corey thought.

The church lady came back to Corey's table to announce that the food was ready and that the family should assemble their plates. Corey pulled back his mother's chair and followed her toward the wide countertop between the kitchen and the large hall. The sight of all the traditional church basement fare brought instant memories of meals past and a mouth-watering anticipation to taste those distinctive delights from his youth. Corey handed empty paper plates to his mother and grandma, then took one for himself.

The first thing he grabbed was a freshly baked white bun, already cut and covered inside with a tab of butter. Flipping it open, he placed a healthy mound of thin-sliced, honey-cured ham along with a dollop of yellow mustard. He scooped German potato salad and creamy coleslaw onto the plate, along with a spoonful of St. Bridget's infamous calico beans—a sweet concoction of bacon, ground beef, brown sugar and four different kinds of beans (lima, baked, butter, and kidney). He also saved enough space on the plate for two full squares of seven-layer Jell-O, each topped with a thick coating of whipped cream.

He returned to his seat and began devouring the items on his plate. He was focused on the food and half-listening to his uncle talk about how the price of corn had gone off a cliff when he felt a tap on his left shoulder.

"Oh, Carol. Julian. Hi." He finished swallowing the mash of beans and ham sandwich half-digested in his mouth. Nick stood quietly beside Julian.

"Sorry to interrupt. We thought we'd take this chance while the food line is so long to come by and greet your mother."

"Sure, good idea."

He waited a moment for Ginny to finish what she was saying to her own mother before asking her if he could introduce her once again to his friends.

"Oh, of course." She pushed back her chair and started to stand.

"Please don't get up on our account," Julian said to no avail. Corey then rose as well.

"Mom, these are my friends, Carol and Julian. Guys, this is my mother, Virginia Fischer."

"Yes, we met at the visitation. And please, call me Ginny. You two are from the Cities, right?"

"Yes, we live in Minneapolis," Carol said.

"Julian works at the bank with Nick," Corey explained. "And Carol and I have been friends since college."

He sensed a flash of recognition in his mother as she warmly shook hands with Carol. He wondered whether she remembered him mentioning Carol's name all those years ago, when Frank had challenged him in Ginny's presence to name the woman whom he had allegedly taken to bed.

"Thank you for this lovely meal," Carol said. "We're sorry to interrupt your dinner but wanted to come over and say hello."

"And to tell you again how sorry we are for your loss," Julian added.

"Thank you. I appreciate that very much. And this is no intrusion at all. I don't really know any of Corey's friends, so it's been my pleasure to meet the two of you."

"Well, we've certainly heard nice things about you. We had dinner with Nick and Corey the night that they learned the terrible news. And both of them spoke of you so fondly."

Corey winced at Carol's words. While he didn't question the kindness of her intent, he couldn't help but feel embarrassment at her revelation. Upon hearing that Frank had died, Corey had callously gone out to dinner with friends instead of racing home to comfort his mother.

"That's kind of you, Carol. Say, can the two of you join us tonight for dinner? I'm making Corey's favorite—beef stroganoff. In fact, it's mostly made already."

"Thank you, Mrs. Fischer, but we need to head back to Minneapolis."

"Are you sure? There's plenty."

"Yes, Julian needs to work in the morning."

Nick poked Corey with his elbow.

"All right then. But thank you so much for coming all the way down here."

They shook hands, then Ginny sat back down in her chair. Carol led Julian toward the food line. Corey pulled Nick aside.

"Hey. I'm going to catch up with Billy after the luncheon. I'll meet you back at the motel later, then we can go together back to the house for dinner around six. Okay?"

"Fine. I'll find something to do. I guess I can tolerate one more night in this sleepy little town. But then we need to get on the road after your meeting with the lawyer tomorrow. Got it?"

"Sure."

Nick walked over to join Carol and Julian in line for lunch. Corey sat down again next to Ginny and finished what was left on his plate. Once the reception neared its end and only a few close relatives remained in the parish, Billy made his way over to Corey who was trying to find a graceful exit from his conversation with cousin Janice.

"And then Marge says—and you can just picture her saying this, right? She says, 'for garsh sakes, Jimmy, I was talkin' 'bout the curve of her ears!' You see, Jimmy thought Marge was sayin' something about her, you know, her boobies."

Corey tried to interrupt before that last word was uttered, but there was no chance. He didn't know what to do next other than offer a polite but uncomfortable laugh. Thankfully, Billy intervened.

"Can I steal this guy away from you? We've got a lot of catching up to do."

Corey and Billy walked up the musty church stairwell and out into the crisp November air. The day was scripted perfectly for an autumn funeral—sunny, a faint breeze, only cool enough to don a light jacket.

"So, I won't bother with all that 'I'm sorry for your loss bullshit.' Tell me, how are you doing?"

"It's surreal, to be honest. For the past twenty-four hours, at the funeral and the visitation, I've been accepting expressions of sympathy. And I don't feel one bit of sadness. Is that strange?"

"Not at all, man. It's normal. I hope you don't mind me saying this, but the sad part isn't that Frank died, it's what he said to you last year in his house. And even more, how your father treated you all the years he was alive."

They walked away from the church, toward the harbor at the bottom of Main Street. The magnetism of the river attracted them strongly as kids, and it drew them toward its shores once again.

"Well, this is certainly new," Billy said.

"Huh?"

"Me walking faster than you. As kids it was always the other way around."

Corey laughed. He remembered how Billy frequently tried keeping up with him when they were young. Back then, it wasn't much of an issue, except that one time in the early spring of fifth grade. Corey had been marching home from school in the gutter adjacent Monroe Street as melting snow flowed beneath a thin veneer of ice in the thirty-five-degree air. Crash, crackle, splash. Corey smashed through the tantalizingly thin ice. Cold brown water covered the soles of his boots. The thrill of the crashing ice led him to ignore Billy's pleas of "wait up!" from behind. It was only when Billy shouted "Corey Francis Fischer, stop this instant!" that he finally halted and laughed at Billy's imitation of Ginny's voice, his feet an inch deep in dark run-off. He remembered turning his head like an owl and then playfully responding in kind. "William Arthur Preston, what do you want?"

Billy yelled that Corey should slow down and wait for him. As a kid, Billy was stocky—like his father Larry—not as fast a runner as Corey. It may have been the only source of friction between them as boys—Corey's clear advantage in speed. As soon as Billy explained how Corey was crashing all the best ice and leaving little for Billy to step on, Corey quickly fell in line behind and followed Billy the rest of the way home.

"So, how are things with Nick?" Billy's question brought Corey back from that memory.

"Normal, I guess. Normal for us, that is."

"Are things better? Is he acting less like an asshole and more like the partner you deserve?"

"Come on, Nick isn't a monster."

"He's not exactly as good as you deserve either."

Corey couldn't argue with that. "Well, you know how it is after you've been with someone for that many years."

"Actually, I don't. Remember? Amanda and I divorced after ten. Best decision I ever made. It's an option for you too, you know."

Corey nodded. "Yeah, especially given Nick's penchant for living the not-fully-committed life."

"Oh," Billy said softly. "Is that still going on? I thought you guys addressed that in therapy."

"We did, but I'm guessing he hasn't changed his sneaky ways. I went looking for some cash in his wallet recently and found a piece of paper with a name and number I didn't recognize. And he'd never dream of letting me near his password-protected phone. Who knows what I'd find in there." He then told Billy about the damp towels in the hamper.

"Corey, buddy. Is that how you want to live your life? Always chasing after Nick to see if he's cheating on you?"

Corey shook his head no. All of a sudden, Billy grabbed him by the arm.

"Hey, what's that on your other wrist?" Corey held up the bandage more visibly and lifted his pant leg to reveal the one on his knee. "Jesus, man. Did he do this to you?" Corey laughed. "It's not funny. Did he? Cause I'll confront that bastard and make it right."

"No, Billy. I fell while running last Friday night. Nick may be a lot of things, but physically abusive isn't one of them. Besides, if he were, I could handle him on my own. I'm not afraid of him that way. I'd fight back."

"I'm glad to hear it. You know I support you, Corey. Completely. I'm proud of you. If more people faced their problems like you did last year, we'd all be better off. Hell, I could've been more self-aware myself. It might have even saved my marriage, though probably not."

"I thought you loved the single life?"

"I do, don't get me wrong. But sometimes I think we could've made it work if I had tried a bit harder. I admire you for going through counseling together. Amanda and I were too angry for that."

"Well, I'm not sure how successful our sessions really are—when Nick shows up that is."

"Tell me something. Do you still love him? Or do you just think you love him?"

Corey uttered a small laugh, thinking that Billy was posing one of his infamous riddles. "Is there a difference?"

"Yeah, there is. There really is. And if you don't know that, then I think you've answered my question." Corey considered what Billy said. "So then answer me this."

"I think you've exhausted your daily allotment of questions."

"Why do you stay? I know Nick is handsome and all. Successful, maybe even good in the sack. But so are a lot of other guys, and one of them could offer you the thing you really need, the thing that Nick can't."

"And I suppose you're going to enlighten me on my deep psychological longings?"

"I'm serious, Corey. You know it as well as I do. You want what you never got here in Pepin, at home. Someone to love and defend who you are, no matter what. To be there for you when you need it the most. That's not who Nick is. I'm sure I'm not the only one aware of that. Don't your other friends see it too?"

"Not at all. Everyone thinks he's a saint. Mr. Perfect. They all tell me I'm the luckiest guy in the world. We travel, live in a great condo, and never miss an opening of the newest restaurant. I live a charmed life, as my friends all say. If only they could see deeper inside."

"Then let them. You gotta open up, let 'em see the truth— that appearances can be deceiving."

"Maybe," Corey said while looking toward the pavement, "but living up to their expectations is a hell of a lot easier than revealing Nick's sins. And mine. Besides," Corey said a bit more lightly, "having my friends' envy is a far better salve than their sympathy."

They walked for another two blocks. As they passed the bank, Corey didn't look inside the large window to see where his father had worked for nearly forty years. At the corner of Main and Pine, they instinctively stopped, Corey wondering whether they should continue down toward the marina, or head back toward their respective childhood homes.

They turned their backs to the river and continued walking.

"You know what I'm gonna say next, don't you?"

Corey nodded yes and smiled.

"You gotta come visit me. Stay as long as you like." Billy repeated this request at the end of every conversation.

"I will. This time, I really will. Let me get through the inheritance stuff and healed up from these hideous wounds." He held up his hand and pointed to his leg. "Then I promise. For real."

"Okay. I'm gonna hold you to it this time. If you're not out there by winter, I'm gonna kidnap you." They laughed. Then Billy stopped Corey's forward momentum with the gentle grip of his hand on Corey's. "And please, don't wait for Nick to change. I know you're hoping for an answer, but it's never gonna come from Nick. I think the only one who will change in your relationship is you." Billy pulled him into another hug. "Have I said too much, maybe gone a sentence or more too far? Wait, don't answer that."

They both smiled, then walked another half-block before passing in front of the Hometown Diner, the only remaining café in Pepin. Billy stopped and pointed toward the door. "You know, Amanda took all my money in the divorce," he joked. "I'm technically broke. But if you've got five bucks, let's go inside. I'll let you buy me a cup of coffee."

"Some things never change, I see. You never seem to have cash when we go out."

"The method to my madness, dear boy. I'm a cheapskate to the core, but always open to the generosity of friends. How do you think I got so filthy rich?"

At that moment, Corey heard the clanging of the railroad crossing bell behind them and seconds later the roar of a freight train bearing down on Pepin, heading north. He remembered that this was one of the thrilling aspects of living here in the middle of nowhere—a hurtling engine carrying scores of box cars and a tiny caboose at the end, usually red.

"Hey, wait a minute!" Corey shouted. He turned his head away from the café, and from Billy, so he could watch the train cars speed past one by one, in a constant rhythm of clickety-clack, clickety-clack. He remembered how, as a boy, he tried imagining the inside of those flying boxcars—not what they held but rather whether there was room for him to stow away. He'd been fascinated by stories of hobos who rode the rails across America, jumping on and off in random places, seeking their true home in the world. He used to day-dream about doing the same, his backpack filled with personal possessions and money stuffed securely into his underwear.

In the brightness of this November afternoon, Corey could see the river just beyond the train tracks and all the way across to the other shore. He spied a train traveling south along the Minnesota side of the river. He nudged Billy and pointed to the far shore before shouting, "Double Train!" Billy nodded with approval, smiled wide, and flashed a thumbs-up sign in return. The roar of the locomotive cars passing in front of them was too deafening for conversation. But Corey instantly remembered their childhood belief that when two trains crossed at the same time in front of downtown Pepin, you could make a wish that would magically, eventually come true. Corey thought about all Billy had just said and then he made his wish.

Corey's thoughts returned to the passing trains, the hobos inside, and the endless possibilities if only he could jump on the next locomotive heading out of town, a thousand miles in any direction. And, as far away from his troubles as the train and his money would take him. Suddenly, Corey's distant impulses attached themselves to the caboose as it flew off in the distance and eventually out of sight. They stood watching the empty tracks for a moment longer, the sound of the receding train still faintly reaching them.

"Come on," he said, turning back toward Billy and urging him into the café. "Let me buy you that cup of coffee."

Corey and Nick showed up at Ginny's house at six. On the short drive over, Corey tried engaging Nick about the conversation he had partially overheard through the basement vent the day before. Nick had been too drunk to be quizzed about it last night, after arriving back at the motel with Carol and Julian around midnight.

"I don't remember talking about anything serious, to be honest. It's not like your mother and I are the best of friends."

"She said you two had a conversation regarding our marriage, and that I should ask you about it."

Nick appeared to be thinking.

"Well?"

"I guess we did talk about the fact that we got married in a rush up in Canada, and that she and Frank weren't even invited or made aware of it until later."

Corey strained to remember the exact words he had heard through the vent. Nick's explanation didn't fully make sense.

"Swear to God, that's all I remember."

Corey pulled the Jeep into the driveway, and he decided to let it go until later. Maybe he could get more information out of his mother before confronting Nick again. By the time they arrived at the house, Ginny had finished making the stroganoff. Corey smelled that delicious, familiar scent of meat and mushrooms as soon as he walked in the door. He could already taste the savory sauce and perfectly tender strips of meat spread across thick egg noodles. Over dinner, they recapped their respective experiences and conversations from the funeral and the lunch at St. Bridget's. Afterward, Corey resisted his mother's plea to "let the dishes be." He and Nick washed every pot, plate, and spoon by hand, then joined Ginny in the living room and sat down.

"So, Mom. Last night, you said that you had something to tell me?"

"Yes, Corey. I'm sorry for being so abrupt yesterday. You stirred some feelings that I needed time to think about."

"I'm sorry too. I wasn't trying to upset you."

Nick interjected. "If you'd rather, I can go back to the motel so you two can talk in private."

"No. You should stay. It's high time we speak more openly in this family and that we stop holding onto secrets." Corey shuddered in reaction to the intensity of his mother's stare toward Nick. He noticed how slowly and emphatically she uttered the word "secrets." Neither Corey nor Nick said another word. Instead, they let Ginny speak.

"Last night you mentioned that both of us were locked into battles with Frank across the years. I can't disagree with that." Ginny reached for a tissue from the box atop the end table. She wasn't crying or suppressing a sneeze. Corey figured she was keeping the tissue handy or reaching for something to hold.

"But you also said that I had a choice, that I chose to spend my life with Frank. I suppose on the face of it, you're right. I was an adult when we met, though just barely. And I was a grown-up throughout our marriage. That was a meaningful difference between your situation and mine, Corey. And I want to affirm that in your struggle, at least until you turned eighteen, you were a child and that it was Frank's responsibility—not yours—to make things right. I'm sorry he never did that."

"Thank you."

"But when you made that reference to me having a choice, I want you to know it wasn't that simple. In fact, it was far more complicated than you could ever imagine."

"Mom, you don't owe me an explanation."

"Let me finish, Corey. This is something I haven't been able to talk about for forty years, something I've been carrying my entire life. And it's time to set the record straight. I want you to understand the choices I did or didn't make. I'm not making excuses or shifting the blame to anyone else. But I need you to hear this once and for all."

This was not the direction Corey anticipated their conversation would go. He had been sitting at the edge of the sofa, with Nick to his right. But he settled himself back against the cushion and listened to the words flow from his mother's slightly trembling lips.

"In the summer of 1972, I graduated from high school. I had a job at the ice cream shop and spent my free time hanging out with friends. I was planning to attend community college in the fall. I had the grades to attend a university, like Eau Claire or Steven's Point, but my parents didn't have the money. My dad insisted that learning secretarial skills and living at home was the best course for me.

"One day that August, my friend Susan told me about a picnic being planned southeast of town. We both had the afternoon off, so I said what the heck. We convinced two more friends to join us and then drove out to a secluded gravel-covered parking lot on a bank above the Chippewa River twenty minutes outside of town. Frank used to tell the story that he noticed me the second I stepped foot on the sand, walking in the middle of my group of friends. He was a junior at UWEC, intent on obtaining a degree in business and under pressure to complete his studies in four years. His father wasn't about to pay for a single semester more.

"I remember him approaching me and introducing himself. I was surprised when he asked if I worked at the ice cream shop near the college. I guess he had seen me there before, but I didn't remember him. Anyway, my friends withdrew a few yards down the beach, but still close enough to eavesdrop on every word. Frank did most of the talking, at first—about his studies, being an accomplished hunter, and his dream of one day moving far away and running his own business. I remember feeling inadequate. Here was this handsome older guy clearly motivated toward a successful career, and he seemed more worldly than anyone I'd ever met. I mean, I still shared a bedroom with my sister and worked part-time jobs year-round since ninth grade. I even had to earn enough to buy my own prom dress. My father called purchases like that 'extravagances,' beyond what his salary from the factory could afford. Within minutes, I sensed that Frank had grown up with privilege. His dad bought him a car at sixteen. There were annual trips to Chicago, and he had also owned a cabin in the woods. We did have one important thing in common though—a devout Catholic faith.

"He asked if we could take a walk, and I agreed. I remember the skies being slightly menacing. The sun was still high atop the trees, but there were distant rumbles of thunder. We saw some guys run off in search of firewood for a bonfire. Others formed an exclusive circle and lit a joint. There was loud music and voices filled the river bottoms, echoing off the nearby hills. A few couples paired off, finding privacy beyond the reedy shoreline, or near the random oak trees amongst the tall grasses. I remember turning back to look at my friends who made shooing motions with their hands. I swung back around and kept walking with Frank."

At this point Ginny looked down into her lap. Corey was happy not to make eye contact, unsure where this story was headed.

"I dated a few boys in high school but was still a virgin. I was intimate with my prom date, but nothing serious. Among my friends, I was the lone holdout from letting a boy go all the way. I was raised to save myself for the man I would marry. In a way, I guess that's how it all worked out."

She paused again, this time to take a long sip of water from a tumbler on the end table.

"Later that month, on the day I discovered I was pregnant, I called in sick from work and told my mother when no one else was at home. She shook her head, then sternly told me that I was going to have that baby." Ginny looked up at Corey. "I want you to know that I never considered any other option." She paused, then continued. "Mom told my father that very same night. When the two of them called me into the kitchen and sent my sister to her room, I was terrified. If you remember, Corey, my father had a very booming voice. Anyway, as soon as he finished yelling about my sinful behavior and his disappointment, he demanded Frank's address, then drove straight over to the dorm. Somehow he convinced Frank to return with him to our house. With my mother standing behind him for support, my father sat us both down in the living room. He explained that he would arrange for us to get married at the courthouse the following week. Frank tried to express that while he cared for me, he wasn't ready for a lifelong commitment. That's when my father explained that he was giving an order, not asking a question."

"What about your feelings, Mrs. Fischer? Did you want to get married?"

Corey glared at Nick for asking such a blunt question, a question that was in his mind too, but that he felt should remain unasked.

"I don't know that I even thought about my own wishes at that point. I was terrified of my father and unsure about Frank. Plus, I had a baby on the way and wanted to do the right thing. What choice did I really have?"

"Well, no offense, but you were eighteen and old enough to make a decision for yourself," Nick said.

"That's not fair, Nick. Try putting yourself in her shoes for one second."

Corey and Nick stared at each other with looks of contempt. Ginny filled the awkward void by telling more of her story.

"I remember things weren't entirely settled when my father drove Frank back to the dorm, but they were by the next day. You see, my dad tracked down Donald Fischer in Pepin. Once Dad explained the situation, the two of them agreed that their children would do the right and Catholic thing. We got married at the Eau Claire courthouse the very next week. We rented an apartment for Frank's senior year, and I got a job instead of attending community college. After that, we moved here once your grandfather got Frank a job at the bank. We've been here ever since."

"Mom, I had no idea. I mean I figured out long ago that I was born about seven months after you were married. But I always assumed, well, I'm not sure what I assumed but it certainly wasn't this."

"So, then Corey was to blame for you having to get married, right?"

Ginny practically leapt to the edge of her chair.

"No, you are not right at all, Nick. Corey was the best thing I ever did in this life. Nothing about what I've said is his fault."

"I'm sorry. I wasn't trying to blame him. It's just that you began this conversation by saying you didn't have a choice about spending your life with Frank. If it's not about an unwanted pregnancy, then are you talking about how your parents forced you to get married?"

Ginny looked at Nick, then at Corey, and then began to weep.

"Mom, you don't need to say any more."

"Maybe not," Nick said, "but I think this is exactly the type of thing you two should be talking about. For God's sake, we've endured years of unhappiness in our own relationship because of the emotional baggage you've carried from childhood. At some point you two need to get everything out on the table, once and for all."

Corey protested Nick's remarks, though deep inside he recognized grains of truth.

"Is that what you meant, Mrs. Fischer? Even though you have no regrets about Corey, you feel you had no choice in marrying Frank?"

It took a while for her tears to wane, to answer Nick's question with words.

"No. I don't blame my parents. They were trying to do what was right under the circumstances. I would have done the exact same thing in their position. And I'm the one who said 'I do' at the courthouse."

Ginny paused to blow her nose into the tissue.

"This is difficult, but Nick's right. It's time we stop hiding things from each other and instead share what's been in the shadows for too long." She breathed deep. "There were other choices too. Some I made, and some were made for me."

"Which were?"

Nick was like a dog with a bone. Corey was about ready to slap him.

"At the picnic, Frank and I walked down the beach, talking. At first, I thought it was nice. I remember glancing back at some point, and all the others looked like ants milling about in the sand, fading along with the day's disappearing light. That's when Frank steered me up a small hill into the tall grass between the beach and the woods. He said he was tired and that we should sit and rest for a few minutes. Frank spread his slick blue windbreaker on the ground, stretching it as wide as possible and urging me to sit and relax against the base of a large river birch. I snuggled into him and gazed up toward the sky. We sat that way, touching, for several minutes. I began to feel comfortable wrapped in his arms—safe.

"I was caught off guard though when Frank made the next move. His lips pressed firmly against mine, with far more determination than my prom date. It felt forceful but, if I'm honest, not entirely unwanted. His tongue surprised me, thrust into my mouth. I'd never kissed a boy like that before. I remember having to breathe through my nose because I couldn't free my lips. I turned in the direction Frank seemed to be pushing me and soon I was flat on the ground. For a moment he lay beside me, but in one swift move he lifted himself on top, his weight pinning my arm beneath my back. I could feel the windbreaker against my shoulders and legs, and the slippery blue padding whined ever so slightly as it rubbed against the grass."

Ginny looked up at Corey who stared back with a pained face. She continued.

"I felt my skirt rise higher on my hips, and I thought about how far away I was from my friends. Frank's aggressive open-mouthed kissing continued, but I needed a break. With my prom date, it seemed so different, much more of a back and forth. With Frank, I felt as if I were square dancing in the gymnasium back at school, awkwardly following someone else's lead and unsure of what comes next. Everything happened so fast. It wasn't until afterward that I realized there wasn't time to choose whether I wanted it at all. I heard his dangling belt buckle slapping against the ground a moment before feeling my underpants being pushed aside."

Corey looked at Nick who was now white as a ghost. Ginny lifted the tissue to both eyes. Her words came out haltingly, through barely-veiled distress.

"I tried to say something, I really did. But I couldn't. Frank's overpowering jaw sealed our mouths together. My right hand was locked with his left against the ground. Before I could free my pinned left arm to signal that I wanted to slow down, he was already fully inside me. I remember feeling Frank's deep sigh echo in the back of my throat, drowning out my own attempt to speak. When he moaned more deeply, I think it awakened me from confusion. I found some inner strength and freed myself from his mouth, regaining enough breath to cry out his name. At that same moment, he lifted his mouth from my face and exhaled with exhaustion, then rolled onto the grass."

Now Corey was crying too. Nick sat in silence, his hand covering his mouth and chin.

"Mom, you were raped."

She shook her head, no. "Things were different then, Corey."

"Things may have been different, but you were forced against your will. That's called rape."

Ginny didn't say a word. She sat still and cried. Corey got up from the sofa and joined her in the chair, just like he did as a boy. But this time, he trembled with rage. He put his arm around her and pulled her into his side. She accepted the embrace, but eventually motioned for Corey to return to the sofa next to Nick.

"Thank you. I'm fine, really. I know it doesn't look like it, but I am. I got over this many years ago. It's just difficult to tell you now, because I'm embarrassed."

"Why are you embarrassed?"

"This isn't the type of thing you want to tell your son, to explain to him that he was conceived like this."

Corey collapsed into the back cushion of the sofa. He rubbed his palms against his forehead, then ran his fingers through his hair.

"Mrs. Fischer," Nick said. "That's a terrible burden to carry all these years."

"Yes, and no. Whenever I'd get down about it, I'd think about the blessing I got with Corey. And I can say without a doubt that I have zero regrets."

"That's… I don't know what to call it. I guess I'd say that's brave. But why didn't you tell anyone?"

"I did. I told my good friend, who convinced me not to tell my mother. 'She won't understand' my friend told me. I thought she was right. So I never told another soul until today."

Corey listened intently.

"I only told you this story so you'd have a better appreciation for my choices in life. I'm not trying to sidestep responsibility for my actions, or at least the ones I could control. But sometimes things aren't black and white. Sometimes you take what life hands you."

Corey thought of several things to say in rebuttal, but now wasn't the right time. What his mother needed was affirmation. He rose from the sofa once more and walked over to her, lifting his mother from her chair. He enveloped her in a long, firm embrace. Neither of them was crying any longer, for it seemed that their relief came in the telling and in the hearing of her story.

Nick stayed seated on the sofa.

6

Tuesday

On Tuesday morning, Nick left early for Eau Claire. His bank had a large branch there, and he said it was a good opportunity for a surprise visit from HR. Besides, he complained, "I've got nothing else to do all morning while you go see the lawyer."

Corey and Ginny drove downtown to meet Larry Preston, the biggest legal fish in the small pond of Pepin. Though warm enough to walk the nine blocks from the house to Main Street, Corey sensed his mother's exhaustion from the tumult of the past two days. They drove instead, arriving promptly at nine o'clock.

The office building sat on a corner, one block from the bank where Frank sold insurance. Corey parked in front of First National. He looked into the large front window, straining to see the interior wall behind which Frank ran his business. He remembered how his father used to talk animatedly about the thinly veiled connection with bank officers. He could almost hear Frank's bragging still today. "They come in for a home loan? Bob refers them to me afterward for homeowner's insurance. You say you need to borrow money to buy a car? Well, you're gonna need auto insurance too. Congrats on depositing your first paycheck. Say, you're gonna need to buy life insurance, son!" Nothing about it was untoward, Frank assured Corey. He claimed to be doing folks a favor with one-stop shopping. Such details of the business world were lost on Corey as a boy. Not that he couldn't grasp them; rather, he simply didn't care.

The receptionist greeted them and offered coffee before showing them in to see Larry. He had a corner office on the third floor, with a large window and clear view of the marina two blocks away. Beyond that, Corey could see the river and the bluffs of Minnesota in the distance. What a contrast to his windowless work cubicle in Minneapolis.

"Come in, come in. Have a seat at the conference table. It's more friendly than talking across this big old desk."

They obliged. Corey scanned the framed photos and credentials hanging on the wall. *Impressive*, he thought—a law degree from Marquette. Pictures of the entire Preston family on various camping vacations adorned the walls. Corey recalled being envious as a kid—hearing about Billy's trips to Door County, the Black Hills, and Yellowstone. The farthest Frank ever took Corey and Ginny was to see Frank Lloyd Wright's famous house, Taliesen, near Spring Green. In those days, Frank attended his annual out-of-town insurance conferences alone, leaving Corey and Ginny at home.

He looked closer at the photos. Corey smiled at the one taken at an unidentifiable campsite when Billy and his siblings were small—the family around a fire pit cooking their breakfast and Billy feigning self-immolation by jumping near the fire. What a goofball. Turning to face Larry, who was standing in front of his desk, Corey wondered if this was how Billy was destined to look someday... worn down like his old man.

"Ginny, that was a lovely service. Real, real nice. I'm sure Frank was looking down upon it all and smiling."

"Thank you. I'm sure he was."

Corey looked away and rolled his eyes. If Frank was indeed up there looking down instead of down there burning up, then it only confirmed that heaven and a church were the last places Corey ever wanted to be.

"Did Linda offer you coffee?"

"Yes, thank you," Ginny replied. "But we already had ours back at the house."

"Fine. Let's sit down. I have the papers right here. This shouldn't take long. As I'm sure you know better than me, Frank was a man who didn't miss a beat. Maybe that's why he was so successful in business over the years and his customers kept coming back for more insurance. He looked after every detail."

"Yes, he certainly did." Ginny's replies were delivered in monotone. Corey attributed it to her being tired from the past few days, especially after last night. He was a bit apprehensive too, over what was in his father's will. Surely Frank did the right thing, at least for Ginny. But then again, Corey wasn't confident of anything right now.

"Okay then. Let's see here." Larry donned his reading glasses and shuffled through the file, scattering papers across his end of the table within seconds. Corey glanced at the large mahogany desk and shuddered at the random piles strewn about the surface, extending onto the credenza. He wondered how anyone responsible for important legal affairs could be so disorganized. Were deadlines ignored? Key documents misplaced? Entire matters forgotten? He'd read somewhere that this kind of disorder was actually the sign of high intelligence and an orderly mind. If that were the case, Corey mused, then he'd rather be considered an imbecile.

"Here we go—Frank's last will and testament. Are you ready to hear it?" After Ginny and Corey each nodded their heads, Larry began to read. The words were straightforward. No emotional farewells or personal wishes, just business laid out in clear, understandable terms. Larry summarized them after reaching the end of the document.

"It's pretty simple. Most of Frank's estate reverts to you, Ginny. The house, all the bank and investment accounts, and Frank's personal effects. I'd roughly estimate those assets to be worth about five hundred thousand."

"That doesn't sound like a lot," Corey said. "But maybe for living in a small town it is?"

"Given your mother's age and expected longevity, that number is a bit on the light side. But there's more to the estate than that. Being an insurance salesman, Frank walked the walk and followed his own advice. He carried both term insurance and a whole life policy that has a substantial cash value. All together, Frank Fischer's estate is worth around two million dollars."

"Jesus Chr—" Corey said.

"Ginny, you're a wealthy woman. You won't have to worry about a thing, moneywise. If you prefer, I can recommend a financial advisor who can guide you on what to do with the money, especially the large insurance payout. That is, unless you want to manage it by yourself, or with Corey's help?"

"I can certainly balance a checkbook and pay bills, but I don't know the first thing about investments or managing that kind of money."

"Neither do I," Corey added. "Nick does all of that at our house."

"Okay," Larry said as he moved papers from one side of the folder to another. His voice trailed off, unsuccessfully trying to suppress a sneeze that finally overpowered him. Ginny offered him God's blessing.

Corey fidgeted in his seat, uncomfortable with the gap in the conversation. He looked at his watch. Nick was probably on his way back from Eau Claire by now. They needed to wrap this up.

"Well, thank you, Mr. Preston. Everything seems straightforward. I assume you'll help my mother with changing names on bank accounts, title to the house, all those sorts of details?"

"Of course. However, I can help. I'm here to assist in any way I can."

"Great. Then I guess we'll leave you to the rest of your day. Thanks again for all you've done." Corey pushed back from the conference table and started to rise from his chair.

"Well now, hold on," Larry said. "There's two more items." Corey sat back down. "First, your father's estate also included the cabin in Barron County. Frank willed that to you, Ginny. But here's the thing, Corey. Your mom already indicated she has no interest in keeping it. Is that right, Ginny, or have you changed your mind?"

"That's correct. I'd rather it go to Corey, if he wants to have it."

"Just to be clear," Larry jumped in to explain, "if you decline the bequest of the cabin, Ginny, there's no contingent beneficiary in Frank's will. Corey isn't mentioned. But as Frank's only other direct heir, Corey would receive the cabin under Wisconsin probate law. Or, we can simply have you quit claim it to him. Either way."

Ginny turned in her chair to face Corey. He suddenly realized what was being said and was on the verge of yelling "no," but resisted upon seeing the imploring look on his mother's face.

Larry interrupted. "Now, son, you don't have to make any decisions right now. The place is paid for, of course. So, let me know if you want the title changed into your own name or if you'd like me to help you list it for sale."

"Oh, I don't need any more time, Mr. Preston. I haven't been to Barron County in twenty years. And I'm definitely not the hunting type. Go ahead and list it for sale tomorrow morning for all I care."

"That's what your mom figured, but I wanted to be sure."

Corey looked at his mother with a slightly furrowed brow and squinted eyelids. What else had been discussed about him before he returned to Pepin?

"I understand," Ginny said. "I wasn't necessarily hoping you'd keep it. I simply wanted to let you make that choice, seeing as you did spend time there as a boy."

"Those weren't happy memories for me, if you remember."

"I know. But even if we sell the cabin, I'd like you to drive up there and collect your father's things. Our car is there along with whatever he left at the cabin when he died."

Corey didn't know what to say.

"There are also personal mementos inside that I'd like to have brought back to Pepin—family pictures and what have you. I guess we can leave the rest and let the realtor sell the cabin as is, fully furnished."

Corey paused, riven. Why couldn't she ask her brother, or a friend? Why must this burden pass to him? The last place in the world he wanted to go was Barron County—to that cabin. The pleading look on her face led him to resist an instinctive "no." The blunt reality that his mother wanted him to retrieve her only vehicle from the cabin led him closer to uttering "yes."

"Well, you think about that for a minute. I need a few signatures from Ginny on these documents."

Mention of the cabin led Corey to think about his latest painting—a depiction of that same damn cabin. Had he willed this whole sequence of events into existence by simply casting visions of that lonely place onto his canvas with brush strokes? He had tried painting that cabin several times over the years, but only recently had he found the right angle, the right light, the right perspective. Why now? And what might happen once he arrived in Barron County? Would the actual cabin scene blow apart the picture that had formed in his mind of that place over the past twenty years? Would he have to begin his painting anew?

Corey shook his head to clear his thoughts. He watched his mother dutifully sign her name in a dozen places. Corey's mind then drifted off to the last time his mother asked him to travel to Barron County. It was a Saturday in mid-November during his senior year of high school. He had slept in till ten, as usual, then rose to start on homework and chores. With his stomach rumbling, he pulled on a green and gold hooded sweatshirt and matching sweatpants, then hobbled down the hallway using impressive gymnastic moves to pull white tube socks onto each foot by the time he hit the kitchen's linoleum floor.

He remembered his mother sitting at the table drinking coffee and perusing the Wisconsin State Journal. She greeted him and said that she had pancakes warming in the oven and bacon on the stove. Frank was apparently up early and had gone into the office for a few hours. Unsurprisingly, Ginny also let Corey know that Frank had left a list of chores for him on the counter. Looking back, it was probably something typical for that time of year—

rake the leaves, clean the gutters, or bring in a stack of wood from the shed.

He remembered Ginny asking about his crabby morning mood. He explained that Frank was trying to get Corey to go deer hunting with him. Ginny encouraged him to go, saying that it would mean a lot to Frank. Corey remembered his own snarky reply—"What, so he has someone to beat in the competition for biggest kill? Well, he's won that battle already because I refuse to pick up a gun much less shoot a goddamned deer." He recalled Ginny dropping her newspaper and sternly telling Corey to watch his mouth. "You may be technically an adult, but as long as you're in this house you'll show respect and not take the Lord's name in vain."

He had apologized, saying that he did respect her, but he couldn't say the same for Frank. He remembered expressly using his father's first name rather than "Father" or "Dad." By that time in Corey's life, those labels had begun to feel too familiar and accepting. Ginny reminded him that Frank was the only father he would ever have, like him or not. In a year's time Corey would be off to college, beginning his own life. She said that the next nine months might be the last chance he would have to forge a better father-son relationship. Corey reminded her that having a relationship required that both sides try, and he didn't ever see Frank trying. He remembered her reply. "The man feeds, houses, and clothes you, Corey. He buys what you need and agreed to pay half your college tuition. I'd say he's trying."

Corey held his ground, telling her that both of them were treated less than they deserved. Then he remembered looking directly at his mother. "Frank may well provide me with life's necessities, but relationships demand a lot more. Why can't he be kind to me, like you are?" He remembered seeing his mother's eyes well up as she said, "he tries."

"Yeah, he tries to change me by criticizing my every move. I'm a bad hunter. I should be getting better grades. If I were a real man, I'd be on the football team." Tears had come to Corey's eyes too. Ginny took a moment and seemed to be reaching for the right words to say. She reminded Corey what a tough upbringing Frank had as the only son of Donald Fischer, especially after Lillian died. He had no one around to help him develop a softer side. Corey remembered asking her how long she'd let that be an excuse for Frank to berate his only son and an excuse for letting him demean Ginny as well.

As he sat in Larry Preston's office now, watching his aging mother finish signing documents, he wondered anew how this demur, kind woman had remained so fiercely loyal to that man, especially in light of what she had revealed last night. Then he remembered her chilling answer from all those years ago, explaining that she had taken a vow to be a supportive wife, a vow that she intended to keep. She even quoted scripture, something about wives submitting to their husbands just as the Church submits to Christ. It was from Ephesians—Corey remembered looking it up. He also remembered how he felt as his mother finished reciting that Bible verse all those years ago—he had lost hope. He resigned himself to hunting with his father at the cabin and enduring it as best he could. He would bide his time until the following August and then get the hell out of Pepin on the first train heading north. He had no doubt at the time that he could pull it off. After all, he'd been masking his feelings and true self for the better part of his life. What would be so difficult about acting the role of dutiful son for another nine months?

"Corey? Have you decided?" He looked over at Larry and then to his mother. He had the sense that they'd been trying to get his attention for a few moments before he answered.

"Fine. I'll go, but then I want it listed for sale." Images of the cabin raced into his mind. The outdated furniture, the same old photographs adorning the walls, the bedspreads, towels, and décor that graced the cabin as long as he or anyone else could remember. Nothing about the cabin ever changed, he mused. What a perfect metaphor for his father's life, and one of the reasons Corey couldn't stand to go there. That cabin represented everything he loathed about Frank, and he recalled nothing but uncomfortable memories of the place.

"There's no rush on the cabin ownership and sale, unless you really do want to list it immediately."

"Well..." Ginny started to say something. Both Larry and Corey waited for her to continue. "I know there's no rush on selling the cabin, but I do need my car."

He sympathized with his mother's plight—it was her only vehicle. But he also envisioned a battle with Nick, once Corey explained the necessary detour on their way back home, to retrieve Frank's belongings from Barron County and to honor Ginny's request.

"Here's an idea," Larry said as if reading Corey's mind. "What if Billy rides up there with you tomorrow and drives Ginny's car back to Pepin? Then you and Nick can continue on toward Minneapolis."

That's a great idea, Corey thought. He'd get to spend a little more time with Billy and less time alone in the car with Nick. Before he could answer, Larry said more.

"Son, while you're thinking about that, there's one more thing—another reason you need to visit the cabin."

Corey turned from his mother back toward Larry, his mind blank as to what the lawyer might say. "And that is?"

"Remember now, I said there were two things to discuss. The first is ownership of the cabin. The second is that Frank wrote a codicil to his will earlier this year, specifically leaving you a personal gift." Ginny and Corey sat back in their wooden chairs. Corey held his breath.

"You father bequeathed you his hunting guns. It says here he had two—a Marlin 336 rifle and an H&R Handi twenty-two Hornet."

Corey looked at his mom as he strained to understand what Larry just said. Her face gave no clues.

"Are you familiar with those, Corey?"

"Yeah, I guess. Those are the rifles he hunted with when I was a kid, but I haven't seen them in twenty years. Why did he give 'em to me? He knew how much I hated hunting."

Corey directed his question toward Larry who simply shook his head, then unfolded and lifted up his hands. Both Larry and Corey then looked at Ginny. She shrugged her shoulders. "I have no idea."

"Well I want nothing to do with them."

"That's fine, son, but as of right now they're legally yours."

"Then give 'em to someone else."

"I can't really do that, Corey. Frank gave them to you in his will. Only you can dispose of them."

Corey's mind raced as he tried to understand his father's bequest. It made no sense. The only two things Frank gave him in the will represented the part of his childhood that Corey perhaps loathed the most.

"You can certainly sell those guns, Corey. If they're still in good shape, you can get decent money for 'em. I assume Frank had the guns with him at the cabin when he died?"

Larry's question pulled Corey back from the flood of questions inside his mind. "How would I know?"

"They're not in the gun case at home," Ginny said. "I saw him stow them in the trunk of the car before he left on Friday."

Larry nodded his head. "That's what I thought. So, it's up to you whether you want to keep or sell those guns, Corey. But either way, they're yours now. And, you're going to have to drive up to Barron County to get them for yourself."

Deliverance

November 2013

1

Wednesday Morning

Corey looked to his left. There was Nick, with his hands gripping the steering wheel and looking not so different from Frank driving this same route all those years ago. If someone had told him a week ago that he'd be returning to Barron County, Corey would have said they were nuts. Nothing about that place felt appealing. And traveling there with Nick? Frank would roar from deep in his grave at the thought.

He looked to his right and watched as his hometown faded into the distance. The dramas of the past few days were now behind him—the running accident, the funeral, seeing his mother again for the first time in over a year. And yet, confronting the spiteful inheritance from his father still lay ahead. At least the drive up would be pleasant, with Billy along. Corey turned toward the back seat.

"Thanks again, Billy. We really appreciate you coming with us."

"No worries. Glad to help out."

"Yeah," Nick interrupted, "you're doing us a favor saving us from driving all the way back to Pepin."

His head still turned toward the back of the vehicle, Corey offered Billy a pair of raised eyebrows and a smirk. It may have been the first nice thing Nick had said about Billy, ever.

"Not at all. You probably saved the Preston family's holiday dinner too."

"How so?" With furrowed brow, Nick glanced at Billy in the rear-view mirror.

"I'm heading back to California Friday night, and my sister's family is going to her in-laws Thanksgiving Day, so Mom's having our holiday meal in Pepin tonight. She was already cooking when I left. I'd for sure have been put in charge of a few side dishes if I had stayed home."

"Uh oh," said Corey before he and Billy began laughing.

"Did I miss the joke?" Nick glanced between Corey and the road.

"The joke is that everybody might end up with food poisoning if I cook."

"You remember the mushroom incident?" Corey asked.

"Of course. No one will ever let me forget it."

"Mushrooms?" Nick asked.

"Yeah, the mushrooms. We were camping one summer down at Governor Dodge State Park west of Madison. My father had this crazy idea that us kids all had to find food from nature to contribute to the campfire meal one night. I think he was trying to give Mom a break from preparing all the food. Anyway, my brother caught a few sunnies off the pier and my sisters gathered berries from the woods. Those berries were pretty sour, if you ask me."

"Sounds more like sour grapes from you than sour berries from them."

Billy playfully whacked Corey on the arm before continuing his story.

"Yours truly was the most industrious of the kids. I went out and found some delicious looking morels. They're not easy to find, you know. They only grow near elm trees and in a limited season every year."

"I believe that season is spring, not summer. Yes?" Corey asked with a knowing smile.

"Hey, I was only like ten years old. These things looked just like the morels we used to find out on the edge of town. You'd have been fooled too, my friend."

"So, what happened? Did you eat them and get sick?" Nick asked.

"Not right away I didn't. I brought them back to camp, and we kids all began making our respective parts of the meal. I can still smell those filleted sunnies roasting over the fire. Mom came out of the camper after everything was set on the table and asked about the strange-looking black things—my morels. 'Those aren't morels,' I remember her yelling. 'Those are the poisonous look-alikes that grow in summertime.' Only my brother had stuck some in his mouth by then. He got up, spit 'em out, then raced toward the water bucket to rinse 'em out."

It surprised Corey to see Nick laugh at Billy's self-deprecation.

"Yeah, maybe it's best you leave the Thanksgiving meal prep to your mom."

"Agreed. But I still can't stay long once we get to the cabin. I pretty much need to turn around and drive right back. Otherwise, I'd stay and hunt with you guys."

"Yeah, the hunt." Corey's voice betrayed his lack of excitement.

"I see you're just as eager now as the last time you headed this way—with Frank."

"Well, I for one am looking forward to it," said Nick. "I've hunted with my dad and brothers since I was a kid. I tried to get Corey to join us a couple times, but he wouldn't go."

"Why on earth would I sit out in the cold all day waiting for the opportunity to kill something when I could be painting instead?"

"I'm guessing that your idol Frida Kahlo went hunting at some point. Her deer painting seemed pretty realistic to me."

Billy looked puzzled. "So are you hunting or not? I thought you said you guys planned to try out the guns your father left you."

"Oh we're hunting all right. Corey owes it to me for missing work the past three days and driving so far out of our way."

Corey sat twisted, with his back up against the vehicle door and his arms crossed in front of him. He could see both Nick and Billy directly. His injured knee was pulled up onto the seat with his foot resting against his other leg. He rubbed the wounded one out of recent habit but recognized that it no longer throbbed like before.

"He just has bad memories of hunting with his father. With me it'll be different."

Corey didn't disagree with what Nick said. His final trip to Barron County with Frank had been a parody of father-son bonding, especially his father's stunt in sneaking Corey into the Foxtails Lounge despite being underage.

"Why you heading back to LA so soon? Why not stay in Wisconsin for the long weekend?" Nick again looked at Billy in the rear-view mirror.

"I gotta get back. Things are a bit crazy right now at work. I only flew out here for Frank's funeral. I wasn't planning to come home for Thanksgiving this year."

"You really surprised me. And I'm thankful you came."

Billy nodded. "Yeah, I've got two construction projects at a critical stage that need attention. Plus, I'm finally listing my place for sale. I got it in the divorce, but it's too much house for me. Besides, I think I'd rather get a shitty bachelor apartment close to the beach."

"You'll be a walking cliché," Nick said. "Congrats."

Corey rolled his eyes. Billy gave a laugh.

"Tell me again. Why are you in construction?" Nick asked.

"As opposed to… selling drugs?" Corey's facial gestures matched the sarcasm in his voice. "What the hell kind of question is that?"

"Calm down. I just wanted to know how he got into that line of work. Wasn't your degree in economics, Billy?"

"No, business."

"Did you get your MBA, like I did?"

"Just a Bachelor's, I'm afraid. Once I graduated, that was enough school debt for me. Besides, Amanda wanted to go back to

California after college and be closer to her family. So, I followed her west."

"Do you regret that now, given how things didn't work out?" Nick always asked the questions that Corey never would.

"Not at all. I love Southern California—the weather, the vibe, everything. Housing's a bit expensive, but that's why I ended up in construction. Jobs are plentiful, and the demand for new projects never ends. I forget how many people they say move to LA every day on average. But they definitely keep on coming, and they all need a place to live."

Nick looked at Billy in the mirror once more and nodded his head.

Corey screamed, "Look out!"

His head hit the side window as Nick swerved violently toward the median, then back across the road and onto the gravel shoulder. Billy's head hit the glass too, but he wasn't seriously hurt. The Jeep missed a full-sized doe by inches. It clipped an immature button buck directly on the hip. Nick came to a stop alongside the road. He was now breathing heavily.

"You guys okay?" Nick asked.

Corey and Billy each nodded yes. All three of them turned to look out the rear window. Corey got sick to his stomach. The small buck was clearly injured, dragging his hindquarters with two wobbly front legs. The doe stood in the nearby grass, facing her gravely wounded offspring.

"What are we gonna do?" Corey demanded.

"We're going to get out and see if the impact damaged my Jeep."

"No, I mean the deer. Look at it. The poor thing is hurt."

"Well, there's nothing I can do about that," Nick said sharply. "He was in the wrong place at the wrong time. I'm more concerned that he might've busted my headlight."

Nick opened the door and walked around to the front of the vehicle. Corey looked at Billy who shrugged his shoulders, then Corey unbuckled his seat belt and jumped out to pursue Nick.

"Looks like there's no damage, thank God. We can get back on the road." Nick didn't look up from inspecting the front of the Jeep.

"So, we're just going to leave it there, to suffer?"

"Do you have a better idea? We don't have any guns with us, so I can't put the thing out of its misery."

"What? That's not what I meant. We need to call someone, like the sheriff."

"Be my guest. But I can tell you what he'll say—do nothing. Here, go ahead." Nick thrust his phone toward Corey.

"Then we need to bring it to an animal shelter, or a local vet."

"Did you hear that, Billy?" Nick shouted toward the open back door. "Corey wants you to make room in the backseat for the injured deer. Heck, maybe once he's healed they'll even let us adopt him."

Billy stepped out of the vehicle, motioning for Corey to get back inside. He walked toward Nick. Corey returned to the front seat but left the door ajar.

Billy looked back at Corey, then turned to face Nick. "Listen, maybe you should cut him some slack, huh? His father just died and we're driving to a place he never wanted to see again in his life."

Nick started to say something, but Billy talked over him.

"Then this happens. It's clearly upsetting to him, all right? Do you think it might be best to take it down a notch or ten?"

Nick and Billy stood face to face. A car traveling the same direction slowed down. Its passengers gaped at the injured deer and hovering doe on the side of the road. They inched forward, lowered the passenger side window, and came to a stop.

"Everything okay here? You guys need a lift?"

Nick moved his gaze off Billy and turned toward the motorists. "No, thanks. We're fine."

"Alrighty then. Good luck." The window rolled back up, and the car took off down the road.

Nick turned back to face Billy and said, "I don't need to be told how to speak to Corey."

"I disagree, and not just about today's incident."

"You might want to watch yourself and your tone, William."

"My tone is exactly what I intend it to be. I'm not mincing words with you, Nick."

Nick stared back at Billy without saying anything for a moment.

Corey watched the confrontation through the windshield and heard it through the open door. Nick's body language was clear, and Corey worried they might come to blows. He couldn't remember seeing either of them getting physical before. The only instance of violence he'd ever witnessed up close was between his parents, and that was always a one-sided bout. He particularly worried for Billy. Corey had never seen anyone defy Nick before. He certainly hadn't dared.

"Listen, Billy. You're a guest here and doing Ginny a favor. We appreciate that." Nick spoke slowly and deliberately.

"It's not about me or Ginny. This is about Corey."

"I know. I know. I'm getting to that."

"Fine. Then get to it."

Nick took a deep breath. "I suggest you get back inside the Jeep while I wipe this fur off my bumper. You and Corey can dial up the local animal control office and report what happened."

"I think that is a stellar plan."

Corey could see the sneer on Billy's face.

"Then, once we get to the cabin, you can turn right around and drive back to your family's Thanksgiving. Okay?"

"Yeah. If only I'd have thought of that."

Billy stared at Nick for a moment, then returned to the Jeep. He dialed the game warden and reported the incident. Corey listened intently while also glaring at Nick.

"Thank you, officer," Billy said. "I appreciate that you'll be sending someone out to take a look."

Ninety minutes later, the landscape triggered faint recognition.

Rolling hills sheltered farms, fields, and groves of hardwood forest. Aging farmhouses randomly dotted the countryside—their matching barns either purposeful and restored or falling into themselves beyond repair. Billy was asleep in the back seat.

"So, does it look familiar?" Nick asked.

"What?"

"The road, the scenery, the whole thing. Do you remember any of it?"

"I guess. I mean, a road is a road. Rural Wisconsin looks just about the same north to south—hills, farms, woods. And a tavern in every town."

"Huh. I guess the state does have one redeeming quality."

"I do remember an eerie comment my dad made as we drove along this road though."

"Yeah? What'd he say?"

"He had one hand on the wheel and the other rubbing his chin, then fiddling with a dial. I was reading a book, and he kept chiding me to lift my head, to enjoy the scenery."

"And you found that eerie?"

"No. If you'll let me finish the story, Nick, I'll get to that."

"Be my guest."

"Anyway, I marked my page and closed the book. I stared out the window at the same boring scenery as an hour before. My father pointed out a hawk diving for prey. Then he went on and on about the hidden nooks and crannies around this stretch in the road, or that. The land was 'full of unexpected surprises,' he said. And that humans had probably never walked on parts of this land. I think he made half that shit up to impress me. I was about to pick up my book when he stopped my arm with his. 'Look,' he said, pointing toward the forest. Then he said the oddest thing. 'It'd be the perfect spot to hide a body. Nobody'd ever find out.' I didn't know what to say, so I just shook my head."

"How bizarre." Billy had awakened from his back-seat nap. "I wonder who he wanted to knock off."

"No one, I'm sure. The idea had probably been cooking in

his two-burner brain for half an hour. He probably thought it was clever."

"Well, if anyone comes asking about a missing person while we're up here, I guess we'll direct them toward the pines," Nick said. "What a sick motherfucker."

"That wasn't all. He also pointed out a pair of does grazing in a corn field on the edge of the woods, a few hundred yards back from the road. He said they probably didn't know what's comin', and that they were enjoying one final meal."

"Charming," Billy said.

"Speaking of food, anyone getting hungry?" Nick asked. "I am."

"Me too," Billy said, "though I'm not sure what we'll find this far from civilization."

Corey hadn't eaten anything since a stale Danish and a sugary cup of yogurt at the motel earlier that morning. He had passed on an offer of bacon and eggs from Ginny before leaving Pepin.

"It looks like there's a place coming up." Corey pointed to the large billboard alongside the road before reading it aloud. "Stop at Sam's for a Sumptuous Sandwich."

Five miles north of Wheeler, Nick pulled into Slippery Sam's and parked. While walking toward the entrance, Corey looked through the window and saw a patron gorging on the advertised house specialty—shaved roast beef spread across slices of white bread, smothered in brown gravy with two scoops of mashed potatoes. He prayed there'd be a healthier option.

"Seat yourself, fellas." A waitress at the counter waved her hand in a circular motion across the café once they entered. "I'll get ya some menus."

"Okay, this is something I do remember," Corey said. "I've been here before—with my father."

"Weird. Are you sure?" Billy asked.

"Yeah. The name on the sign might be different, but everything else looks the same. I don't think the interior has changed one bit in twenty-five years."

"I agree it's no Chez Toulouse." Nick said. "But it's our only option, and I'm starving."

"Maybe, but look at that ripped upholstery." Corey pointed toward a booth.

"Keep your voice down or they'll hear you," Nick said.

"So what if they do?"

"Billy and I are hungry, and there's no place else to eat. I don't want to get kicked out or have these rednecks spit in my food."

Corey chose a faded red leather booth along the back wall. Away from the front window, flickering fluorescent bulbs did little to brighten the rest of the room. The dim lighting was probably a conscious choice. It gave the tired furnishings another decade of life.

The waitress brought menus and plastic glasses of ice water. When Corey asked about napkins and utensils, she pointed to a bevy of mixed forks, knives and spoons inside a metal cup adjacent the napkin dispenser. He wondered how many customers' hands had fondled the protruding fork tines in search of a spoon. The waitress left, saying she'd be back in few minutes.

Corey watched as she walked away. The waitress didn't look familiar, but this place sure did. The memory of that prior visit came rushing back as he looked around the café. He and Frank had stopped here for lunch on the way to Barron County when Corey was a teen. Back then, Corey ran ahead into the café as much out of hunger as an immediate need to pee. The host pointed toward the back, and Corey walked quickly to the men's room. Before reaching the door, he jerked his head toward the front to see who had screamed "Frankie!" as his father entered the café. He saw the backside of a woman dressed in a pink and white server's uniform. She held a notepad and rested her hand comfortably on his father's shoulder. Corey pushed open the restroom door and exhaled loudly after reaching the urinal and unzipping his fly.

He remembered coming back into the café and seeing that same waitress walking straight toward him. She asked Corey if he was Frank's son, and he remembered nodding yes. She introduced herself as Judy and said that she had "put you boys over there in my section, so I can keep an eye on ya." He recalled heading in the direction she had pointed, spotting the back of his father's head and plopping down into the booth. The red leather bench released a whoosh of air the moment his butt hit the seat. He asked his father how he knew the waitress, but remembered how Frank acted coy, asking Corey who he was referring to. "The waitress. She knew your name as soon as you walked in the door." He remembered Frank's sudden spark of recognition. "You mean Judy? Oh, I'm sure she recognizes all of the regulars."

Looking back now, Corey couldn't believe how he had continued quizzing his father. He pointed out that they lived far away, so they couldn't really be considered regulars. Frank said that he'd seen her a few times over the years when he stopped here on the drive north. Corey persisted. He asked Frank if they were related to her because she seemed pretty friendly and kind of grabby too. He would never forget his father's reply and quick change of tone. Frank looked up from his menu and straight into Corey's eyes. "You already know all of our relatives, Corey, so your question's kinda dumb. Now, what are you going to eat?"

Nick and Billy each ordered a hot beef sandwich. Corey asked for a bowl of chili and side salad. When the food arrived, he was disappointed. He picked at the limp lettuce and pondered the choice of unidentifiable dressings in the trio of metal containers the waitress had set on the table.

"Would it kill them to have balsamic vinegar and olive oil?"

Nick shook his head while swallowing mashed potatoes drenched in brown gravy. "I know, right? How uncouth. I mean, look at those people eating patty melts with their hands instead of cutting them up with a fork and knife!"

Corey ignored Nick's mockery. Billy kept eating.

"Why's everyone staring at us?" Corey asked.

Nick looked left and right before locking eyes with Corey.

"Maybe because you're the only one in the entire place eating rabbit food? No one's looking at us. But who'd care if they did?"

"Me. We don't exactly fit in here."

"Well, I do," Billy said. "I dressed the part—jeans and work boots." Corey appreciated Billy's attempt to keep things light.

"Yeah, but none of us are wearing baseball hats."

"Look over there," Nick pointed. "The three women at the bar aren't wearing baseball caps either."

"Very funny, but they're definitely more butch than we are, Nick."

Nick shook his head. "Amazing. You make up these dramas in your mind."

"I just don't want to become Barron County's first hate crime victims, do you?"

"You're neurotic sometimes, you know that?"

Corey's silverware clanged abruptly against his china as he locked eyes with Nick. "I'm going to the bathroom." He asked Billy to move aside, then slid out of the booth. Billy let Corey pass, then sat back down and stared across the table at Nick. Corey heard part of their conversation as he walked away from the table.

"I don't want to hear it," Nick said. "This is none of your business."

"Corey is my business. He's my best friend. And I don't like how you speak to him."

"Hey, my words may not always be the most sensitive. But they're always true. I won't apologize for that."

Corey returned to the table just as Nick was swallowing his last mouthful. The waitress dropped off the check. Billy put a ten-dollar bill on the table and Nick took care of the rest. After leaving the café, Nick began walking across the parking lot toward the convenience store.

"What do you need in there?" Corey asked.

"If we're going hunting, we need licenses. That all right with you?"

"Fine. I need some gum anyway."

Billy and Corey followed Nick into the store. The café and Mini-Mart complex sat at the crossroads of two state highways, far from any nearby town. Several cars were parked at the gas pumps or adjacent to the store. Inside, the Mini-Mart offered everything someone visiting cabin country might need—food, tobacco, alcohol, sporting goods, and licenses to hunt or fish. They waited their turn in line, then Nick told the clerk what they wanted.

"Okay, darlin'. You'll each need to fill out a form. When you're done, I also need to see ID and proof that you've completed a hunting safety course. Oh, and a fifty dollar fee per person."

"I have a picture of my Minnesota hunting safety certificate in my phone," Nick said. "Will that do?"

"Let me see it."

Nick handed his phone to the clerk who replied that it was fine. Then she looked at Corey.

"I took a hunting class when I was sixteen, but I don't have proof. I'm sure the certificate got thrown away long ago."

"Then I guess you won't be getting a license today."

"Now hold on," Nick interrupted. "He took a class. His best friend from high school's back there getting a soda. I'm sure he can vouch for it."

"Not good enough, sorry."

Corey looked relieved.

Nick leaned across the counter and spoke in a softer, friendlier tone to the clerk. "Listen. I'm an experienced hunter, and I guarantee you he'll follow the rules. We'll be hunting on private land. And we're only here because his dad died last week at the family cabin up the road. They found him in the yard."

"You mean Frank Fischer? I heard about that. What a shame. He came in here a lot to buy stuff. Great guy." Turning to look at Corey, the clerk said she was sorry for the loss. Then she rubbed her chin and said, "Okay. I'll take your word for it. But don't tell anyone I gave you a license without showing proof of a completed hunting course. I could get in a lot of trouble. I'm only doing this out of respect for Frank."

"Thank you," Nick replied. He grabbed the two license applications, then directed Corey over to the far end of the counter.

"Just my luck," Corey said. "Frank's number one fan is the one doling out licenses."

"Come on." Nick handed him a pen.

Respect for Frank? Is that what the clerk really said? Obviously, the woman didn't know him all that well, didn't know what Corey had endured the first time he applied for a hunting license all those years ago. The clerk's mention of the hunting course requirement brought it all back in Corey's mind as he filled out the form. Prior to his first real hunt, Corey had to complete a boring week-long hunting safety class at the Sportsman's Club outside of Pepin. The class was supposed to teach inexperienced hunters how to handle a gun, deftly ascend and alight from a tree stand, and make sure that new hunters shot at animals, not people.

After the course ended, Frank drove Corey straight to the hardware store back in Pepin to get their licenses. Corey remembered that blessed event being far worse than he'd expected, the humiliating conversation that still rang in his ears across the years.

The clerk in Pepin filled out Corey's license application, asking pointed questions as he went along, such as whether it was his first time. Corey affirmed it was. "A hunting virgin, I see. Boys, we've got ourselves a first-timer." Loitering near the counter with cups of coffee in hand, an assembled group of grizzled-looking men laughed at the joke they'd likely heard a hundred times. Frank laughed too. Corey remembered providing nothing more than a polite reply to the clerk's annoying questions and lame jokes, simply hoping to get it over with.

"But fellas," he recalled the man saying to his audience, "he's not inexperienced at all. Isn't that right?" Corey remembered turning toward his father, hoping for a sign of what to say next. Frank looked back at him with a wide grin, while the other men egged on the licensing man as if he were an evangelist preaching the Word. "Yeah, you were engaged all week in huntercourse. I just hope you had a young lady in the class. It'd be pretty awkward if it was just a bunch of fellas doing huntercourse."

Corey got the joke at the first mention of the made-up word. He didn't need to hear the innuendo twice. The men in the store laughed unabated for a full minute. Then the clerk continued. "Let me ask you—can you tell a doe from a buck?"

Corey recalled answering the clerk plainly. "Yes sir, the buck has a rack, hopefully a big one."

"That's right, son. That's right. The exact opposite from humans. Isn't that the case, Frank?" His father simply said "Yep."

Corey remembered standing there, confused. "Sir?" he asked.

"Geez, Frank. Haven't you taught him about the birds and the bees?" The clerk stared directly at Corey to deliver the punch line. "You see, son, in humans it's the females that have the big rack."

Corey remembered feeling flush. He turned and left the shop, away from the chorus of laughter behind him. He didn't wait for the man to finish issuing his license. He walked slowly, but on a bee-line toward his family's green car in the lot. He pulled a portable radio from his pocket and placed headphones on his ears. He didn't hear Frank approaching from behind. Frank pinched Corey's arm and held a tight grip. He'd never forget Frank's cruel words. "Don't you ever embarrass me like that again. Do you understand?"

Corey simply stared into his father's eyes.

"Jesus Christ, Corey. Where are your manners? Those guys are my clients and they're just having a little fun. Your sissy stunt might've cost me some business. Is that what you want?"

Corey shook his head no. He wanted to lash out, to tell his father how thoroughly embarrassed Frank had made him feel. But all he could do was apologize, softly. After a few seconds, Frank let go. Corey placed the headphones back over his ears and rode home with his father in silence.

West of New Auburn and north of Sand Creek, Nick pulled off Highway 25 onto a gravel township road marked V. He slowed to a crawl, looking at each driveway for number 457.

"That's it. There's my parents' car in the yard." The silver Chevy Malibu provided the only vibrant color within eyesight against the sallow browns of the cabin and surrounding woods. As they entered the gravel drive, Corey took in every detail and searched for familiar things. There stood the cabin and matching shed, as well as an outhouse near the woods. All three structures were made from cut timber, two-by-ten-inch plank siding that was sorely in need of painting. If he were still alive, Frank would insist on another coat of dark brown—the color it had always been.

Nick parked next to the Malibu and turned off the ignition. As Corey stepped onto the lawn, he detected scents of damp and dying vegetation. The clerk at the convenience store said that Barron County had received plenty of rain over the past month. The first wave in September mercilessly ripped the leaves from every tree but the oaks. Corey could feel how all of that moisture had turned the softening ground into a slick, soggy plane with a thin coating of ice.

"It doesn't look like much, no offense," Nick said.

"Well, it wasn't meant to be a castle. My grandfather built it in the 1950s as nothing more than a hunting cabin."

"Looks solid though," Billy said. "The foundation's level. If it's in decent shape on the inside, you'll get some offers, if only for the land value alone."

"Yeah, I'm sure fifty acres in Barron County is worth something to someone. Just not to me."

Billy declined the offer to take a look inside. "I really do need to get back and help with the meal."

"Are you sure? I'll bet we could find some tasty mushrooms out behind that shed."

Billy laughed. Corey handed him the keys to the car. Ginny told him they'd been found in Frank's pocket when he was discovered dead in the yard. Who knows where the man was headed when he died in the middle of a solo hunting weekend.

Corey and Billy came together in a hug. Nick waved goodbye from several feet away. Billy fired up the car, adjusted the seat and mirrors, and drove away. He gave a final thumbs-up out the window as he turned onto the county road and disappeared.

2

Wednesday Mid-Day

Corey walked toward the cabin, pulling a tarnished gold key from his pocket. After a strong push with his left shoulder, the door opened. What little light remained outside at two o'clock in the afternoon on the overcast November day was blocked by the blue and white, plaid-patterned curtains, one of the few remnant touches from his grandmother.

He turned to Nick who remained standing outside. "Why don't I open things up in here while you unload our stuff and check out the shed?"

"Sure."

Corey entered the three-room cabin and stood still in the entry. Spread across the entire front of the cabin was a great room including a kitchenette and Formica-topped dining table with four metal chairs. A scattering of random furniture filled the rest of the space—a mid-century sofa and two recliners from the 1970s. A pale green end table sat between the chairs, topped with a lava lamp that Corey remembered his father buying at a flea market somewhere nearby.

Hideous, he thought.

He then stepped deeper inside. He observed every detail with four of his five senses. The air smelled musty. Dust covered the countertops. Floorboards creaked with every step. Prints depicting random scenes from the forest hung on the walls. He winced at the amateur mattings and frames. Corey then did a double-take, walking closer to view the painting hanging above the TV. He hadn't seen this particular work of art in over twenty years. He didn't even know that it was hung here at the cabin, or why. The framed painting depicted a sandy-haired boy near the top of a hardwood in the middle of an island in the Mississippi River near Pepin. Corey smiled at seeing his own faint, cursive signature in the lower right-hand corner of the canvas. It was the same painting that had won him third prize at the Stockholm Art Fair in ninth grade. He had forgotten all about it. Corey shook his head, wondering about it hanging here at the cabin.

He entered the lone bedroom in the back. Knotty pine covered the ceiling, and a pair of twin beds and a dresser filled the room. The same old matching bedspreads lay untouched upon them. Corey's father didn't have a chance to sleep here before he died. Frank had apparently begun to unpack his bag, though. A pair of recent sport magazines sat on the nightstand. A weekend's worth of shirts and underpants stuck out from an unclosed drawer. His wedding ring lay flat atop the dresser. Ginny had mentioned to Corey her suspicion about the ring's absence from Frank's hand when she first viewed him in the casket. Corey had called the Barron County EMTs to verify that it wasn't misplaced or stolen. They assured him that they delivered Frank back to Pepin exactly as they had found him in the yard, positioned as though he were heading for his car.

Corey perused the four corners of the tight room, noticing the rustic construction and masculine décor. Though the cabin was built soundly enough at the time, attention to detail was lacking—nails pounded into the wood at odd intervals, no trim along the base where wall met floor, and uneven wooden framed windows with some that no longer opened as the cabin had settled over time.

Yet Corey appreciated the allure of this place to his father and to his grandfather before him. It reflected their personalities, their desires—simple and masculine, nothing flowery or colored in pastel. The walls were solid wood, the bedspreads and curtains held tartan patterns and dark hues. The only interior décor consisted of framed photographs from past hunts, or of family and friends.

This cabin was a place for the Fischer men to escape and act like men. Hunting, occasional fishing in a nearby trout stream, felling trees or chopping wood from their own forest, and maintaining the structures they had built with their own hands. Nothing changed here at the cabin, or in all of Barron County for that matter. It was probably why this place captivated Corey's father and grandfather but held no attraction for him.

He entered the bathroom. A white metal water heater showed signs of rust flowing from its fixtures down toward the floor. A wrinkled towel hung from a hook next to the shower, and a pile of discarded men's clothes lay on the floor near the sink. Frank must have showered after arriving here last Friday, not all that unusual for a man who prized cleanliness and looking his best.

Nick's noisy entrance interrupted Corey's thoughts. He carried their bags along with a box of food from Ginny, then dropped the bags with a thud, set the box atop the kitchen counter, and looked around.

"The 1950s called. They want their furniture back."

Corey laughed. "Yeah, well some of this shit is making a comeback if you've seen the latest design magazines. Retro interiors are all the rage."

Corey's eyes were drawn to the patterned linoleum covering the floor of the entire cabin. Diamond shapes colored baby blue, vanilla, and brown flowed from one end of the building to the other in a never-ending loop for the eye to follow in and out of every room and onward to the entryway leading to the lone outside door.

"Man, I'm guessing this place hasn't changed much since your grandfather built it. Get a load of that couch. It might even be an antique," Nick said with a smirk.

Corey considered the plaid sofa with the long gray patch of duct tape encircling the entire right cushion. It felt good to laugh. There had been far too little laughter between them the past year.

"My grandfather bought that sofa with life insurance money when grandma passed. Or so I'm told."

"That's the one you never knew?"

"Yeah, Lillian. She died when my dad just was a kid. Grandpa raised my father all on his own."

"Well it certainly showed—not having a woman's touch."

"You mean this cabin or my father?"

"Both. This place screams of alpha male hunter."

"You're right, Nick. I guess we'll fit right in."

Nick pointed at three framed photographs hanging on the great room wall. "Is that your dad?"

"No, my grandpa. But they sure did look alike."

"Spitting image. Count your blessings. You broke the mold."

"I'm not so sure. At the visitation, people remarked how much I resembled him. I wasn't offended. Despite everything, Frank was a handsome man."

"I guess so. But being a world class asshole certainly made his half-way decent looks irrelevant. Too bad your mother couldn't see that sooner, or..."

"Or what? She could've found someone better? Maybe, but then I wouldn't be here, right?"

Nick nodded his head. They turned to unpack their bags.

"So... where are the guns?"

Corey hesitated, then looked toward the entryway. "They're in the hall closet. Or, at least I saw gun cases there, and I assume they're inside."

Nick walked toward the front door and looked inside the closet. "Well, it's only two thirty. We still have time for a quick outing before dark."

"You mean, to hunt? Today?"

"That's the idea, Corey. What do you say?"

"I say I need a shower first."

"You took one at the motel before we left."

"Yeah, but I feel dirty from the long ride. The whole deer incident, then stopping at the café and getting our hunting licenses wore me out. I can't go outside again until I recuperate first."

"Fine. You shower and get all dolled up for the hunt. Then meet me in the yard. We'll do some target practice before heading into the woods. Okay?"

"I guess."

Nick picked up the gun cases and left the cabin. Corey returned to the bedroom and lay back on one of the beds. Even though he had been sitting for most of the day, Corey felt tired. And, his knee and wrist began to throb once more. He was reluctant to remove the bandages for fear of seeing that his wounds were infected. But he would need to change them if he intended on showering again. Earlier that morning, he had taken a brief shower, adeptly avoiding getting water on the bandages. They got a bit wet in the process, however, and were now damp and itchy while he lay there atop the bed.

Why was everything such a struggle? Why couldn't Nick give him a break and wait until the next morning to hunt? What happened to the patient, accommodating Nick he met back in college? Long before they arrived in Barron County, Corey knew that he and Nick had changed, in ways both good and bad. The intensity of their sex had waned, conversations had grown more taciturn, suspicions replaced excitement. Nick worked late... Corey drank. Nick traveled for work over the weekend, and Corey resumed a childhood passion. His commitment to running gave him a lean, lanky physique. An aversion to being inside a gym, especially after finding Nick in the steam room with a stranger doing God knows what, left Corey without much muscular definition in the arms or chest. But his legs were handsomely developed and delivered him wherever he wanted to go.

Today, he wished those toned thighs would carry him down miles of dusty country roads. Restless since first turning into the cabin's driveway, he felt an irresistible need to escape. The tensions rising in him urged Corey to flee. But his wounds bound him to the cabin, and to Nick.

Corey anticipated that some difficult issues might come to a head this weekend—here, far away from the distractions of daily life. With all that had happened the past few days and particularly after his conversations with Ginny and Billy back in Pepin, Corey knew it was time to confront the couple's unspoken tensions. He had given significant thought of late to the prospect of living alone. He pictured having his own place and spending his own money, albeit with far less income than he enjoyed commingling his financial life with Nick's. Corey made enough to survive on his own, but not enough to fund the life to which he'd become accustomed—dinners at Chez Toulouse.

What he couldn't quite see, though, was a path from here to there. Nick might leave Corey for someone else, of course. That would be the easiest solution. But why hadn't it happened already? Why had Nick stuck by him after all of the drama from the year before? Corey suspected that Nick still slept around, probably with guys at the bank. Most likely, with Evan. How rich, Corey thought to himself. The guy in Human Resources fooling around with fellow employees. What would the execs think of that? But Nick was smart and knew how to circumvent rules. That, and he was a fantastic liar. If he was mostly able to elude getting caught by Corey over the years, he could certainly evade detection at work. And when challenged, Nick always had a viable excuse. "Evan's married," he reminded Corey whenever suspicions arose. But Corey knew it wouldn't be the first so-called straight guy to be bi-curious, or the only closeted gay man to marry a woman in order to hide and deflect from someone he didn't want to be.

So, what was holding Nick back from racing for the exits? It was a question Corey had asked during therapy. In front of the counselor, Nick spoke about stability, a feeling of safety and security in their long-term bond. He said that Corey filled a void that had been present throughout Nick's life—someone to be there for him through thick and thin and never leave his side despite Nick's unworthiness. Corey remembered being floored by that candid declaration, but he also wondered if it were true. Nick had repeated his claim of deep insecurity more than once during therapy. He said that he liked having someone to come home to, someone who would be there at the end of a long day or in troubled times, a person who would love him and stay by his side no matter what. These answers felt genuine at the time, so Corey accepted them. But a constant, nagging doubt remained. Nick may well need the positive things that a long-term relationship provided, but his answers rarely spoke to anything unique about Corey as the provider.

Therapy, then, gave Corey no lasting comfort that their relationship would endure. He expected one day he'd be dumped as soon as a more attractive, stable person came along. It was only a matter of time. What Corey couldn't foresee was a picture of him gathering the strength to leave on his own. Not that he feared surviving. Rather, his hesitation had more to do with logistics, figuring out how and when to leave.

He walked over to the living room window and pulled back the curtain to see what Nick was doing outside. The shed door was ajar, and Nick had pulled a small folding table onto the lawn. Atop the table lay the two hunting rifles. Nick had removed them from their cases and appeared to be checking them out one by one. He saw Nick load bullets into the long rifles before disappearing into the shed for what seemed like a minute, then emerging with yet another case, this one a bit smaller and very flat, limber like a soft-sided briefcase. Corey knew what hid inside the burlap case but continued to watch as Nick placed it upon the table. He unfolded the pouch in two swift moves. He saw Nick lift out the hunting knives, inspecting them individually and admiring the silver blades, rubbing them against his thumb to test their serration, their strength.

Corey let the curtain fall back across the window and walked to the bathroom. After a fifteen-minute shower, he cleaned his wounds with antiseptic and bandaged them anew with fresh gauze and tape. After dressing in as many layers as he had packed,

Corey looked at his own autumn jacket and wondered if it would provide enough warmth for hours deep in the woods. He looked in the front closet and saw an Upland Hunter's Field coat. Most certainly it belonged to Frank, but Corey was surprised his father had spent money on such a fine jacket. He reluctantly tried it on, and of course it fit—he and his father had essentially the same build. The tan coat had a water-resistant nylon exterior with a fleece-lined flannel inner layer. Several pockets lined the front of the coat—upper hand warmer slots, two large button-front cargo compartments, and dual zippered pockets underneath for extra storage.

He felt a bulge in the deep right front pocket and lifted the flap to feel inside. He knew what it was even before he saw it— his father's Colt Woodsman, the hunting handgun that Frank had inherited from Corey's grandfather and that his father had promised to give to Corey someday as well. But Larry hadn't mentioned anything about this gun in the will. Corey decided on the spot that it now belonged to him. He remembered play-acting with this gun as a kid, up here at the cabin, though his father always insisted that it first be emptied of its shells before Corey ran outside to pretend that he was pursuing an enemy or to take aim at an unsuspecting squirrel. Corey had completely forgotten about his pre-teen gun-fixation phase. In those dramas played out at the cabin and in the nearby woods, Corey had cast himself as the hero each and every time, bringing swift, hard justice to the villains in his mind as he vanquished each foe with deadly aim.

He placed the Woodsman back into the front coat pocket, then walked into the kitchen. He shoved a granola bar from Ginny's food box into his pocket, then stepped outside the cabin. He saw Nick across the yard, assembling a target made from corn stalks, and walked toward him.

"Let's get this over with."

"I see you're still excited about learning to fire a gun."

"I know how to shoot, Nick. I just haven't held one in a long time."

"It's like riding a bike, as they say."

"And that's exactly what I'd rather be doing."

"We need to see if these things even work before you put them up for sale, right? Or maybe, if they fire nicely, I'll keep 'em for myself."

Corey kept the "Hell No" reply inside his head. After today, these guns would either be sold or thrown away. He wasn't going to let Nick keep a single one. No way.

"I made a target, atop that old stump." Nick grabbed the first rifle, the Marlin. More muscular than the H&R Handi, Frank always said that the Marlin was the gun most appropriate for an experienced hunter, for a real man. "Here. You start with the H&R. It's easier to handle than the rifle and was designed for more inexperienced hunters."

Corey's stomach fell. Nick's comment instantly brought back a voice from the past. "Even your mom could kill something with this one," Frank had explained while holding the H&R. "Blindfolded." Now, all these years later, Corey held the same weapon in his sweaty right hand. Frank used to brag about the H&R with its deadly accuracy and easy handling. Holding it again, here at the cabin, Frank's voice replayed in Corey's head. "You got the safety on? Good. Check your clip." As a kid, he had tried to comply with his father's demands with limited success. "For God's sake hold it tighter. You're letting it slip. Don't be such a quiche-eater." Corey adjusted his grip, then and now. "Yeah, like that. Now take off the safety, lock onto your target, and shoot."

Today, the voice barking instructions had changed, but the message endured. "Corey, you've got to hold it steady. Center your target just above the tip of the metal scope."

He took aim at the bunched corn stalk thirty yards away. He missed.

"Here, let me show you." Nick raised the Marlin to his shoulder, resting it comfortably in the crease of his armpit. His left hand extended to steady the rifle, and Nick quietly used his index finger to press the safety off. He then placed his right eye up to the edge of the steel scope. With his left eye closed, Nick gazed at the make-shift target for no more than two seconds before firing a perfect blast.

"That's how it's done. Man, this is a classic. You see that le-ver-action? Forged steel and side-ejection cartridges. What a beauty. Here, try this one." Corey took the heavy rifle from Nick. "Pretend the target is your father," Nick said, "and you'll never miss."

Corey stood tall once again on Nick's mark. After loading a bullet into the chamber, he steadied the rifle with both hands. Hopefully he had worked out his rusty jitters on that first, failed shot.

"That's it. Focus. Take your time."

All he wanted at this point was for Nick to shut his mouth. The attempted encouragement was distracting. Corey gazed through the scope and felt drawn to the power of the gun itself, even more than the target. So cold, so powerful, so revolting. Not even his father's bullying could lift Corey's hand to that instru-ment of death more than a few times as a kid. And yet, here he was again—learning how to kill anew, fondling the brutal metal gun as if it were a tempting vice.

"You gonna shoot or stare at the target all day?"

Simultaneously focused in both the present task and past memories, Corey blocked out whatever Nick said next. He felt the gun and saw the target. He heard Frank's whispers and smelled the dampness in the nearby woods. He tasted a drop of salty sweat that ran down his cheek. And then he pulled the trigger.

Another miss. After a few seconds, he dropped the rifle to his side, shook his head, and laughed.

"How poetic. I've walked right into his fucking trap."

"What do you mean?"

"My father left me these guns in his will to see if I had the balls to come out here and shoot. And I followed the script per-fectly. This was his taunting attempt to prove I'd never be the manly son he wanted. For once, I didn't let him down."

Nick walked away, into the shed, then returned with a pair of blaze orange vests to pull over their jackets. Hunting licenses were attached on the back.

"We're all set. What do you think?"

"No self-respecting gay man would be caught dead in that hue."

"Well, you can't hunt without it, Corey. It's state law."

"But the DNR won't even know."

"That's not the point. You need to have your license displayed on the back of something orange. Besides, it's for your own safety."

"We're on private land. We won't be in danger of getting shot. What's the point?"

"The point is that people trespass or can misjudge where they walk."

"Then we'll have 'em arrested and charged."

"Not if they put a bullet through your chest first, you won't."

Corey put on the vest, picked up the Handi, and led the way across the lawn. The Fischer property consisted of thirty acres covered by woods and twenty of clear-cut tillable land rented to a local farmer who planted and harvested field corn. Corey had heard it was an arrangement first made on a handshake between his grandfather and the current farmer's dad. Frank always said it was the deal of the century. A hard-working farm family paid them for the right to grow corn while creating a setting that enticed deer into the open where the Fischers could shoot the biggest one each year.

The sun sank low in the southwestern sky as they approached the edge of the grass. Though it was only three o'clock, darkness came early to northern Wisconsin in November and would arrive within the next two hours. Corey saw a large stone adjacent to a weathered wooden cross at the edge of the woods below a towering oak.

"Hey, what's that?"

"What?" Corey asked.

"That rock and cross. Over there."

Corey stopped, gazing at the familiar sight.

"That would be a gravesite."

"A grave? For who?"

"That's where they buried Frank's boyhood dog, Beau. Or should I say, where my grandfather buried him."

"I thought your dad hated pets."

"He did. At least he never let me get one as a kid. 'Too much work,' he always said. I was willing to do it all—feeding, walking, grooming—if he'd have let me get a dog of my own. But Frank wouldn't hear of it. Maybe it had something to do with Beau."

"Did the dog die at the cabin or something? Is that why he's buried here?"

Corey took an awkwardly long time to answer. The story of his father's dog seeped back into his mind. He had only heard it once from Frank, but never forgot.

"Yeah."

"What's the story?"

"The way my father told it, Beau was almost thirteen—a ripe old age for a retriever. Two years younger than my father was at the time, in fact. Anyway, I guess Beau had slowed down a bit that final summer, wasn't as eager to jump into the river to chase sticks. By the time school started in the fall, Beau didn't do much other than eat, sleep, and shit in the yard, Frank said, but that dog slept by his side every night all the same. My grandma had been dead a few years, and grandpa Donald wanted little or nothing to do with Beau."

"So, what happened?"

"According to Frank, they came to the cabin for deer opener. I guess that would've been almost fifty years ago now. Wow." Corey shook his head. "Anyway, my dad said Beau couldn't get down from the truck on his own. Frank lifted him out and helped him onto his feet. Something was wrong with him—bad hips or joints or some other old dog malady. Frank asked my grandpa if they could take Beau to the vet, but Donald wouldn't let him. Grandpa said that Beau was an old dog, and his time was near. Why waste money paying a vet who would just say the same thing?

"According to Frank, when they arrived at the cabin Beau seemed to be in more distress than usual. My father slept on the living room sofa that night with Beau while Grandpa took the bedroom. When Frank awoke the next morning, he was alone in the cabin. Beau was gone. Dad said that he jumped up from the couch at the sound of a gunshot outside. He figured that my grandpa was practicing with his new rifle, the same one you're carrying right now. Frank apparently checked for Beau at the front door but couldn't see him in the yard. He put on his coat, then headed outside. That's when he saw my grandfather at the edge of the woods—right here by that stone. Donald just stood there, I guess, looking toward the ground and leaning on what Frank thought was a rifle. After walking closer, he saw that Grandpa was actually resting on a medium-sized shovel and gazing at a pile of dirt mounded below that oak tree.

"When Frank told me this story, I swore he was emotional. We were standing in this exact spot. I noticed the stone just like you did, and I asked him what it was. It was the only time I'd ever seen him cry. It made me uncomfortable. I think I cried when he told me the rest of the story, even though I never even knew the damn dog. I can still see my father standing right where you are now. His shaky voice is as clear to me as it was back then. He mimicked my grandpa's words and tone when Donald told him that 'Beau died early this morning, son. It was his time. Now go back to the shed and grab two pieces of wood so you can make a cross. Then roll that big gray rock over here and let it rest on this mound of dirt. We don't need any critters digging him up and having his carcass for lunch.' With that, my grandpa turned and walked toward the cabin, made breakfast, and later shot a decent-sized doe. He and Frank never spoke of Beau again.

"I remember asking my dad 'why not?' Why didn't he ask Grandpa if Beau had died naturally or if he was shot? 'We both knew what happened, and there was no point in bringing it up,' I remember him saying. 'You don't ask Donald Fischer a question like that. No sir. No good would have come of it.' I just stood there in the cold autumn wind, looking down at the grave marker, while Frank turned away from the makeshift grave and walked back to the cabin, alone."

"Well that's depressing. But it certainly says a lot about your grandfather, and your dad too, for that matter."

"How so?" Corey asked.

"It explains why your dad was such an asshole. Look who his role model was."

Corey agreed, then turned to enter the woods. After a hundred yards, Nick identified a fallen tree they could use as a perch for their afternoon hunt. The log sat at the crest of a small knoll, with a well-worn deer path crossing a few feet behind. Corey cleared a layer of wet leaves, then mimicked Nick's movement as he kneeled onto the ground and rested his elbows atop the dead tree, aiming his rifle toward the path ahead.

Thirty minutes into their silent, seated observation, Nick pointed at movement in the distant hardwoods, then looked into his hand-held scope.

"Corey," he whispered, without moving his head. "There's a deer coming down the trail from the right. Pick up your rifle, slowly. Don't make a sound."

"But the deer's too far away."

"Just pick up the rifle."

Corey did as instructed, secretly hoping that the animal would turn and walk the other way.

"Okay, it's coming closer." Nick continued to whisper. "Another thirty or forty feet and you'll have a decent shot. Ready?"

Corey's quiet, affirmative answer defied the response inside his head. He lifted the rifle to his shoulder. As he rested the barrel in the palm of his left hand, he firmly gripped the gun with his right. He first looked in the direction Nick was pointing, then closed one eye and squinted into the rifle's scope with the other.

He couldn't see the deer. Trees aplenty, but no deer.

"He's in range. You got him?"

"No," was Corey's soft reply. He looked up and saw the deer at a distance of one hundred yards, plenty close to shoot. But when returning his right eye to the scope, nothing. The gun now felt sweaty in his hands as he frantically went back and forth between natural and magnified vision. One view saw the deer, the other inexplicably blocked.

"He's right there," Nick said through clenched teeth.

Corey had to act. He couldn't just sit there and fail to pull the trigger. Nick would accuse him of weakness—or worse, insurrection. He scanned the wooded horizon one last time and pointed the rifle in the most accurate direction he could. He returned one last time to the scope. Despite having nothing visibly in the crosshairs, he pulled the trigger with his right index finger and produced an ear-shattering blast. It nearly knocked him backward off the log.

The deer tore off in the opposite direction. Corey had missed.

"Damn! That was at least a ten pointer. Didn't you have him in your sight?"

"I did," Corey lied. There would be no way to explain wasting a bullet on a pure guess. He was surprised when Nick left it at that, saying nothing more about the horrible shot.

3

Nick shot a deer an hour later.

"That's how you do it!"

The twelve-point buck hit the ground hard. Nick bounded over the log and ran to the site of his kill. Corey lagged several yards behind. They arrived in time to hear the hollow, raspy groan of the buck's last breath. It was the sickest sound Corey had ever heard.

"Is he dead?"

"Yeah he's dead. What a beauty. Twelve points… count 'em!"

Corey did. Focusing on the deer's antlers was a welcome distraction from watching the pool of blood forming on the ground.

"Now what?"

"We need to field dress him."

Corey had forgotten how awful this was to watch. Memories of his father's field dress routine were buried deep. He watched with increasing horror as Nick methodically placed his rifle against a tree and removed a series of knives and other tools from his pack, laying them out on the ground like a surgeon next to the still-warm deer.

"Are you sure he's really dead?"

"Well, he certainly isn't gonna make a miraculous comeback."

"I mean, do you think we should wait a minute, to make sure he can't feel any pain before you cut him?"

"My bullet caused him more pain than he's ever gonna feel again. Cutting him can't be any worse. He's not breathing, see?"

Corey placed his hand gingerly in front of the buck's large snout. He felt a slight wisp of air but couldn't be sure if it came from the animal's cold, damp nostrils or from the day's slight breeze. The buck's eyes were open, glassy, and staring straight ahead. Corey stepped away from the carcass, facing the other direction as Nick kneeled in the dirt and began to work.

"Here. Hold his back legs up away from the body, so I can get a better angle on his chest."

Corey did as he was told, reluctantly. He tried looking away but couldn't help seeing Nick stab the jagged edge of a large knife into the deer's protruding rib cage. An audible burst of air gushed from the slit, the final remnant of life held deep within the buck's chest. Corey gasped a moment later, sucking into his lungs the same air he imagined that the deer had just expelled. And then he held it inside, willing himself not to exhale for as long as he could muster. He finally released one steady stream of exasperation—the air, the tension, the regret. He hadn't been the one to pull the trigger but felt just as bad as if he had.

Corey continued holding onto the deer's stiffening legs as Nick forcefully cut through the animal's thick hide from the bottom of its breastbone through the soft underbelly. The sound was impossible to avoid. Like a thick notebook of paper being torn in half, the deer's hide was ripped wide open, inch by horrible inch. After placing rubber gloves over his hands, Nick methodically opened the deer's body cavity, inserting two fingers along each side of the blade in the shape of a V, cutting all the way down to its pelvis.

Nick declared the animal "about to lose his manhood," then cut away its genitals with one swift slice. Corey felt a phantom pain in his own crotch and once again tried without success to look away. He was thankful for a few temporary breaks from Nick's knife work on the deer, each time Nick stopped to clean the blade with alcohol wipes. Then he switched tools altogether, grabbing a small saw to split the deer's pelvis in two. He returned to the sharp hunting knife for the rest of his work, more fully cutting open the rib cage, pulling it apart and slashing free the dead buck's diaphragm.

"Okay, now pull his top leg toward me and tip him sideways. We need to roll him fully over to spill out his guts."

Corey obliged, shocked into silence at the gruesomeness. Nick made a few additional cuts, loosening connective tissue within the deer's body, then reaching inside and removing its internal organs. Anything soft and pliable was removed, then thrown into a growing pile three feet away. Corey looked once more toward the woods for distraction. But his senses took over, pulling him back to the disembowelment occurring before him. The worst was the smell. At first, Corey feared that he might have shit his own pants. Feeling behind himself, those remained thankfully clean. Still, the odor of feces and raw flesh filled the air. He heard an unfamiliar noise and looked down to see Nick remove two plastic bags from his duffel, then place the deer's heart and liver inside.

"Why are you bagging those up?"

"My brother loves the taste. I'll boil them tonight and take 'em to my sister's tomorrow. I don't care much for the kidneys, so I put them in the discard pile, but I'll save 'em for you if you'd like." Nick wiped his brow with his coat sleeve, then looked up at Corey with a knowing smile.

Corey shook his head.

Nick laughed. "I didn't think so."

Nick opened up the pack and put the harvested organs inside. He placed the safety on his rifle and strapped it to his pack.

"Okay, if we each grab a leg, we can drag him back to the cabin."

Corey complied. Neither of them spoke as they tugged the carcass through the woods and across the lawn. Thankfully they were hunting only three hundred yards from the cabin, and the deer slid smoothly across the damp ground. Corey tried to imagine that he was already back inside the cabin, drinking a mug of hot tea and working a crossword puzzle. Upon reaching the shed, Nick asked Corey to take the weapons and backpack inside while Nick began fastening the dead buck to a pulley and rope system attached to the shed in order to hoist it for hanging overnight.

"I also cut off a tenderloin," Nick said, pointing toward the pack. "You'll find it when you unload inside. I saw a grill in the shed. If you season the meat, I can cook it once I get everything here cleaned up."

Corey grabbed the rifle and strap from Nick's shoulder, then lifted the pack from the ground. He walked back toward the cabin. Once inside, he went straight to the bathroom and washed the dirt off his face. He returned to the kitchen and looked in the fridge at the food Ginny had sent with him earlier that morning. She had packed coleslaw, baked beans, and hamburger patties. He removed the first two items, transferring them to ceramic bowls. He also placed a pair of plates, some silverware, and glasses for water on the table, then opened the bottle of sparkling cider Ginny had packed as well. He retrieved the bottle of Belvedere from Nick's bag—Nick brought it with him on every overnight trip, it seemed. Corey mixed a vodka tonic with lime for Nick and was tempted to take a swallow. He brought the edge of the glass to his mouth and was reminded of the fond scent of grain alcohol. He let the bubbles of the tonic water barely touch his lips but set it down when he heard Nick's approaching footsteps on the front porch. He found a few basic seasonings—pepper, onion powder, and salt—and pulled the two tenderloins out of Nick's pack. Corey avoided directly touching the other organs inside the plastic bags, simply placing them in the back of the refrigerator.

Nick looked approvingly at the seasoned meat, then took it outside to be grilled over a charcoal flame while sipping his drink. Ten minutes later he returned with the well-done steaks, and they sat down for dinner.

"You're going to cut right through the plate, with all the force you're putting on that knife. Careful, or you'll strain your tender wrist." Nick stared at Corey who kept cutting his almost burnt venison steak.

"Well, I'm used to it being a little less done."

"Hey, I cooked the damn thing with that poor excuse for a grill from the shed. You want more tender food for your delicate palate? Then next time help me out or grill it yourself."

Corey stopped cutting, dropped his utensils atop the dinner plate, and met Nick's stare, eye to eye.

"Why do you have to be like that?"

"Like what? You're the one who criticized my cooking."

"No, Nick, I didn't. All I said was that this is a little overdone. I didn't say it was your fault."

"You implied it."

"What are you talking about? I implied no such thing."

"It's your tone, Corey. Sometimes it's like that knife you're holding in your hand—a bit sharp and edgy, pardon the pun."

Nick grinned widely. Always the funny guy and always in the right.

"You can assume whatever you like, but I'm telling you that was not my intent. You're the one who chose to turn this into an argument, talking about my delicate wrists, whatever in the hell that means."

"I'm calling it like I see it. You've been testy ever since we got here. So when you complain about the dinner in front of you, that I provided, excuse me if I assume your snarky comment is directed at me."

Corey took a deep breath. For the second time today, he summoned his calming mantras.

> Universe, I belong to you.
> Deep in my soul, I am love divine.
> Words in my ear, nothing will conquer my heart.

It didn't seem to work. He had to say something.

"I just sat here and told you my intent. Despite all of your brilliance, Nick, there's no way you can read my mind. Instead of assuming the worst in me, as you always do, perhaps for once you could give me the benefit of the doubt."

"Give you the benefit of the doubt? Isn't that exactly what I've been doing for the past year and a half? When you lost your job, I continued to support you, even though it took months to find a new one given your lack of focused effort. And who stood by you as everything fell apart? Me. I gave you the benefit of the doubt that recovery was a possibility. And what thanks do I get? Criticism over how I cook your fucking food. I've been giving you the benefit of the doubt longer than anyone else would. So don't sit there and talk to me about giving you a break. I'm the one who deserves a break."

No mantra or meditation could stem the anger that burst. Corey violently bumped the table with his thighs as he pushed himself back in his chair before storming off to the bedroom and slamming the door. He heard Nick get up from the table soon after and pour himself a second vodka tonic before retreating to the great room and turning on the TV.

An hour later, Corey emerged from the bedroom, figuring enough time had passed so they could ignore their earlier argument and move on to something pleasant. He brewed a pot of green tea and settled into the great room recliner with last Sunday's *New York Times* crossword puzzle. Nick lay prostrate on the sofa. The TV was now off, and he appeared to be streaming a college basketball game on his phone.

"Her blank, from Miss Saigon." Corey's question sounded more like a statement.

"Say what?"

"Do you remember a song from Miss Saigon called Her something? Four letters."

"Or me." Nick held his phone up in the air, moving it in a vain attempt for a better signal.

"Her or me? I loved the musical but that doesn't sound right. It does fit, though."

"It's right, trust me."

"We should go to more musicals… that was a nice night."

"Yeah, it was."

"Okay, how about this? Keeper of the flame, six letters. If your 'or me' answer is right, then this one ends in an E and starts with an S."

Nick typed on his device.

"Any luck?"

"No, I can get the U of M basketball site, but when I click on the live game it goes blank."

"I meant with the clue. I thought you were looking it up. Come on, help me here. Keeper of the flame. Six letters—begins with S, ends with E."

"Séance."

"Hmmm. That fits and makes sense. Thanks."

Using Nick as a live dictionary had been a fond routine over the years. It suited them as a welcome beginning to their Sunday mornings—one of the many exclusive things they did, together. Except for weekends when Nick was away on business, Corey and Nick rarely spent their Sundays apart. They would peruse the farmer's market for fresh produce, then jointly prepare a meal for friends, rent cross-country skis and traverse the riverside trails, or leisurely sip a late morning espresso followed by an afternoon matinee. The settings may have varied, but the inseparability remained constant, at least in the early years.

Corey returned to his puzzle yet distracted by Nick who was fiddling with his phone. Nick was still strikingly handsome with his dark hair, though Nick now wore it long. He could almost pull it into a small tail. Wouldn't that be something, Corey mused… Nick in a ponytail. Wouldn't that go over well at the bank?

Nick wasn't as fit as Corey, though. For him, work always came first, ahead of exercise, ahead of his hobbies, and ahead of his relationship with Corey. That order of priority probably helped Nick rise to be the bank's youngest Vice President of Employee Relations. He was supposedly respected up and down the bank's chain of command—for his good judgment and uncanny discretion with the daily barrage of scandalous employee screw-ups from across the country. Such prudence bothered Corey to no end, for Nick wouldn't share details of the juiciest stories, even in strict confidence. He proclaimed himself bound to an unbreakable bond of ethics and trust. What happened at work, stayed at work.

"By the way, it's sconce."

"Sorry, what?"

"Keeper of the flame. It was sconce, not séance," Corey clarified before adding with a trace of condescension, "but I wouldn't have figured it out without your help."

"No problem." Nick set his phone down on the end table with a thud, then raised himself up onto one elbow, facing Corey.

"So what's with the beer sign?"

Corey looked at the wall near the door, toward the familiar neon sign depicting a busty, barely clothed woman holding two overflowing mugs of foamy beer. He rose from his chair, walked over toward the sign, reached down to plug it into the wall, then stepped back to watch it light up in four different neon colors.

"You don't think she's hot?" Corey asked, returning to his chair.

"Uh, no. But she certainly fits the décor of this man-shack deep in the woods."

"That's for sure. And it matches my father's personality whenever he came up here."

"You mean like flirting with that waitress at the café? What was her name again, Judy?"

"Not just her. I'm certain Frank was a cheater, and he certainly didn't try and hide it from me—up here, at least."

"Oh?"

"Yeah. In fact, I know where he got that sign because he took me there on our last trip here together."

"Do I know about this already? Doesn't sound familiar."

"I doubt I ever told you. It's not something I wanted to remember." Corey returned to his puzzle.

"So... are you gonna tell me, or what?"

"If I must." Corey set the newspaper and pen on his lap, freeing up his hands to help retell the story. "Like I said, it was our last trip here, when I was seventeen and a senior in high school. It was the last night of our stay, and he said we were going out. 'For dinner?' I asked. He said yeah, the place had frozen pizzas but that it was somewhere we needed to go for my initiation into manhood." Corey put those last three words in air quotes. "We drove about thirty minutes, then pulled into a gravel parking lot in front of the Foxtails Lounge."

"Oh boy," Nick said. "I see where this is headed."

"I remember the building clear as day. It had faux log siding and a green metal roof with no windows to speak of. There were a handful of neon signs just like this one, advertising varieties of beer. We got out of the car, and I followed him toward the Lounge. The closer we got to the door, the more I sensed what was inside. I could hear the muffled sounds of hooting and hollering echoing through the walls and reverberating off the roof. A fat, gruff-looking man, bearded and sporting a baseball cap with the Packer's logo, greeted my father by name, then asked him if there was any ID for the new guy." Corey pointed toward himself.

"Frank told him I was his son and had just turned twenty-one. He explained that I had stupidly left my wallet back at the cabin and gave the guy a wink. The bouncer looked me up and down suspiciously, then told me I could go inside."

"Sounds like Frank got around up here in cabin country. A lot of people seemed to know his name."

"Yeah, and they all apparently believed his bullshit too. I was four years away from being legal. Anyway, once we got inside, Frank made a beeline for the stage and found us a pair of bar stools. Over the loud music he shouted to me, saying that I was becoming a man soon and that it was time to introduce me to the benefits that come with it. I remember the room reeked of cigarettes with a blue haze of smoke filling the air, obscuring what little light shone from the random neon signs scattered along the wall. Through the cloudy air I saw him smile wide."

"Is this the same guy who reacted violently to your mother's cigarette-smoking in the house?"

Corey nodded and continued his story. "I remember Frank flagging down a waitress wearing nothing more than tight cut-off jeans and a bikini top even though it was mid-November. He ordered a bourbon and branch for himself and a beer for me. A topless blonde on the stage held onto an aluminum pole with the crease of one leg and the grip of one hand as she swung around. She successively stared into the eyes of every patron, with a plastic-looking smile. All of a sudden she stopped, brought her elevated foot back to the ground, then straddled the pole with rhythmic thrusts of her groin in sync with the encouraging hoots and cheers of every guy in the joint.

"A second woman with jet black hair appeared at the rear of the stage, then lowered herself onto a hard-backed wooden chair, facing backward. Her arrival inspired commentary from the two bearded men to my right. One of them complained how old she looked, how her breasts practically touched the floor. They joked about how the Foxtails' entertainers had really gone downhill. Then they debated how much, if anything, they should offer the women on stage for a lap dance. I'll never forget the asinine line one of them shouted to the other—something like, 'If you want to bag a ho after shootin' your doe, you're gonna need big bucks to get her to fuck.' Both of 'em laughed as if it were the funniest thing they'd ever heard. I turned around to see if my dad had heard it too, but he was gone."

"Where did he go?" Nick asked.

"I'm not entirely sure, but I overheard those same two guys talking about some booths in the back where the girls gave something more than a lap dance." Corey looked at Nick's expression. He couldn't tell if Nick was surprised or getting turned on. "Anyway, Frank returned a while later with a pizza and asked me what I thought of the Foxtails Lounge. I told him it was okay. 'Just okay?' he shouted. 'It's a goddamn red-blooded American male paradise!' He proceeded to tell me how he was about my same age when his father first brought him there and that I should appreciate it.

Not every father would do this for his son. I didn't know what to say, but I'm sure he could see my hesitation, and disgust. In fact, he said he knew what I was probably thinking—that this type of thing degrades women or goes against the Bible. Then he assured me that it was perfectly fine and moral. 'As long as you play by the rules,' he explained 'it's actually good for a marriage—makes you appreciate your wife that much more once you get home.' I think he was trying to convince himself as much as me."

"Unbelievable," Nick said. "What a piece of work."

"I remember one more thing about that night that always stuck with me. Toward the end, he pointed to the dark, back corner of the bar, at a few tables with men in the shadows far from the stage. 'You see those guys hiding back there?' he asked. 'They're ashamed of themselves, and for no good reason. Embrace who you are, I say, and your God-given rights as a man. Don't be a pussy, a douche bag, a queer. Man up, for Christ's sake.'"

"Your father was rather fond of that word queer, it seems."

"Right. Well, I didn't flinch. Those words may have been directed toward the men in the back of the bar, but I think they were also aimed at me. I had heard him say things like that before, like at football games when he pointed out guys he deemed weaker men. Flower, Bugger, Flamer, Bender, and Puff. Frank knew all of the degrading names, and occasionally much worse. I don't know for sure if he was testing me for a reaction or not, but I never let him see one. I kept it all inside. My father was never going to get the satisfaction of seeing the scars that his bullets left behind. And now that he's dead, he never will."

Later that night, Corey awoke with a start, sensing that something or someone was moving across the darkened cabin bedroom. November's new moon meant an absence of light piercing the tattered cloth curtains. Feeling a hand brush across his thick mane, he sucked in an audible breath, then turned to see Nick's face hovering over him. Nick leaned over Corey's bed fully naked.

Corey was limp, though that would soon change. Sex hadn't crossed his mind during their brief stay. He and Nick hadn't touched each other that way for weeks. Neither had made a move or seemingly had the desire, for each other at least.

"You want something?"

"Isn't it obvious? You know how nature gets me worked up. And that Foxtails story? Hmmm. Come here."

Nick pulled Corey's head a bit closer and then pushed himself fully into Corey's mouth.

Corey didn't stop to think about whether he wanted to satisfy Nick this way or not. Oral pleasure had become so routine by this point in their relationship that it felt like a blend of habit, desire, and obligation. As Nick intensely thrust himself back and forth through tightly pursed lips, Corey detected Nick's musky scent and tasted the salty veneer of his skin.

He suddenly pulled his head back and turned to the side, gasping for a breath of air. Nick shoved his hand under Corey's legs and turned him over with one abrupt move.

"I was actually thinking about doing this out in the woods today, before that deer came along." Nick massaged Corey's buttocks with both hands.

Surprised and slightly aroused by Nick's unexpected forcefulness, Corey raised himself onto both elbows, so he was no longer face down in the pillow. "That would've been something new. I've never done that outdoors before." He wondered for a moment whether Nick could say the same.

"Something about the earthy smell of these woods gets me going." Still straddling Corey's thighs and balancing one hand on his lower back, Nick leaned over to grab a small plastic bottle on the nightstand that Corey didn't remember being there when he got into bed.

"I'm not ready for that, tonight."

"Relax. It'll feel great in a minute."

"How would you know? You're always on top."

"We all like what we like, and I guess my needs are more manly. Now, lift your ass, and relax."

Corey twisted underneath Nick's weight and managed to once again turn face up. "I'm not into that tonight, okay?" He could see the disappointment on Nick's face despite the darkness in the room.

"Fine." Nick threw the bottle from his hand, and it landed on the other bed. He shuffled up close once again toward Corey's face. "But you're gonna take me, one way or the other."

Pent-up, nature-driven desires didn't take long to explode. Corey felt Nick's body quiver and heard him exhale with a distinct grunt. Then he tasted the shocking, bitter effluent of Nick's body, but refused to swallow—both as a matter of safety and of spite.

Without a hand from Nick, Corey then erupted onto himself. They remained in that position for a few moments while Nick gingerly removed himself from Corey's mouth and audibly exhaled with gratification. Nick jumped off the bed and searched the dark room, finding and the putting on the T-shirt and boxer shorts he had previously shed and discarded to the floor.

Within a minute, Nick was back in his own bed buried under wool blankets. Corey got up and walked awkwardly toward the bathroom, then quietly closed the door. There, he found a fresh washcloth in the metal cabinet hanging above the stool. Dampening it with warm water, he cleaned himself up. Then he spit Nick out.

After drying his skin and brushing his teeth for the second time that same night, he placed both hands on the rim of the porcelain sink and stared into the silver-framed mirror. Questions flooded his mind, but he spoke none of them aloud. The hollow-core walls separating them was permeable to every sound, something Corey keenly recalled from his last trip to this cabin with his father. The memory of Frank's disgusting farts seeping through the bathroom door still brought a wince to his face as he stood there now, staring at his own reflection. His full head of hair was trimmed short, complimenting trendy, longer sideburns framing his boyish looks. He had the smoothest silky skin that money could buy. Hazel-green eyes stared back at him as questions circulated in his mind. Am I still appealing to Nick? To anyone? Did he come over to me tonight, or was I just the most convenient outlet? And, am I still attracted to him? The sex was okay. Not terrific, not unwanted. Just okay.

Corey couldn't pinpoint a singular point in time when his feelings for Nick had changed. It happened gradually, without warning. Part of him wanted to recapture their sexual magic though another part couldn't muster the effort to try. Tonight's episode was no different from those of the past year, and yet it was different in one significant way. He and Nick had reached orgasm together innumerable times over the years, but Corey sensed deep inside his heart that tonight just might be the very last one.

4

Thursday Morning

Nick awoke first in the late autumn darkness. Corey heard him enter the bathroom, turn on the faucet, and gargle. Then he heard Nick in the kitchen knocking around the cupboards. The next several minutes were quiet before the sound of a shrieking kettle pierced the air. He heard Nick zip his hunting jacket and don his boots, then finally the gentle slam of the back door.

Corey got out of bed and parted the frayed bedroom curtain to observe Nick on the lawn sipping a cup of tea and surveying the coming dawn. Corey noticed how the light in Barron County was filtered, casting a pall across the land. He felt a mix of calm and foreboding. He was no psychic and chalked the competing feelings up to anticipation of the day ahead. He knew that Nick looked forward to hunting, but not necessarily with Corey. Nick likely wanted to get out in the woods and hunt alone. Given the increasing acrimony of their relationship over the past sixteen months and yesterday's squabbles, Nick might think something would set Corey off today, triggering an overdue reckoning on their most difficult struggles, something more potent than the su-perficial spats of the past year.

Corey went back to bed and pulled the covers over his head. He fell asleep but awoke when Nick returned to the cabin. He would have stayed in bed a bit longer had Nick not been banging pans in the other room. He got dressed and left the bedroom.

"Geez, I think you could've awakened the dead."

Nick looked Corey up and down. "I think I just did."

Corey let it pass. "So, what's for breakfast?"

"Looks like your mom packed us store-bought doughnuts and canned fruit. Want some?"

"Yeah, thanks. What time are we heading out?"

"As soon we eat and you get dressed."

After they ate, Corey lingered in the cabin longer than he should, eventually joining Nick in the yard. Both rifles were once again laid across the folding table near the shed. Nick's hands held his cell phone, as he appeared to be typing one last message. Corey wondered who Nick was texting, whether it was personal or related to the bank. In a way the answer didn't really matter, because Nick's attention was focused elsewhere—away from here, away from Corey.

For the past year, Nick always seemed distracted, preoccupied with something other than the TV show they were watching, the party they were attending, or the conversation in which they were engaged. Corey estimated that Nick heard roughly one-third of what Corey said. Admittedly, he had his own distractions too, but the sense of disconnect with Nick that started as a tiny bit of frayed cloth at the moment of Nick's first infidelity now felt like a chasm, as though the fabric of their relationship was being torn right down the middle.

"So, what's the plan?"

At the sound of Corey's voice, Nick stuffed the cell phone into his jacket.

"I thought we'd start out sitting in the tree stand you were telling me about. Do you remember how to get there?"

"Yeah, it's the opposite direction of where we went yesterday—over that way and down the hill. That is, if it's still standing."

"Let's find out. You take the H&R again today, and I'll use the Marlin. We can always switch later if you want."

"I'm bringing this Colt Woodsman along too." Corey lifted the handgun from his pocket and showed it off to Nick.

"Where'd you get that?"

"It belonged to my father, and to my grandfather before that. As a kid, it was the only gun that interested me."

"Is it loaded?"

"Not sure. I didn't look." He handed it to Nick who shifted the cartridge and looked inside.

"It's a .22—same bullets as the rifles. I've got extra in my pocket if we need more. Bring it along. It'll come in handy if we need to shoot something up close." Nick handed the gun back to Corey.

They walked across the dormant, leaf-strewn lawn, heading toward a grove of hardwoods that blanketed twin halves of a small valley separated by a gentle stream. A barely perceptible frost coated the sod, releasing crunching gasps as they headed toward the woods. Corey looked up into temporary blindness. The sun rose steadily in the southeastern sky, sending desirable warmth on this crisp fall morning. Perhaps it would be easier to spot deer today, the sun casting its rays into every corner of the forest, unencumbered by foliage that had long since fallen to the ground.

"Soak it in now. We'll be under a thick cloud cover all afternoon," Nick shouted from behind. He always seemed to know exactly the right thing to say to break up Corey's otherwise perfectly zen moments. Who was this man behind him, Corey wondered, the man he had known for nearly twenty years? And what was on his face this morning? Was Nick trying to grow a beard? Corey didn't even notice the mixed brown-gray stubble when they left the cabin. In the course of their entire relationship, Nick had never gone more than a day without shaving.

It took them fifteen minutes to reach the deer stand. A mere half-mile from the cabin, it stood at the edge of a vast hardwood forest and a wide-ranging corn field that had been harvested several weeks before. The stand blended into the wooded divide, despite a leafless canopy surrounding the man-made structure. It had stood for thirty years, constructed by Corey's father out of fresh cut lumber delivered from a mill in Chippewa Falls. It looked like it had been reinforced at the joints sometime in-between and appeared bent but unbroken. The stand was affixed to a unique trio of tall stumps, leveled off with a handsaw.

"Ladies first." It was Nick's tired joke, as he motioned for Corey to lead the way.

The stand wobbled as he rose half-way to the top, and especially after Nick joined the climb. A bench provided the only modicum of comfort.

"I guess we'll sit here and wait?"

"Yep, and stay as still as possible," Nick said.

"I know that. But seriously, are the deer smart enough to look up and see us? Isn't all of their food source on the ground?"

"Yes, but they notice motion. You could sit here as quiet and still as a mouse and they'd never see you. Even with that bright orange vest. But move a muscle, and they'll detect you and run."

"Okay, but at some point I'll need to pee."

"Well, you can hustle down and back up the stand quickly. Or better yet, let it all hang out right here, over the edge."

"You'd like that, wouldn't you?"

"I'm good. Got my fill last night."

Corey gazed off toward the horizon, or what he could see of it through the trees. The deer stand sat on a downward slope toward the nadir of a narrow valley looking out to the far bank and onward to another field of corn at the top of the next ridge. Corey noticed a dead ash tree to his left that was receiving violent penetrating blows from a pileated woodpecker. The ash had long ago surrendered to the ravages of time, insects, and the harsh change of seasons.

Several of the trees were encumbered, he soon observed. Thick brown vines entangled most every hardwood within sight, large or small. He marveled at the blind ingenuity of these plucky climbers, fortuitously attaching themselves to young saplings, by accident or design, then symbiotically growing and shadowing their hosts as each reached ever closer to the sun. The dependent vines clung to their towering landlords, forever at their mercy.

When he looked more directly beneath the deer stand, Corey noticed a salt lick on a platform a few yards away. He calculated that it was probably a couple of years old, worn down to a mere shell of its original size by rain, deer tongues, and time. Mesmerized by the rounded white pillar of salt, Corey was drawn to it like a deer, wondering about its allure, its attractive satisfaction.

"You see that big elm tree over there?" Corey whispered a few minutes later. "The one with the splotch of missing bark?"

Nick nodded.

"That's where my dad missed his mark, shooting the damn tree instead of a ten point buck just beyond." Still whispering, Corey then forced a reminiscent exhale of air through his nose. "I thought it was pretty funny at the time, but Frank didn't. I was sitting where you are now and tried to suppress a laugh. That pissed him off. I'm surprised he didn't haul off and whack me. It didn't help that he came up empty-handed on that trip. I remember it was a quiet ride all the way back to Pepin, but I didn't mind. I had a hilarious story to tell Billy once we got back home—about how Frank Fischer shot a hundred-point elm tree."

Nick smiled but didn't laugh.

"Just so we're clear, we have permits for two bucks, which means we can also each take a doe, but I doubt the roof of the Jeep would support more than two carcasses. Since we already bagged a good one yesterday, let's make this second one count. Only shoot a big buck."

Corey felt the abrupt transition, from telling a joke to being reminded of their purpose in the woods. He watched the path with expectant eyes. Yet, he was torn. Part of him wanted the deer to all flee unscathed while the other part of him longed for Nick to snag a buck so they could get down from the cold deer stand and leave.

"What time do the deer arrive?"

"Funny. You'll have to be patient."

"What happens if we see one? Do we each take aim and then decide who shoots? Or take turns? My father always insisted on taking the first shot."

"How about you shoot at anything coming from the left and I'll take the right. That way we aren't trying to shoot past each other. Or at each other." The absence of levity in Nick's hushed voice made Corey wonder whether that last part was a joke.

"So, you only came out here hunting with your dad twice?"

"Oh, I sat in this stand several times as a kid, but I was only up here twice with a gun."

"Why?"

"Do we need to get into that topic again? I think it is a well-worn path."

"Regardless, it's beautiful here. Much more so than my family's land in Minnesota."

"This is Wisconsin, Nick. Home of beautiful landscapes and beautiful men." Corey glanced sideways for a reaction but saw none.

"Speaking of family," Nick said, "I told my sister we'd be at her house in Hudson by six, so we'll have to wrap up here by five at the latest."

Corey gnawed on his fingernail, formulating words to match the thoughts in his head. "Yeah, about Thanksgiving. Do we really have to go to your sister's?"

"What? Yes, we have to go. We made a commitment."

"I was thinking maybe we've had enough family for one week, with all of the time spent in Pepin. I'd prefer to drive straight home."

"What we had this week was a lot of your family, Corey, not mine. I think you can put on a happy face for one evening. I did that for you the past five days."

Corey relented. It wasn't worth a fight. "Anyway, I agree with you. It is peaceful here. If it weren't for the family ties, I might consider keeping this place rather than selling."

Nick laughed. "Isn't that ironic? Most people try to keep cabins and hunting land in the family across generations to preserve a legacy. Here you are getting rid of it."

"Hey, if I had a sibling or a cousin who wanted it, I'd say more power to him. But I don't. And I refuse to feel bad about selling."

"And yet another irony." Nick cracked a wide smile. "You are the end of the line for both the cabin and the Fischer family name."

"How's that?"

"You don't have any kids, and I'm guessing you're unlikely to impregnate anyone."

"We could always adopt." Corey regretted letting those words leave his lips, especially *we*. He knew the debate it might spark, but Nick had opened the door.

"Not with me, you're not. We've had that discussion. You know I don't want kids. So that's the end of that."

"The end of what?"

"The end of talking about kids."

"Well you brought it up by mocking me for being the end of the line."

"Fine. And now I'm ending it. I also think we should end this futile time in the deer stand. Nothing has passed through here in the last hour and a half, not even a raccoon. And with this argument, I'm guessing we've scared off the deer as well."

"So we're done for the day?"

"No, I'm gonna keep hunting, up on that ridge overlooking the far corn field. We need to go our separate ways. This isn't working. You can go back to the cabin or stay here in the stand. But I'm going to get a deer by myself."

Corey bit his tongue, shoved the Woodsman into his pocket, strapped the Handi to his shoulder, and turned to descend the ladder. It was getting cold in the stand anyway. Thirty feet above the ground, and just below the treetops, he'd been exposed for the past two hours to a bitter wind that brushed across his face and forced a tear. In the brief moment between looking down to the first step and glancing across the platform at Nick, they locked eyes.

"I've told you before, Corey. It isn't sexy when you cry."

He didn't bother explaining that the wetness on his face wasn't induced by emotion. Instead, he resumed the descent, his head disappearing beneath the floor of the stand.

He leapt from the ladder, skipping the final two rungs, and headed downhill. He considered turning back toward the cabin but didn't want to cross paths again with Nick. At least, not yet. Corey needed a good hike through the woods to make up for not being able to go for a run. He forded the stream with an easy step onto a limestone rock bisecting the rivulet's flow that together with fallen branches created a gentle ripple whose sound could lull a listener into peace, if only he were attuned to hear it.

As he reached the top of the hill, Corey felt the vibration of the phone in his pocket. Maybe Nick was texting an apology. He looked down and read the text from Carol. She wished him a happy Thanksgiving and asked how the rest of his week was going. He sent a brief reply, saying that he'd have to fill her in once he got back home. There were too many details about the inheritance and driving to Barron County for him to fully convey in a text. They made plans to meet for coffee on Saturday back in Minneapolis.

He continued walking, with a comforting feeling having heard from Carol. Like Billy, she was a true friend. And yet, his relationship with Carol was far more complicated. After all, Corey had never been naked with Billy. Trudging alone through his family's private woods, Corey soon lost any interest in walking softly or searching for deer. His thoughts raced back to when he had first met Carol. Their initial encounters had been awkward, to say the least. Thankfully, they survived that and ended up as friends. In hindsight, perhaps Carol's only failing was that she was the one who introduced him to Nick.

As he walked through the woods, not caring if he ever saw another deer in his life, Corey reflected on his relationship with Carol and how they had created a lasting bond given its disastrous beginning. They had met during freshman year at the Phi

Beta Upsilon Halloween party. Once the friend Corey showed up with disappeared, Carol approached and offered him a drink. He remembered telling her that he wasn't yet twenty-one. She got him a hard cider anyway. Carol led him by the hand, providing a quick tour of the main floor and then up the back stairs to her single room on the top level of the house. She told him to sit on her bed while she refilled their drinks. He drained his second one while listening to her recount salacious sorority stories. Carol made the first move. Collecting the empty bottle from Corey's hand, she pulled him in for a kiss. Her tongue slipping past his own lips was unexpected. Neither excited nor disgusted, he simply followed her lead. Wordlessly, she lifted his hand, placing it under her shirt. He left it there without doing more—no attempt to caress her breasts or feel for a clasp to unclip. She reached for his crotch, deftly unzipping his jeans and moving her hand seamlessly past the elastic band of his briefs.

She grasped limpness, straining to hold him in the palm of her hand. Corey pulled his mouth away from hers, then jumped off the bed. Carol implored him to relax and come back. She said they could take things slow. He remembered his face feeling hot, and a voice inside saying that this was wrong, all wrong. He should have been erect by now.

He walked into the bathroom and closed the door, then sat down on the toilet, letting his head fall into his open hands. He turned on the faucet letting water run untouched into the sink, hoping Carol wouldn't worry that he had fainted. Corey remembered the momentary thrill upon first being touched, but also how it ended once he had opened his eyes. When she said his name at the bathroom door, he turned off the faucet, wiped his dry hands on a towel, then reentered the room. Despite her mild protest, he insisted he had to leave. He told her he wasn't feeling well, and that it was getting kinda late. The lameness of those excuses now made him shake his head. He also remembered taking a very long and erratic route back to his dorm that night, the scene from Carol's bedroom playing repeatedly, unavoidably in his mind. While crossing the street, he nearly got hit by a city bus. The driver had honked, jolting Corey from his self-reflection long enough to notice that the bus had the green light.

Now, as he continued walking along a well-worn deer path in the woods and reflecting back on that night, Corey also thought about Billy's role in the whole debacle, and how he once again had proven to be the best friend Corey ever had. He and Billy had met for breakfast the morning after the Halloween party, just as they had every Saturday morning during freshman year. They attended different colleges but only a few miles apart. Bonnie's Café had the best pancakes Corey ever tasted, far better than the ones Ginny made at home. His mouth watered even now at the thought of those steaming hotcakes lathered in butter and maple syrup.

He recalled how Billy had been already seated and sipping coffee when Corey arrived that morning long ago. Billy spent the first several minutes recounting his heroics from a football game the night before. Corey promised to attend the next home game. They caught up on their respective classes and a little news from home. Billy also mentioned that he had a date that night with an attractive co-ed, Amanda, who was near the top of her sophomore class. Corey remembered teasing him, saying that a girl who sounded that hot, smart, and fun must be doing charity work if she agreed to go out with Billy.

When it was Corey's turn to talk about life outside the classroom, he spontaneously mentioned the Halloween party and that he had "met a girl." He regretted that revelation the moment it left his lips, but something inside him instinctively compelled him to compete with Billy's news about Amanda. He'd never forget the look on Billy's face. "You what?"

Corey explained, providing a play-by-play account of the night. Down deep, he realized his need to talk to someone, and Billy was the best choice. Billy would understand... he would have something wise to impart. But that required Corey to confess every detail of that fateful night—every embarrassing detail.

He remembered Billy's reply. "That was sorta expected, don't ya think?" Corey must have looked confused. Billy said more. "Maybe girls aren't your thing. Maybe you're gay?"

That memory made him feel anxious, even today. Corey remembered his face turning bright red, like it had the night before in Carol's bedroom. Billy had taken the conversation to a place Corey wasn't ready to go. "What the hell, Billy? I'm not gay," he recalled saying loudly. "Why are you saying that?" Billy had tried to calm him down, but Corey didn't want to hear it. He placed a five-dollar bill on the table and walked out of the café.

That was one of those life moments Corey had regretted ever since. At the time, he remembered needing to flee. Corey remembered showing up at the sorority house the next night. Carol opened the door and pulled him inside from the cold, saying how glad she was that Corey had called. She was worried that she'd done something wrong. They ascended to the top floor and settled once again into her room. She had placed a series of pillows on top of the bed, against the wall facing the TV. Corey asked if she had any more hard cider, even though he had already consumed two with his roommate before leaving the dorm. Carol popped *Ghost* into the VCR, and they settled onto the bed. He was on his fourth drink of the night by the time Patrick Swayze's character bled to death on the street.

Once again, Carol made the first move, pulling Corey's arm around her and snuggling into his chest. He didn't resist. He also complied when she placed her hand on top of his pants, reciprocating by rubbing her breasts through her shirt and then boldly underneath. He focused intently on the idea of sex, on the anticipated acts that would lead to an orgasm. With her back now to the TV and neither of them paying attention to Whoopi Goldberg faking a séance, Carol pulled off Corey's pants and underwear in one graceful move. He showed no sign of hesitation. He arched his back, closed his eyes, and waited tensely to be touched. She urged him to lie back, then gently placed her lips in a place no girl ever had before. It felt nothing like the excitement of his first and only sexual encounter in high school, with a boy.

He exhaled loudly and sank into the pillows. Corey wasn't sure what to do next, so he simply did nothing and let Carol lead him wherever she wanted to go. Competing images flooded his mind. He couldn't erase a single one—Carol, the drinks, and the memories of his mocking father. Then he thought about a Latino guy from English 101 whom Corey caught staring in his direction several times. He even willed himself to remember the porn video he had watched repeatedly on his laptop, Corey's eyes always magnetically drifting across the screen, from the woman underneath toward the man on top. His body remained tense.

He begged himself to stay hard, the alcohol in his system keeping his fears and resistance at bay. He would do whatever Carol wanted and then tell Billy and Frank that yes, he had sex with girls. And no, he was not a virgin. As she stroked him with greater force and more persistence, Corey desperately wanted to explode. His eyes shut tight as could be, he thought of the most erotic and arousing things he could imagine, all involving men. Then he willed himself over the finish line.

Thinking of that scene now, Corey reflected on the person he used to be, often going against what he felt to be true inside in order to prove a point to everyone else. Was he really all that different now, twenty years later? He wasn't certain. He was glad that things worked out in the end with Carol. Despite an initial awkwardness, he eventually explained why he couldn't see her again, romantically at least. He remembered her taking it far better than he had feared. She was the one who insisted that they be friends.

Corey also made things right with Billy. They met at the same café the following Saturday. They hadn't spoken in a week, other than the hurried message Corey left with Billy's roommate midweek. Within seconds of sitting down in the booth, Corey apologized for his previous abrupt exit. Billy accepted and offered one of his own for getting out of line with what he had said.

"No, you weren't," Corey remembered saying. Then he told Billy that he was gay, the first time Corey had said those words aloud—to anyone. Billy reached across the table and touched Corey's trembling, folded hands. He thanked Corey for telling him. Then he said no more, allowing Corey to do the talking. Corey told him about the second night with Carol. Then he told him about Enzo from high school. Billy nodded without any indication of surprise, even upon hearing the vivid description of Corey's overnight experiences with the foreign exchange student back in Pepin.

Corey explained that it wasn't until he was on the bed with Carol that he really understood the sensations he felt with Enzo. It was as if everything came flooding back to him at once—how Enzo smelled, how Corey's body tingled from head to toe, how his heart felt like it would beat right out of his chest, and how he didn't want the moment to end. Corey never forgot Billy's next words. "I think you're describing what everyone feels about their first time having sex. This is great, Corey."

Their conversation continued for nearly two hours. He remembered the waitress repeatedly asking if they needed anything else. Corey recalled telling Billy that even though he felt such exhilaration when he and Enzo were in the moment, Corey also felt ashamed at the time. Enzo was a boy, and everything Corey had learned growing up taught him what they were doing was wrong. It wasn't something he could accept, or talk about with anyone, not even Enzo. At school Enzo had barely acknowledged him, as if what they did was a dirty secret and they couldn't give away a single clue.

Billy expressed sympathy with Corey's plight and said that he wished he'd known what Corey was going through back then. In typical Billy fashion, he also reminded Corey that the future doesn't have to mirror the past, that Corey was living on his own in college now, and that he could be more free. Corey remembered a period of silence where he reflected on all that had been said. Billy eventually asked him what he planned to do now, perhaps start dating guys or look for an LGBT group on campus. Corey wasn't sure. It was all too new. But eventually, yes. He wanted to live more openly, at least here at college. He couldn't fathom sharing the news with his parents back home.

As Corey walked through the woods in the mid-day muted sunlight of Barron County, the rifle safely strapped to his side, he marveled at how he had survived that long-ago drama. He remembered the sense of relief he felt at recognizing his sexuality and the gratitude for having a friend who could tenderly expose Corey's truth. The skies above him had filled with a passing mass of gray clouds, but off toward the western horizon it looked like the sun might break through. Corey kept walking. And, he grew hungrier. The donut and fruit he ate for breakfast clearly weren't enough, and they hadn't packed anything for lunch. Perhaps some deprivation was good and would leave him room to gorge out when he and Nick arrived at the Parkers that evening for dinner.

Corey thought about the last time he had been home to Pepin for a Thanksgiving meal. It was 2003. He and Nick had been together for eight years, but Corey had yet to tell his parents about his sexuality and the true nature of the relationship with his roommate, Nick. Ginny's meal had been as good as ever. It was the one unchanging aspect of Pepin that he liked. While watching yet another football game after dinner, Corey remembered the news break at half-time. How could he forget? A special report told how Bush's political strategist was leading an effort to have gay marriage bans placed on the ballot in several states before the 2004 general election. A combination of his father's reaction to the news story and Corey constantly thinking about Nick combined to stoke his desire to finally come out to his parents. With the benefit of hindsight, though, Corey wondered whether his decision wasn't in fact borne from the presence of relatives that day. There's no way Frank would get too verbally abusive with all those witnesses.

Corey remembered reaching for the remote and pressing the mute button. Frank protested. "Hey I'm watching that." Corey summoned his mother from the kitchen where she had been doing dishes with her sister. As soon as she entered the room, Corey announced in a firm voice that he was gay. Frank fiddled with a loose string on his armchair. Ginny looked directly at Corey but didn't say a word. Uncle Jim offered to leave the room and take Grandma with him, but Frank told everyone to stay right where they were.

Corey recalled that his father looked serious but not upset. He also remembered the stern series of hurtful questions that emerged from his father's mouth, with everyone listening in stunned silence. "You're telling us this now, on Thanksgiving?" Ginny tried to interject with "it's okay," but Frank held his hand toward her face. She stopped talking. Corey remembered explaining that he only decided to make this announcement upon hearing the news report on TV. It seemed like an invitation from the universe. Then he told them about Nick.

Frank said something snarky about the news "getting better by the minute." His father's hurtful questions continued. Even ten years later, Corey could still hear them. "How do you know for sure? Have you ever slept with a woman?" Ginny tried again to intervene. Uncle Jim suggested that they take a break and get dessert. Frank wouldn't have it. He wanted answers to his questions, and nobody was leaving the room until Corey provided them. "How does he know he's gay if he's never had sex the right way?"

Corey remembered feeling defensive. He was tempted to blurt out the highlights from his encounter with Carol. After all, wasn't that one of his motivations way back then—to sleep with a girl so he could later use that as a shield against his father? But why did he feel protective of his experience with Carol when the time had finally arrived to use it? He only told them the basics— yes there was a girl in college, and no he didn't enjoy it at all. That's how he knew he was gay.

His answer wasn't enough. Frank wanted to know her name. Corey tried to deflect. Ginny made another run at getting them to calm down. Frank insisted on a name. Corey told them her name was Carol and that it happened in college.

"Satisfied?"

"No," Frank said. "But if she was any good, you would have been."

At that point, Uncle Jim got up from his chair, and Grandma followed him into the kitchen. Frank stood, then walked down to the basement without saying another word to anyone. Corey heard his father turn on the television in the workshop and figured he would be down there stewing, formulating new arguments against Corey's declaration of homosexuality. That or he'd drink himself to sleep on the basement sofa. When Corey awoke the next morning, Ginny told him that Frank had left early on a last-minute hunting trip to Barron County. Corey stayed to visit with his mother for another day, then drove home to Minneapolis.

5

Corey didn't know for certain where Nick had gone. He assumed that Nick had taken the well-worn trail up and to the left at the fork in the path where Corey veered to the right. After leaving the deer stand, those were the only two options for heading deeper into the woods.

As a kid, Corey had walked these paths with his father, mostly during hunting season. At other times of the year, Corey explored the trails alone, without wearing bright orange clothing or the fear of getting shot. He remembered being enchanted as a boy meandering through this vast forest, all of the paths worn smooth by deer and other creatures traveling to and from the stream that traversed their land. Corey learned to navigate those paths quickly as a kid and never got lost.

Today he kept walking west, away from the cabin and toward the open corn field he knew lay at the top of the ravine. Little did Nick know, but his trail would bring him to the opposite side of that same field. Eventually, they'd cross paths and Corey could confront Nick anew, then make him answer for the state of their relationship. Worst case, there'd be a marriage-ending fight. But even then, Corey fantasized about ditching Nick deep in the darkening woods and taking a shortcut back to the cabin, leaving Nick lost in the moonless autumn night.

He reached the crest of the hill, breathless from the steep climb. His leg began to throb again. Despite being a frequent runner, Corey was unprepared for the challenge in ascending a thirty-degree slope wearing hunting gear and carrying two guns—the rifle strapped to his shoulder and the Colt Woodsman nestled in his coat pocket. At the top of the ravine, he welcomed the sight of a fallen elm that provided a spot to rest. The trunk lay mere feet from the edge of the woods. Much of the elm's outer skin had long ago rotted away. He set the rifle against the trunk, then peeled away some loose bark to create a space large enough to sit. The smooth surface felt comfortable. He removed another chunk of bark, then observed it from both sides. A line of five beetles on the underside surprised him. They were either dead or hibernating, each one frozen to the husk of the bark.

Corey sat down and caught his breath. He beheld a fantastic view of the field beyond the intervening hardwoods—an uneven plane of arable farmland. It would be far easier to traverse than the wooded ravine. The cultivated plot bowed upward like a blanket held at its corners by four children, billowing in the middle from a gentle breeze. He gazed outward from the forest and toward the field ahead. Surely this was the spot to find a deer grazing unwittingly. Corey put his hands inside his pockets for warmth and felt the snack he had stowed away when leaving the cabin yesterday. He pulled the granola bar from his pocket and ripped the package open with his teeth. The bar had disintegrated into crumbs after being tossed and bruised in the course of Corey's climb up and down the deer stand and from the rubbing of the package against the hard metal handgun.

He sat and ate granola remnants from his cupped palm. Then he watched and waited for something to appear. Patience was never Corey's strong suit, but today there was motivation to prove his hunting bona fides—to Nick, to his dead father, and to himself. He heard the muted ring of the phone in his pocket. He reached for it, answering as soon as he recognized the number.

"Hello?"

"Corey, it's Mom. I just wanted to call and wish you a happy Thanksgiving."

"Thanks. Same to you."

"Are you guys on your way to Nick's sister's house?"

"Nope. Still at the cabin—in the woods, actually."

"Oh. Billy brought the car back yesterday. I thanked him for going so far out of his way and for missing half a day with his family."

"I think he was happy to do it."

"So, how's it going?"

"Here? Okay, I guess. Nick got a deer yesterday. It's a long story."

"That's good. And you? Did you go hunting too?"

"I sure did."

"Corey, is everything all right?"

"Great. Why do you ask?"

"I don't know. You sound, well, distant—more than usual."

"I guess it's been a long day. A long week, in fact, but I'm sure it's been the same for you."

"Oh, I'm doing fine. Grandma, Jim and Mary came for lunch and just left. It was nice having them here. It gave me a distraction, someone to cook for."

Memories of Ginny's turkey and wet dressing simmered in Corey's mind. He could taste her home cooking, and it deepened his hunger.

"I'll bet it was terrific, as usual."

"We had a nice meal, but now I'm a bit tired. Like you said, it's been a long week."

"I should've stayed another day and helped you out with Thanksgiving dinner, Mom. It's just that we promised Nick's sister and, well, Nick can be adamant about keeping plans."

"Corey," she interrupted, "it's okay, really. I appreciate all you're doing, all you've done."

"I'm not sure I did that much."

"No, you did. More than you had to. I know how difficult this week must've been for you."

He didn't know what to say. It had been a shitty week.

"Corey, you still there?"

"Yeah, Mom. You caught me off guard, that's all."

"Well, maybe I'm surprising myself a bit too, since Frank died. I finally feel free to say the things that I want to, out loud—things I should have said a long time ago."

"It's not your fault, Mom. Dad was, well, he was Dad. There wasn't much room for either of us to speak our minds."

"True, but I saw how you tried to stand up to him at times. I'm sorry I didn't speak up too. I owed you more support than I gave."

He couldn't hear what she said after that.

"Mom. Mom? I might be losing reception."

"I said you know you're always welcome here. In fact, I'd like it if you came down for Christmas. Bring Nick too."

"Okay. I'll get back to you."

"That's fine. But Corey, please come alone sometime too. There are things I'd like to talk about with you—just the two of us—including some things about Nick."

He listened attentively to what his mother might say next, but the phone went dead. What things? He looked at his cell phone and saw the "No Service" message. What could his mother possibly want to talk with him about? What did she have to tell him about Nick?

He stayed seated atop the log. A mink scurried past him—jumping over the elm—so close that it caused him to gasp. He worried that it might bite him. Corey kept watching the horizon for Nick, thinking that they would cross paths again in the woods or the field, if only he sat there long enough. Regardless, there'd be another confrontation. The unfinished squabble in the deer stand opened up old wounds, including the idea of adopting a child. Corey had thought about having children ever since he and Nick got married. It seemed like the next logical step. Six months of couples counseling had built a firm footing beneath the foundering edifice of their relationship, one they had initially jumped into head-first based on mutual attraction and lust. The decision to marry arose from a joint need for security and recognition. With no support from Corey's parents and nominal encouragement from Nick's, they relied heavily upon validation of their union from friends. Yet, it didn't seem enough, especially when Nick's confession of an indiscretion came to light in therapy. Corey yearned for something more secure—proof that Nick had changed and that he had chosen Corey above all others, in lieu of all others.

The clouds soon parted in the western sky, broken wide open by penetrating rays of sunlight. He first noticed the scenic change while gazing upon the field. Shadows raced toward him, chased from one side to the other by the expanding brighter ground, like a herd of buffalo loping atop the land. He marveled at the images unfolding before his eyes, a once hidden kaleidoscope of colors and patterns now visible, no longer camouflaged by overcast skies. Muted yellow corn stalks lay crisscrossed atop the dark brown dirt, as if placed there by an artistic mathematician. Not one looked out of place. The rough stalks lay in a geometric design across the entire field, in pre-arranged rows occasionally divided in a rolling pattern by the deep ruts of a tractor tire.

For a moment Corey forgot about hunting, instead marveling at the unexpected beauty of this place. The eerily patterned field reminded him of Escher's famous works of mind-numbing design. As the moments turned into minutes, his thoughts drifted to another comparison—*The Cornfield near Argenteuil*, a virtual replica of the scenery now before him. Corey was intimately familiar with the works of Sisley and his fellow Impressionists. It was one of his favorite genres of painting. Created in 1873, the lesser-known work of oil on canvas reflected the very same scenic images as far as he could presently see. A vast blanket of yellow stalks filled half the canvas and half of Corey's present line of sight. At the edges of both the painting and the field lay a forested grove of hardwoods, with gently rolling hills in the distance. While Sisley's sky was bright blue with few clouds, the one above Corey today was the reverse—mostly teeming with billowy white and gray, only a few spots of blue and emerging sunlight in between.

He smiled while recalling long-forgotten memories of the Sisley painting and other works he had studied with such passion in college. He also remembered his father repeatedly questioning why Corey would pursue a major in art history. "What in the hell can someone do with an art degree? Who's going to hire you with that?" Wouldn't his father have loved being present today, hearing his only son explain how the perfect light cast down on this lonely corn field in late November mimicked the painting by Sisley, and how it evoked in Corey the very same happy emotions as when he first beheld that great work of art in Hamburg's Kunsthalle Museum?

He grinned with broad satisfaction.

Then, in an instant, his smile disappeared. A large buck emerged from the trees at the far edge of the field. Corey hesitated. He didn't immediately position the rifle for a shot or even attempt to spy the animal through the scope. The buck had appeared from a part of the woods where he calculated Nick would possibly appear. It was the perfect position at the end of a trail that Nick most likely had followed.

And yet, Corey heard neither a shot nor a sound.

This was his chance to shoot a deer and prove his worth. In truth, he didn't want to fire the gun, or to shoot any innocent creature. Yet the time for backing out had passed. He simply couldn't look away. The alternative would be to return empty-handed, feigning ignorance of this unique opportunity. "I never saw a deer," he could say. "Nothing crossed my path." But what if Nick killed a deer? Or this deer? Corey knew that a buck with this sized rack would be a prized kill, one that he estimated at eighteen points. This was the one to shoot. Resigned to his fate, he lifted the rifle from the ground and brought the scope to his eye.

The beast was even more majestic once magnified. The buck lifted its head and looked straight at Corey. Did it spy him sitting motionless atop the fallen elm? Did it know what was about to transpire? Perhaps, for the deer slowly disappeared from the scope and walked toward the crest of the field.

Corey looked beyond the rifle and followed the buck with his eyes until the deer stopped once again, dropping its head toward the ground, grazing on remnant corn cobs with their residual nourishing kernels. Suddenly the buck jolted, startled by the snap of a branch under Corey's foot as he moved into a better position by stepping gingerly onto the edge of the field.

The deer ran at a loping pace to Corey's left, back toward the woods in the direction where Corey expected Nick might emerge. The buck slowed to a crawl and Corey followed him once again through the scope. He made a decision quickly. He brought the rifle level with his face, arms extended just a foot, and it all happened at once—in slow motion for the hunter, in an instant for his victim. Corey pulled the trigger and felt the jolt of the gun. He reloaded. He righted himself, then pulled the trigger once more before refocusing his sightline in the scope. He then spied an orange hunting vest just beyond the deer. Peering through the lens atop the rifle, Corey swore he also saw a burst of blood. He looked up and witnessed the massive buck thrust its two front legs violently into the unforgiving brown dirt, pivot, and drop to the ground. He saw the orange vest fall as well.

"Jesus Christ," Corey whispered before staggering backward and then collapsing to the trunk. The shots were already fired, and he couldn't retrieve them. He sat on the frozen elm for what seemed like minutes. A brisk November wind brushed across his face. His hands felt bone cold from the freezing temps. Winter-proofed clothing and a brand-new pair of chestnut brown boots shielded the rest of his skin from the elements. He summoned the courage to stand, then peered across the field. He felt like vomiting but swallowed instead, forcing a bitter taste back down his throat.

Corey looked up with dread to confirm the cold-blooded killing he feared he had just wrought. He noticed sudden movement. His jaw dropped heavily to his chest. The deer seemingly gathered strength enough to stand and released a painful whimper. Staggering to its feet, the buck limped off toward the woods. The loathsome rifle dropped from Corey's right hand. He never wanted to touch the brutal metal device again. He stepped cautiously onto the cornfield, then stopped with sudden alarm.

"Corey! Goddamn it. Did you just shoot at me? Corey!"

He couldn't find the strength to answer with words. He had no capacity to do anything other than stand—exposed—wondering what to do next. He tuned out Nick's hollering.

For God's sake, why did I come here in the first place, he wondered. A moment of calm befell him. Then he recalled the reason with clarity. Corey came here to resolve years of unspoken tension, to reconcile in the waning light of a November afternoon the truth about Nick.

And, he came here for the killing.

Deep down, Corey wanted to exorcize a host of demons and, in the process, to snuff out a life. He knew what needed to be done. He picked up his gun, brushed the leaves and water droplets from his pants, then began to run across the field.

Corey set his sights on the middle of the barren cornfield, on the downslope just beyond its apex as he winced in pain with every step. Straw-colored stalks rose a mere foot and a half from the ground, remnants of a final harvest three months before. Row upon row of miniature yellow soldiers stood stoically above the unyielding ground. Shorn off at the knees by the blades of a mechanical picker, these vestiges of once tall, green plants were destined to face the agony of a Wisconsin winter before being mercilessly plowed under the softened black soil in spring.

Nick caught up to Corey and grabbed him from behind.

"Jesus Christ, you scared me," Corey said. "You're lucky you didn't get shot."

"For a minute there I thought I did. Didn't you hear me yelling?"

"Yeah, but no more than usual."

"That's not even funny. I had that deer in my sights, ready to shoot, and the next thing I know a bullet grazed past my head."

"Now who's being dramatic, Nick? You think I was shooting at you?"

"How in the hell do I know? I fell to the ground and hit my knee on a boulder. Thanks a lot. It hurts."

"I'm sure you'll be fine, but maybe you need to go to urgent care?"

Nick shook his head and changed the subject. "So, what happened?"

"I shot one."

"One what?"

"A deer, what do you think?"

"You did?"

"Yes, didn't you see him fall over, then get up and run?"

"So you missed?"

"No, didn't you hear what I said? I shot him. He fell but then got up and staggered off toward the woods."

"Didn't you aim for the heart, like I showed you?"

A salty taste of humiliation rose in Corey's throat. For a fraction of a second, he contemplated placing the blame where it belonged—with Nick, the one who had probably spooked the deer and caused Corey's shot to miss.

"So he ran off into the woods?" Nick looked toward the trees. "Shit."

Corey felt nauseous.

"What's wrong? Why are you sitting down?"

"Jesus, Nick, give me a fucking break. I just shot something for the first time in my life. I feel sick."

Braced momentarily against the reedy corn stalk, Corey fell completely onto his back against the dirt. Queasiness remained. Fully level with the ground, his body was protected from the cold breeze. He reluctantly thought back to the moment when he pulled the trigger. It was as awful as he had imagined, and yet so easy and intentional once he followed Nick's advice. It played over and over again in his head as if tape-recorded from the day before. "Pretend the deer is your father. And then you'll never miss."

As for expelling his father's ghost, however, the blast was a failure. Corey's self-torment persisted. He closed his eyes and simply breathed. He reached into the recesses of his mind, blocking his surroundings and grasping for the Ayurvedic meditation he learned from Doctor Carnes. "The deer is alive," he murmured to himself. "I haven't yet ended a life." He repeated the mantra over and over. The holistic healer had taught Corey well—"Get out of the moment and into yourself." Such a simple concept, one that he routinely practiced. As long as no one interfered, repeating a soothing truth in a recurring rhythm usually removed Corey from pain.

He rose slowly but concertedly from the ground, without a gesture of help from Nick. The rifle lay beside him against the corn stalk as Corey rolled to his right. First up to his knee, then bracing his arm against his extended leg, he willed himself upright. He pulled the blaze orange stocking cap back down to cover both ears and tugged at the base of his jacket. Reaching down, he picked up the Colt handgun, which had fallen out of his pocket. Then he turned to face Nick, upwind.

He waited to hear something snarky, but Nick didn't say a word—at least not out loud. Instead, Nick rubbed his kneecap and scoured the edge of the woods for any sign of the deer. Corey focused on an ash tree above Nick's shoulder and fifty yards in the distance. Another soothing thought entered his mind. *Perhaps I only grazed his caramel-colored coat. The deer will be just fine.* Over and over silently, this time without moving his lips.

Nick broke the silence. "You know, I saw that buck before you did, but he was walking toward your end of the field. An eighteen pointer from what I could see."

From Corey, silence. The calming, recurring meditations were more powerful than Nick's innocuous banter.

"I should have taken the shot myself. The damn deer was in range for each of us. Now we have to track him."

The momentary comforts of Corey's contemplation fled like a startled rabbit. "Track him? What do you mean track him?"

"I mean, we have to follow the buck to wherever he collapses so I can finish the kill." Nick pointed dramatically toward his own chest.

"But you didn't even see me shoot him, you said. I might have completely missed."

"Oh, I saw it. You missed the target but definitely hit the deer in the leg."

"Then why did you grill me about shooting the deer, if you saw the whole thing?"

"Because I wanted to hear you say what you did out loud, to own up to shooting an animal in the wild. I know you, Corey. This is a big deal. I wanted to hear you say it."

"But I didn't see a thing after firing two shots and noticing blood spurting into the air. I closed my eyes, dropped the rifle and fell to the ground." Corey surprised himself at being so forthcoming about his own frailty. That kind of honest vulnerability had been absent from their relationship for quite some time. "So what did you see, Nick?"

"I saw blood erupt from the deer's leg too."

"Then maybe I only grazed him. Even in humans, flesh wounds often bleed the worst."

"Oh, you more than grazed him, Corey. That deer is mortally wounded."

"How do you know? You were as far away from him as I was."

"That buck was tail down as he ran away, a sure sign he was seriously injured."

"But he ran into the woods. We'll never find him. And what sense would it make if we did?"

"His trail of blood will be easy to follow."

Nausea returned. Corey clamored for a reassuring meditation, but nothing stuck. Nick's stark picture flooded his mind with morbid thoughts. There seemed no escape from what was to come. He stood in the middle of a barren Wisconsin corn field, hopeless. He foresaw Nick calling the shots, with Corey playing out a role cast for him by some unconquerable fate.

"Now, pick up your rifle, pull yourself together, and let's go find that deer."

They walked but a few yards before the next argument started.

"You have the flashlight, right?" Corey felt both jacket pockets multiple times but knew his failing the moment the question left Nick's lips.

"Uh, it must've fallen out of my pocket back at the elm tree. I don't remember having it when I got up to run across the field."

"Great. Well one of us has to go back and get it. We're not going on without it." Nick and Corey exchanged imploring looks. "Fine, I'll go, but you're going to carry the damn thing the rest of the way. Now, where was that tree?"

Corey pointed. Nick laid his rifle on the ground and jogged with a slight limp toward the fallen elm. Corey exhaled. His lungs felt tight against the cool breeze, suffocating him in the open field. He sat down on a pile of abandoned corn stalks, his only barrier from the cold, hard dirt. He removed his hat and set the rifle on the ground. The Woodsman still rested inside his coat pocket. He used all ten fingers to rub the day's exhaustion from his face. He saw Nick one-third of the way across the open space, still heading toward the woods. He figured that he had a few minutes before Nick returned. Then he gazed in the other direction, the same one in which Nick had pointed, indicating the wounded deer's path of escape. He saw nothing besides the expansive corn field and the beginning of another dense hillside of wood.

As he leaned back and placed his hands on the ground behind him for support, Corey felt something pleasingly smooth but for no more than a second before it slipped from under his grasp. He saw the two-foot-long garter snake as it slithered away from him. Though he knew the snake was harmless, Corey uttered a slight scream. Thankfully, Nick couldn't have heard it.

The snake halted its escape after only a few feet. Corey regarded the small reptile with amazement. Its shiny skin looked wet, the green and black coloring of its body vibrant. He also noticed a foot-long trail of translucence, something the creature had just left behind—a desiccate, pale shell of its former self. Once its primary layer of protection against the outside world, the old skin was now shed, unneeded. Corey reached for the snake's remnant, fingering the delicate discarded membrane. He was surprised at its lightness, its vacuous feel, its uselessness. He pondered the ease with which the reptile left so much of himself behind. The snake slithered away and out of sight.

Nick stood at the edge of the field, bent over the tree stump looking for the flashlight. Corey knew he had little remaining solitude. Solitude—there had been plenty of that in his life lately. Other than Friday night double dates, watching various TV shows together and sleeping in the same bed, Nick and Corey's intimacy had diminished over the years as there seemed less to talk about, fewer things in common. He frequently wondered whether this trajectory was normal among married people—growing apart, something to be endured along the journey toward twenty-fifth or fiftieth anniversaries. Or was it a sign that their relationship had simply run its course?

They had no children whose feelings needed considering. Their only obligation was a joint mortgage on the condo. Even their cars were paid for, each one titled in their own name. Fewer and fewer tangible ties bound them together. In years past, especially before they were legally married, Corey took comfort in that arrangement. The fact that Nick stayed despite the freedom to flee at any moment felt affirming. Nick hung on because he wanted to, or at least that's what Corey thought. Even at his worst, in the midst of Corey's debilitating depression and hospitalization a year before, Nick had endured. He wasn't always pleasant and certainly lacked a compassionate bedside manner. But he kept on, even when there was every reason and opportunity to leave.

Yet, their relationship felt ambivalent the past few years. No one was running for the exits, but neither was there much burning desire to stay. Dinner conversation was minimal, each of them alternating between bites of food and scrolling through social media newsfeeds on the phone. The talks they did have were often mundane—schedules, work, condo building gossip. Politics was a safe topic, something on which the two men saw eye-to-eye.

But the pressures and pains from years of acting the part began to weigh on Corey—the good son, the supportive husband, the responsible employee. Always striving to ensure the happiness and approval of others, his subconscious started down the path of a slow-approaching crash. His body and mind needed more than others' approval. As he learned through his month-long stay in treatment and subsequent therapy, he also needed approval from himself. Something about turning forty and being a year removed from treatment for alcoholism and depression spurred in him a growing need to stand tall. He felt compelled to defend himself in the face of unwarranted criticism from anyone—most of all, from Nick.

Corey watched as Nick half-jogged, half-walked toward him, the daylight still sufficient to see three hundred yards with clarity. Within a minute, Nick returned breathless but not stopping to rest.

"Here. Put this in your pocket and make sure it doesn't drop out. Let's go."

"I need to sit here for a minute. I don't feel well." Corey was unable to lift himself off the ground. Nick's unsympathetic reply was as predictable as the coming sunset.

"We don't have a minute. I've got to fix your mess. Pick up your gun, and let's go before we lose him." Corey dragged himself up from the barren surface. As he rose in the coming finale of daylight, he navigated each step forward. After securing the flashlight in his left-hand pocket, he cocooned the Woodsman in his right. The rifle was strapped to his shoulder. By the time he looked up, Nick was ten yards ahead, and Corey struggled to catch up.

Nick was the first to reach the stain marking Corey's imprecision. "There." The trajectory of Nick's finger pointed to a splash of cherry-tainted corn stalk, a splotch of like-hued liquid pooled on the ground below. "He ran that way."

Corey felt like puking once again. Then he did. The partially digested granola bar came streaming out of his throat, overcoming his vain attempt to keep it inside. Nick looked away.

"You okay?"

Bent over, Corey repeatedly spit on the ground, wanting to rid his mouth of the foul taste. He then wiped his open lips on the sleeve of his suede hunting jacket, a far better taste on his tongue than the putrid vomit that passed through a moment before.

"I will be. Gross."

"Good. We've got to get going before he gets too far." Nick turned and walked away without saying another word. Corey followed him across the downslope of the slightly bowed land. At the lowest point of the five-acre plot ran a narrow chasm the length of the corn field. Corey had seen it once in springtime, filled with snow melt carrying the remnants of a disappearing white blanket that had covered the ground since fall. The rest of the year it lay dormant, occasionally providing a basin for torrential rainwater running randomly through the rows of growing corn. The droplets that weren't trapped by the thirsty ground sought escape toward this ravine before being carried on to the Red Cedar River and eventually the Chippewa, the Mississippi, and finally to the Gulf of Mexico and beyond.

Corey's pace soon left him further and further behind. Nick's apparent thirst for the kill propelled him onward while Corey's guilt held him back. Something had to give. At this rate, Nick would reach the dry creek bed and then disappear in the distant woods, unless he stumbled upon the deer while still in Corey's line of sight.

Corey picked up his stride to a jogging pace. At least he was heading downhill. Between running up the wooded rise to reach this field and the emotional toll of the past five minutes, Corey was nearly exhausted. And yet, Nick ran on ahead. So Corey ran too. What other choice was there? They forged onward, as if magnetically pulled toward their fate. Corey strained to keep pace with Nick traversing the field, the taller man's legs unfairly longer, and Nick's injured knee barely an impediment to his fast-paced stride. That disparity in speed was a constant source of aggravation whenever they walked any distance, but especially today—much like Corey trying to keep up with his father as a boy.

6

Thursday Afternoon

By four o'clock in the afternoon, daylight had faded. The northern Wisconsin skies turned cobalt gray, the thick layer of remaining clouds racing east as the sun headed west, opening up the heavens. Woods to their backs and another grove of trees ahead, Corey and Nick traversed the open plot of dirt which itself turned darker by the minute, light no longer reflecting off the corn stalks scattered randomly across the ground.

Corey looked behind him and saw how the trees in the distance had caught the few remaining rays of sunlight, illuminating their spidery network of branches. The oaks, gripping their tan leaves deep into winter, were aglow with hues of pink, orange, and red. Some appeared set aflame by the waning star, its fire magically extinguishing itself upward, inch by inch. Sunlight soon left the grasp of each tree's uppermost fingers, gone until a new day, returning those branches to their stale autumnal gray and brown.

A trail of deer blood led to the edge of the harvested field. As light fled the western sky, the adjacent woods turned opaque. The forest that lay ahead was coniferous. This portion of the Fischer land was noticeably darker than the leafless hardwood forest behind them where the hunt began. The wounded animal must have fled toward the pines, seeking hidden shelter from Corey and Nick.

"He entered the grove, right there," Nick said.

"It looks dark. Maybe we should turn back."

"You still have the flashlight, right?"

"Yeah, but..."

"Let's go," Nick interrupted.

"C'mon, we're never going to find him in there."

"Yes, we will. But if we don't find him soon and before this flashlight burns out, we'll resume searching in the morning. That means calling my sister and canceling dinner." Nick pulled the phone from his pocket. "Shit, my battery's low."

Corey's gut writhed. He didn't want to spend another minute in this wretched place—the cold, the fading daylight, the exhausting arguments with Nick. He yearned to escape and never return. Yet, to achieve that, the deer must be found, then put out of its misery—and Corey's.

At the edge of the lonely field stood a rusted fence. Nick deftly bent between the barbed wires, avoiding its jagged spurs. Gingerly, Corey tried the same.

"Nick, look."

He did, then touched the bloody flesh and wisps of brown hide dangling from the fence.

"Ouch. The deer caught its underbelly on the top wire. I think your shot to his leg weakened him. He couldn't clear the fence. He won't get far now."

"Isn't it possible the bullet went straight through? Maybe he'll recover and get away?"

"Uh, no. This isn't some feel-good movie, Corey. That deer was mortally wounded. You must've hit the femoral artery. We either find him and put a bullet through his heart or let him die a slow, painful death all night."

Nick's splash of reality brought Corey back to the deer they hit on the road the day before. Lingering over that memory, he fell farther behind Nick as they entered the pine grove. He could see the outline of Nick's body ahead of him. He also saw Nick stop and turn around.

"Come on. You're holding us back, and it's getting dark."

"Give me a second." Corey struggled for air and craved water. He dreaded the moment when the gap between them and the deer would narrow, then disappear. How could Nick continue the pursuit so eagerly? How could he even see where he was going? Corey's mind raced. The landscape was full of shadows, the trees posing as motionless predators waiting to strike. Corey's only confidence in moving forward was that he still knew these paths from memory, from the many times he had traversed them as a boy. He also knew that their current course was taking them farther from the cabin. Even if they did find and kill the deer, it would be a monumental task to drag the damn thing all the way back to the shed.

"I think he's slowing down. Shine the flashlight over there." Corey did. Nick pointed to the ground. "Yeah, the blood is bright red, and there's a lot of it. We're getting close."

Corey kicked himself for being out there in the woods with Nick—the blood-thirsty hunter who lately acted as if he didn't care what Corey did, if he lived or died. What a change from their earlier days. Maybe the tipping point was the incident in Miami last year. Corey's lingering suspicions about Evan finally seemed to be proven true. Yet once again, he had no evidence, and Nick steadfastly maintained his innocence. All the drama of Corey's suicidal close call was for naught. Months of individual and joint therapy followed, leaving Corey riven between the instinctive truth within his gut and the paucity of evidence for his fears. In the wake of his hospitalization, he often felt as if he were going mad. The questions lingered and paranoia ruled. At times, he suspected nothing and assumed their relationship was secure. But other times things seemed amiss, like when Nick was distant in thought. Corey wondered who Nick was really with on those late-night business dinners. He worried that he might lose it again. He never wanted to return to that dark place and hoped despair would never sneak up on him again like a hidden virus.

"I need to rest," he yelled. "I can't keep up."

Nick walked back to where Corey stood against a pine tree.

"What's the point of following him, Nick? He'll be impossible to find in the dark."

"If you'd hunted with your father a bit more, you'd know it's unethical to abandon the hunt once an animal's been hit."

Corey uttered a defensive laugh and let the comment pass. "How can you even hunt, anyway? You'll lose your membership in the Gay Men's Club of America." He meant it as a joke, one last attempt to diffuse the escalating friction.

"I'm not a walking gay cliché like you, Mr. Artiste. Hunting is something I grew up with, something I like to do. Maybe for once you could be supportive? I supported you through all of your shit. I was there for you in the hospital."

Humor bolted from Corey's mind. "How dare you? What happened last year is in the past. You promised it would stay there."

"Maybe so, but you seem to forget how I've sacrificed, how I was there for you when even your own parents didn't come to visit."

"You didn't come to see me either, not until the next day!"

"I was in Miami. On business. You knew that. And then when I did show up you refused to let me into the room."

"Right, you were in Miami on business. Over the weekend, with Evan."

"Oh, give me a fucking break. Not this again. You know that trip was critical to my job, and nothing happened. I couldn't tell you Evan was at the conference because you'd go off the deep end. And I was right. Besides, I needed my job once you so carelessly lost yours."

"That's not fair. I was depressed. I couldn't go back to work. I can't help it if my past finally overwhelmed me."

"Yes, you could have helped it. I did. I've had my share of hurts and abuse too, Corey. But the difference is that I never let mine affect anyone else."

"Seriously? Your fucked up background totally affected me. And us."

"Here we go again. Let me see. My being abused led to rampant promiscuity and an inability to commit and then to all of our conflicts as a couple. Did I get that about right?"

"You can be a real son of a bitch, Nick."

"Yeah, well at least this son of a bitch handles life head-on instead of repressing emotions to the point where they require hospitalization."

"Oh, I forgot. I'm supposed to mimic your masterful control of emotions. Forgive me for not living up to your example of fucking perfection."

"Well, that's what you were supposed to learn in treatment, wasn't it? To let go of the past and finally man up?"

"Man up? Jesus Christ, you're just like my father."

"I'm like your father? That's a laugh. You're the spitting image of Frank Fischer, and not just in looks."

"What's that supposed to mean?"

"It means the apple didn't fall from the tree. Or should I say, the damaged apple?"

Corey gripped the handgun in his coat pocket. For the first time in his life, the idea of harming another human being crossed his mind. His right hand flexed involuntarily around the gun.

"Damaged? How so?"

"Come on, Corey. Your family's messed up. A domineering, abusive father and passive mother. Half the time you're like Ginny, half the time like Frank. You brought a lot of baggage into this relationship."

Corey laughed. "I brought baggage? That's rich, coming from you."

"My problems are no worse than the average person, but at least my family functioned normally."

Corey began a defense, but Nick interrupted.

"You should thank me. A lot of guys would've turned and ran once you pulled that stunt with the pills—the attention-seeking suicide attempt. But I stayed. And do you think that was easy for me? Dealing with your depression and family-induced despair?"

No answer from Corey.

"I mean, how long am I supposed to carry the burden of someone else's life, huh? I've tried doing the right thing for you, Corey. You needed stable support, and I gave it to you."

The rage inside Corey's head obliterated the words forming in his mouth.

"Now, enough of this pointless *déjà vu*. Let's go."

Nick resumed the hunt. Shoving aside pine branches, he tracked the bloody trail. Corey cast his gaze left and right into the trees as he shadowed behind. Unfamiliar noises swarmed. Something rustled in the fallen leaves. A pair of wings swooped close to Corey's head. He reached for a branch of tamarack, holding on to it for a moment while walking past, as if protecting someone behind him from getting whacked.

Nick's voice broke the silence, as the path they followed started a gradual descent. "What's at the bottom of this hill?"

"There's a spring-fed stream, about four feet across. Why?"

"The deer will definitely be heading toward that creek. Losing blood is making him crave water. We'll find him at the stream, just like Frank said."

Corey stopped.

"What do you mean, just like Frank said?"

Nick stopped too. He turned and looked at Corey. "What are you talking about?"

"My father. You referenced Frank, as if he gave you some important advice from beyond the grave about tracking a wounded deer."

"There you go again, making up fantasies in your mind. I said no such thing."

Corey knew he was right, 100 percent. Just like when he heard Evan's deep voice in a Miami hotel room through the phone. He heard what Nick had said. But why? When would Nick and Frank have talked about anything, let alone hunting?

He had a weird hunch.

"You went hunting with my father?"

"Like that would ever happen." Nick laughed. "Think about it."

"That's the only way you'd have known what my father would say about a wounded deer seeking water."

"Listen, forget it. Let's get down to the stream. We gotta locate that deer before we get lost."

Corey remained standing while Nick continued ten feet farther.

"I won't just forget it," Corey yelled. "You said that because it happened, or in some sick attempt to mess with me. Which is it? Are you a sneak or a son of a bitch?"

Nick's silence told Corey all he needed to know.

"So it is true. When was this?"

"When was what?"

"When did you go hunting with my father?"

"I already told you I didn't. Now cut this shit, and help me find the deer."

Corey didn't budge.

"You clearly said you heard about tracking a wounded deer at a stream from Frank. When did you hear that? You owe me an explanation."

"Fine. If you really want to know, it was last year when you were in the hospital, but I never went hunting with him. That idea is absurd, if you really think about it."

"What do you mean, when I was in the hospital?"

"I mean when I got back from Miami and you refused to let me in the room. I called your parents to let them know what happened. Frank hung up on me and refused to answer when I called back. Not knowing what else to do, I drove to Pepin and told your parents that they needed to visit you. I was doing it for you, Corey."

"For me?"

"Your father had set the whole thing in motion when he said those horrible words. I wanted him to come to Minneapolis and apologize to you in person. Despite his bigoted views, I was hoping he'd at least meet you half-way."

"Half-way? As in, he only had to accept me and our rela-tionship half the time? Or, better yet, maybe I could've agreed to only be gay half the time? You knew my bastard of a father was never, ever going to accept me. I read it myself in black and white thirty years ago. My father hated queers. And that means he hated me."

"Give me a break. You had just tried to take your own life, and I didn't know what else to do or how to help you. I went there to appeal to your parents' sense of decency."

"Yeah? And how'd that turn out? I don't remember seeing my loving father in the hospital."

"Not so well, obviously. He did let me in the house, once I yelled through the screen window that you had tried to commit suicide. We all sat at the kitchen table and I told them what I knew, which wasn't a lot at that point. Your mother listened and cried."

Corey felt a deep pang in his heart. He and Ginny had yet to speak directly about that awful night.

"Then I told them how Frank's cruel words had sparked the crisis. That's when he got defensive, and our conversation took a nasty turn."

Corey looked at Nick in disbelief. "In all of the therapy we had last year, you never thought to mention this once?"

"There was no point, Corey. My efforts didn't do any good, and I knew you'd be upset that I even went there, like you are right now."

"Of course I'm upset, and not just about your ill-conceived visit to Pepin. On top of that, you've proved to be a massive liar—yet again."

"As usual, you're missing the point. I went to see your par-ents out of a desire to help you. And a lot of good it did me—all I got was chastised and rebuked."

"How so?"

"As soon as I brought up your father telling you to never come back to his house, he denied responsibility and turned the blame back on me. Frank said that you were wounded the minute you arrived back in Pepin that day, and that you were clearly bothered by something else, something obviously to do with me."

Corey could hardly believe what he was hearing. For the past sixteen months he had no idea of this confrontation between his father and Nick, a heated moment that was solely about him.

"He said that I must have done something to upset you and accused me of changing you over the years from a polite compliant son into someone who rejected his religious upbringing, someone who could utter cruel, disrespectful things about Frank being a shitty husband and father."

Corey listened without reply. The story confused him—who was the actual bad guy in this tale, Nick or Frank?

"He blamed me for turning you against them, and for influencing you to rarely come home to Pepin. Frank surmised that your unexpected, last-minute visit was a cry for help, and that you were obviously fleeing from me or something I had done. Frank said that you coming home to Pepin that day was like an injured animal in search of a sip of water, like a mortally wounded deer desperately seeking to quench its thirst."

This part of Nick's explanation was the first thing that seemed to make any sense. Of course, Frank would equate the situation to hunting. As a kid, every lesson he taught Corey, every story meant to convey a serious message, was told using examples from hunting or the natural world.

"That's why I mentioned your father's comment about the wounded deer likely heading toward the creek, and now I regret that I did," Nick paused. "But who cares? It's no big deal."

"No big deal? Are you kidding me? You shouldn't have gone, and you know it. You went there and begged. You gave Frank the chance to reject us once again, and he took it."

Nick turned away, moving silently into the darkening forest. "Yep, and now he's dead, so what's the big fucking deal?"

The biting utterance was aimed away from Corey, toward the trees ahead, but he heard every word. That was Nick's style. Never a deep cut, his words were meant to prick like a sneaky sliver, irritating for hours beneath a single layer of skin.

"It is a big fucking deal," Corey yelled. "And it explains why I felt like you'd been in my parents' house before, you lying son of a bitch. I'll bet that's what my mother wanted to talk to me about in private."

"What do you mean?"

"Never mind." A mix of reactions flooded Corey's psyche—anger at his father, contempt for Nick, and a hatred of them both equally. The hatred ran so deep that it blocked his mind from forming coherent thoughts. Instinctively, he followed Nick who once again walked deeper into the woods. Corey's subconscious mind took over as he struggled to keep pace, raising his physical and mental temperature so high that all he could feel was heat, which in turn generated a deep thirst. He craved nothing more right now than a deep swallow of cold water. Corey struggled to find a meditation to calm his mind. He began repeating another series of silent chants.

> I am worthy of love.
> And I will claim it no matter what.

Soon, he was breathing more calmly, in and out. What remained at the forefront of his awareness was still the hatred. But it was no longer an intense loathing that burned like a thunderbolt. Instead, Corey felt a resolute enmity that simmered toward a powerful boil. His son of a bitch father was dead. There would be no reckoning for all his sins, the sins that caused Corey so much anguish throughout his life. But Nick was here, in front of him. Corey had the most leverage he had ever felt in their twenty-year relationship. He knew where he was going on these paths, despite the darkness, and for the first time in his life he felt he had nothing to lose. And, he remembered his wish after seeing the passing double trains back in Pepin.

Finally, he spoke.

"Our relationship is over, isn't it?"

Nick stopped and turned around.

"Is that a question or a statement?"

Corey wasn't certain. And it didn't really matter. Nick's reaction is what mattered. He pondered Nick's snotty reply—"Is that a question or a statement?" Corey had asked it in his own mind countless times. He had even answered it—sometimes yes, sometimes not yet. He cleared his throat and gave his reply.

"It's a question. I want to know if our relationship is over."

Nick deflected with a snicker. "Maybe you should shoot me first and ask questions later."

Corey thrust both hands into his coat pockets, one set of fingers gripping the flashlight, the others clutching the Woodsman.

"Because if it's over, Nick, then we're splitting everything down the middle, fifty-fifty."

"And I suppose you've got a sound basis for that? Even though we're not legally married?"

"What? What are you talking about?"

"I'm talking about the fact that we're not married."

"Yes we are. It happened in Thunder Bay four years ago. You were there, remember?"

"Yeah, I remember. But so what?"

"We got legally married, that's what. And any marriage performed outside the state is now valid in Minnesota for same-sex couples, as of last summer. Remember attending the rally at the State Capitol?"

"Oh, I'm aware of the law, and I was there, but your facts aren't exactly correct."

Nick's reply unnerved Corey. "We each said 'I do.' Julian performed the ceremony. He was definitely official because I saw the ordination certificate myself. I think you're the one who's got his facts mixed-up."

"You're right about Julian getting his credentials on-line to perform weddings. But his status was only valid in jurisdictions that allow for internet certification."

"So?"

"So, Julian never registered with the Ontario government as a licensed provincial officiant. The marriage wasn't finalized in the eyes of the Canadian government, so there's nothing for the State of Minnesota to recognize. You might have been there to witness something, but it wasn't a legal marriage."

Corey stood, speechless. A flood of questions formed in his mind. Finally, he verbalized one.

"You knew our marriage was a sham the entire time and never said a word? What kind of sick bastard are you?"

"Actually, it was your sickness that brought it to light, Corey, when I tried to get into the psych ward to see you last year. Remember?"

"What are you talking about?"

"When I got to the hospital, you and Billy instructed the staff to refuse me entry. I told them we were married and that I was legally entitled to enter that room. They asked for proof. I was so pissed off and let every nurse and doctor within earshot know that they would be sued for discrimination. But they wouldn't back down. So I drove home, found our signed marriage certificate with Julian's name as the officiant and Carol as a witness, then went back to the ER."

"I don't see the problem, then."

"Long story short, what I showed them wasn't good enough. They said I had to produce a marriage license authorized in Minnesota. I guess the poor-quality printing gave them pause. I searched our files for ours and had Julian search his too. I finally called the courthouse in Ontario to try and get one on a rush basis. I was on hold for at least twenty minutes. The woman was nice, but eventually she came back and said she had no record of either our ceremony or of Julian being registered. I called him right away, and together we figured out what had happened. He felt horrible that he never registered. He didn't even know he was supposed to. Voila, the ceremony wasn't authorized, and we were never married."

"But you still wear a ring. You've got it on right now."

"I paid good money for this ring, and I like it. That doesn't mean it has to symbolize anything."

"You son of a bitch. You kept this from me for over a year?"

"Like I was going to drop that bombshell right after you tried to take your own life? I may be heartless, Corey, but I'm not cruel."

"In your case I see little difference. You could have found a way to let me know before now."

"There was never a good time to tell you. Anyway, in retrospect, it's for the best. That little oversight will make our break-up that much easier."

"Maybe so, but I still get an equal share once we go our separate ways."

Nick paused and appeared to be thinking. "Don't worry, Corey. You'll get what you deserve."

"I know, and I deserve half. I've contributed to this relationship just like you."

"Not even close. While I worked forty plus hours per week, you chose to work part-time at the museum and spent the rest of the time pursuing your hobby—art."

"You supported that plan."

"What choice did I have? You were adamant and whining."

"You said my paintings showed promise and encouraged me to take a chance at being a break-out success."

"Look, I'm no art expert. I only went along with it because you cried like a little girl in order to get your way."

"That's not true. Regardless, the fact that you're the bread-winner doesn't make your role any more valuable than mine. I cooked your meals and hosted countless parties for your co-workers."

Nick gave a mocking snort. "Okay, whatever you say. Good luck with that argument in court without actually being married."

"Well, if not half, then what do you think I deserve?"

Nick stared at Corey and seemed to be thinking carefully about a reply.

"Come on, how much?"

"I'm not going to answer that. Not right now."

"Typical—failure under pressure. Well I'll tell you this. Once I inform the judge about your multiple indiscretions, I might just end up owning everything we've got."

"That ain't gonna happen, Corey. The only way you'll get it all is if I die this weekend, before returning home to change my will. After that, you won't be entitled to a goddamn thing."

Nick's utterance of that last syllable coincided with a thunderous crash, followed by the sound of something writhing in the leaves nearby. Nick turned and looked behind him.

"That's our buck. He must've fallen. Let's go."

Nick turned and resumed a torrid pace. Corey trailed reluctantly, still in shock over all he'd just heard. Of course, he remembered telling the hospital staff to keep Nick out of his room. At the time, Corey was enraged and upset about hearing Evan's voice on the phone. Billy was there in the psych ward to support him, and that's all that mattered. In retrospect, it was the right decision. Nick wasn't Corey's husband after all. He was nothing more than a stranger—a stranger who repeatedly cheated and lied.

Corey kept his hands firmly in his coat pockets grasping the gun and the flashlight. Tall pine trees obscured light from the night sky. Shadows impersonated bear and wolf. His mind began playing subtle tricks as they moved deeper into the unknown. The graying landscape created new dangers with each passing minute. He wondered whether in fact the deer knowingly led them into this forest as a trap, for revenge.

A harried voice jolted him to attention.

"Get up here and hand me the flashlight. I can't see where the trail of blood runs next."

Corey could barely see Nick in the darkness.

"A 'please' would be nice," Corey snapped.

Nick spun an abrupt 180, taking one loud step toward him. Corey instinctively thrust both hands back into his pockets. There was security in having something to grasp—the flashlight a ray of hope, the gun a means of self-protection.

"If you'd rather just give up now and go home by all means go right ahead. But give me the light 'cause I'm moving on."

"Give up? You think I'm the one who's given up? You checked out of this relationship the day I checked into the hospital."

"Enough with the psycho bullshit, Corey. I'm talking about the goddamn deer!"

A deep, mournful groan pierced the air.

"What's that?"

Corey knew the answer to his question before Nick spoke a single word. The wounded creature wasn't far away. Perhaps crouched behind a fallen jack pine, or sheltered in a shallow divot on the needle-laden ground contemplating a counter-attack with his antlers and a valiant fight in the waning moments of his life.

"Give me the handgun," Nick demanded. "You shine the light on the deer, and I'll finish him off. It's too hard to shoot up close with the rifle."

Nick abruptly lunged his hand toward Corey, with an angry gaze that chilled him more than the cold air seeping into his jacket. He stood, unmoved. If he succumbed to Nick's demands, the deer would be found, and killed.

"No." The tone of Corey's reply was simultaneously defiant and defeated.

"Waaauuuuuuuhhhhhhh."

The gruesome, carnal cry was now louder than before. The deer couldn't be more than ten yards away. Suddenly Corey could see it in the distance. Urgency seized him.

"Fine," Nick shouted. "I'll shine the light, and you kill him. Your father gave you that handgun for exactly this purpose. Now, man up and use it."

Corey's mind raced between admitting defeat or standing his ground. Inside he was riven. The deer moaned again. Its hooves thrashed the dry, fallen leaves in a vain effort to stand. The buck writhed with desperation, then once again wailed in fear, twisting its antlered head, struggling to gain a footing to rise.

Corey closed his own eyes, as if that would stop the agonizing din. His hands remained deep in his pockets, clenching both the flashlight and the gun. An image appeared in his mind—one he didn't expect. He saw his father clear as day, standing before him, a wry smirk across his lips. Behind closed eyelids, Corey stared back at the man who had given him life, who vainly tried raising him to be tough—like father like son. Corey continued his make-believe stare, then silently spoke words that turned Frank's imaginary expression from satisfaction to fear. "You're dead. Your time has passed, old man. You had your chance at redemption, at making things right. And you blew it, you son of a bitch. I hope you rot in hell."

Corey opened his eyes. He could see the struggling deer, momentarily empathizing, mistaking it for a struggle of his own. Turning his head, the man standing in front of him for a moment looked just like Frank. He was barking like Frank too.

"Stop yelling. Please."

Nick either didn't hear him or chose not to. "Give me the damn light so you can kill the deer. Right now. He's in pain."

Nick closed in. Corey's thoughts raced to extremes—surrender, resist. I love him, I hate him.

"No."

His pounding heartbeat was louder than his voice. His hands reacted subconsciously, grasping rival solutions to this painful climax.

"For the last time, give me the goddamn flashlight and pull out your gun."

Give up, man up. I love him, I hate him. Corey could barely breathe. All he could muster was a defiant nod of his head.

"Give me the fucking flashlight!"

Twigs snapped under Nick's angry feet as he reached for Corey's jacket.

Instinctively, Corey drew the flashlight from his left pocket and the Woodsman from his right. Nick grabbed the light from Corey's hand, then rapped him on the side of his head and yelled, "It's about goddamn time!"

Without another conscious thought, Corey pointed the shaking gun at Nick and shot him.

Reckoning

November 2013

1

Thursday

Corey watched Nick fall and saw blood spurt into the air. He was gasping and looking around, stunned, like what the fuck? A voice inside Corey's head said shoot him again—finish the son of a bitch. Instead he turned and ran, the Colt Woodsman heavy in his hands.

A few minutes later he stopped to look back but heard nothing more than his own heavy breathing. The handgun was still in his palm, feeling as though its weight had doubled. He shoved the Colt into his coat pocket. Different choices flashed through Corey's mind before he settled on one. He turned once again in the direction of the cabin, and he ran. He kept on going, bobbing and weaving between the trees. Pine branches whacked him in the face. Visible breath flowed from his mouth, snot from his nose. The temperature had dropped steadily since sunset, and a bitter wind slapped his face. His lungs barely held rapid, successive gulps of air, his body recoiling at each inhalation. Surrounded by darkness, he instinctively took a shortcut back toward the cabin, following familiar landmarks. He crossed the ravine and rushed past the deer stand he had abandoned hours earlier. He also passed the gravestone for his father's dog, then emerged onto the lawn. Despite a renewed throbbing of his injured leg, he didn't slow his pace. The sight of the cabin drew him forward.

With the heft of his shoulder he thrust the door open and

headed straight toward the kitchen sink. He held his mouth open and gulped cold water directly from the faucet. Then he moved to the bedroom and threw his meager belongings into a duffel. There was no time to gather items of value for his mother as he'd promised. That lapse would remain his failure. He grabbed Nick's keys from the table, then left the cabin, pulling the door firmly shut behind him.

He got inside the Jeep and started up the reluctant engine. He pounded the dash with his fist, urging the defroster to function. Finally, the windshield cleared of rime, the heater drying up the accumulating moisture faster than Corey's hot breath replenished it. He pulled the gear into drive, turned a tight 180 in the lawn, then sped out the driveway without looking back.

Five minutes down the road, the phone rang, and his back straightened. He glanced between the pavement and the passenger seat, then drew the device from his bag. The name of Nick's sister flashed on the screen. He forcefully sent the call to voicemail. A minute later, he listened to her message.

"Corey! What's going on? I got a call from Nick, but the reception sucked before the line went dead. I did make out 'Corey' and 'shot.' I called back, but it just rang and rang. I did get a text, showing a location north of Barron. What's going on? I'm really worried. Dad and I are getting in the car to drive over there. We'll call 911 along the way, just in case. Please call me as soon as you get this message."

He had forgotten all about Thanksgiving dinner with the Parkers. But the voice message made him think that an ambulance or sheriff's car might rush past him any minute. Corey noticed his seventy-five-mile-per-hour speed. What if he got pulled over and had to explain carrying a firearm with no permit? And where was he was rushing off to, alone on Thanksgiving night? He slowed to sixty. Questions and answers swirled in his mind. Did he actually shoot Nick? Yes. Did he leave Nick in the woods? Yes. Is it possible Nick might bleed to death? Hell, yes. Then Corey blurted out a question that he couldn't answer. "Oh my God, what have I done?"

He began inhaling deeply, reciting a familiar meditation from his new age therapist.

> Spirit of the world.
> I belong to you.

He abandoned the chant after twenty repetitions, unable to slow the pace of his breath no matter how many mantras he uttered. He considered pulling over to regain his bearings. His eyes darted between the winding country road and the dimly lit screen of the phone still resting in his quivering hand. He scrolled through most of the alphabet until he found the name he wanted. He pushed the "send call" button with his thumb, then listened to a series of rings while drumming the steering wheel with the fingers of his other hand.

"Hey there—"

"Thank God you answered," he interrupted.

"Corey? What's wrong?"

Silence filled the call for several seconds as he choked back a flood of emotions. He managed to utter only one sentence before the dam burst.

"Billy, I need your help."

Through sobs, he told a halting story of what had happened in the woods. Twice Billy asked him to slow down, to repeat what he'd just said. Corey heard a muffled side conversation through the phone. Then Larry's voice replaced Billy's. Corey explained things again, this time a bit slower and without tears. Larry didn't interrupt, but frequently said, "uh huh."

When his story caught up with the present, Larry spoke. Larry told him to call 911 and drive straight to the nearest police station.

"No." Nick's sister had already taken steps to save her brother, if that were even possible.

Larry then advised him to pull into the nearest gas station

and wait for Larry and Billy to come get him. Once again Corey was defiant. He wanted to get far away from Barron County, and fast.

Larry's final suggestion was for Corey to turn south and come home to Pepin. He could figure out the next steps with the people who cared about him most. Corey abruptly said goodbye and turned off his phone. He needed time to think about what he had done... and what he would do next. If Nick died in the woods, Corey would be arrested for murder. His life would be over. How would his mother bear such shame? He considered turning down a remote dirt road, pulling into the dark woods, and killing himself there amidst the trees. If he had already killed one man tonight, why not two? Like his father said years ago, it was the perfect place to hide a body. No one would ever find him.

He cracked the window to let in cool air. The feverish defroster not only cleared the front window, but also overheated the interior of the Jeep. The raw gust slapped his reddened face, reminding him that his feet still felt like ice. A sudden chill traversed him as he awkwardly shook his upper body. Alert from the chilly blast of night air, he summoned the empowering mantras that his therapist had indelibly engraved into his mind.

I am worthy of love. And I will claim it no matter what.
Universe, I belong to you. Deep in my soul, I am love divine.

After repeating those affirmations, a plan came into his mind. He would return to Minneapolis and gather a few things. From there, he'd drive someplace where no one could find him— for a while, at least. Whether Nick was alive or dead no longer mattered. What's done was done.

He pulled into the garage just after seven, alighting from the Jeep, then rushing toward the old brick building where he had lived with Nick for the past ten years. His knee ached, stiff from his run through the woods and the two-hour drive. While riding the elevator to the top floor, he checked his phone for texts or missed calls. Then he remembered having shut off his phone after the frustrating conversation with Larry. He powered it back on.

As he waited for the elevator door to open, he prayed silently. *Please, God, don't let me bump into anyone. Not tonight.* He petitioned an unfamiliar being. It was universalist meditation rather than prayer that typically brought him relief over the past year since his hospitalization. But now, he instinctively reverted to the method of his childhood, a petition to the Catholic God who had yet to grant a single one of his crisis-driven appeals.

He fumbled with his keys at the door. They all looked the same. He had a foreboding sense that someone was waiting on the other side of the threshold. He opened the door and stepped inside, then stumbled over the Hoover vacuum and fell to the tiled floor. He picked himself up, flipped on the hall light switch, and hustled toward the bedroom, intent on packing a few belongings and clean clothes though still unsure of his journey's ultimate destination. He shoved shirts, pants, and underwear into a suitcase, not worrying about wrinkling them. He emptied his personal drawer into a cardboard box—listening as bracelets, eyewear, and coins from foreign lands fell with a thud. Somewhere down the road he'd sort out the true necessities from this pile of possessions. He did the same in the bath and hall closets, emptying shelves and drawers wholesale into another suitcase. He was careful not to take anything belonging to Nick. He wanted no reminders of his former lover.

And then Corey saw it—Kahlo's "Wounded Deer" hanging on the bedroom wall. The painting's image brought him back to Barron, to the carnage he had left in the woods. Deep pain stared back at him from the painted face on the wall. He had seen that look before. He saw it in an injured, anguished eighteen-point buck. He saw it in the enraged, cruel countenance of Nick. Corey even saw it several times in a reflection from the rear-view mirror earlier tonight, as he had sped away from the cabin.

He carried two suitcases to the garage, loading them into the trunk of his Prius. There was relief at the prospect of driving his own vehicle. He hated Nick's Jeep. For the longest time, he had wanted to drive something sporty, more fun—like an Audi TT. But Nick had insisted Corey buy something practical—and used, as well.

He went back upstairs to get the cardboard box. As he burst out of the elevator and into the hall, he ran straight into Mrs. Randall.

"Oh, Corey." She clutched her breast. "You scared the daylights out of me."

"Sorry, Mrs. Randall. I'm in a bit of a hurry."

"I can see that. Why the rush on a holiday? Nothing's really open, you know."

"I'm... uh... I'm hauling some things out of the condo."

"I was wondering about that. I heard you come and go a few times. I even looked out the peephole to see who was making all that ruckus."

"Sorry to have bothered you. This is the last load." He moved toward his own front door, willing the conversation to end.

"Isn't Nick helping you? I haven't seen him lift a finger all night."

He paused, then turned back around to face her. "He's at his sister's for Thanksgiving, so I'm moving stuff all on my own."

Mrs. Randall cocked her head. "It's a shame you two aren't together for the holiday. That's not good for a relationship, you know."

"Yes, that's true." The walls in their building were not soundproofed. Mrs. Randall certainly listened in on his quarrels with Nick. On occasion she had dropped nuggets of wisdom into their hallway conversations based upon squabbles she had clearly overheard.

"Do you want to join me for a piece of apple pie, seeing as you and I are all alone tonight?"

He scoured his mind for an excuse. Despite growing hunger pains, stopping for a slice of dessert was not in Corey's plan.

"No thank you, I've really got to finish taking out these boxes."

"Well, maybe when you're through?"

"How about a rain check, Mrs. Randall? I've got to unpack everything over at the studio. I won't be back until late."

"Are you okay, Corey?"

He squinted his eyes and turned his head, wondering if she had detected the bulge of the gun. He stuck both hands into his coat pockets and hugged the Colt tighter to his side.

"Me? Yeah. Why do you ask?"

"You seem a little jumpy, that's all. Sweaty too. I haven't seen you in such rough shape since, well, you know."

He assumed she meant the night the paramedics wheeled him out of the building a year before. His pause allowed her an opening to continue.

"And I heard about your father. I'm sorry for your loss. I haven't had a chance to tell you in person. This is the first time I've seen you since I learned of it."

"That's very kind, ma'am. But I'm fine. I just need to finish this work and then rest."

"Suit yourself. Maybe tomorrow? I'll be home all day."

"Sure thing. Save me a slice."

Back inside the condo, he briefly considered taking a shower. He sniffed his armpit and winced. Corey longed to be clean, to wash away the layers of grime he acquired in the course of this unusually long day. But he didn't want to linger in the condo any longer than necessary, and the unexpected hallway chat had already cost him five minutes. A good long shower would have to wait. He paused before leaving home for what he presumed would be the very last time. It dawned on him how little this space appealed to him. He saw Nick everywhere—in the fixtures Nick selected, in the way the furniture was arranged, even in the artwork adorning the walls. None of it was Corey's creation. Nick had insisted on hanging only the works of known artists in their condo. Corey turned off the light, grabbed the cardboard box from the floor, and left.

He got in the car and drove ten blocks. The condo was nice, but his art studio was home. Beyond canvases, brushes, and paint, there he also kept his most personal possessions—a tackle box full of fishing lures he had accumulated with Billy, a packet of ribbons marking his grade school track and field victories, and two county fair medals he won alongside his mother for their home-made raspberry jam. There were also several notebooks, the journals he had kept since age nine. They held his most secret and personal thoughts.

In a safe tucked behind a series of stacked poster boards, Corey had also hidden a substantial amount of money he'd saved from random art sales over the past fifteen years —for emergencies or a rainy day. Nick had no knowledge of the cash because Corey never told him. He opened the safe and dropped his head closer toward its dark interior. He smelled the mustiness of old papers and of the greenbacks that had been fingered by thousands of hands. He removed the entire stack, totaling almost ten thousand dollars, and placed all of it into a faded leather pouch.

As he scanned the studio once more, he stopped and stared at the poster from last year's art festival in Marfa. That was it— Marfa, Texas. That's where he would go. It was a two-day drive, but no one would suspect him to be there. He knew some resident artists and gallery owners, people who might take him in for a few days or help him get what he needed. From Marfa, he could cross into Mexico and from there, who knows? He didn't have to plan the rest of his life tonight.

He packed everything into the car, including as many art supplies as the trunk would hold. Though he wanted to take every work in progress, there was only room for one large canvas. He left everything else behind, along with a cryptic note for Carol, saying that he was escaping for a while, perhaps forever. He promised to call from somewhere down the road. His note said that she could either have or donate his things. Rent was paid through the end of the year. He scribbled his name, drew a heart, then closed the door and left.

2

Thursday

Corey placed the last load of art supplies in the trunk, then got into the front seat. He drove away, clutching the steering wheel tightly while crossing through a dozen city intersections. He lightened his grip after joining the freeway, the odometer rapidly recording each satisfying mile.

An hour and a half outside the city, he looked down at the dashboard.

"Shit."

The fuel gauge rested near empty. Like him, the car was close to running on fumes. He spotted a barely lit sign advertising a truck stop five miles ahead. Surely it would be open on a holiday. It was. As he pulled off the freeway and into the station, he wondered for a second if there was another choice for filling up with gas. The place looked as though it hadn't changed one iota in thirty years. There was but one outpost for cars with no overhang covering the pumps. The others offered diesel for large trucks. Two large streetlamps sitting atop a single metal pole illuminated the entire lot. A shabby, one-story building sat several yards farther away from the road.

He pulled up to the pump and shut off the engine. The place seemed almost deserted. Of course, this was the middle of nowhere on Thanksgiving night. Corey's was the only car parked in either the gravel lot or at the pumps. A few semi-trucks and trailers were convened to the left of the run-down building. He was surprised that a place like this still existed—no security cameras, no music blaring from a speaker, and no option to pay by credit card there at the pump. That last part was fine with Corey. Card transactions could be traced. He was paying for everything now in cash.

He walked inside the shop to pay for fuel in advance. While waiting for the clerk to return to the front counter, Corey scanned the interior of the truck stop which offered shelves filled with candy, gum, and nuts near the register, paired with a small diner all in one room no bigger than his condo. A few men sat alone in booths. Two were at the counter. He assumed they were long-haul truckers. Their appearance reminded him of the red-necks at the Sportsmen's Club where he obtained his hunting license as a kid—the men who mercilessly laughed at him when he was the butt of those humiliating jokes. He also thought that each of those truckers looked pathetic, spending the holiday together like a group of orphans, staring at their individual plates and saying nothing—solitary, in a sea of collective loneliness. Part of him longed to sit down and enjoy a hot meal too, perhaps the turkey and mashed potato special advertised on the white board. But he just wanted to keep going, to get farther away from all he was leaving behind. He noticed that one of the men made eye contact for longer than seemed natural. Corey looked away once the clerk approached the register. He handed her three ten-dollar bills.

"Put this on pump number two, please. And I'll take a pack a gum."

"That'll be another dollar, even."

He fumbled in his wallet for a dollar bill and handed it to the clerk. Before returning outside, he stopped in the men's room. He froze at the sight of someone standing astride one of the two close-set urinals with no barrier between. From behind, the guy looked like Nick, though several years younger. Corey approached the second urinal, then reached down and unzipped his fly. He shifted his eyes to the left, looking at the man standing next to him, and caught him staring back—first at Corey's face, then a bit lower. It was the same guy from the dining counter who had been staring back at him. From the front, the man looked nothing like Nick and everything like the bad boys in Corey's fantasies—pierced studs in both ears and his nose, some sort of tattoo running up and down the left side of his neck, and an enchanting goatee of bushy brown hair. He could have been the twin of innumerable porn stars Corey watched in videos when Nick was out of town, the type of man worthy of masturbatory imaginings, and the kind of guy Corey hadn't hooked up with in almost twenty years.

He once again fixed his gaze straight ahead toward the wall, but soon couldn't resist looking down and to his left. The man produced no stream of urine. Instead, he was erect and tugging his foreskin back and forth. All of a sudden, the guy pushed himself back into his jeans. He washed and dried his hands at the sink, then walked toward Corey at the urinal and leaned in close.

"My truck is the silver one with red trim. Meet me there."

Corey felt the man's finger trace the outline of Corey's shoulder blades through his jacket, then heard him walk across the tiled floor and exit the restroom. He looked down to his own waning stream of urine, then finished and zipped up fast. He had always found southern drawl's a bit intriguing, and on a rough-looking guy it was downright erotic. He was distracted trying to picture the guy swishing his finger across Corey's back, imagining that same finger summoning him toward the truck. He forgot to stop and wash his hands on the way out the door. The guy stood at the register paying for his evening meal as Corey left the building and walked toward the fuel pumps. He stuck the unleaded nozzle into his gas tank and listened as the car began filling up. He saw the guy from the restroom exit the building, staring intently at Corey as he walked toward the semi-trucks parked and idling at the far end of the complex.

Corey jumped at the sound of a hard clunk and looked up to see the meter on the pump which showed exactly thirty bucks. He returned the nozzle to its holster, then dropped into the front seat and ignited the car's engine. He sat for a moment, deciding which direction to turn. He could see the large silver rig ahead and to the left, parked a few spaces away from the others, with faint light emanating from the cab. To Corey's right was a dirt road leading to the freeway and his intended escape from today's hell.

He imagined Nick lying dead in the woods. Then again, maybe the Parkers arrived in Barron in time to save him, and Nick might still be alive. One way or another, he thought, the bastard was out of his life for good. Corey was free to do whatever and with whomever he pleased, until the law caught up with him of course. Then his freedoms might evaporate. This could be the last opportunity to do exactly as he desired. His thoughts flowed quickly back to the men's room and the stimulating touch of the pierced man's finger on his back. How long had it been since anyone touched Corey that way, expressed desire for him like that? He didn't care any longer that his body reeked from sweat and grime. Something primal drew him toward that truck. He pulled the gear into drive and turned left.

He parked on the far side of the silver rig and turned off the car's engine. Corey found a tin of breath mints in the center console and then popped two of them onto his tongue. Would the guy want to kiss? Maybe, and he'd better be prepared. He bit down hard on the white tablets. Sucking them would take too much time. He cringed as the peppermint oil stung inside his mouth.

Corey exited the Prius, then stepped up to the passenger side of the semi and opened the door. The driver drew a curtain across the windshield, then looked at Corey and nodded his head before disappearing into the sleeper compartment. With the same finger that summoned Corey from the men's room, he was now beckoned to follow the guy into the back of the cab. He climbed up the steep step and onto the passenger seat, banging his coat and the protected gun against the metal door. He forgot the damn thing was still in his pocket, his hand reaching out as if to protect the brutal device or to make sure it had not gone off. He pulled the door shut.

The cab smelled like a high school locker room. A pair of paper coffee cups sat in a holder between the two front seats, one filled with sunflower seeds still resting within their black and gray husks, the other half-full of empty shells. He noticed the music, Brantley Gilbert's virile voice flowing from the speakers directly into Corey's accepting ears.

The guy grabbed Corey by the shoulders and pulled him into the back of the cab. He moved in with an open mouth for a kiss, and Corey let the guy's tongue come inside. He tasted the tang of nicotine, barely covered up with a trace of wintergreen. He sensed a trembling in the bearded stranger's body, then felt his pants being unbuttoned. He lay back against a hard pillow as the man dropped his head toward Corey's lap. He heard a belt buckle slap against the side of the compartment and the unzipping of the trucker's pants. Corey flicked away the man's baseball cap and placed both of his hands atop the guy's cleanly-shaven head. He closed his eyes and imagined being swallowed whole, as the trucker stroked him with his dorsoventral stud. Corey closed his eyes and strained his neck. The stale smell of the cab gave way to whiffs of pungent male sweat, the trucker's body producing pheromones that made Corey simply want more.

"Okay," Corey said as he lifted the guy's sweatshirt over his head. "Get on your knees. Now."

The trucker turned toward the opposite end of the bunk before pulling his pants the rest of the way off. Corey removed his hunting jacket and hung it over the front seat. He left his shirt on. His jeans and underwear bunched at the ankles.

"I got condoms in the glovebox. Can you grab one?" The trucker pointed toward the front dash.

"Not tonight," Corey replied. "I'm going in raw. If you want me, this is how it's gonna be."

The trucker opened his hands in wide surrender, then readied himself for Corey's uncommon, quiet aggression. For the next several minutes there were guttural utterances of carnal gratification. Corey recognized in himself a power that had lain dormant for a very long time. He took it slow, felt the trucker's bald head and caressed the black metal gauge in his left earlobe.

Corey briefly closed his eyes. When he opened them, he noticed something in the front of the cab. Though dark in the sleeper compartment, a dome light illuminated the dashboard. His eyes were drawn to the visor. Elastic bands held a few unremarkable scraps of paper, possibly route information or punch cards for a favorite place to get coffee and donuts. Corey couldn't read them from where he was kneeling behind the trucker's ass. But he clearly saw a picture strapped to the visor. It looked a bit worn, as if touched too many times. In the photograph stood a pretty woman and a young girl. The truck driver was behind them both, smiling. As if needing confirmation, Corey glanced at the gold ring encircling a finger on the man's left hand, which was being used now to bear some of the trucker's weight. The confusing pleasure of the moment evaporated. Corey looked down at the man whose head was pitched to the side and facing backward to consider his dominator. In that face, Corey no longer saw the inked, pierced bad boy of his dreams, but rather the faces of two familiar cheaters.

"I gotta go," Corey said as he extricated himself from the trucker, then sat against a pillow and pulled himself back inside his jeans. The trucker turned his body to face Corey, then rose to his knees.

"What? Just like that?"

"This isn't right. I need to leave."

"Come on. We'll try something different. What do you like?"

"What I'd like is to leave, so move."

The trucker was blocking the only path for Corey to squeeze between the seats and climb into the front of the cab. The guy refused to budge. Corey pushed him, and the guy shoved him right back. Corey hit his head on the rear compartment, on the same spot where Nick had whacked him with the flashlight hours earlier.

"Ouch!"

"What the fuck's your problem, dude? You're the one who came over to my truck and got inside."

"Yeah, and now I want out. You're married, and I'm not gonna be part of your deceit."

The truck driver still refused to move or allow Corey to pass. He sat between the two front seats, blocking the way and breathing heavily. "So what if I'm married? It's better than being a full-fledged faggot."

Corey looked around the sleeper compartment, silently searching for a way to escape. He grabbed his coat from the back of the passenger seat.

"Who the fuck are you to judge me anyway? My life is my own business."

Corey awkwardly placed his arms into his coat sleeves as he desperately tried to think how to get out of this mess.

"You're the one who came here lookin' for anonymous sex. No one held a gun to your head."

As he rebuttoned his open coat, Corey remembered what rested in the pocket. He leaned forward slowly while looking the trucker straight in the eyes, then pulled out the Colt Woodsman and pointed.

"Get out of my way."

"Whoa, whoa." The guy backed up and let Corey squeeze through to the front. Then he grabbed Corey's arm from behind, trying to wrest away the gun. Corey fell forward onto the passenger seat, landing on his left shoulder while gripping the gun even tighter with his right hand to hold on. They struggled for a few seconds before the Colt fired inside the truck. Corey brought his hands up to instinctively cover both ears, realizing that the gun was still in his grasp. A dull sound of bells rang in his ear. He couldn't hear anything else.

He shuffled toward the door, then opened it and jumped out onto the gravel-covered ground. He landed on his feet before falling onto his knee, bracing himself with his already injured free hand. The gun fell from his other hand to the ground. He grunted through clenched teeth the minute the searing pain from the scabbed injuries on his wrist and knee took the brunt of the unco-ordinated landing. He rolled onto his back and clutched his knee with both hands, rubbing himself near the reopened wound. He felt a trickle of liquid pooling at his kneecap before it began run-ning down his leg.

The semi blocked the streetlamp, but there was just enough light for Corey to see his surroundings. He reached around the gravel until he located the gun. He stuffed it back into his coat pocket, then gingerly rose to his feet.

He looked up toward the semi, expecting to see the truck-er climb down and come after him. But there was no movement from inside. And he heard no sound, other than a buzz from the nearby freeway and a still-faint ringing in his ears.

Corey stumbled to his car, then got in and drove away.

3

Thursday

The Colt Woodsman remained in his right coat pocket. Corey couldn't help but repeatedly feel the bulge created by that despicable instrument of death. He also worried about it accidentally going off, again. With his eyes fixed on the road, he gently removed the gun from his pocket and placed it underneath the seat, then drove on.

Back on the freeway, he set the cruise control to the posted limit. He didn't trust himself to abide by the law, and the last thing he wanted now was to be stopped for speeding. With both hands gripping the steering wheel, he stared straight ahead, replaying in his mind what had happened back at the truck stop.

A large sign alongside the freeway welcomed him to Iowa. It would be two more hours to Des Moines, another five to Kansas City. His gut told him to keep driving, to put as much space as possible between him and the trail of destruction he'd left behind. He also wanted to get to Marfa. Corey willed himself to focus on the road, fighting exhaustion and anguish and fear. But his body and mind were spent. He also started questioning his ability to make decisions. His conscious choices today felt universally disastrous—each and every one.

When a road sign heralded an upcoming off-ramp for Mason City, Corey ignored his instincts and exited the freeway instead. If his gut told him to drive on to Marfa via the fastest route, then it was probably best to get off the main road right away. By now, the trucker might be coming after him or radioing to a buddy up ahead—unless the gunshot had incapacitated him, or worse. Corey felt exposed here on the freeway and figured he'd have more anonymity on a darker two-lane road. At the top of the exit, he brought up the GPS on his phone, expanding and moving the screen with shaky fingers until he found a county road that would take him east, then connecting to a state highway where he could turn south through Iowa.

Just after eleven, the car entered Charles City. He had driven for two hours since leaving the truck stop. Fatigue overwhelmed him. He simply couldn't drive another mile. He noticed a motel on the south end of the town. "Hunters Welcome," boasted the flapping sign below the marquee. The drowsy clerk emerged from a room behind the front desk after Corey entered. She hesitated when Corey offered cash and refused to show ID. He assured her that he had lost his wallet while hunting and was driving home with only a meager cash donation from a friend. He watched as she examined him from head to toe, still adorned in his dirty hunting clothes. His request for a bandage and explanation of having fallen on a rock and wounding his wrist and knee provoked a relaxation in her voice and sudden openness to accepting cash.

"Here you go, hon." She handed him the room key and a first aid kit, then returned to her back office as Corey walked out the door.

The room was basic—a double bed, lamps on the nightstands, and worn-down wall-to-wall carpet. Corey forgot to ask for non-smoking. He regretted the omission once he smelled that distinct odor held tightly in the woven fabric of the tattered curtains hanging across the window. It reminded him of the truck driver's breath. But he was too tired to go back and ask for a different room. He'd be asleep within minutes, anyway—not alert long enough for the disgusting scent to matter.

He turned the deadbolt behind him and strung the safety chain into its slot. He wasn't expecting visitors. No one knew he was there. He took the cell phone out of his pocket and sat down on the bed. He had felt it vibrate several times since leaving Minneapolis. But he had let everything go to voicemail. He scanned through scores of missed calls—from Billy, Larry, Nick's sister, and several unexpected ones from Carol. He longed to hear a friendly voice, but he wasn't ready for others to tell him what to do. So he decided against listening to any of the messages, for now. He also wasn't eager to talk with his mother. There would come a day when he might need to explain things to her, but not tonight. He would rather let her fall asleep with the burdens she already carried.

He set the phone on the nightstand and connected it to his charger, then plugged that into the wall. He shed his clothing piece by piece, tossing each item into the plastic laundry bag from the hotel closet. His discarded shirt and jeans would need to be washed thoroughly in hot water. They reeked like never before. He wondered for a moment if he should simply throw them away, especially after considering the bountiful red stain covering one of the pant legs. He climbed into a steaming hot shower and stood in the tub for a quarter of an hour. It was the most mindful bathing he had experienced since a week ago after falling hard on the pavement, just before learning that his father had died. That seemed like years ago now, though it had been less than a week. *How fast life can change*, he thought—*how fast, and how much?*

Corey stepped out of the shower and dried himself. He lifted his foot onto the toilet seat and dabbed tissue on the knee injury until it felt sufficiently dry. He reached for the first aid kit the motel clerk had provided, pulling out a roll of gauze and some tape. He was grateful to find a small tube of antibiotic gel in the kit and applied it generously to his gash. He then covered the injury with several layers of the gauze, ripped three pieces of medical tape from the roll with his teeth and finished dressing his wound.

He emerged from the bathroom wearing only a thin white towel. He sat down on the bed, torn between competing urges—

feeding his hunger and calling someone. Corey was famished, having eaten nothing since the granola bar in the Barron County woods. While hurrying to leave the cabin in a panic, he hadn't thought of food. Even when racing through the condo and passing by the refrigerator, he never gave eating a single thought. Only now did he acknowledge his appetite, here alone in the motel room in a town where he knew no one by name. He thought about ordering a pizza but doubted anything was open as it neared midnight on a holiday. It was just as well—he didn't want to see another human being unless absolutely necessary. Interacting with the motel clerk for three minutes was already enough.

Instead, he grabbed his cell phone and scrolled down to find a familiar number, then lay back on the unforgiving mattress. He recoiled after butting up against the headboard and landing directly on the spot where he'd been struck, by Nick in the woods and by the trucker in the back of the cab. After rubbing his skull to soothe the sting, he sent the call, put the phone up against his ear, and waited for Carol to answer.

"Corey? Where are you?"

"In a motel room."

"By yourself? Do you still have the gun?"

His heart sank. How did Carol know about the gun? He heard the panic in her voice and understood she was fearing the worst.

"I guess you heard what happened?"

"Yeah. Julian got a call from Nick a couple hours ago."

"From Nick? He's alive?"

"Of course he's alive. Haven't you listened to any of my messages?"

"Actually, no. I haven't."

"He's in a hospital in Chippewa Falls. Julian drove there to be with him and his family." She paused, then asked, "Did you really shoot him, Corey?"

"Yes, but it's a long story—too long to get into right now. Listen, I called because I needed to hear a friendly voice, and you're the first person I thought of."

"I'm glad, Corey. Now tell me where you're at, and I'll come get you."

"I'm pretty far away—too far for you to drive tonight."

"You must be scared and upset. I'm worried."

"Please don't, Carol. That's the last thing I want. I just need time to think. I 've pretty much hit rock bottom."

"Tell me the truth, Corey. Have you been drinking?"

He recoiled from her question. "No, the thought hadn't crossed my mind, but now it has."

"Good. And the gun?"

"It's in the car. I'm not gonna hurt myself, if that's what you're thinking."

He heard a sigh, then a faint whimper through the phone. "That's exactly what I thought when you didn't answer my calls."

"I get it, but don't worry. I'm okay. Well, I'm not really okay. But I won't shoot myself. Or anyone else either."

"What?"

"Never mind. Bad joke." Under his breath Corey added, "Sorta." He shook his head and continued. "Anyway, what's Nick's condition?"

"Julian called a while ago from the hospital. I guess they're keeping him overnight. The doctors are treating his flesh wound."

"Nothing life threatening?"

"No, but he's really pissed off."

"Yeah. And I'm sure everyone there is demonizing me and stoking his rage."

"Maybe," she said. "Listen, I don't know what happened in the woods, and I don't need to. But I know what a shit Nick can be. Hell, there've been plenty of times *I* wanted to shoot him."

For the first time all day, Corey laughed.

"But here's the thing. You're only gonna make things worse if you run away. If you have a story to tell, you should come back and tell it. That's the only way you'll resolve things or gain any peace."

"You're probably right. But I could also end up in prison. I shot someone, and potentially left him to die."

"But he's not going to die. Nick'll be fine, at least from what Julian told me."

"I know, but..." He paused. "You don't understand."

"Maybe not. And I can't tell you what to do. But I can say that I love you, Corey—like a brother."

Carol had uttered that phrase countless times before—that she loved him like a brother. And every time, he felt those words in his gut. They also triggered a predictable response.

"Like a brother? Not like a lover?"

"We tried that, Corey. Didn't work out so well."

He couldn't believe that he and Carol were both laughing, after all that had happened on this horrible day.

"So, what are you gonna do?"

He stayed quiet for a moment as Carol gave him time to reply.

"I'm gonna hang up and make one more call before I crash on this bed. I promise I'll be in touch tomorrow, okay?"

"Okay. But call me any time, all right?"

"All right. Good night."

He ended the call, set the phone down, then rubbed his eyes and temples with both hands. He laid back against two worn bed pillows and exhaled deeply. Nick was alive, not mortally wounded. That made for one calamity avoided. Corey looked at his phone, opening up the map showing the route to Marfa. Damn, that would be a long way to drive. He was no longer certain he had the urgency or energy to flee. Instead, he felt exhausted. What he needed now was a good night's rest. He could decide his future in the morning. There was still one call to make, though, and he dialed the number. Billy answered after the first ring.

"Corey?"

"Yeah, it's me."

"Thank God. I've been going nuts here. You okay?"

"I will be, Billy. I'm sorry for ignoring your calls. It's been a helluva night."

"Where are you?"

"Listen. I need you to do me a favor and trust me that things are gonna be fine. I'll explain everything when I can. But for right now, I need to speak to your father."

Corey heard an exchange of muted voices on the other end of the line. He also heard Billy say, "Here, he wants to talk to you."

In contrast to their earlier conversation that night, Corey took his time and explained to Larry most of what had happened since leaving Barron County. They agreed upon a plan, then said their goodbyes. Corey closed his phone and turned off the light. He slept more soundly that night than he had in a very long time.

4

Friday

He grabbed a black coffee and cinnamon roll at the Kwik Star before leaving Charles City the next morning. Then he got on the road. By seven thirty he reached Marquette, Iowa. He remembered traveling through there years ago on a family trip to see the famous Native American burial site at Effigy Mounds National Monument. It might have been Corey's favorite camping trip as a kid and definitely one of their most active family outings. The Fischers camped at Wyalusing State Park, paddled a canoe down the Wisconsin River, and tracked wildlife at the Cedar Creek Wildlife area.

He also recalled a rented boat ride into the flooded Spook Cave. His mother had looked pale as the tour operator propelled them forward into the dark cavern with a low ceiling. Ginny loathed confined spaces. Once she saw where they were headed, Ginny made the guy turn the boat around and let her out, despite Frank's chiding. Corey and his father ended up taking the tour without her. That was the first time in his memory that Ginny had ever taken a stand over Frank's objection, advocating for what she wanted or needed.

He left Iowa behind and steered the car onto the Marquette-Joliet bridge, the massive tied-arch steel structure that would deliver him across the Mississippi and back into Wisconsin. He gripped the steering wheel tight. Traveling over bridges thrilled him as a kid, the ever-present possibility that the driver could wrench the car over the guard rail and straight into the river, or that the whole damn thing could collapse.

He watched his hands, as if waiting to see if they would obey his desire to drive straight across, or instead act on their own volition and careen the Prius over the barricade. His hands remained steady. He also noticed the wedding ring on his left hand. He hadn't even thought about it until this moment. He was wearing something that meant absolutely nothing, a reminder of what never was. At the high point of the bridge, Corey rolled down the window, yanked the gold band from the ring finger and chucked it out toward the river.

A large sign at the end of the bridge welcomed Corey back to the state from which he had fled the day before. He turned north on the familiar river road of his youth. It was the main route running up and down Wisconsin's western coast, first hugging the St. Croix River in the north and then the Mississippi from Prescott to Prairie du Chien. Classic river towns dotted the landscape, none of them all that large, but each with the same quintessential traits of an incorporated Wisconsin city—a town hall and licensed tavern.

He drove for another hour, ravenous but not seeing anything open and worthy of his refined tastes. By the time he reached La Crosse, the lack of food over the past twenty-four hours caught up with him. He was hungrier than he'd ever been before. He remembered there was a charming café downtown, a place where he had stopped with his parents on their way home from that long-ago camping trip. He found the Bavarian Bistro and instantly recognized the green awning from years before. The woman at the counter recommended a fresh-made quiche with cremini mushrooms, locally picked ramps, and Swiss cheese. Corey bought two slices along with coffee and rye toast, then took a seat near the window looking out into the city. He took a forkful of quiche into his mouth. He closed his lips and then his eyelids, fighting competing impulses—savoring the sweet assault on his taste buds or getting nourishment to his stomach as fast as possible. Upon opening his eyes, he noticed the quaint décor of the café, including pictures of the Alps and of steaming hot bread. It reminded him of that trip to Munich long ago, with Nick. There was an older couple sitting at a small table at the far end of the bakery. They reminded him of the man and woman he saw in the emergency room just one week ago. The couple in the corner were sharing a pot of tea and a cinnamon roll. The woman's right hand rested atop the round table, and the man's hand lay atop hers.

Corey finished his breakfast, paid the bill, and got back on the road heading north. He was on track to reach Pepin for his eleven o'clock meeting at the law office, but found himself exceeding the speed limit, anxious to meet with Larry and begin to put the pieces of a new life together. A few miles out of town his car caught up with a semi-truck who seemed to be in no rush to get wherever he was going. Corey veered toward the median and saw no traffic coming at him, so he pulled out into the oncoming lane and pressed down hard on the accelerator. As he passed the truck, he couldn't resist looking up at the driver. The man looked nothing like the trucker from the night before. He was fair-skinned with a thick, ginger-colored beard and a baseball cap on his head. The man nodded in acknowledgement. Corey looked toward the road, made sure he was fully past the truck, then pulled back into the northbound lane.

As he put more distance between himself and the truck, Corey repeatedly glanced into the rear-view mirror. He could still see the man behind the steering wheel of the truck, though the driver got smaller and smaller with each receding mile. As Corey steered into a curve in the highway, he looked back once more, but the truck was out of view. Instead, he saw an image of the trucker from last night glaring through the back window, holding onto the car with both hands and struggling to get inside. Corey gasped and almost drove the Prius into the ditch. After regaining control, he looked into the rear-view mirror once more and saw nothing but the empty road behind him.

The repulsive vision triggered a memory from a trip down this same highway as a kid, a hunting trip with his father and one of Frank's friends. He remembered that it was a Sunday afternoon. Corey was behind the wheel of the car with his father fast asleep beside him. Driving toward home, the plan was to arrive by five when Ginny would have a mouth-watering meal for them—probably pork chops with herb sauce. Focused on the road ahead on that long-ago day, he felt happier with every mile speeding away toward home. He wouldn't have seen anything if he had tried to look back anyway. Blocking his sight line in the rear-view mirror was the carcass of a large buck strapped to the trunk of the car. Field-dressed on the spot that morning, the deer's lifeless body looked as if it were merely asleep and taking a long, cold ride atop the full-sized sedan. Later, just before reaching home, Frank delivered the buck to a professional processor who turned the animal into a bevy of sausages, steaks, and jerky.

Today was different—there was nothing atop the car. And the day was cloudless and bright, a clear contrast to the entire past week. The sun was rising in the southeastern sky. Music played softly from the car radio—an '80s station broadcasting from La Crosse. Though forty degrees outside, the car's heater kept him at a comfortable sixty-eight. The highway jutted inland, away from the river for a stretch and through the heart of rural Wisconsin. He passed a farm and pasture several acres wide, bordered by a chest-high rail fence stretching from the edge of the road back until it disappeared into a distant forest. Corey's eyes darted back and forth between the alluring pasture and the asphalt road. The sun shining upon the faded green grass gave the land a deceptive feeling of spring. If he didn't know better, he might have mistaken this moment for April instead of November, with nature ascending rather than shutting down for the year.

In the pasture, he saw a quartet of black stallions, standing together along the fence adjacent the road, as if watching the cars go by and making commentary about the scene passing before their eyes. Corey wondered if horses could communicate with their own kind. These strikingly tall animals looked as if they owned the world, like four young men hanging out, musing about life. At the far end of the pasture, he spotted a lone brown-and-white-splotched horse. It stood facing west, away from the four stallions, either oblivious to their presence or willfully choosing to look the other way. The horse appeared to be gazing across the fence toward a different herd of animals penned up on a neighboring ranch. A near twin of its neighbor, this second field looked a bit smaller, but outfitted with the same feeding troughs as the first and patches of grass with just a hint of their slow and impending change to brown. In that second field stood a small herd of cattle, milling about and grazing. A few of them chased each other in the grass. It appeared to Corey as if the lone horse wanted to join the cattle but was blocked by the wooden fence.

Corey drove on.

He had passed through Trempealeau County, and the highway turned back toward the river. The music station had become mostly static. He switched to an AM news channel broadcasting out of Winona across the river. Through the speakers he heard a muted bell, then listened as the broadcaster read the nine o'clock news.

"According to the National Turkey Foundation, forty-six million birds ended up on dinner tables across America today. Minnesota is the United States' top turkey-producing state, followed by North Carolina, Arkansas, Missouri, Virginia, Indiana, and California. Americans also ate a record number of potatoes, pumpkins and cranberries yesterday. By the way, our neighbors in Wisconsin lead the nation in growing and harvesting cranberries. And, according to AAA, an estimated thirty-nine million of you traveled more than fifty miles on this Thanksgiving holiday. That's about a 1.5 percent decline from 2012."

"In local news, authorities are investigating the death of a truck driver south of Albert Lea. Police say the thirty-two-year-old man was found early this morning shot to death inside his semi, parked at a remote truck stop off Interstate 35. The man's name is being withheld pending notice to next of kin.

"In sports, the Green Bay Packers..." Corey reached over and turned the radio off. He quickly pulled off the highway onto Waumandee Creek Road and steered the car violently toward the shoulder. He jumped out. He ran, then stumbled down an embankment, puking onto his coat and into the tall grass. There wasn't a car or person in sight. He collapsed to the ground and slammed his fist against the earth, yelling.

"Fuck!"

"I didn't mean to—"

"Jesus!"

Corey began hyperventilating. He hadn't taken in a breath since exiting the car. He looked around the dying greensward ditch. For a minute he couldn't remember where he was, only what he'd done. Questions and agony battered him from inside.

How did this happen?

It can't be true.

Why am I having this nightmare?

His thoughts soon turned. He willed himself to remember as much as possible from his time at the truck stop. Were there any cameras? Did the store clerk ever look him in the eye? Had he left anything behind inside the semi? How much of his own blood spilled out onto the ground when he leapt from the truck?

Corey instinctively reached for his phone. He needed comfort from a supportive voice—Carol, Billy, his mom. He stared at the screen, then put the phone back into his pocket. For now, he chose not to tell a soul.

A van slowed to a crawl on the road above where Corey sat, then picked up speed again after passing his car. He decided not to linger there any longer. He uprooted several blades of large prairie grass and used them to wipe the vomit remnants from his coat, then he spit out the taste of bile. He ascended to the road and returned to his car, popping several breath mints into his mouth.

Back on the highway, Corey drove north and tried to focus on nothing more than the road ahead of him. An hour later, he spotted the welcome sign for Pepin. As he drove through town, he noticed light in the Preston's living room window but kept on going. He had agreed to meet Larry in the downtown law office at eleven, so he had a little time to spare.

A few quick turns brought the car in front of 430 Pine. He parked in the driveway, then turned the engine off. He detected no movement inside the house, so he sat a few minutes longer. Soon a hand brushed open the curtains in the kitchen window. He figured that it took her a few moments to recognize the car bearing Minnesota license plates.

Corey got out and walked to the side of the house. Ginny opened the back door. They beheld one another before moving closer, each with arms extended toward the other. Corey's emotions spilled out from inside him, and he began heaving his shoulders, weeping in his mother's arms. She wrapped him in a tight embrace, each of them now crying and refusing to let go.

5

Friday

Corey walked downtown, arriving at Larry's office just before eleven. The wind whipped eastward off Lake Pepin. His face felt hot, boiling to the touch, and the chilly breeze cooled him a little, making him feel thankful for such a small gift from nature. As he walked the nine blocks, there was hardly anyone on the street. He assumed people were still hunkered down with their loved ones for the holiday weekend. The signs in all of the Main Street shops read "Closed."

After ringing the doorbell, Corey impulsively felt the bulge of his coat pocket, reminding himself that he'd remembered to bring the handgun as Larry instructed. He then reached inside the other pocket and touched the bullets that he had removed from the gun's chamber last night. When he looked up, Larry was already at the door, unlocking it from inside.

"Good morning," Larry said, while pushing the glass door outward, then reaching toward Corey and pulling him into a tight embrace.

Corey's chin rested on the old man's shoulder. Their cheeks touched, and he couldn't speak.

"I'm glad you're here. Come on in."

They took the stairs up to the office. Corey entered but did not sit down, waiting for a cue from Larry, who closed the door behind them.

"Let's sit over here at the table. I'd offer you coffee, but Linda's not in today and, well, you wouldn't want to drink anything I'd brew."

Corey smiled, then turned toward the table wondering where to sit. "Will Billy be joining us?"

"No. You and I need to meet alone, one-on-one. Having Billy here would jeopardize the confidentiality of our attorney-client conversation."

"Of course, that makes sense." Corey's smile quickly faded as he pulled back the chair and took a seat at the end of the table. Larry took the next closest one, with the corner the only thing between them. He reached out and rested both hands on Corey's, which were folded atop the table.

"So, how are you feeling, son? I mean, considering all that's happened."

"To be honest, I'm worn out."

"That's understandable. You've been through a lot, and I'm not just referring to the past twenty-four hours." Larry released his grip and reached into his lapel pocket for a silver fountain pen.

"And I'm nervous about what happens next."

"Well, that's what we're going to figure out this morning. I thought we could take it slow, make sure we go over everything in detail."

Corey nodded.

"I don't have any other appointments today, so we have as much time as we need, okay?"

"All right."

"And when we're done, Billy wants us to call him so he can come down and take you out for coffee or something before he leaves for the airport. I'm not sure what's open today, but you'll figure something out."

"Does that mean I'll still be a free man after this meeting? That my next stop isn't the county jail?"

With his fingertips, Larry drew a yellow legal pad toward him and opened his custom pen. He then leaned back in his chair and waited until Corey looked up.

"You aren't going to jail today and hopefully no other day either. Look, I'm gonna be honest with you, Corey. You've been involved in a serious altercation, one in which Nick was shot. By you. But every case is unique, and there are definitely reasons to conclude that he's as much to blame for what happened as you."

"So you think I can claim self-defense?"

"I don't want to get too far ahead of ourselves. We need to go through everything clearly, before we go to the police."

"The police?"

"Yes, sooner or later. And sooner is a better choice."

"I see."

"I, um, put in a call to George Stevens last night, after I spoke with you."

"The Pepin County Sheriff? Why?"

"I've known George since we were kids. Your dad knew him too. I explained the circumstances in sketchy detail, then asked him to check with his colleagues up in Barron to see if anyone had reported an incident."

"And?" Corey's hands were clammy and clasped together, folded underneath his chin as if supporting the weight of his head.

"And, while an ambulance responded to one emergency call last night involving a shooting, the sheriff wasn't immediately involved. They did receive a referral this morning from Chippewa County, once the man was treated for a gunshot wound to the buttocks at St. Joseph Hospital in Chippewa Falls. The investigating officer at the hospital referred it back to Barron because the man said that's where he got shot."

Corey sat back in his chair, his folded hands now resting on the edge of the table in front of him. His gaze dropped to his lap. Since his call with Carol the night before and given the passage of time with no word from Nick, he had grown slightly complacent, convincing himself that the worst was behind him—for that crime, at least.

"Nick gave them your name, address, and phone number. But from what George said, the Barron County investigator hadn't yet tried to make contact." Larry paused to breathe before he continued. "Corey, George pretty much knew why I was calling, but he didn't ask me where you were. He simply suggested that if I spoke with you that I should encourage you to contact Barron County before they contact you. George also suggested that if you happened to be here in Pepin today, then he'd be happy to call the guys in Barron himself and maybe even persuade them to come down and interview you here in town."

"Mr. Stevens pretty much knows I'm here, doesn't he?"

"Yeah. Even though I didn't tell him directly, I'm certain he knew I was calling on your behalf. He might have even driven by and seen a car with Minnesota plates at your parents' house after you arrived."

Corey looked toward the window but couldn't see down to the street from where he was sitting. He envisioned the sheriff's patrol car cruising past the building as they spoke.

"The good news is that according to George Stevens, Barron is investigating this as an accident, at least for now."

"That's good news?"

"Yes. It means that Nick may have given them the same story you told me over the phone last night, including about him hitting you with the flashlight before he got shot. Either that, or he's not pressing charges—at least not yet."

Corey nodded his head but said nothing, his eyes still cast downward.

Larry stayed quiet for a few moments as well, yet Corey could feel Larry's eyes boring into him.

"So, you really shot him in the ass?"

Corey looked up to see a broad smile.

"I guess I did." He exhaled, and his shoulders dropped an inch. He returned Larry's smile.

"Well, now don't get me wrong, son—I'd never advocate hurting another person. And as your lawyer, I'm gonna advise you to be very remorseful in front of the investigating officer and, God forbid, a judge. But here in this office? And just between us? I think Nick got what he deserved."

They spent the next hour talking in detail about the past forty-eight hours. Larry took pages of notes. Corey repeated every excruciating detail from the time he and Nick arrived in Barron County until he fled to Minneapolis. At Larry's request, Corey also removed the Colt Woodsman and bullets from his coat pockets, handing them to Larry who then carried them in a handkerchief over to the safe behind his desk and locked them up.

"So, I think I've got it all down. I can't promise anything, and I don't get involved in many criminal matters, but this really sounds like classic self-defense. Nick hit you, you felt threatened, your instincts took over, and you protected yourself. And although there's no eyewitness other than you and Nick, we've got other circumstantial evidence in your favor."

"Which is?"

"First of all, I already took a statement from Billy."

"From Billy? But he wasn't there."

"You're right, but he was the last person to see either of you before the incident. If needed, he'll testify to Nick's behavior the day leading up to the accident. He told me all about Nick mocking you for wanting to help the deer that you guys hit on the road, and about his inappropriate taunts when you stopped for lunch at Sam's Café. It may or may not help, but we have it just the same."

Corey considered Larry's words and hoped they wouldn't need to drag Billy into this mess any more than necessary.

"Do you have questions about any of this?"

Corey rubbed a fingertip across his closed lips.

"Yeah, a couple."

"Shoot." Larry grimaced. "Sorry, poor choice of words."

Corey laughed. "No worries. That's actually the focus of my questions."

"Oh?"

"Yeah. What I'm wondering about is what justifies shooting someone. How do I prove that I was acting in self-defense and not out of a desire to kill?"

"Well, like I said, it's a combination of the actual events that led up to the incident as well as the bigger picture of the two people involved—their interactions and obvious or not so obvious motives."

"So, like if I was under attack?"

"Yeah, that would matter."

"What if I felt threatened, you know, sexually?"

"Are you saying that Nick tried to assault you out in the woods?"

"No. I was talking about... I mean, suppose I didn't have hard proof that he threatened me, and there was only my word to go on?"

"You mean, like if Nick denied hitting you?"

"Sure. Or, I don't know, if he were dead."

"But he's not dead. Everything I've heard from you and from George Stevens is that Nick will be just fine."

"I know. But what if he weren't?"

"Well, I suppose we'd still have the bump on your head as evidence, though I guess there's no proof it wasn't self-inflicted."

"I would never..." Corey didn't finish the sentence.

Larry leaned in and put his hand on Corey's shoulder.

"Don't worry about things that might've been, son. I think it'll all be fine in the end, really. Remember, there's nothing we can do now to change the past. Just tell the truth, and let the chips fall where they may."

"But I really didn't mean to kill anyone."

"I know, Corey. And you didn't."

"But..." He looked at Larry with pleading eyes. "I, uh, I just... I'm not sure how to ask this."

"It's okay. Take your time. We're not in any rush."

Corey put his palms and fingertips together, as if in prayer. He rested his elbows on the table. Larry maintained his light touch on Corey's shoulder.

"Does running away from a crime scene make my case worse?"

"Well, in this situation, probably not. Nick's sister got him to the hospital, and it sounds like he'll be fine. Now, if he had died and you ran away without taking any action to save him, yeah, that would have made things a whole lot worse for you."

Corey slowly opened his hands. His fingertips rubbed each eyebrow, and his palms held the weight of his head.

"I'm sorry," Larry said. "I shouldn't have added that last part. Nick didn't die, and he's not going to. So, you running away probably doesn't add to your legal jeopardy."

Corey sat there, rubbing his face.

"Are you okay, son? Is there something else you're trying to tell me?"

Corey looked up.

"No. Just trying to take it all in."

"Good. I get it." Larry looked down at his notepad. "I do have a few more questions for you, unless you need a break?"

"No, I'm fine. Ask away."

"All right. How did you end up in Iowa, so far off the interstate?"

Corey looked at Larry, then shifted his gaze back to the table in front of him.

"I was heading toward Texas but couldn't drive the whole way in one night. I got off the freeway to look for a motel, and I guess it just took several miles before I found one that was open on Thanksgiving."

"Did anyone see you along the way, between leaving Minneapolis and arriving back here in Pepin?"

Corey scratched the top of his head, then rested both arms on the table.

"There was the motel clerk, of course. We interacted for about two minutes, tops. I also stopped for breakfast this morning in La Crosse. Other than that, no one."

"What did you and the motel clerk talk about, besides the essentials of course?"

"I don't know, not much. I asked for a room and told her I was paying in cash."

"Cash? Why?"

"I guess at that point I didn't know Nick was alive. I was trying to avoid leaving a credit card trail. You know, in case..."

"Okay. But how far did you think you were gonna get just using cash?"

Corey explained the funds from his art studio safe.

"Ten-thousand dollars? Jesus."

Corey shrugged his shoulders and lifted both upturned palms in supplication.

"I see. Well, my advice when you talk to the Barron County sheriff is not to volunteer that piece of information unless of course they directly ask for it. It might make you look shady."

"I'm sorry. In retrospect I guess it was a stupid thing to do, hiding that money all these years."

"It may be irrelevant, Corey. Don't worry about that for now. Okay, let's see. You talked with the motel clerk. Anyone else?"

"I don't think so."

"You didn't stop for gas or any other food along the way?"

Corey refused to look up. "Nope."

"I guess I should get one of those hybrid cars too. Sounds like you rarely have to fill 'em up."

Corey nodded.

"Oh, I almost forgot. I also made an appointment for you at the hospital over in Wabasha this afternoon. I need them to examine your head."

Corey looked at Larry with furrowed eyebrows.

"We need a doctor to assess your injury, where Nick hit you. You said it was a harsh blow, right?"

"It drew blood and left a mark. See?" He turned to show Larry the crown of his head.

"Ouch, it still looks swollen. That's good. Well, you know what I mean."

"Yeah, I know. You've been incredibly kind, Mr. Preston. I don't know what I'd have done without you. I didn't know where else to turn."

Larry shook his head. "I think of you like one of my kids, Corey. I'm glad you trusted me."

"This is all so embarrassing—my best friend's father witnessing how badly I've fucked up my life."

"Listen," Larry said, once again reaching over to touch Corey's hand. "Don't think that for one minute. I'm here to support you no matter what... all of us Preston's are. And what you're going through is definitely serious and difficult, but it is what it is, and you're gonna get through it. We're gonna get through it. Okay?"

"Okay."

"Good. I think we're done for now. I'll call Billy. And here, take this business card with you over to the hospital. Remind the doctor to send his report to me as soon as possible."

"Will do." Corey paused. "Sir, do you mind if I call my mother? I'd like to let her know that I won't be home for a while."

"Of course. You talk to her in here. I'll go out to Sally's desk and call Billy. Then I'll place a call to George Stevens and see if he can't arrange a meeting with the detective from Barron for some time tomorrow. Does that sound all right?"

"Yeah. It'll give me one more night to worry, but I guess what's done is done. I'll find out soon enough where things go from here."

Larry turned to leave his office, but paused at the sound of Corey's voice.

"Mr. Preston?"

"Larry."

"Larry? What should I do if Nick tries to call?"

Larry leaned against the door jam, stroking his chin with his hand.

"For now, I'd say don't speak with him. Who knows what his mood or his mindset will be. Let's talk with George Stevens first. That sound reasonable?"

"Definitely. I don't want to hear from Nick or even see him at this point anyway."

"Okay. And Corey, you're doing the right thing. I hope you know that. As long as you tell the truth and are firm in your answers like we discussed, I'm confident that everything will be fine."

6

Friday

Billy pulled up to the office building in his rental car. Corey got in the front seat while Larry opted to walk home in the cool sunshine.

"So, where to?" Billy asked. "I've got about two hours before I head to the airport."

"I think the only thing open today is the Kwik Shop. We could get something there to snack on—for old times' sake."

"Perfect. Junk food sounds awesome after eating nothing but leftovers the past two days. I'm gonna need a good, long run on the beach once I get back to California."

"From the looks of it, I'd say you ate *all* of the leftovers. You might need to run for five days straight."

"Ha ha."

They entered the Kwik Shop long enough to get a bag of chips, two candy bars, and a fountain drink apiece. Corey couldn't remember the last time he had a meal like this, but it was probably in this very spot with Billy, a long time ago.

"You wanna go back to my parents' house?" Corey asked. "I'm sure my mom would like to see you before you go."

"Yeah, I'll stop in when I drop you off. But first, there's somewhere we need to go."

"Oh? Where's that?"

"You'll see. We'll be there in about ninety seconds."

Corey sipped his soda and watched while Billy drove west, toward the river. As promised, the car came to a halt in a parking space at the marina within a few minutes. Corey alighted from the passenger side and began walking toward the pier with junk food in hand. He turned and looked back toward the car upon hearing the trunk pop open. He shook his head and smiled. Billy balanced his soda in one hand and two fishing poles in the other, while somehow also closing the trunk.

"I can't believe you. And yet, I sorta can," Corey said. "Where'd you get all that?"

"My parents' garage. They still had my old pole, and an extra one for you."

"You know it's too cold for fishing, right? And I'm pretty sure that nothing's still legally in season."

"Well, well. Look who's concerned about adhering to the law all of a sudden."

Corey couldn't believe he was laughing at Billy's stupid wit, and at himself.

"Yeah, that's me—Corey the convict. Wait till you see my new wardrobe—nothing but orange jumpsuits."

Billy laughed too.

"Come on, lawbreaker. Let's catch us some fish before the law catches us."

They traversed the rocky promontory jutting into the wide river. Near the end of the man-made pier, they wandered down to the water's edge, each finding a suitable boulder upon which to sit and cast their lines. The shoreline showed signs of the coming winter. A narrow veneer of ice surrounded the rocks at the river's edge, but a foot out from shore the water flowed freely. By January, the entire river would be frozen over. But today, the Mississippi rolled past them, her muddy brown water fleeing the cold north.

For a while, Corey and Billy fished in silence, each of them casting their gaze toward the water, or in search of eagles, or to be the first to spot a train barreling down the tracks across the river.

Corey appreciated these moments of quiet solitude sitting next to his best friend, both today and all of those times in this same spot as a boy. It was a quiet that brought both peace and comfort, the security of an unspoken bond.

Corey took in the panoramic view of immense Lake Pepin. To the north he saw Maiden Rock flanking the river valley on its eastern front and Point No Point directly across the gorge. Scanning downstream to his left, he considered the symmetrical bluff tops of the Minnesota and Wisconsin embankments—land that had once been part of a vast plain, ripped apart by a glacier that carved this substantial chasm. At the far southern end of his sightline, Corey saw the geologic end of Lake Pepin, hemmed in by a series of grass and tree-covered islands. He remembered navigating them by canoe as a kid with Billy, and with Frank. In contrast to his companions on those adventures, Corey's focus was exploration more than fishing. In those meandering channels he scouted a bountiful bevy of creatures with eccentric-sounding names—the Blanding's turtle, Massasauga rattlesnake, cerulean warbler, and ruffled grouse.

As he looked upon those islands now from afar, his thoughts drifted once again to Arshile Gorky and the museum exhibit Corey would likely never see. It was only running through the end of December, and he didn't expect to return to Minneapolis before that, if ever at all. The grassy atolls at the end of Lake Pepin evoked memories of *They Will Take My Island*, the first Gorky painting that had captured Corey's imagination. It was back in 2010, when writer and blogger Paul Vermeersch beckoned the public to pen their own lines of verse about what truths lay within the surrealist painting. Hundreds responded to the call. Corey was one of them. He still carried a copy of the poem on a folded piece of paper in his wallet. Corey retrieved it from his back pocket and opened up the tattered note.

"Can I read something to ya?"

Billy looked over at Corey who held his pole in one hand and a piece of paper in the other that was being flapped by the wind.

"Of course. Is it your written confession that I've always been the better fisherman?"

Corey laughed. "Not quite. It's a poem inspired by a painting."

"One of your paintings?"

Corey attempted to describe *They Will Take My Island*. The painting was Gorky's late-life reflection upon the idyllic landscape of his youth, living near the shores of Lake Van in what was then central Armenia, land that Gorky never saw again after fleeing the Turkish invasion. In the middle of Lake Van stood an island.

"Reading about that landscape reminded me of this." He pointed south toward the end of Lake Pepin. "It's funny. I never told anyone about the poem, not even Nick. It got published online with all the others. I guess I always considered myself a painter not a poet, so I kept it to myself."

"Read it to me, Corey."

He did.

> They will take my island
> Her offspring, her beauty, her time
> They form no defense to fate.
>
> The soldiers march on
> Their goal, their role
> Cruelty betrays its own suffering.
>
> And yet, she lies in wait
> Her strength, her patience
> The vanquished always rise.
>
> Armies falter
> Their arrogance, their greed
> Darkness defeated by light.
>
> Yes, they will take my island
> Her offspring, her beauty, her time
> And yet, she will return again
> To me.

Billy had been staring at the distant islands while Corey read aloud. After Corey finished, Billy turned his head and looked Corey in the eye. "That's beautiful, man. You're really talented, you know that?"

"Thanks, Billy."

Both of them shifted their gaze back toward the water, watching fishing lines that showed no sign of action.

"You're pretty talented yourself, you know."

"Yeah?"

Corey shook his head in affirmation. "Yeah. You're the second-best storyteller I know."

"Is that right? And I suppose the best storyteller you know is sitting here beside me?"

"I'm glad we see eye to eye on that, Billy."

"Huh." Billy appeared to be thinking. "You know, if you do end up going to prison, this might be your last chance."

"Last chance?"

"Yeah, your last chance to finally catch a bigger fish than mine. Do you know how boring it is to beat you at this every single time?"

"Ha, that's not how I remember it. I recall catching fish much longer than yours, at least once or twice when we were kids."

"Yeah, but those were sturgeon, not real fish. I'm talking about ones that count, the kind you eat or can brag about back in town."

"Well, then I guess there's two things I'll be missing out on in prison."

Billy looked at Corey with an imploring smile.

"I won't be catching fish, and I won't be living by your dim-witted, made-up rules."

They fished for half an hour. Billy didn't ask a single question about Barron County. Toward the end, Corey saw Billy repeatedly checking his watch.

"What time's your flight?"

"Not till five, but with the drive back to Minneapolis, allowing extra time for security and returning the rental car, I should probably be heading back to my parents pretty soon to say goodbye."

"Yeah. I don't want you to miss your flight because of me. And nothing's biting on these lures anyway. Too cold. Let's get going."

"You're right. Come on, lawbreaker, I'll give you a ride home."

"Is that my new nickname or something?"

"It has a nice ring to it, don't you think?"

"Not so much. But if I'm getting a nickname, you need one too."

They ascended the rocky pier and walked side-by-side toward the car. All of a sudden, Billy reached out and halted Corey's forward progress with the fishing pole attached to his hand.

"I got it."

"Got what?"

"My nickname. You know—if we become criminals and live a life on the lam."

"You always were the creative storyteller as a kid, Billy. Oh wait, did I just guess it—Billy the Kid?"

"Nope. Billy the Kid is too obvious. Besides, he mostly worked alone. No, we're a team like Redford and Newmann. We're Butch Lawbreaker and the California Kid."

Corey placed his hand on Billy's shoulder.

"You know what I think? I think you'd better keep your day job and forget about a career in comedy."

"You just keep thinking, Butch—thinkin's what you're good at," Billy said. "That's a quote from the movie, you know."

"You clearly need help. Come on, California Kid, let's go."

As Billy drove toward Ginny's house, they reminisced about a couple stories from their youth. Soon they reached the Fischer driveway. Billy pulled up to the edge of the garage and turned the engine off.

"Before we go in to see your mom, I have something serious to say."

"Okay, and I know that I still owe you an explanation."

"That's not what I meant. Hear me out. I knew you'd have a heavy conversation with my dad back at the law office, so I tried to keep things light. Clearly, a lot of serious shit happened, and there's probably a bit more still ahead of you. But I want you to know I'm proud of you, Corey, and that I support you 100 percent."

"I already knew that Billy. I don't deserve it, but I knew it."

"And the serious thing I want to say to you is this. Check your e-mail."

"Check my e-mail? That's the serious advice you've been building up to all afternoon?"

"Check your damn e-mail, will ya?"

"Okay." Corey pulled the device from his pocket. "Shit, it's dead."

"For fuck's sake, Fischer. Here, use mine. You can read the e-mail I sent you this morning."

Corey laughed at Billy's faux anger, then took the phone from his hand and tapped the message addressed to himself. He read it silently.

"Billy, this is really generous but totally unnecessary."

"Is that your way of saying thank you?"

"Thank you, of course. But I can't accept it."

"Sure you can. I cashed in all my credit card points, and they gave me this free flight voucher. But I'm adding one condition—you can only use it to come to California. It's good for a year, so you can stay as long as you like. Hell, maybe you should just fly one-way and start a new life out west."

"You don't know how appealing that sounds right now, escaping to a new place."

"Then do it. This is exactly the time of year to get the hell out of Wisconsin and move to the beach. You've been promising me you'd visit for a couple years now, remember?"

"I do. And I will come see you Billy. But for now, I've got to stay here in Pepin. I need to make a few things right. After that, I'll be on the first flight to LA, and I'll stay as long as it takes to make you sick of me."

"So I guess you're moving to LA permanently, then?"

Corey laughed.

"Maybe, California Kid. Maybe."

7

Friday

Ginny held a book as Corey approached. She looked as though she hadn't moved in the forty-five minutes since he left her to enter the examination room.

"Oh, you're done. How'd it go?"

"Fine. The doctor said I probably had a mild concussion and should've been seen right away. For now, she recommended ice to reduce the swelling and ibuprofen for pain."

"I'm sorry this happened to you, Corey. I wouldn't have guessed Nick to be the violent type."

"I didn't think I was that type either, but we know how that turned out."

He sensed his mother's unease. After arriving at her doorstep this morning, he provided only the barest of details of what had occurred in the Barron County woods and nothing of his night after that. Ginny had listened with a rapt silence and asked no questions. Corey appreciated that. He had answered enough of those with Larry already. There'd be time to explain everything to his mother, at some point, but not right now.

"The good news is—the doctor also stitched up my knee."

"From your accident last week? I would've thought it had healed by now."

"It started to, but I reopened the wound yesterday when I fell on the gravel."

"At the cabin?"

Corey hesitated before saying, "Yeah."

"Oh, I'm sorry. Well, at least you're on the mend now, right?"

"Indeed."

"Say, are you hungry? We could stop at the market here in Wabasha. I'll make you anything you'd like back at home."

"What I'd like, Mom, is to take you out for dinner. Maybe we could find something on this side of the river, somewhere we won't run into anyone we know."

"That sounds lovely, Corey."

"How about that place on the golf course up the road? We had a great meal there once. I think it's called the Tavern on the Green or something?"

"Yes, they had excellent food. Sadly, those owners sold it and moved on a few years back. Let's try Waterman's in Lake City."

"Okay."

They drove north along a highway that hugged the river bluffs. The conversation returned to small talk—about casseroles and pies that neighbors continued to bring to the house, and a retelling of the Thanksgiving that Ginny hosted with her mother.

It was only late afternoon, still a bit early for dinner. Corey impulsively pulled into the gravel lot in front of a geological land-mark that doubled as a river overlook.

"Is there something wrong with the car?" Ginny asked.

"No, it's fine. I thought we'd stop and see what this marker says and take in the view."

He belatedly noticed a semi-truck parked in the corner of the overlook, at first blush hidden behind a row of trees. Corey parked the car at the other end of the lot. They emerged from the car and walked toward the viewing platform. They looked across the wide body of water, back toward Pepin slightly upriver. From this vantage point, they could see the geographic end of expansive Lake Pepin. This was the point where the steep and fast Chippewa River emptied into the Mississippi, continuously dropping its sandy sediment to form a series of islands and sand bars, many of them covered with trees and tall grass. Corey also spied the unmistakable white steeple of St. Bridget's, upriver in Pepin.

"Spectacular," Ginny said.

"Yeah. It's pretty here, and such a beautiful, sunny day."

"A bit windy, though. Brrr." Ginny pulled a scarf snug around her neck and the collars of her coat in tight.

"Look. An eagle." Corey pointed east. "You can see it through the trees."

"Wow. Looks like he's got something in his talons. A fish perhaps?"

"Probably."

"Oh, I hate seeing an innocent creature swooped up and killed like that, but I guess it's a necessary evil."

"Hmmm."

Once the eagle flew out of sight, Corey motioned toward the marker.

"Let's go see what the sign says."

They walked a few feet and stood directly in front of the black metal placard with gold lettering. Each began to read silently.

"Mom?"

"Yes?" Ginny turned to face him.

"Would you read it to me, like when I was a kid?"

"You remember when I used to do that?" She laughed. "I haven't read to you in thirty years."

"Come on, please?"

"Oh, for goodness' sake. I've got a better idea. Why don't you read it to me?"

"All right," he said, before turning his gaze back toward the signpost. "City dwellers need go no farther than this if they seek romantic solitude, wrote panoramic artist Henry Lewis in 1848. One cannot imagine a more lovely expanse of water than Lake Pepin in quiet, clear weather, and no wilder scene than when whipped by the storm, its waves bound against the rocky cliffs. Between the towns of Red Wing and Wabasha most of the rugged valley of the Upper Mississippi is filled by this river widening known as Lake Pepin. Long before the European explorer Father Louis Hennepin discovered what he called the *Lake of Tears* in 1680, it served as a highway for Indian people of many cultures."

Corey finished reading and looked at Ginny. He felt warmth in his heart, upon seeing her smile. From this angle, his mom looked a bit younger and definitely more content than in the days when they first reunited after Frank's death, only one week ago. He also realized she was now the only parent he had left. Once she died, he would have no family at all. Corey decided that he didn't want to live the rest of his life without knowing his mother more deeply, and for her to know him. She had opened the door to a closer dialogue days earlier, and he intended to embrace it.

"Mom, I want to tell you what happened at the cabin."

"Corey, you don't have to tell me anything you don't want to. I understand you're going through a difficult time."

"You're right, I don't have to. But I want to. That is, if you're interested in hearing it."

"Of course." She looked around the overlook before motioning off to one side. "Here, let's go sit on that ledge."

Once seated, Corey told his mother far more than he had intended. He detailed the ride north and his feelings upon arriving back at the cabin. Ginny listened silently as he gave an in-depth account of shooting the eighteen-point buck and the ensuing chase as darkness descended. Without pausing to let her react or respond, he also provided a moment-by-moment account of his penultimate argument with Nick, as the buck lay writhing and crying in the dirt.

When she said nothing, but only nodded her head with perceptible understanding, he then jumped ahead to his morning session with Larry, explaining the legal pitfalls that lay ahead of him, both the criminal investigation and then figuring out what to do about Nick.

"I'm sorry to be dumping all this on you. These are my problems, not yours."

"Corey, I need to tell you something."

"Oh?"

"Yes." She paused. "I knew your marriage to Nick wasn't valid. He told us last year, the day after they rushed you to the hospital."

Corey nodded, looking down.

"That's what I was urging Nick to tell you when you were down in the basement the other day. I should have told you myself right away. Corey, I'm ashamed of myself."

"That was Nick's fault, Mom, not yours. And it doesn't matter now anyway. It all worked out for the best, really—me finding out when I did."

"It still must've been painful to hear about the marriage and that Nick kept it from you for over a year."

"Yes, it was. Still is. I mean, I understand his logic—not telling me while I was recovering and going through therapy. But it was the way that he told me, in his threatening, condescending tone. That really stung."

"You deserved better than that, Corey—from all of us." She paused a moment, then continued. "You know, that's why I was crying the other night, when I told you and Nick about getting pregnant and then marrying your father so quickly."

"How do you mean?"

"I mean that I wasn't crying about Frank or about my parents forcing us into marriage. I was crying about you, Corey, about how my greatest failure was not standing up for you against your father. I had the strength. I just didn't use it. I hope you'll forgive me."

"There's nothing to forgive, Mom. We're here now and have a chance to start again. Maybe it's time to put the past behind us where it belongs."

"You know what? I'm proud of you, Corey. I really am."

"Am I finally your favorite child?" he asked through laughter.

Ginny laughed. "You are your father's son, Corey. Always quick-witted and funny when you want to be. I like this side of you. I hope to see more of it in the future."

He looked at her and smiled, nodding his head.

"If I may ask, honey, what are you going to do now?"

"Right now I'm gonna take you to dinner."

"No, I mean..." He interrupted her with a playful nudge.

"I know. I guess I'm going to wait and see what Nick's reaction is, whether or not he decides to press charges. Then, either way, I'm going to end our relationship and sever whatever remains of our financial ties, which isn't all that much. We own the condo together and a few joint bank accounts, but the cars are each titled in our own names, and our retirement accounts are separate too. Of course, Nick's is much, much larger with him being the breadwinner and all. Larry says I've got no chance of sharing in that or any of the investment accounts in Nick's name since we were never legally married."

"You're still young. You'll bounce back."

"I hope so. It sucks to be starting all over at my age. I guess I shouldn't have relied so heavily on Nick for financial security. That didn't work out so well."

"You know you can stay with me as long as you like, right? In fact, I'd really welcome that. With the life insurance Larry tells me I'll be getting, money won't be a problem."

"Thanks. I would like to stay with you for a while—to work everything out, if that's okay."

"Yes, that's okay. I could sure get used to going out for dinner like this, with you here. And I'm paying tonight, by the way. Your father wasn't much for dining out. It was the curse of him liking my cooking—I always had to make meals at home."

"I'm willing to be your date any time you wanna go out." Corey laughed. "Maybe there's some justice in spending Dad's life insurance money to wine and dine you like you deserve."

Ginny laughed too.

"And I'll try not to involve you too much as I sort things out with Nick."

"You can talk to me any time, you understand? Although, I may not be the right person to give you advice. My marriage was far from perfect, and I haven't dated in forty years."

"I know," he said.

"But I can tell you this. I've made mistakes too. And what I've learned is that you can't take them back. All you can do is move forward."

"You're right." He stared at his mother for a moment, then smiled. "You know what? For a small-town girl from Wisconsin, you're pretty wise."

Ginny returned his smile with one of her own before standing up and shifting her gaze toward the river. Corey stood as well but continued looking down at her face. All of a sudden, her eyes showed concern.

"Corey, look."

Her voice had turned somber. She pointed out past the trees and into the river. He saw it too. An older man was piloting a small motorboat halfway across the channel. A young girl sat up front, donning a bright orange life vest while holding on tight to the gunwales. Between them, two long fishing poles stuck upward from the floor of the boat, the lures at the end of each line flapping violently in the wind.

The man struggled to navigate his little craft. A combination of wind, wave, and tide kept pushing them farther into the current as he seemingly tried steering them closer toward shore. Though he was traveling in a straight line toward land, the wave patterns in that direction powerfully rocked the boat from side to side. The little girl appeared to be shouting toward the man, twice standing up from her seat. But, with one hand gripping the controls of the outboard motor, he gestured with the other for her to stay seated right where she was.

Corey reached out for his mother's hand.

"Do you think they'll be all right? Should we call someone?"

"Let's give 'em a minute. I think they'll be fine." Ginny cocked her head. "That's Jeff Olson out in the boat."

"The grocery store owner? I remember him."

"Yeah. And I think that's one of his granddaughters. Geez, I hope they don't capsize."

Corey gazed toward the river and saw the little girl pull the hood of her coat over her head. River water splashed in her face each time the boat hit another wave. She hunkered down as low as she could in the front seat, but still with much of her body exposed to the recurrent splatter. Corey saw the fisherman pull the cap on his own head tighter. Then, in one hasty move, the man turned the boat ninety degrees, and they headed downstream instead, toward a large sand bar covered with trees and tall grass in the middle of the river. Soon, the boat no longer pitched up and down with each wave. Instead, the river carried them in a calmer direction.

After several more minutes, the tiny boat had sailed onto the leeward side of the sand bar. With waves tapering off, the man motioned for the girl to climb over the bench seat and join him at the back. She did this gingerly, hands alternatively outspread for balance or grabbing hold of the gunwales. Cory held his breath. "Don't fall in the river," he whispered. The fisherman then dropped a rope and anchor, and the boat came to rest in the calmer waters of a lagoon on the near side of the island. The man reached for a fishing pole, cast its line into the river, and handed it to the girl; he then did the same, but keeping this second pole in his own hands.

Corey realized that he still held his mother's hand in his.

"I think they're going to be all right, Mom."

"Yes, I think so." She squeezed his hand. "Corey, you see that sand bar behind Jeff Olson's boat, with the large oak tree?"

"Hmmm mmm." He had an idea what she might say next.

"That looks like the setting of your ninth-grade painting, the one you submitted for the Stockholm Art Fair."

She was right. Corey had stood in this very same spot twenty-five years ago to paint a surrealist scene about a boy clinging to the uppermost branches of a hardwood in the middle of an island, staring into the distance toward a town with a tall, white steeple.

"It's one and the same. I came out here with my art class on a field trip."

"I remember how upset your father was when you only got third place."

"Yet another cause for his disappointment in me. Well, he wasn't the only one that thought I got screwed."

"Corey, he wasn't disappointed. Exactly the opposite. He was proud of that painting. That's why he built a frame and hung it at the cabin."

"But you just said he was upset."

"Yes, with the judges, not with you. I remember how he drove straight over to Stockholm and gave the Art Fair coordinator a piece of his mind."

"He did? I never knew that."

"Well, maybe you've got selective memory where your father's concerned. He was proud of you, you know. And he did love you."

Corey stared back at her with twisted, pursed lips.

"I recall him telling me afterward how he got the coordinator to admit that yours was the best painting in the high school age group and that the judges didn't seem to know a Rembrandt from a River Trout. That's a direct quote."

Corey laughed. Despite his father's many shortcomings, the ridiculous saws he came up with were memorable.

"But the results had been posted, and there wasn't going to be a correction. Frank gave the guy an earful and told him that you were going to make it big as an artist someday, even if the judges in Stockholm couldn't see it."

"Frank said all that? Frank Fischer?"

"Yes, Corey. He did. And it wasn't the only time he expressed pride in your work, or in you."

"Well, it mighta helped if he'd have given some of that praise to my face."

"I know, I know."

They both looked again to the river, checking on the fisherman and his boat.

"Say, you should take a mental picture of this scene and paint it."

"What?"

"Yes, the squall on the river and Jeff Olson out there fighting the wind and the waves to save himself and his granddaughter. You should paint it, Corey." He looked askance at his mother, then returned his gaze toward the river. "And once you're done, we'll submit it to the Stockholm Art Fair next summer. I just know you'd win. It might even provide some redemption for getting robbed of first place back in high school."

Corey laughed. "I think you and Dad were more upset about the third-place ribbon than I was. But that painting was pretty good, I guess. Huh. Maybe it's time I paint this scene again. But instead of a faceless boy climbing a tree and looking out toward the horizon for answers, I can paint the grit of the fisherman's face and his determination to get the young girl safely back to shore."

"I did notice the art equipment in your car. You've certainly got plenty of time to paint. And we can set up space for you in Dad's old office, now that it's been cleaned out. Come on, Corey. This feels right. It might even be good for you."

He looked at his mother and grinned. "All right, all right. I'll start in the morning."

Corey and his mother looked yet again in the direction of the river. The sun had dropped below the tips of the empty treetops. Golden light beams brought soft color to the little green boat. The fisherman and the little girl now sat side by side, each casting their gaze toward the water, waiting to catch a fish.

Acknowledgements

Panic River began during a writing prompt in a Master Fiction course at The Loft Literary Center, Minneapolis, in the Fall of 2015. It continued to develop under the relentless support and direction of my "Unreliable Narrators" writing group: Rosanna Staffa, Susan Schaefer, Amit Bhati, and Drew Miller. I then spent two intense years on the book with significant mentorship from award-winning authors and teachers Peter Geye, Sandra Scofield, and Ian Graham Leask. Panic River would not have been published without the genius and generosity of these brilliant writers. To each of them, I'm grateful.

Many others deserve acknowledgement for promoting my writing life: Sue Zumberg at Subtext Books, Rachel Anderson of RMA Publicity, Kevin Fennel's website design, Gary Lindberg, Mike Kelly, Rick Polad and Ian at Calumet Editions, and to all those affiliated with the Rural America Writers Center. I also appreciate a pair of men who generously shared personal stories with me that were woven into this tale.

Panic River was written during a three-year period of significant trials in my personal life, a period in which I received enduring encouragement from family members and friends; while too numerous to mention, know that I appreciate the role you played in carrying me and this book into 2019.

Finally, I'm grateful for the loving support of my father Ken and sons Isaac and Jason, as well my mother Millie who reviewed a first draft before she passed. Last, but not least, for Marco: thank you.

About the Author

Elliott Foster is the author of *Whispering Pines*, a 2015 Indie Book Award national finalist. His poetry has been published in *The Green Blade* literary journal, and he co-authored the 2019 memoir *Retrieving Isaac & Jason* with his father, Ken Flies. Elliott lives in Minnesota with a dog named Louie to whom he reads excerpts from his forthcoming work, a sequel to *Panic River*. So far, Louie approves.

Made in the
USA
Monee, IL